MW00686234

THE NEW MIDDLE AGES

BONNIE WHEELER, *Series Editor*

The New Middle Ages is a series dedicated to transdisciplinary studies of medieval cultures, with particular emphasis on recuperating women's history and on feminist and gender analyses. This peer-reviewed series includes both scholarly monographs and essay collections.

SEXUALITY AND ITS QUEER DISCONTENTS IN MIDDLE ENGLISH LITERATURE

Tison Pugh

SEXUALITY AND ITS QUEER DISCONTENTS IN MIDDLE ENGLISH LITERATURE
Copyright © Tison Pugh, 2008.

First published in 2008 by
PALGRAVE MACMILLAN™
175 Fifth Avenue, New York, N.Y. 10010 and
Houndmills, Basingstoke, Hampshire, England RG21 6XS
Companies and representatives throughout the world.

PALGRAVE MACMILLAN is the global academic imprint of the Palgrave Macmillan division of St. Martin's Press, LLC and of Palgrave Macmillan Ltd. Macmillan® is a registered trademark in the United States, United Kingdom and other countries. Palgrave is a registered trademark in the European Union and other countries.

ISBN-13: 978–1–4039–8487–6
ISBN-10: 1–4039–8487–5

Library of Congress Cataloging-in-Publication Data

Pugh, Tison.
    Sexuality and its queer discontents in Middle English literature / by Tison Pugh.
        p. cm.
    ISBN 1–4039–8487–5
    1. English literature—Middle English, 1100–1500—History and criticism. 2. Gender identity in literature. 3. Heterosexuality in literature. 4. Homosexuality in literature. I. Title.

PR275.G44P84 2008
820.9′35380902—dc22   2007026994

A catalogue record for this book is available from the British Library.

Design by Newgen Imaging Systems (P) Ltd., Chennai, India.

First edition: February 2008

10 9 8 7 6 5 4 3 2 1

Printed in the United States of America.

For Rachal and Jim

CONTENTS

ACKNOWLEDGMENTS

The solitary work of writing belies how much fun it really is, especially given the wonderful community of medievalists and other scholars who support me at every turn. A list cannot do them justice, but it must suffice for the moment: Susan Aronstein, Martha Bayless, Carrie Beneš, Louise Bishop, John Bowers, William Burgwinkle, Michael Calabrese, Stephen Mark Carey, Holly Crocker, Glenn Davis, Martha Driver, Jim Earl, Siân Echard, Laurie Finke, Christina Fitzgerald, Joseph Gibaldi, Amy Gorelick, Stephen Guy-Bray, Cynthia Ho, Cary Howie, Kathleen Kelly, Anna Klosowska, Kate Koppelman, Anne Latowsky, Clare Lees, Scott Lightsey, Marcia Smith Marzec, Gretchen Mieszkowski, Vin Nardizzi, Barton Palmer, James Paxson, Regina Psaki, William Quinn, Lynn Ramey, Martin Shichtman, Lynn Shutters, Shira Schwam-Baird, Barbara Stevenson, Richard Strier, and Angela Jane Weisl. In Bonnie Wheeler, I have found an editor who sees merit in my work while simultaneously helping me to improve it; one could not ask for a better combination. I have not yet personally met Christopher Baswell, Jeffrey Jerome Cohen, or Robert Sturges, yet they each know how much they have helped me in various ways, and they stand as testaments to the blind collegiality so generously available in our field. Thanks also to Paul Szarmach and the participants in the 2004 National Endowment for the Humanities Summer Institute at Trinity College, Cambridge, with whom I enjoyed a summer of fellowship and intellectual engagement. I was able to complete this book (and to start my next project) while on a sabbatical leave from the University of Central Florida, and I thank José Fernandez, Dean of the College of Arts and Humanities, and Dawn Trouard and Tom Krise, Chairs of the Department of English, for their support of my scholarship. My research assistant, Kelly Hould, provided cheerful and efficient assistance with many tasks. And finally, thanks to my family and friends for their patience throughout the writing process.

Chapter 3, "Queering Harry Bailly: Gendered Carnival, Social Ideologies, and Masculinity under Duress in the *Canterbury Tales*," originally appeared in *Chaucer Review* 41.1 (2006): 39–69. I appreciate the editorial guidance of Susanna Greer Fein, David Raybin, and the anonymous peer reviewers; I am also grateful for the generosity of Pennsylvania State University Press in allowing me to reprint this work in slightly altered form. Also, I was generously allowed access to the resources of the Huntington Library, which greatly facilitated my research.

CHAPTER 1

INTRODUCTION: SEXUALITY
AND ITS QUEER DISCONTENTS
IN MIDDLE ENGLISH LITERATURE

To adapt an immortal line from Shakespeare's *Twelfth Night,* some are born queer, some achieve queerness, and some have queerness thrust upon 'em.[1] In this book, my interests lie with those who have queerness thrust upon 'em—the male agents and actors who, through their interactions and affinities with others, become marked with and/or compelled to embody queerness before being identified as normatively (hetero)sexual males.[2] The construction of normative masculinity depends upon the possibility of the queer, as queerness provides the binary Other that normativity hierarchically opposes. Rather than flip sides of the same coin, queerness and normativity oscillate in respect to each other in the construction of sexual and ideological subjects. In this manner, queerness often constitutes a necessary tactic in disciplining certain male subjects into the prevailing ideological order.[3] One might think of the queer as the abjected alternative to, if not as an escape route from, cultural normativity, but queerness can be appropriated and systemically deployed to tame disruptions to the prevailing social order by reconstituting the genders and sexualities of men who might otherwise upset the status quo. Assuming a normative masculinity is a task fraught with queerness, and men must frequently contend with queerness to realize such an ideal masculinity, if such culturally viable masculinities are indeed available to them at all.[4] Heterosexuals are created through ideological interpellation as much as they are born as unique individuals, and queerness foundationally constitutes certain heterosexual subjects in myriad ways. The queerness of heterosexuality creates conditions in which discontents are bound to fester, as the imposition of ideological normativity upon otherwise resistant subjects subjugates their queerness yet can never ultimately squelch it. As Sigmund Freud famously declares, "The two urges, the one towards personal happiness and the other towards union with other human beings, must struggle with each other in every individual."[5] It is easy to see the relevance of Freud's words for homosexuals, whose desires for personal happiness, when directed toward sexual fulfillment with a member of the same sex, often conflict with the desire to participate more widely in a homophobic social community.

This tension between the individual and society in relation to sexuality is not unique to homosexuals, as heterosexuals are likewise capable of experiencing queer—although not necessarily homosexual—desires. *Queer* connotes a wide range of cultural stereotypes and identities, from defamatory condemnations of sexual diversity to celebratory proclamations of personal freedom. As the connotative range of *queer* traverses between damning and laudatory, its semantic range elicits further taxonomical crises. When exactly does a sexual act or actor become queer? Are sodomies and sodomites intrinsically and transhistorically queer? Sodomy laws have defined a wide range of heterosexual erotic practices as illicit, which raises the question of whether a given sexual act—fellatio, for instance—is queerer when performed by homosexuals than by heterosexuals.[6] The answer to this question hangs upon given ideological conditions in effect during a particular time and in a particular culture, as responses to sexual acts shift—sometimes imperceptibly, sometimes seismically—throughout history.

Concomitantly, as queerness fails to communicate a clear cultural meaning, heterosexuality too can never signify precisely. For along with questioning when a sexuality transgresses into queerness, we must also ponder when a sexuality metamorphoses into ideological acceptability as representative of that cluster of licit acts known as heterosexuality. Such philosophical musings point to the essential feature of sexuality in regard to its ideological function: its amorphousness. If sexualities were defined in absolute terms, their potential to construct subjects into ideology would be hamstrung because everyone could recognize them in all situations, both historical and contemporary. The definitional haziness of sexuality enables its ideological function, in that all members of a given community must feel its disciplining effect as a constitutive factor in their social position that is then tied to their sexual desires. Fluctuating in regard both to sexual acts and to cultural normativity, sexuality refuses to be taxonomized into epistemological certainty, and its murky range of meaning carries the potential to cast many subjects under clouds of sexual suspicion.

Given the murkiness of queerness and its concomitant function to undermine normativity, many homosexuals resist its power to construct them as the Other. "Should a homosexual be a good citizen?" ponders Leo Bersani.[7] Hinting at the fundamentally antisocial potential of queers who resist a marginalized construction as debased Other, Bersani's question limns the almost ubiquitous smoldering antagonism between homosexuals and discriminatory societies.[8] However, homosexuals do not hold a monopoly on antagonistic stances between self and society, and this question could as readily be asked in regard to heterosexuals who face the ideological constraints of sexual normativity and chafe against the discontents that erupt due to the pressures between civilization and eros. When heterosexuals resist normative constructions of their subjectivity, they inhabit a queer position of conflicting with a social system that would otherwise reward them for their normativity. Queerness refuses to function monologically, as it frequently defines and constructs normative masculinities for heterosexuals by allowing a space of pleasure that must be foresworn in the advent of the discontented heterosexual subject.[9] Of course, neither does heterosexuality function monologically, yet its ideological weight allows it the pretense of ubiquity; with its ostensible omnipresence, its fantasy of normativity goes largely unnoticed. Normativity surrounds a culture, as "natural" as the air we breathe, and it polices sexuality by enveloping heterosexuality and excluding queerness. Consisting of both sexual acts and breaches of normativity, queerness comprises sexual, amatory, and gendered practices that ostensibly depart from prevailing cultural norms. However, its tense relationship with cultural norms does not necessitate that queerness *always* subverts ideology: it rebels against ideological identity codes in some instances while quelling such resistance under other circumstances.

Despite the apparent paradox of using queer theory to analyze normative sexualities, such an approach underscores the fundamental queerness at times necessary to inhabit normative positions. Ideological constructions of heterosexuality and heteronormativity dismiss questions about their ontological value as unworthy of critical inquiry, if not as altogether inane, because heterosexuality bears the standard of unquestioned normativity. It is culturally constructed as the natural foundation of all sexuality, and its more strident supporters present it as naturalizing and normatizing as well.[10] As David Halperin demonstrates,

> The crucial, empowering incoherence at the core of heterosexuality and its definition never becomes visible because heterosexuality itself is never an *object* of knowledge, a target of scrutiny in its own right, so much as it is the *condition* for the supposedly objective, disinterested knowledge of *other* objects, especially homosexuality, which it constantly produces as a manipulably and spectacularly contradictory figure of

transgression so as to deflect attention—by means of accusation—from its own incoherence.[11]

Heterosexuality is no more natural or unnatural than homosexuality. It is more widely experienced, yet numerous scientific studies document the naturalness of homosexuality as well.[12] The cultural responses to hetero- and homosexuality diverge greatly depending on the ideological conditions in effect in a given society, especially in that heterophilic cultures imbue heterosexuality with normative valences. In such instances, the construction of heteronormativity often depends upon the debasement and denigration of queer desires.

In cultures predominantly antithetical to queer desires such as medieval western Europe, queerness threatens constructions of cultural normativity in regard to a given person's social privilege. In its crudest incarnation, the queer path to ideal masculinity depends upon the power of ideology to ostracize the queer. "Don't be a fag": this harsh playground taunt has taken many forms over the centuries, and its discordant contempt for sexual nonnormativity peppers myriad historical and literary texts including (but by no means limited to) biblical injunctions, classical amatory satire, and medieval monastic discourse. To look briefly at some examples, Leviticus admonishes, "Thou shalt not lie with mankind as with womankind: because it is an abomination" (18:22).[13] In his *Ars Amatoria*, Ovid teases effeminate men while giving grooming instructions: "[Going] Beyond [these directions] is for wanton women— / Or any half-man who wants to attract men."[14] Peter Damian coins the word "sodomia" in the eleventh century to castigate sexual sinners in his *Book of Gomorrah*.[15] These diverse authors and texts, representative of vastly different cultural conditions, clearly teach proper sexual masculinity through their negative injunctions. To be a functioning male member of society, as these texts coercively conceive of masculine sexual normativity, one must assiduously avoid any associational relationship with queerness as marked by sexual acts, effeminacy, or other nonnormative behavior. A crude tool, homophobia nevertheless efficiently communicates overarching societal preferences for normative sexuality.[16]

Negative constructions of same-sex desire are but one side of continuing cultural discussions about sexuality and homosocial relationships, and along with these representative voices disdainful of homophilia, one can readily find resistant voices describing homosocial relationships and desires in laudatory, sometimes hungry, terms. In the Bible, the imprecations of Leviticus are balanced by the tender friendship of Jonathan and David, as attested by their covenants of loyalty and great love for each other.[17] Ovid's sly digs at sissies find a counterpart in Martial's blunt desires for anal intercourse with a male slave ("And unless I say under oath 'I'll give it,' you withdraw those buttocks that let you take many liberties with me"),[18] and Peter Damian's and Alain of Lille's condemnations of sodomy sharply contrast with voices of other monastic men, such as Marbod of Rennes and Baudri of Bourgueil, who praise male beauty in highly eroticized terms.[19] The dominant voices of biblical, classical, and medieval cultures at times drown out encomiums to homosocial relationships, but these homosocial desires nevertheless created a broad enough social space to warrant their own traditions, as documented in the historical and literary record.

In this cursory overview of cultural conversations about male homosexuality and homosociality from the biblical, classical, and medieval periods, the primary congruency arises in the lability of homosociality and same-sex activities within various cultures such that they never communicate precisely. The examples cited earlier all concern homosocial behavior, and many of them concern homoerotic behavior, but which of these relationships, if any, were queer? Same-sex relationships do not necessarily disrupt cultural normativity when couched within prevailing social codes of male friendship and hierarchical association. It is difficult to envision that David and Jonathan's homosocial affection queered biblical norms;[20] likewise, assuming that Martial's or Marbod's sexualities disrupted cultural normativity appears an ahistorical and anachronistic view of homosocial relationships, as these men would be unlikely to speak candidly about their desires if they faced severe social reprobation for them. The queerness of these relationships, if any queerness exists in them at all, appears in their eroticism, yet male eroticism in itself does not always and transhistorically register as disruptive to societal norms. Such homosocial relationships cannot be definitively construed as queer, yet queer potential is nonetheless latent in homosocial structures of male friendships. In the amorphousness of queerness and its convoluted relationship to heterosexuality, normative men can enjoy homosocial, and possibly homoerotic, attachments.

Such conflicting paradigms of queerness challenge scholars to categorize accurately the meanings of same-sex desires throughout history. One cannot necessarily equate same-sex desires with ideologically queer ones, as systems of heteronormativity are balanced by systems of homonormativity—the social practices of people of the same sex that are endorsed by the governing ideological regime as reinforcing necessary cultural values. Laurie Shannon suggests that same-sex friendships should be understood within the framework of homonormativity, a theoretical concept that "evoke[s] the strange blend of ordinariness, idealization, and ideology entailed in this rhetorical regime" of homosociality;[21] her conception of homonormativity captures the amorphous relationship between social practice and social ideal, which sets the stage for queering potential. The paradox of homonormativity, however, is that it may either obscure queerness or reflect true social normativity, depending on the circumstances of the relationship. For example, Mathew S. Kuefler asserts that "throwing suspicion on male friendships as breeding grounds for sodomitical behavior suited the goals of the men of the ecclesiastical and royal hierarchies" in twelfth-century France.[22] Medieval male homonormativity, as evidenced through studies of male friendships and homoerotic verse, bespeaks a radically different conception of male-male relationships from that in the modern era, but we can still attempt to identify the parameters of the normative within the period.[23] The confused space that simultaneously separates and envelops homonormativity, queerness, and heterosexuality necessitates deeper investigations into their interrelationships. Again, if sexuality registered with a uniform valence in a given society, its cultural meaning would always be clear; however, queerness—in its ambiguity and amorphousness—potentially marks every man, including heterosexuals, as nonnormative.

What, then, makes a man queer and/or homosexual? Lee Edelman observes how perceived differences overwhelm similarities in constructing men and male sexuality:

> For if...the cultural production of homosexual identity in terms of an "indiscreet anatomy" exercises control over the subject (whether straight or gay) by subjecting his bodily self-representation to analytic scrutiny, the arbitrariness of the indices that identify "sexuality"—which is to say, *homo*sexuality—testifies to the cultural imperative to *produce,* for purposes of ideological regulation, a putative difference within that group of male bodies that would otherwise count as the "the same."[24]

Differences construct identities, and identities are thus phantastically synthesized in response to sexual variances among men. Any man could be subsumed into queerness, depending on how cultures scrutinize and construct a range of possible sexual signifiers and correlate these signifiers to a given human male. Likewise, although men could be viewed as equals in ideological normativity regardless of their partners in sexual acts, they are nonetheless rendered different from one another in service to ideological regimes dependent upon the creation of this very difference. Edelman indicates that such policing bears the potential to produce straight or gay men alike, and it is critical to realize that heterosexuality, like homosexuality, is produced through social forces as well as generated by biological and hormonal influences.[25] The resulting classification of sexualities—and of the men who enact and embody them—differs according to the varying levels of social approbation or disapprobation in conjunction with their sexual identities. Queerness is embodied and experienced in vastly different ways among men who register as normative—or not—in regard to their sexual desires and acts.

Edelman's analysis of the fundamentally similar cultural production of gay and straight men points to the necessity of queer theory in analyzing both homosexuality and heterosexuality. Indeed, queer studies is evolving as an analytical tool of cultural ideology by shifting its primary focus on homosexuality to a more ecumenical perspective. As David Eng, Judith Halberstam, and José Esteban Munoz suggest, queer studies must be "ever vigilant to the fact that sexuality is intersectional, not extraneous to other modes of difference, and calibrated to a firm understanding of queer as a political metaphor without a fixed referent."[26] This study participates in such an expansive view of the queer, in that none of the men under scrutiny are homosexual or express a desire to experience sexual relationships with other men. They are nonetheless ideologically queered from the masculine privilege of western society precisely because their gendered identities and sexual desires are rendered suspect in a manner congruent to the construction of the sexually queer. Here we see the power of "regimes of the normal," as Michael Warner labels them, to confer upon some subjects the ideological benefits of normativity and upon others the opprobrium of the queer.[27] With its conscriptive bent, ideology deploys queerness to pursue its own normative ends. Creating queerness interpellates heterosexual men into social structures that they might otherwise resist, and their queered position as debased Others thus mitigates the possibility of resisting such ideologically hierarchical systems. Normativity inculcates cultural values into individuals, yet such normativity can frequently only be realized through queerness.

How could normative regimes of sexuality function during the Middle Ages if concepts of homosexuality and heterosexuality did not exist in this time period, as some scholars argue? Michel Foucault famously observed that sexualized perceptions of personal identity formulated in response to the medical discourses of the nineteenth century, which radically shifted social constructions of and reactions to sexual acts and actors.[28] Foucault is certainly correct that perceptions of sexual identity changed markedly in response to cultural shifts in this era, and scholars such as Karma Lochrie and James Schultz persuasively argue that we cannot rely on formulations of heteronormativity, as well as on modern conceptions of heterosexuality and homosexuality, to facilitate analyses of medieval sexualities. Quite simply, sexual norms do not function transhistorically, and medieval and modern norms frequently conflict. In

her coinage of the term "heterosyncrasies," which adumbrates the culturally particular construction of sexualities and subjects, Lochrie explains
the vastly different conceptions of medieval and modern sexual norms:

> Desire for someone of the opposite sex in modern norm-speak is natural
> or normal because it is the most widespread sexual practice and, second-
> arily, because of religious ideology that is likewise dependent on the
> concept of norms. Desire for someone of the opposite sex in medieval
> nature-speak is natural in the corrupted sense of resulting from the Fall,
> but it is not in any sense legitimated by its widespread practice or idealized
> as a personal or cultural goal.[29]

Schultz ponders the vacuity of heterosexuality as a critical concept: "There
would seem to be a trivial sense in which any sexual act involving a
woman and a man could be called heterosexual. The designation is trivial
because *most* sexual acts involving more than one person involve a man
and woman. What's the big deal?"[30] Lochrie and Schultz demonstrate
that ostensibly heteronormative desires of the Middle Ages do not, in
fact, mirror medieval perceptions as much as they reflect modern preconceptions, and they rightly condemn the facile deployment of modern
heteronormativity in studies of medieval sexuality. Historical constructions of sexuality vary intrinsically from modern ones, and scholars
of medieval sexuality must take into account that modern eyes tend
to blur the contours of medieval normativity. From this perspective,
heterosexuality and heteronormativity cannot be identified as a meaningful tool of ideology within the sociotemporal and cultural field of the
Middle Ages.

  While I agree with Lochrie and Schultz that constructions of sexuality
and normativity differ intrinsically between medieval and postmodern
cultures, must we then throw out the baby of a queer critical lexicon with
the bathwater of anachronism? As Foucault himself cautioned, "The term
[sexuality] itself did not appear until the beginning of the nineteenth
century, a fact that should be neither underestimated nor overinterpreted."[31]
With this observation, Foucault points to the possibility of transhistorical
similarities in constructions of sexualities as he simultaneously upholds
their differences. Jonathan Goldberg and Madhavi Menon embrace the
chaos of studying sexuality in their vision of *homohistory*, a history
"invested in suspending determinate sexual and chronological differences
while expanding the possibilities of the nonhetero, with all its connotations of sameness, similarity, proximity, and anachronism."[32] I embrace
the potential for anachronism in homohistory and address it to the construction of heterosexuality and normativity in the Middle Ages. The

critical terminology of contemporary queer studies can still be usefully, if anachronistically, applied to analyses of medieval sexualities when these terms are carefully contextualized. If normativity is used as a critical rubric in analyses of medieval sexuality, it must be situated among the norms of the Middle Ages in regard to sexual acts and personal identities, while simultaneously highlighting the vast lability of normativity throughout the centuries.

For example, medieval concepts such as spiritual and chaste marriages highlight how certain social systems register either as normative or as queer depending upon the circumstances of their enactment of hetero-sexuality. Spiritual marriages must be construed as normative within medieval ideology since these relationships met with cultural approval (although marital chastity today broaches heteronormative Christian prac-tice in marriage).[33] The normativity of medieval spiritual marriages nev-ertheless opens possibilities of gender play, as medieval women accorded themselves great spiritual power—often greater than their husbands—through the practice. Precisely because of the normative valence of spiri-tual marriage, medieval women could exploit its contours to wield authority over their husbands, as evidenced in Chaucer's *Second Nun's Tale* and *The Book of Margery Kempe*. In these narratives, the normativities of spiritual marriage and of male gender roles collide, resulting in the possibility of ideological subversion. In the *Second Nun's Tale,* Cecilia's husband Valerian accepts his wife's spiritual guidance, and both husband and wife find greater holiness as exemplary (and thus normative) Christian subjects who choose martyrdom for their faith.[34] Margery's husband, in contrast, wonders hypothetically whether she would sleep with him to save him from imminent murder; she famously concludes, "For-sothe I had leuar se yow be slayn than we schuld turne a-yen to owyr vnclen-nesse," to which he resignedly concludes, "Ye arn no good wyfe."[35]

In these conflicting depictions of spiritual marriage, heteronormativity fails to function transhistorically, and thus if heteronormativity is to be used as a critical tool to study the past, it must take into account the ways in which men and women entered into sexual relationships adhering to or disruptive of medieval—not modern—constructions of normative behavior. Normativity nonetheless functions in spiritual marriages to regulate identities, in that Valerian finds proper Christian submission with Cecilia while Margery's husband is queered from his patriarchal privilege by her demand that he renounce his sexual desires and join her in chaste—and normative—marriage. Margery's adroit manipulation of normativity in spiritual marriage allows her to undermine the ideological construction of feminine subservience in medieval marriage, in obvious contradiction to her husband's desires. Because they straddle the fence between normative and queer, spiritual marriages must be analyzed on a case-by-case basis, but scholars can nonetheless employ normativity and sexual hermeneutics to uncover who is and who is not experiencing queerness in the construction of a nonetheless heterosexual identity. Spiritual marriages expose the conflict between opposing senses of cultural normativity, thus highlighting the phantastic construction of normativity itself: normativity cannot be maintained against its inevitable confrontation with its multifarious and contradictory constructions, yet neither should it, therefore, be dismissed as irrelevant to discussions of medieval sexuality.[36]

Both heterosexual and queer desires were frequently proscribed in the Middle Ages, especially since an unmarried state was in some instances thought preferable to sexually active lifestyles, in line with Paul's admonition that "it is better to marry than to be burnt" (I Corinthians 7:9). Yet such proscriptions could never contain or delimit desire; the queerness of medieval spiritual marriages thus arises in the possibility of gender deconstruction through one's very participation in normative social structures, as Margery so strikingly illustrates. In its ostensibly oppositional stance to normativity, the queer is thus foundational to any purported construction of normativity: the normative needs the queer to establish itself vis-à-vis its apparent ideological adversary. But when related yet distinct normativities collide, queer potential almost inevitably comes to the forefront to expose the contradictions inherent in normativity. Scholars should use such terms as *queer, homosexual, heterosexual,* and *heteronormative* in referring to medieval sexualities with care and should contextualize them for the sociocultural environs of the Middle Ages. In this regard, Judith Bennett's suggestion to use "lesbian-like" to describe certain medieval women and their communities strikes me as a reasonable solution to the difficulties of using modern words to describe medieval sexualities,[37] and I ask my readers to supplement the suffix *-like* to *heterosexual, homosexual,* and *heteronormative* in the ensuing analysis to spare both of us the weight of clunky neologisms. Heterosexuality, homosexuality, and heteronormativity did not exist in the Middle Ages as we know them today, but sufficiently similar ideological weight was placed on sexual acts and actors so that a current critical lexicon can be used to describe the past when such terms are used with appropriate caution and contextualization.

Heterosexuality demands gendered actors to embody its naturalized position in ideology, yet as heterosexuality is built upon a foundation of queerness, so too is gender phantastically constructed by imbuing biological sexual differences between men and women with normatizing assumptions. Studies of gender in the Middle Ages reveal the period's ostensibly rigid gender categories that police individuals yet frequently

fail to regulate gendered acts and actors successfully.[38] Jo Ann McNamara
contends that the cloudiness of medieval gender categories springs from
conflicting depictions of humanity's creation in Genesis, which relates
first that God created man and woman in his image, but then indicates
that Eve is incarnated through Adam's rib.[39] In this foundational moment
of Judeo-Christian history and thought, gender (as incarnated through
sexual biology) both does and does not exist, and McNamara trenchantly
remarks that the "gender system requires strong institutional support to
resolve the tensions" inherent in cultural constructions of masculinity
and femininity.[40] Gender potentially defines a person's place in medieval
society, yet it is built on such an unstable foundation that it continually
falters when its basic parameters are questioned.

In regard to masculinities in the Middle Ages, the illusions of gender
continually deflate their pretensions, and again, we see the queer tension
inherent in conflicting constructions of normativity.[41] For example,
courtly heteronormativity appears to fortify constructions of knightly
masculinity, but this heteronormativity is itself predicated upon the
impossibility of its realization. Similar to Zeno's paradox, the enactment
of gender demands that men continually approach and adhere to a model
of masculinity that can never be fully attained. Because the people of the
Middle Ages frequently defined social orders and identities through rites
of initiation, masculinities were performed and reiterated in public spec-
tacles. As Ruth Mazo Karras declares, "Medieval society was one of col-
lectivities, in which identity came from membership in particular groups.
Many of these groups—knights, monks, apprentices, guildspeople—
underwent particular initiation ceremonies that marked their selection or
separation from the rest of society."[42] In this manner, social relationships
mark a man as a representative of a given social order, whether his masculinity is that of son or father, or of king or commoner, or a combination
thereof.[43] By proclaiming a masculinity as encoded through a social role
or identity, however, a man confronts the likelihood of that masculinity
experiencing duress in response to other cultural forces. Such circumstances occur frequently in romances when a knight's loyalty to his lord
conflicts with his love for his lady. Both relationships are normative
within the ideological construction of heterosexual masculinity in the
Middle Ages, yet they bear the potential to queer the knight depending
on his response to antithetically gendered tensions. Such conflicting
masculinities reveal the ways in which genders can never shore themselves up against every daily condition. Because neither the relationship
with the lord nor the lady should be jettisoned in favor of the other, the
pressures inherent in serving a male lord and a female beloved often elicit
queerness that colors the contours of knightly identity.[44] Ideological

visions of gender and sexuality phantastically insist upon normativities, yet they are social impossibilities at the same time that they are modeled as social ideals: the utopian construction of normativity is tantalizingly visual yet nonetheless phantastic. Queerness almost inevitably seeps into the process of constructing heterosexuals because gender and sexual regimes are built on such shaky foundations.

When queerness is attached to heterosexuality, when queerness enables heterosexuality, the façade of heterosexual superiority is revealed as an agent of ideological control not merely of homosexual men but of many heterosexual men as well. Such queerness compels ostensibly masculine and normative subjects to inhabit sexual otherness, to abandon normativity, and to confront the failures of masculinity in order to be reconscripted into proper ideological and culturally normative manhood. Given the potential for normative masculinities to undergo duress when conflicting ideological pressures converge, a man and his masculinity are often broken down in a crucible of queerness to then form again in response to normativity. Adrienne Rich exposes the ways in which compulsory heterosexuality regulates and monitors female identities and erases lesbian existence, yet queerness can also be deployed in such a compulsory manner to delimit and curtail a vibrant range of viable alternate sexual identities.[45] Compulsory queerness paradoxically serves as a stage in the construction of (hetero)normative masculinity, although such an ostensibly normative masculinity may not be what the man desired in the first place. Whereas Rich exposes the ways in which compulsory heterosexuality creates discontent among lesbians, compulsory queerness functions in a paradoxically similar manner to create discontented heterosexuals.

In this manner, heterosexual interpellation into the prevailing ideological order is revealed to be a queer and queering process. The strength of Louis Althusser as a theorist of the ideological order arises in that many of his readers almost intuitively recognize the ways that hailing and interpellating function in regard to their own experiences. The ideological order creates subjects, and in so doing, Althusser argues that these subjects learn the values associated with various thoughts, actions, and identities:

> Throughout this schema we observe that the ideological representation of ideology is itself forced to recognize that every "subject" endowed with a "consciousness" and believing in the "ideas" that his "consciousness" inspires in him and freely accepts, must *act according to his ideas*," must therefore inscribe his own ideas as a free subject in the actions of his material practice. If he does not do so, "that is wicked."[46]

The moral lessons of ideology inculcate and indoctrinate subjects as proper citizens of a community, and these lessons include social mores defining licit and illicit sexualities. Althusser is primarily known as a Marxist critic, yet his class-based analysis of ideological power connects in a deeply personal way to gendered and sexual subjects as well. He notes that we are born into sexuality in that "the former subject-to-be will have to 'find' 'its' place, i.e. 'become' the sexual subject (boy or girl) which it already is in advance."[47] Ideological constructions of sex and sexuality, so strongly in place even before a child is born, would appear to conscript each subject into heteronormativity from the moment of conception.

Interpellation works to construct ideal subjects, those who accept their place within the ideological order, but critiques of Althusser's theories highlight the possibility of individual disruptions to the prevailing order. For instance, Judith Butler limns the likelihood of disruptive subjects who undermine the ideological status quo: "Although [Althusser] refers to the possibility of 'bad subjects,' he does not consider the range of *disobedience* that such an interpellating law might produce. The law not only might be refused but might also be ruptured, forced into a rearticulation that calls into question the monotheistic force of its own unilateral operation."[48] Similarly, Warren Montag notes the apparent paradox at the heart of interpellation: "For how could ideology be simultaneously imaginary and material, and how could the notion of the 'imaginary' be conceived, except in reference to a consciousness whose illusions, whose false ideas, prevent it from knowing or perceiving the real?"[49] Subverting ideology by taking advantage of its inherent paradox, subjects find new possibilities of identity antithetical to the social world in which they find themselves.[50]

By theorizing the compulsory nature of queerness in creating heterosexuals, I do not wish to suggest the impossibility of ideological resistance, bleakly arguing against Butler's and Montag's positions and positing an ideological regime resistant to any hint of subversion. At the same time, it is essential to explore how ideology conscripts resistant subjects through deployments of the queer. If ideological subversion were truly impossible or merely a quixotic quest, disciplinary regimes in place during the Middle Ages would likely still hold sway today. Nonetheless, queerness in some ways provides a "back-up plan" for ideology to discipline recalcitrant subjects into normativity or to reconfigure otherwise problematic masculinities. When the ideal interpellative process fails to create normative subjects, disciplined subjects can still be constructed through queerness. As the initial discussion of the connotative register of *queer* demonstrates, queerness indeed bears transformative powers to upend restrictive ideologies, yet restrictive ideologies also bear obfuscatory powers to wield queerness in furtherance of their own ends. It behooves any scholar of queer culture to study not merely the queer's revolutionary potential but the ways in which queerness quells rebellions as well, and a discontented heterosexual affords an opportunity to understand queerness on a different yet no less essential level.

This tension between masculinity and queerness is familiar in contemporary entertainment, and it is instructive to look briefly at some examples of men voluntarily assuming queerness in twentieth-century popular culture to gauge the difference between voluntary and compulsory assumptions of queerness. When a heterosexual man puts on a dress in a Hollywood comedy, for example, he frequently becomes a better heterosexual as a result of this queering process. In such films as *Some Like It Hot* (1959), *Tootsie* (1982), and *Mrs. Doubtfire* (1993), circumstances necessitate the male protagonist's rejection of masculinity and assumption of a female façade, but this disavowal of masculine privilege sets the stage for a subsequent reemergence as a better heterosexual male, one more finely attuned to feminine desire and thus at least potentially more successful in heterosexual courtship. By deciding to don women's garb, these protagonists find redemptive possibilities through gender minstrelsy and conquer any discontent that spurred them to drag in the first place.[51] Other artifacts of recent popular culture similarly highlight how queers construct ideal masculine aesthetics and the bodies necessary to incarnate these aesthetics. In a particularly engaging example, the transvestite mad scientist Frank N. Furter of *The Rocky Horror Picture Show* sings of his fantasy model of manliness, whom he has built from scratch:

> "He'll do press-ups, and chin-ups, do the snatch, clean and jerk.
> He thinks dynamic tension must be hard work.
> Such strenuous living I just don't understand—
> When in just seven days, oh baby, I can make you a man."[52]

This outrageously queer character ascribes to himself divine powers of male creation, as evidenced in his reference to the seven days of creation. Godlike in his queer creative potential, Frank N. Furter thus represents the subversive potential of queers to construct men who reflect homoerotic images of desire. Likewise, makeover programs such as *Queer Eye for the Straight Guy* showcase the power of the queer to define heteronormative male beauty and to make men "better" heterosexuals. In these instances, the aesthetic construction of the male form depends upon queer men visualizing and then constructing new images on the raw materials of heterosexual male bodies. Here we see the production of a perk and chirpy heterosexual contentment, and never is heard a discontented word.

Compulsory queerness functions in a similar yet radically different way in that normative masculinity is defined as a goal that can be realized only through queer intercessions. In compulsory queerness, however, we do not see queer agents building masculinities in service of their own desires; in contrast, we see ideology deploying queerness for its own ends. The queer frequently hums with resistant potential, but not when it is shackled in service of the creation of proper heterosexual subjects, who find themselves under the forceful sway of compulsory queerness and indoctrinated into heterosexual normativity. Agent of both rebellion and discipline, queerness cannot be contained under an overarching interpretive rubric designed primarily to celebrate transgression or to resist bigotry. Through the construction of heterosexuality, queerness shores up the very hierarchical systems that position it as debased Other. Only by understanding the ideological deployment of queerness in all of its complexity, however, can its radical and revolutionary potential—if such potential exists—ever be fully unlocked.

Because queerness and heterosexuality are constituted within a complex framework of interrelated factors of social identity, they should not stand alone as markers of personal identity. Rather, compulsory queerness relates to the ways in which a person's social class, religion, occupation, personal relationships, and other social factors are linked with sexual identity to construct appropriate ideological normativity; it arises in the chasm between personal identity and social ideal in that the failure to embody the ideal necessarily reveals the falsehoods of gender and the ambivalent power of the queer. None of the literary characters upon whom this study focuses—the Dreamer of *Pearl,* Harry Bailly of the *Canterbury Tales,* Walter of Chaucer's *Clerk's Tale,* the eponymous protagonists of the romances *Amis and Amiloun* and *Eger and Grime*—employ queerness as a resistant practice of individual sexual identity, but all are ultimately rendered queerly normative due to external forces that reimagine their masculinity as little more than a phantastically inadequate performance. "'Medieval literature' creates and occupies the cultural space of secular ideology," Peter Haidu asserts,[53] and the texts under scrutiny in this study likewise participate in the ideological construction of normativity, yet they do so through a decidedly queer process.

Following this Introduction, *Sexuality and Its Queer Discontents in Middle English Literature* continues with "Abandoning Desires, Desiring Readers, and the Divinely Queer Triangle of *Pearl,*" a study of the enigmatic allegorical contemplation of death, loss, love, and salvation enacted by a father mourning his daughter's death. As is typical in medieval dream visions and allegories, the Dreamer's experiences lead him to a deepened awareness of his relationship with the Divine, and in this instance, he comes to this new Christian sense of self through his colloquies with his deceased daughter. The compulsory force of queerness here lies in the poem's realization of the erotic triangle, in which two male suitors compete for the affections of a mutual beloved, in that the Dreamer sees himself as competing with God for the love of his daughter. The Dreamer must learn, from the force of his daughter's lessons, to turn his attentions (with their troubling undertones of incestuous desire) from her and to the Divine, and in this manner the Dreamer is queered into a new understanding of his place in Christianity by revisioning and refocusing desire to its proper ends. Masculine fatherhood and paternal love must metamorphose into proper Christian subservience and humility, and the erotic power of divinely triangulated desire enforces this Christianized queerness onto the Dreamer so that he can ultimately establish his normative identity as a Christian subject. Given the Dreamer's perfunctory recitation of his Christian faith at the poem's conclusion, it appears that his discontent with the loss of his daughter nonetheless still suffuses his newly revisioned Christian self.

The third chapter of *Sexuality and Its Queer Discontents in Middle English Literature,* "Queering Harry Bailly: Gendered Carnival, Social Ideologies, and Masculinity under Duress in the *Canterbury Tales*," analyzes one of medieval literature's most insistently masculine men: Chaucer's host. Harry's overbearing masculinity appears to dominate the other travelers on the Canterbury pilgrimage, but he must also face the compulsory force of queerness in that his masculinity is increasingly subverted by the carnival play he sets in motion. The gendered and queering force of carnival thus actuates a declivitous model of masculinity, revealing chinks in Harry's overbearingly authoritarian governance. Harry's masculinity thus showcases the dual force of the queer in creating subjects: Harry queers his fellow pilgrims through his rhetorical ploys and his play at the border of social classes, compelling them to accept his governance at the expense of their own primarily masculine gendered identities. At the same time, he is also compelled into queerness by the very carnival forces he unleashes. The queered image of Harry's withered masculinity at the end of the *Canterbury Tales* models the power of compulsory queerness to reconfigure agonistic constructions of alpha-male masculinity when a bourgeois man seizes too much power for himself.

Harry's aggressive yet ultimately tamed masculinity models the ways in which compulsory queerness generates tension within the overarching narrative structure of the *Canterbury Tales,* and in chapter 4, "'He nedes moot unto the pley assente': Queer Fidelities and Contractual Hermaphroditism in Chaucer's *Clerk's Tale*," I turn to the ways in which this queering force is revealed within the pathetic fictions of the *Clerk's*

Tale. Reading Griselda as a queering agent who unlocks the ideological power of social structures antithetical to her own desires, we see that she too models the contradictory and compulsory force of the queer: she is both queered from the normative fictions of her female gender through her increasingly monstrous passivity, and she in turn queers her tyrannical husband Walter from his own sense of gendered identity. By forcing him to confront the monstrosity of his masculine privilege, Griselda coerces Walter into a new model of paternal and husbandly masculinity. Both of these characters realize impossible constructions of gender: Walter in his unspeakable cruelty as a husband, Griselda in her unfathomable suffering as a wife. By adhering to her gender role to the point of impossibility, Griselda ultimately compels Walter to realize the limitations of his authoritarian masculinity. The *Clerk's Tale* ostensibly showcases the movement from heterosexual discontents in marriage to perfect bliss, yet the end of the narrative—particularly in relation to Harry's Bailly's interpretation of the tale—highlights the ways in which discontents are sparked despite ostensibly happy endings.

Chapters 5 and 6 analyze romances of homosocial brotherhood, *Amis and Amiloun* and *Eger and Grime.* In these narratives, the primary relationships of the eponymous protagonists arise in their contractually recognized homosocial oaths to each other, yet this vision of brotherhood carries with it the threat of queerness in the very primacy of these fraternal vows. As much as these romances appear to ignore homoerotic desire and to follow fairly typical narrative trajectories—with the knights defeating their enemies and thus accessing greater masculine privilege within the courtly arena—each narrative is nonetheless invested in disproving any queer aspersions to its heroes. Thus, the homosocial oaths that provide the structure and the backdrop to the romances ultimately become a compulsory and latently queering structure that the rest of the romance must somehow undo. In the collision of normativities predicated upon a knight's loyalties to his sworn brother, his lord, and his lady, queerness almost inevitably colors his character because he cannot simultaneously tend to all three relationships that define him and his position at court.

In chapter 5, "From Boys to Men to Hermaphrodites to Eunuchs: Queer Formations of Romance Masculinity and the Hagiographic Death Drive in *Amis and Amiloun,*" the compulsory queerness incarnated through fraternal friendship sparks tensions that are quelled only in death. Amis and Amiloun must, in effect, metamorphose into saints upon their deaths to divest their friendship of its queer aura. Because their homosocial friendship is so intense, so apparently fraught with queer potential, these knights—despite their heterosexuality—are depicted as beyond the purview of the normative, and thus the narrative works to bring them into normativity by disproving any possibility of sexual desire arising between them. The final image of the two men in their celibate graves effectively returns them to the realm of masculine normativity, albeit in a scene predicated upon the absence of sexuality altogether. In this manner, hagiography tames the queer potential of homosocial romance when the two genres—with their opposed constructions of the heroic protagonist—collide.

Chapter 6, "Queer Castration, Patriarchal Privilege, and the Comic Phallus in *Eger and Grime*," analyzes the fraternal relationship between the two titular protagonists, Eger and Grime, which marks them as queer in a manner congruent with the sexual politics of *Amis and Amiloun*. Eger's fractured masculinity, as evidenced by his little finger that is "castrated" in battle with their enemy Grey Steele, appears beleaguered and belittled such that any subsequent performance of credible manliness becomes an impossibility. As Grime assists his friend to reclaim his lost masculinity, the romance questions the meaning of alpha-male masculinity and patriarchal privilege. For an emasculated man to reclaim his lost phallus, the symbolic meaning of the phallus must be resignified as a queer site of communal and intersexual values rather than of agonistic and alpha-male masculinity. The cultural meanings of the phallus create men through its phantastic construction of potent masculinity, yet *Eger and Grime* denudes this fantasy by reimagining phallic power and symbolism. Celebrating female fecundity at the narrative's end, *Eger and Grime* highlights the labile potential of the queer to reify the prevailing patriarchal order as it simultaneously questions some of its most deeply held values. By prefiguring the generic development of the romantic comedy, *Eger and Grime* explores how the humor of phallic masculinity and the taming of the queer prop up systems of masculinity that have been nonetheless ridiculed.

This book ends by considering the place of compulsory queerness in the academy. Chapter 7, "Compulsory Queerness and the Pleasures of Medievalism," points to the ways in which medievalists' identities are queerly constructed through the intersections of past and present, as well as through the intersections of scholarly vocation and pop-cultural preconceptions. Given the obscurity of medievalism as a career choice in today's society, a medievalist's construction of self-identity is refracted through a lens of postmodern prejudice, but queer pleasures can nonetheless be located in the deconstructed genders of the medieval past. The overarching purpose of this book is to expose the complicity of queerness in the creation of heterosexuality, yet it would perhaps be too pessimistic to end without identifying possible pleasures of compulsory queerness as well.

And finally, a brief word about the methodological framework for the ensuing analysis: this study is indebted to Freud's observations regarding the tension between self and society, as the allusion in the title makes clear. However, I do not limit myself to a psychoanalytic approach to the literature in question, and also use insights from Marxist, feminist, gender, deconstructionist, narratological, and queer theories. Such a theoretical bricolage underscores the difficulty of pinpointing queerness and its effects, and it also points to the power of queer theory to resist categorization and to locate affinities among various critical practices. Carla Freccero sees in queer theory a "resistance to its hypostatization [and] reification into nominal status as designating an entity, an identity, a thing"; she advocates that scholars should "allow [queerness] to continue its outlaw work as a verb and sometimes an adjective."[54] If it is indeed possible to dismantle the ideological regimes antithetical to queer desire, we will need every tool in the theoretical toolbox, and then some.

CHAPTER 2

ABANDONING DESIRES, DESIRING READERS, AND THE DIVINELY QUEER TRIANGLE OF *PEARL*

In *Pearl,* what does the Dreamer desire? On the surface level of the text, he unequivocally seeks to reunite with the Pearl that he loves and has lost. The apparent objectives of desire are rarely as clear cut as they initially present themselves, however, and surface desires often conceal covert objectives, which lie hidden from view and refuse to signify monologically and teleologically. *Pearl* affirms the ways in which ostensibly normative desires—a father's heartbreak and mourning over his daughter's death and his longing to reunite with her—simultaneously conceal and reveal other unarticulated and latent objectives. The strangely eroticized familial relationship between living father and dead daughter, in the end, serves as one facet of a multidimensional romance that becomes increasingly and competitively linked with the Dreamer's latent desire for the God who now possesses her. In this divinely queer and erotic triangle that forms around the Dreamer, the Pearl Maiden, and God, desires lead the Dreamer to self-sacrifice and abandon in response to his undeclared amatory competition with God, whose desires can never be trumped. In the formation of normative Christian masculinity, the Dreamer must be queered into submission to the Divine Will.

In a similar manner, we may well ask: what does the reader of *Pearl* desire? If readers desire the Pearl Maiden to signify meaningfully, to teach a Christian truth applicable to daily life, such a desire must be sacrificed to the *Pearl*-poet's metatextual and narratival authority that refuses to palliate harsh truths with easy answers.[1] As part of the *Pearl*-poet's narrative strategy, structures of meaning devolve into structures of meaninglessness, in that the semiotic systems and genres of *Pearl* create conflicting, polyvalent, and ultimately self-destructing readerly desires, which in the end are revealed to be as mercurial and evanescent as the Dreamer's. Analyzing *Pearl* for the indeterminacy of desire within its construction of spirituality and of literary form, we see that in both the divinely queer triangle of Dreamer, Pearl Maiden, and God and in the metatextual triangle of reader, text, and *Pearl*-poet, the dreamer's and the reader's desires dissolve in favor of the divine and of the authorial, which leaves Christian subjects conquered and in eroticized submission to authorities beyond them. In this instance, queerness marks the pathway to normative Christian identities, which must be predicated upon embracing the hierarchical structure of religious belief instead of in response to personal desires.

Desire and the Divine Erotic Triangle

Many contemporary theorists, especially those from cultural, psychoanalytic, and queer perspectives, concur that desire does not seek to sate itself and thus to effect its erasure; rather, desire is viewed as a multivalent psychical structure, always evolving and deceiving in endlessly self-perpetuating sequences.[2] As Slavoj Žižek articulates, "In our daily lives, we (pretend to) desire things that we do not really desire, so that, ultimately, the worst thing that can happen is for us to get what we 'officially' desire."[3] Desire thus involves pretense and self-deception, as we pursue objectives for the very sake of the pursuit, but not to end the pursuit. Rather than directing individuals to the fulfillment of their goals, desire merely structures its repetition and return, an eternal spiral that never reaches its end. "Desire desires, above all, its own continuation, not its fulfillment. We need our discontent in order to feel and enjoy our desire, and if events do not conspire to make us feel dissatisfied, we will arrange our own privations," explains Aranye Fradenburg.[4] The very failure of desire thus emerges as its ontological purpose, and in *Pearl,* desire appears doomed since it is ostensibly directed to the Dreamer's deceased daughter.

Such a perspective on desire is not unique to contemporary theorists, and it can likewise be found in the writings of the Middle Ages. Medieval mystics such as the author of *The Cloud of Unknowing* believe that earthly desires are doomed to failure:

> For not what thou arte, ne what thou hast ben, beholdeth God with his mercyful ighe; bot that thou woldest be. & Seinte Gregory to witnes that "alle holy desires growen bi delaies; & yif thei wany[n] bi delaies, then were thei neuer holy desires." For he that felith euer les ioye & les in newe

fyndinges & sodeyn presentacions of his olde purposid desires, thof al thei
mowe be clepid kyndely desires to the goode, neuertheles holy desires
weren thei neuer.[5]

(God sees with his merciful eye not what you are, nor what you have been,
but what you would be. And Saint Gregory attests that "all holy desires
grow through delays, and if they decrease through delays, then they were
not holy desires." For he that continually feels less and less joy in new
discoveries and sudden appearances of his old purposed desires, although
they may be called proper desires to the good, nevertheless, they were
never holy desires.)[6]

Through the citation of St. Gregory, the author argues that holy desires
perpetually increase and earthly desires necessarily fluctuate; regardless of
whether the desires are holy or not, however, the author sees little possibility of the earthly fulfillment of desire. In distinguishing between holy and
unholy desires, this mystic separates the heavenly and the earthly, but
latent in his argument is the idea that living humans can never quell their
desires.[7] The Christian subject can only experience desires' daily increase,
never their satiation. Death, then, and the discovery of one's eternal reward
through salvation emerge as the only means to quench desire.

Certainly, the dynamics of desire in *Pearl* highlight its foredoomed
teleological failure on earth in a manner congruent with both modern
and medieval conceptions of such longings. When the Pearl Maiden
describes the ways in which God structures desire, it becomes apparent
that divinity purposefully creates in earthly desires their necessary failure. The Pearl Maiden reveals that earthly desires are predicated upon the
impossibility of their fulfillment and that these failures arise in accordance with God's dictates:

"Now is ther noght in the worlde rounde
Bytwene vus and blysse bot that He withdrogh,
And that is restored in sely stounde;
And the grace of God is gret innogh." (657–60)[8]

("Now there is nothing in the round world between us and bliss except
that which He withdrew, and that is restored in the blessed hour. And
the grace of God is great enough [to accomplish this].")

From the Pearl Maiden's viewpoint, God forecloses the possibility of
earthly bliss through the construction of determinate lacks. That which
God withdraws from humans frustrates embodied desires, and, in this
manner, Christianity creates desires that can never be fulfilled except at
the point that desires—and life—cease; then, Christians welcome the
"sely stounde" when heavenly grace is plentifully sufficient to sate (and

thus to erase) all human desires. "Sely stounde" translates simply as "innocent time" or "blessed hour," but "stounde" bears a secondary meaning of
"time of hardship" or "torment."[9] This connotative register of "stounde"
carries a slight hint of human resentment, in that even when heavenly
bliss is granted, a trace of remembered earthly suffering remains. Such a
connotative register is perhaps not surprising, given the Dreamer's obstinate responses to the Pearl Maiden's lessons and his need to be compelled
into proper Christian subservience and sexuality.

From both modern and medieval viewpoints, desires thus appear to be
destined for failure—at least for the living—in regard to their ostensible
ends. Queer theory further outlines the ways in which desires are misdi-
rected and amorphous such that, even when they are explicitly and consciously directed to a particular objective, they often go astray of this
purported end. Within the framework of the erotic triangle, desires that
initially appear normative are revealed to be multivalent, polymorphous,
and queer.[10] The basic structure of the erotic triangle, in which two suitors
pursue a shared beloved, appears to validate normative desire and sexuality, but, as Eve Sedgwick states, "in any erotic rivalry, the bond that links
the two rivals is as intense and potent as the bond that links either of the
rivals to the beloved."[11] That is, if a male suitor succeeds in defeating his
rival for the hand of the beloved, he will supposedly achieve the object of
his desires and thus quench them. But because desires can never be
quenched, even within the confined borders of the erotic triangle, any
attempt to sate them raises the ironic possibility that they were never actually directed at the beloved. Indeed, although erotic triangles typically
illustrate the sexual dynamics between two men and one woman, permutations of this structure abound precisely because desire is so nebulous a
phenomenon and seeks its own perpetuation rather than its fulfillment.

Queer theory has successfully deconstructed the ostensible heteronormativity of the male-female-male triangle and revealed its underbelly of
homosocial desire, but what happens when God Himself competes within
an erotic triangle? When divinity enters into a triangulated paradigm of
human desire, the metamorphoses and latent shiftings of desire between
the divine and the mortal lover destabilize the ways in which we perceive
the human subject's formative desire. God inevitably and organically
alters the polymorphous structuring of desire as incarnated within the
erotic triangle and fractures all constructions of desire and subjectivity
therein because He will—He must—win. The power dynamics within
this conception of the erotic triangle are vastly different from a wholly
human erotic triangle, and to a degree resemble the foundational erotic
triangle of the Oedipus complex, in which the child competes with the
father for the mother's affections. Within the Oedipal triangle, we see

"the situation of the young child that is attempting to situate itself with respect to a powerful father and a beloved mother";[12] within the divinely queer and erotic triangle, we see a variation of this theme, in which the father is the Father. Competition becomes even more impossible when formulated within the divine erotic triangle than within the struggle enacted between earthly child and earthly father as incarnated in the Oedipal triangle. A father will eventually die, and with him his sexual desire for the mother, but the Father—and the Father's desires—will exist forever. In *Pearl,* God as the Lamb enters the poem at its climax, and this moment should compel the Dreamer to cede his interest in this Pearl for a renewed relationship with Christ; nevertheless, the unraveling of this particular erotic triangle showcases the intransigence of earthly desire and the Dreamer's difficulty in replacing his Pearl with the Lamb as the proper object of his erotic devotion.

The chief difference between the human erotic triangle and the divinely queer triangle is that the human erotic triangle reveals desires where they presumably should not exist within a heteronormatively constructed culture—that is, between the two male suitors themselves rather than bilaterally between the female beloved and the male lovers. Because these desires shatter the assumed heteronormativity of the social romance, they reveal fissures in the ways in which society controls and regulates sexuality through its ideological power.[13] The divinely queer triangle, however, discovers desires precisely where they should be in terms of Christian theology—that is, between the human subject and God instead of between the human subject and a human beloved.[14] Within the framework of the divinely queer triangle, the female human beloved serves as a temporary surrogate for the lover's devotion to Christ, and she must be surpassed if the lover is to discover the futility of human desire and the superiority, if not the intransigence, of divine desire. As George Edmondson observes, God's participation enhances the competitive nature of desire in *Pearl*: "The (P)rince too has desire, a preeminent desire that has happened to alight, as the dreamer imagines it, on his own lost object."[15] Within this erotic triangle, the Pearl Maiden teaches the Dreamer that he must become a wife of the Lamb:

> "Forthy vche saule that hade neuer teche
> Is to that Lombe a worthyly wyf.
> And thagh vch day a store He feche,
> Among vus commez nouther strot ne stryf." (845–48)

("Therefore each soul that never experienced guilt is a worthy wife of that Lamb. And although each day he gathers a group, there comes among us neither argument nor strife.")

In this example embodied by her compatriots and herself, the Pearl enunciates the erotic and spiritual telos of the narrative: for the Dreamer to embrace his own position as a Bride of Christ. Every guiltless soul bears the possibility of serving as the Lamb's wife, and the Dreamer must accept such an eroticized and feminized position with the same rapture he feels for the Pearl.

The Dreamer conceives of romance as a competitive venture bearing the structure of an erotic triangle in which he must defeat his rival to win back the Pearl Maiden's affections. Although he does not yet accept his eroticized yet paradoxical position as his rival's bride, he nonetheless accords a place for God within his worldview, but only after his anticipated union with the Pearl Maiden:

> "I trawed my perle don out of of dawez;
> Now haf I fonde hyt, I schal ma feste,
> And wony with hyt in schyr wod-schawez,
> And loue my Lorde and al His lawez
> That hatz me broght thys blys ner." (282–86)

> ("I believed that my Pearl was deprived of her days; now I have found it, I shall rejoice and dwell with it in bright groves, and love my Lord and all His laws that have brought this bliss near to me.")

The Dreamer establishes an "order" to his desires: first, he will reunite with his Pearl in the "wod-schawez," an idyllic location suggestive of an amorous tryst. In this arboreal retreat, the Dreamer envisions himself dwelling with the Pearl Maiden, but God's presence is not likewise adumbrated. Certainly, his love for God is conditional in that only after his reunion with the Pearl Maiden will he "loue my Lorde and al His lawez." The tension inherent in feudalism and romance, in which a man must serve both his lord as a knightly vassal and his lady as a courtly lover, permeates this scene, but it is clear that the Dreamer prefers to concentrate on his service to and love for his daughter as a courtly lady rather than to celebrate his subservient position to the divine. The irony of the Dreamer's words—an irony he fails to recognize—accentuates his belief that God will sate his desire through a reunion with the Pearl Maiden, but God has no such intention of restoring her to him. Rather, the Dreamer must endure the repeated loss of the Pearl Maiden, reenacting the separation rather than moving beyond it. Without doubt, if the Dreamer is to rejoice ("feste") as he desires, it will be a much different celebration than he imagines.

From a courtly love perspective, the Dreamer's view of the competitive valence virtually inherent in amatory affairs is perhaps not surprising, but he merges this amatory paradigm with his construction of Christian salvation, limning both as agonistic phenomena with winners and losers. In commenting on the Pearl Maiden's position in heaven, the Dreamer accords her the status of a victor both in her marriage to Christ and in her position vis-à-vis the other saved souls:

> "Ouer alle other so hygh thou clambe
> To lede with Hym so ladyly lyf.
> So mony a comly onvunder cambe
> For Kryst han lyued in much stryf,
> And thou con alle tho dere outdryf,
> And fro that maryag al other depres,
> Al only thyself so stout and styf,
> A makelez may and maskellez." (773–80)

("You climbed so high, over all others, to lead a queenly life with Him. So many a comely woman beneath a headdress has lived in much strife for Christ. And you drove out all those dear ones, and after excluded all others from that marriage—only yourself, so proud and firm, a matchless and spotless maiden.")

The aggressive lexicon of "outdryf" and "depres" depicts the Pearl Maiden conquering her fellow virgins in an amorous battle royal; the *Pearl*-poet paints a picture of a turbulent conflict, which ultimately results in the Pearl Maiden enjoying the courtly spoils of a "ladyly lyf."[16] The Dreamer's erroneous vision of heavenly love manifested in conquest informs the reader of the ways in which he perceives both courtly romance and Christian salvation as zero-sum games. In terms of his salvific education, he must learn that one wins by losing, by abandoning oneself and one's desires to Christ rather than by defeating Him. As he first sees the Pearl Maiden as the victor in her own divinely erotic triangle, in which she must defeat a throng of competitive virgins to win Christ's love, he must correspondingly learn to embrace the fact that he has lost, with latent rapture, the Pearl Maiden to God.

If we see the Dreamer's relationship with his beloved Pearl Maiden as an indication of excessive, displaced, and confused desires, these desires also bleed into his relationship with the divine. The Dreamer's desire for his lost Pearl overwhelms Christian doctrine, as he reports that

> "I playned my perle that ther watz penned,
> Wyth fyrce skyllez that faste faght.
> Thagh kynde of Kryst me comfort kenned,
> My wreched wylle in wo ay wraghte." (53–56)

("I mourned for my Pearl that was enclosed there with appalling reasons that severely conflicted. Although the graciousness of Christ would have shown me comfort, my wretched will in woe always toiled.")

In this divinely queer triangle, the Dreamer's focus on the Pearl Maiden conceals as it simultaneously reveals his desire for Christ. Desiring the Pearl Maiden denies the Dreamer the comfort that Christ promises, but that the Dreamer sees in his woe and wretched will a failure to adhere to Christ—who would bestow comfort upon him—illustrates the ways in which conflicted desires deny the Dreamer the coherency of his own desire. In blocking his access to solace, the Dreamer reveals his desire to conquer his "wrched wylle" that denies him access to Christ.

Viewing the tensions among the Dreamer, the Pearl Maiden, and God as a divinely queer triangle allows the reader to discern the conflicting tensions in the Dreamer's relationships with his beloved and his savior, but these insights are all the more surprising in that the competition inherent in this particular incarnation of triangulated desire is a moot point: God has won the Pearl Maiden, as God wins all contests and all prizes. The Pearl Maiden declares God's victory to the Dreamer, proclaiming

> "... I am holy Hysse.
> Hys prese, Hys prys, and Hys parage
> Is rote and grounde of alle my blysse." (418–20)

("I am wholly His—His maiden, His valued one. And His lineage is the root and ground of all my bliss.")

And certainly, Christ is a better suitor than the Dreamer, as the Pearl Maiden portrays Him as a courtly and romantic lover who successfully wooed her with a lexicon of courtly love poetry:

> "He calde me to Hys bonerté
> 'Cum hyder to Me, My lemman swete,
> For mote ne spot is non in the.'" (762–64)

("He called me to His goodness, 'Come hither to Me, My sweet darling, for neither stain nor spot is on you.'")

Repeatedly referring to the Lamb as her "lemman" (e.g., 796, 805, 829), the Pearl Maiden clearly indicates that the Lamb has won her as his bride and lover. By depicting the Dreamer's obstinate pursuit of the Pearl Maiden despite the fact that Christ has triumphed, the *Pearl*-poet foreshadows the solution to the crux of desire: abandoning oneself and one's desire. One can only win by losing, by experiencing the instructive lessons of compulsory queerness along the Christian path to spiritual nor-mativity and sexual subservience as a Bride of Christ.

Romancing the Pearls and Queering the Forms of Desire

Before looking in this chapter's final section at the dynamics of abandon within *Pearl*, I would like to examine the ways in which the *Pearl*-poet confuses the reader's desires so that they too, through a similar queer construction of triangulated desire, are virtually incomprehensible. *Pearl* invites readers to participate not merely in the construction of textual meaning, but also in the construction of Christian identity by witnessing the Dreamer's attempts to regain his beloved Pearl Maiden and finding allegorical meaning therein. Madhavi Menon argues that "ideas of veil-ing and circularity...are central to the trope of allegory in which the tropological impulse makes it impossible to arrive at a certainty that does not immediately question itself. Moreover, this deconstruction of cer-tainty is inevitably tied...to the construction of sexuality."[17] Such a dynamic of readerly seduction structures a range of narratives, and alle-gorical fiction invites readers to cast themselves within the narrative as it seductively dissolves boundaries between text and metatext. As in Stanley Fish's memorable quotation of John Milton, we see another example of literature that is "not so much a teaching, as an intangling."[18]

As the Dreamer's queerly triangulated desire for the Pearl Maiden ultimately reveals his need to submit to God as a Bride of Christ because his own desires become amorphous to the point of incoherency, so too do the reader's desires for *Pearl,* to signify through a coherent hermeneutic, reveal the ways in which we must submit to the *Pearl*-poet's artistry. In regard to the compelling force of some narratives, J. Hillis Miller observes, "What happens when I read *must* happen, but I must acknowledge it as *my* act of reading, though just what the 'I' is or becomes in this transac-tion is another question."[19] *Pearl* functions in this manner, conflating the possibilities of personal readings with its coercive force. These tensions are multiplied in dream visions, in that readers are intended to experience the dreamer's narrative journey for themselves. Helen Phillips points out that the narrator of a dream vision is "the surrogate of the reader, gradu-ally experiencing the narrative, and the critic attempting to interpret it,"[20] and this mirrored construction of protagonist/reader establishes a readerly dynamic that closely parallels the Dreamer's experiences. The divinely queer triangle of Dreamer, Pearl Maiden, and God has as its metatextual equivalent the narratival erotic triangle of reader, *Pearl,* and author. On the path to sharing the Dreamer's Christian catharsis, the reader must confront that his (the Dreamer's) desires are in such a chaotic and destabilizing spiral that, before the divine erotic triangle of Dreamer, Pearl Maiden, and God forms coherently, it is quite difficult to ascertain exactly what or whom he (the Dreamer) desires. As the Dreamer discovers the ways in which his desires are misplaced and incoherent in relation to the Pearl Maiden, readers must similarly learn the ways in which narratival desires deceive them in the construction of the text's meaning.

If we see such literary forms as semantics, symbols, and genres as conduits to sating readerly desire through the communication of meaning, it becomes apparent that the *Pearl*-poet manipulates and queers these forms of communicating narrative sense into forms of frustrating readerly desire.[21] Symbols and genres in *Pearl* repeatedly encourage specific interpretations, only to push these interpretations past any reasonable boundaries, thus stripping them of their ostensible meaning through the disciplinary limits of their hermeneutic horizons. For example, what is a Pearl, and how can the reader formulate a coherent epistemological desire about this amorphous and shifting symbol? The Dreamer ostensibly yearns for his "perle," but the metaphoric and linguistic slipperiness of this simple term signifies the ways in which desires trip over themselves and thus render themselves virtually incomprehensible to the poem's audience. The "perle" originally signifies literally, not metaphorically, as the Dreamer bemoans its loss:

> "Perle plesaunte, to prynces paye
> To clanly clos in golde so clere:
> Oute of oryent, I hardyly saye,
> Ne proued I neuer her precios pere.
> So rounde, so reken in vche araye,
> So smal, so smothe her sydez were;
> Queresoeuer I jugged gemmez gaye
> I sette hyr sengeley in synglure." (1–8)

("Pleasing Pearl, a pleasure for a prince in its splendid setting in gold so bright. Out of the Orient, I certainly say, I never discovered her precious peer. So round, so elegant in each array, so small, so smooth her sides were. Wherever I judged magnificent gems, I set her apart as unique.")

These opening lines refuse to foreshadow the symbolic shifts that the pearl incarnates throughout the poem, as it soon signifies the narrator's beloved and later transforms into the kingdom of heaven, as described in Matthew 13:45–46 ("Again, the kingdom of heaven is like to a merchant seeking good pearls. Who, when he had found one pearl of great price, went his way and sold all that he had and bought it").[22] Moreover, the Dreamer himself metaphorically assumes the cast of yet another pearl in the closing lines of the poem (l.1211–12), and this vast semantic range of the poem's central image undercuts the reader's attempts to understand the Dreamer's desires. I am not arguing that symbols function solely on literal or metaphoric levels, as their power lies in the hazy nexus between these two interpretive planes. At the same time, authors frequently encourage readers to ignore the literal/metaphorical link of a given symbol and then surprise them with a shift in symbolic register. Certainly, in the opening stanzas of the poem, the first-time reader of *Pearl* has no reason to suspect that the "perle plesaunte" is so much more than a mere pearl. On first reading this poem, we are in no manner prepared for the text's subsequent semantic shifts, especially since these lines focus so tactilely on the pearl's pleasing contours and invite the reader to revel in its perfect physicality.[23]

Of course, the Dreamer obviously does not desire a "perle" as incarnated in a gem or jewelry, as he soon sees in his vision that

"The grauayl that on grounde con grynde
Wern precious perlez of oryente." (81–82)

("The gravel that one could grind on the ground were precious pearls of the Orient.")

This lavish detail establishes the ways in which desires self-destruct and revive themselves promiscuously throughout the poem: the Dreamer barely mentions this multitude of pearls because they offer no solace to his desires, but, since the reader has no reason yet to look beyond the literal meaning of "perle," this overwhelmingly plentiful landscape, so luxuriously bedecked with pearls, compels the reader to concede the unknowability of the Dreamer's desires. He claims repeatedly that he desires his Pearl, but we can never really know what he desires in the text because we do not know what a pearl is in this narrative; as a result, our readerly desires are continually dashed and reborn and dashed again. Lawrence Clopper notes the *Pearl*-poet's penchant for semiotic disjunction, declaring that "the poet uses misperceptions about language and reality in order to demonstrate the gulf between sign, a word, and thing, an essence."[24] In such a manner, the *Pearl*-poet repeatedly jolts and dismantles word and image, leaving readers unsure how we should interpret the focal image of the allegory. The text's semiotic system thus mirrors its construction of desire in that both entities signify in the failure of signification. If readers desire meaning through words that signify clearly, our desires are likely to be as frustrated and as unfulfilled as the Dreamer's: he wants to *have* her, we want to *know* her, but neither protagonist nor reader will ever satisfy these restless desires.[25]

The shifting semantic range of "perle" serves as an object lesson in desire, as we see that desires are never sated in regard to their initial objectives, at least in the manner to which the reader is introduced to them. As Sarah Stanbury declares, "*Pearl* sets in motion a set of 'category mistakes' that comment uneasily on the very natures of categories: what is a pearl? What is a girl? How do we know or evaluate what we see?"[26] In addition to the questions that Stanbury perceptively raises, it is also necessary to ponder how these semantic shifts interrelate with and inter-ject questions of desire into the text. If "perle" repeatedly changes despite its status as chief signifier in the text, refusing to signify monologically and transforming at least three times from pearl to Pearl Maiden to New Jerusalem, the Dreamer does not desire a single "perle" (despite the fact that he claims "I sette hyr sengeley in synglure" [8]) but many and vari-able pearls, each with direct repercussions to his sense of self and his unfolding narrative quest to quench his desires. Critics typically agree that, within its plentiful semantic and symbolic range, the "perle" signi-fies perfection, but the Dreamer establishes such a variety of meanings to "perle" that we are unsure what incarnation of perfection he seeks.[27] The unknowability of the Pearl confuses the parameters of the divine erotic triangle, and so too does the iconic physicality of the Lamb. The signs of the text ask the reader to see the Lamb as the physical embodiment of an earthly animal:

> "Thys Jerusalem Lombe hade neuer pechche
> Of other huee bot quyt jolyf,
> That mot ne masklle moght on streche,
> For wolle quyte so ronk and ryf." (841–44)

> ("This Jerusalem Lamb never had a patch of other color but beautiful white. Neither stain nor spot might spread on the white wool, so rich and abundant.")

The queerness of the divine erotic triangle, beyond the interpolation of divine desire in a human search for earthly fulfillment, emerges in the polymorphousness of its bodies and signs, in which a pearl is both a pearl and a daughter and the rival is both a woolly lamb and a savior. Concentrating on the animal form of the lamb forces the reader to con-front the impenetrability of Christian symbolism, in which signs promise to clarify religious doctrine yet ultimately obfuscate meaning when presented in their literal incarnations.

As the lexical shifts of "perle" highlight the openness of the Dreamer's desires in the text and frustrate the reader's attempts to understand them, generic shifts likewise subvert efforts to understand the speaker's desires.

Quite simply, *Pearl* cannot be contained by a single generic form.[28] It is frequently read through the lenses of allegory, dream vision, and elegy, and each of these genres establishes readerly expectations about the narrative's purpose. If an allegory, *Pearl* should provide a moral lesson compatible with Christianity;[29] if a dream vision, *Pearl* should depict the Dreamer's discovery of an important truth;[30] and if an elegy, *Pearl* should lament the loss of a beloved.[31] The teleological drives of these three genres overlap and complement one another well, and readers can generate meaningful textual interpretations with them, both separately from and in tandem with one another. This list in no measure circumscribes *Pearl*'s generic possibilities, and such generic frameworks as consolation, meditation, dialogue, and lyric also structure the text. As the vacillating symbolic valence of "perle" suggests, the *Pearl*-poet delights in shifting interpretive frameworks while they are still nonetheless in play, as he simultaneously explores the transfigurations thus effected upon his protagonist's desires. Readers must face the question of how these various generically constructed desires reflect the Dreamer's narrative quest, as they also confront the difficulty of establishing horizons of interpretive expectations when genres clash.

Beyond the ways in which allegory, dream vision, and elegy interplay and complement our understanding of the Dreamer's desires, *Pearl* also deploys the genre of romance, with its tropes of courtly love, to complicate any nascent coalescence of comprehension. In terms of generic structure as it relates to narratival desire, allegory and dream vision typically feature desires that can be fulfilled: allegories depict a desire parallel to the desire for Christ, and these narratives often illustrate the fulfillment of that desire. Likewise, dream visions depict a desire for a moral truth, and such a truth typically comforts the dreamer upon awakening.[32] Elegy and romance, however, feature the impossibility of desire: elegy, in the fruitlessness of desiring the dead; romance, in the unabashed foregrounding of a courtly love that should never be consummated. Such generic generalizations risk oversimplifying the contours of allegory, dream vision, elegy, and romance, but in terms of their individual structures throughout literary history, we can perceive notable distinctions in the ways in which narratival desires constitute these genres. Indeed, genre itself may be understood as a method of inscribing and codifying narratival and readerly desires within a particularly apt literary form.[33] The *Pearl*-poet relies on the interplay of generic desires to reinforce and subvert one another, as the reader is unsure which genre, with its concomitant expectations of narratival desires fulfilled or frustrated, ultimately guides the interpretive process. In terms of the normativity of desire, however, it is crucial to realize that allegory, dream vision, and elegy are insufficient tools for the poet to queer the normativity of the Dreamer's desires. Thus, romance, with its hints of a courtly love that disrupts and complicates the ostensibly normative elegiac longing of bereaved father for deceased daughter, serves a necessary function in further destabilizing and troubling our understanding of the Dreamer's relationship with the Pearl Maiden.

When the genres of allegory, dream vision, and elegy confront the traces of romance within the text, the resulting genre play renders impossible a clear view of the Dreamer and his objectives. For example, when the Dreamer declares "In sweuen / My goste is gon in Godez grace, / In auenture ther meruaylez meuen" ("In a dream, my spirit has gone in God's grace into an adventure where marvels happen"; 62–64), genre fails to signify coherently and thus sabotages the reader's attempt to develop a generic hermeneutic for the text. These lines fracture organic generic form, as the lexicons of dream vision ("In sweuen"), Christian allegory ("My goste is gon in Godez grace"), and romance ("In auenture ther meruaylez meuen") combine and cripple interpretive praxis. Each of these generic paradigms establishes different expectations for the Dreamer's desires: for the moment of revelation typical of dream visions; for the union with God typical of Christian allegory; and for the marvelous events and play of courtly love typical of romance. The textual question of "What does the Dreamer desire?" here merges with the metatextual question of "How does genre influence an understanding of the Dreamer's desire?" Both questions, however, not only refuse conclusive answers but refuse the possibility of any answer that does not immediately undermine its own semiotic coherency.

Indeed, the Dreamer's tone in the opening stanza further establishes the ways in which semantic and generic shifts upset readerly expectations and queer any understanding of his desires that focus on his lost Pearl Maiden. As his "perle" shifts from a literal gem to a metaphorical representation of his beloved, the speaker's words suggest the loss of his beloved first with an elegiac lexicon ("Allas! I leste hyr in on erbere" ["Allas, I lost her in a garden"; 9]) and then with a lexicon of courtly romance ("I dewyne, fordolked of luf-daungere / Of that pryuy perle withouten spot" ["I lament, griefstricken by frustrated love, for that special pearl without blemish"; 11–12]). The union of dream vision and romance also strikingly appears when the Dreamer first sees the Pearl Maiden, in that she embodies a marvel:

> "More meruayle con my dom adaunt.
> I segh byyonde that myry mere
> A crystal clyffe ful relusaunt:
> Mony ryal ray con fro hit rere.
> At the fote therof ther sete a faunt." (157–61)

("More marvels overwhelmed my mind. I saw beyond that fair stream a
crystal cliff exceedingly radiant. Many royal rays rose from it. At the
bottom of it there sat a child.")

Within this dream world, the revelation of a marvel at the fantastic setting
of a crystal cliff falls within the expected purview of romance. This marvelous vision is both dreamlike in its fantasy and romantic in the possible
reunion between Dreamer and lost Pearl, but neither genre adequately
prepares the reader for the ensuing dialogue and pedagogical instruction
on proper Christian subservience.

In a similar vein, the repeated description of the Pearl Maiden's royal
array portrays her within the dual contexts of courtly romance and heavenly queen:

> "That gracios gay withouten galle,
> So smothe, so smal, so seme slyght,
> Rysez vp in hir araye ryalle,
> A precios pyece in perlez pyght." (189–92)

("That gracious maiden without blemish—so smooth, so small, so
suitably slender—rises up in her royal array: a precious damsel adorned
with pearls.")

The repeated romance tropes establish the reader's interpretative focus,
yet this perspective cannot hold. As Jim Rhodes observes,

> In the opening stanza when he tells us that he suffers "fordolked of
> luf-daungere," we are led to expect one kind of poem only to discover that
> it is going to be entirely of another sort. The poet's manipulation of a term
> familiar to love poetry has a calculated effect nevertheless: it acts as a
> verbal prod that disorients us and sticks in our mind because of its incon-
> gruity, both complicating the narrative and individuating the Dreamer. It
> puts the audience on notice that it has to adjust to his way of articulating
> and internalizing things.[34]

In the end, the generic goals of allegory, dream vision, elegy, and romance
unexpectedly complement one another, but only when the traces of
romance within the divine erotic triangle are reconfigured away from
the Pearl Maiden and directed to God. Likewise, readers must sacrifice
their desires for coherent generic form to the metaconsciousness of the
Pearl-poet and submit to his lesson, despite its troubling elements.

Certainly, many readers are unnerved by the Dreamer's sexualized
and possibly incestuous relationship with the Pearl Maiden. As scholars

have noted, the romantic vision of the Pearl Maiden as courtly lady clashes with her image as the Dreamer's two-year-old child. In response, Jane Beal argues that we have no proof for viewing the Pearl Maiden as a child and suggests that "the textual evidence and the historical context of the poem both support the possibility that the Dreamer was the Pearl Maiden's lover in life who now mourns her loss."[35] This vision of the Pearl Maiden bears obvious merits in that it explains the unmannerly use of courtly love language between father and daughter, but it does not adequately address all of the ambiguities of the text. Beal's argument dismantles a full conviction that the Pearl Maiden is a child, but her explanations for the lines that most directly confirm this opposing viewpoint—"'Thow wost wel when thy perle con schede / I watz ful yong and tender of age'" ("'You know well that when your Pearl died, I was quite young and of a tender age'"; 411–12) and "'Thou lyfed not two yer in oure thede'" ("'You lived not two years in our land'"; 483)—do not pass Occam's razor unscathed. That the poet refuses to describe the Pearl Maiden in unambiguous terms and that the same character can be convincingly interpreted as a two-year-old child and as a young woman indicates that the poet expects readers to wrangle with the ways in which this amorphous character challenges the interpretive process and further destabilizes our understanding of the Dreamer's desires, as well as of our own readerly desires. When we first see the Pearl Maiden, the Dreamer describes her in complementary yet distinct ways, first as a "faunt" and then as a "mayden of menske, ful debonere" ("maiden of honor, fully gracious"; 161–62). There need be no absolute contradiction in these lines, as a maiden child may refer to a youth of variable age. At the same time, "faunt" typically suggests a very young child or infant, whereas "mayden of menske, ful debonaire" connotatively implies a child of more mature years, as few toddlers can successfully assume a debonair posture.[36] As María Bullón-Fernández suggests, "Even though from a 'realistic' point of view the daughter might have been two years old, the narrator's language reveals that he does not see her as a two-year-old girl."[37] Furthermore, the Dreamer enigmatically describes his kinship to the Pearl Maiden in a manner to confuse rather than to clarify her age: "Ho watz me nerre then aunte or nece" ("She was closer to me than aunt or niece"; 233). Familial relationships between a male and female that are closer than aunt and niece include mother, wife, and daughter, but the *Pearl*-poet forebears speaking definitively on this key issue. The likeliest explanation for the Pearl Maiden's cryptic embodiment is that she has metamorphosed into her new role as Bride of Christ, but this spiritual rebirth nonetheless leaves her physically unimaginable to the reader, as she is both infant and maiden, both recognizably human and unrecognizably beyond human.

Rather than resolving the paradox of the Pearl Maiden's age and her relationship to the Dreamer, the *Pearl*-poet delights in this tension, refusing to answer the simplest of narratival questions. Because the text forces us to confront the impossibility of deciphering the Dreamer's desires as represented in the enigmatic Pearl Maiden, who serves as the focal point of the narrative and of its divinely queer triangle, she thus highlights the frailty and incomprehensibility of mortal desire. Through the *Pearl*-poet's overdetermined yet nonetheless hazy description of the text's central image, the Dreamer's desires refuse to communicate themselves to the reader. Readers *see* the desired object but cannot *know* her.

Of course, readers should not know her, since she must ultimately remain incomprehensible to the Dreamer and the poem's audience. In terms of Lacanian thought, the incestuous overtones of this relationship reify the necessary distance between desirer and desired: "That which presents itself as a law is closely tied to the very structure of desire. If [the desirer] doesn't discover right away the final desire that Freudian inquiry has discovered as the desire of incest, he discovers that which articulates his conduct so that the object of his desire is always maintained at a certain distance."[38] Both the Dreamer and the reader desire the Pearl Maiden to reveal truths and fulfill desires, but she will always refuse, keeping her distance until all desires are forever abandoned. By setting up insurmountable borders and taboos around the Pearl Maiden through genre, age, incest, and death, the *Pearl*-poet confounds his protagonist and his readers. Both must learn to abandon themselves to the text's controlling consciousness, with the Dreamer submitting to his latent desire for God and the reader submitting to the *Pearl*-poet's moral lesson. Queered subjection is the narrative solution to the crux of desire, and the destruction of semantic, symbolic, and generic codes prepares both Dreamer and reader for the queerness necessary for normative Christianity.

Abandoning *Pearl*: Reading and the Erotics of Submission

In accordance with the Pearl Maiden's declaration "'Now is ther noght in the worlde rounde / Bytwene vus and blysse bot that He withdrogh'" (657–58; quoted previously), we see that God's presence constitutes the fulfillment of bliss in heaven, in contrast to His withdrawal of bliss on earth. The only human solution to the impossibility of sating one's desires and of triumphing in the divine erotic triangle is to abandon them, to realize that desires directed to another person must be sacrificed to the divine in a total erasure of the self. As Jacques Lacan affirms, "The dialectical relationship between desire and the Law causes our desire to flare up only in relation to the Law, through which it becomes the desire for death."[39] Of course, Christianity does not encourage the desire for death as enacted by suicide, but this fracturing desire nonetheless embraces the destruction of the desiring self and its reconstitution into the impossibilities of desireless-ness. Lacan coordinates his insights in response to Paul, as recorded in Romans 7:7: "What shall we say, then? Is the law sin? God forbid! But I do not know sin, but by the law. For I had not known concupiscence, if the law did not say: *Thou shalt not covet.*" Here Paul asserts that the law stimu-lates desires antithetical to its purported ends. As the law creates desires, it then regulates and prohibits them, in a manner similar to the ways in which the Pearl Maiden describes God as creating earthly desires yet frus-trating the realization of bliss. In the conscripting confluence between desire and the law, the human subject is enmeshed and imbricated in desires that destroy the social self in favor of a self that must be freed from earthly desire for the beloved. In this construction of dictum and transgression, the law itself embodies the act it prohibits, as Žižek observes rhetorically: "Is not the 'truth' of the opposition between Law and its particular transgres-sions that the Law itself is the highest transgression?"[40]

Pearl invites this sort of abandon from its protagonist and its readers, a sacrifice of their selves in relation to a hierarchical consciousness. Abandon, however, is not merely self-abnegation to the point of erasure; the loss of the autonomous self paradoxically leads to a self reborn and renewed in conjunction with divine (and narratival) authority. *The Book of Privy Counselling,* for example, cites Christ's teaching in the Gospel to exhort readers to forsake themselves:

> & that more is, in this thou arte lernid to forsake & dispise thin owne self, after the teching of Crist in the gospel, seiing thus: "Si quis vult venire post me, abneget semetipsum; tollat crucem suam et sequatur me." That is, "Who-so wole come after me, late hym forsake hym-self, late hym bere his cros & folow me."... I prey thee, how may a man more forsake him-self & the woreld, & more dispise him-self & the woreld, then for to dedein for to think of eny qualite of here beinges?[41]

> (And what is more, in this you learn to forsake and despise your own self, after the teaching of Christ in the gospel, who says: "Si quis vult venire post me, abneget semetipsum; tollat crucem suam et sequatur me." That is, "If any man will come after me, let him deny himself and take up his cross daily and follow me."... I pray you, how may a man more forsake himself and the world and more despise himself and the world than to disdain to think of any quality of his being?)[42]

The author delimits the necessity for Christians to follow Christ through the call to disdain and condemn all qualities of their very selves. To be

Christlike is thus to resist thinking of the self, to renounce every quality of the self that connects one to that self. Through this method of self-rejection, Christians find Christ, and only then can desire be sated.

The desire of abandon represents the realization of personal needs and lacks that must be filled by another. Through the narratival erotics of seduction and compulsion as enacted in the divinely queer triangle, the Dreamer and readers discover desires of which they were unaware. It is a paradoxical process of conversion to new desires through the regulation and destruction of previous ones, although these new desires are ironically predicated upon their ever-enacted destruction. *Pearl* participates within such a conception of an abandoning literature, texts that coerce readers into a masochistic self-degradation in order to rise phoenix-like from their phantastic immolation.[43] The dialectic between tenderness and torment, between the pleasure of the text and the pain of abandoning, structures the experience of narrative interpellation into ideology. By reading *Pearl* with an eye to the ways in which it solicits readerly sacrifice and abandon, we see that the poet's demand for submission to God's unknowable will both exalts and degrades his protagonist and his readers into a profound new relationship with the Divine.

In the end, the simple but painful Christian realization that truth must be accepted on faith rather than verified through proof forces the Dreamer to abandon his desire because if Christian subjects desire evidence, they do not have the option of putting their hands in Christ's side and enacting the testing process of a doubting Thomas. For certainly, the Pearl Maiden's attempts to teach the Dreamer any sort of moral lesson repeatedly fail, and this spiritually pedagogical failure stresses the necessity of abandon. Complementing his desire for the Pearl Maiden and analogous to his latent and queerly triangulated desire for Christ, the Dreamer also desires knowledge about her position in heaven in relation to its governing structure. His response to her retelling of the Parable of the Vineyard ("Then more I meled and sayde apert: / 'Me thynk thy tale vnresounable'" ["Then I spoke more and declared openly, 'I think your tale is unreasonable'"; 589–90]) humorously showcases his penchant for literal interpretations of complex spiritual truths. The Dreamer's inability to understand even the most basic parameters of the heavenly kingdom reinforces his need to turn to the Pearl Maiden for spiritual guidance, and this excessive ignorance is typical of the dream vision as a genre. Helen Philips outlines the necessity of the oft implausible naiveté of dreaming narrators: "All dreamer-narrators have a tendency to seem stupid to some extent, for the encounter between dreamer and dream, or dreamer and authority figure, is a structure which splits the didactic enterprise in two, into the learning function and the teaching function."[44] Surely the Dreamer of *Pearl* confounds the reader with his frustrating and funny simplemindedness, as when he assumes that the virgins of heaven are forced to live outside and endure the elements: "So cumly a pakke of joly juele / Wer euel don schulde lygh peroute" ("Such a comely group of beautiful jewels were unfavorably treated, if they should lie in the open"; 929–30). This seeming insistence on ignorance complements well the failure of the Dreamer's desires: both earthly desire and earthly knowledge are insufficient tools to comprehend divine mysteries.

Although the Dreamer's inability to comprehend the Pearl Maiden's lesson strikes some readers as a mark of his recalcitrance, Stephen Russell stresses the opacity of the Pearl Maiden's moral lesson: "Like Orwell's dictum that all pigs are created equal but that some are more equal than others, the Pearl maiden's assertion of universal queenship is really a tease, a *via negativa* that enacts the fact that, given the language at our disposal, explaining is the last thing that will explain."[45] If the Pearl Maiden's explanations do not really explain, however, neither can the Dreamer's desires— for her, for knowledge—function meaningfully or teleologically.[46] The Dreamer's desires for the Pearl Maiden are a blind that nonetheless lead him to Christ, and so too are the Pearl Maiden's lectures. In a sense, the Dreamer's desires and the Pearl Maiden's lessons are red herrings, false signposts on the path to salvation, as they can only signify through the failure to signify rationally. In this narrative world, desires are ultimately desireless, and meanings are similarly meaningless, until they are surpassed through abandon.

In seeking a renewal of earthly bliss through his relationship with the Pearl Maiden, the Dreamer must learn to forgo earthly desires and to forge heavenly ones. The troubling eroticism between the Dreamer and the Pearl Maiden finds a proper outlet when the "perle" shifts from Pearl Maiden to New Jerusalem. In this transformation, the Dreamer finds the ravishment he craves in an erotically charged scene that oddly focuses on a city:

> "As quen I blusched vpon that baly,
> So ferly therof watz the fasure.
> I stod as stylle as dased quayle
> For ferly of that frech fygure,
> That felde I nawther reste ne trauayle,
> So watz I rauyste with glymme pure." (1083–88)

> ("When I gazed on that city, its appearance was so marvelous that I stood as still as a dazed quail in wonder of that brilliant vision. I felt neither rested nor anxious because I was so ravished by the pure light.")

Commenting on the apparent paradox in that the Dreamer finds "nawther reste ne trauayle," Glending Olson pronounces the negative utility of desire: "To express the nature of this rapturous state in a negative way is appropriate to the narrator's condition. He cannot fully possess the object of his desires until after death."[47] At this moment of paradox, the Dreamer finds himself ravished. The Pearl Maiden, an inappropriate target of the Dreamer's desires, is momentarily discarded as an object of incestuous eroticism in favor of an urban eroticism, in which a city ravishes as powerfully as any maiden ever could. Obviously, cities are physically incapable of ravishing, and maidens more frequently suffer in the position of the ravished than enact the role of the ravisher. In this instance, when the Dreamer sees himself as ravished by the city's radiance, the *Pearl*-poet plays with the semiotic interplay between ravish and rape. As Kathryn Gravdal notes of rape, ravishment, and romance, "In romance, 'ravishment' becomes aestheticized and moralized."[48] In *Pearl*, we are not meant to imagine the physical enactment of rape as much as the spiritual ravishing, aestheticized, and transcendent, that the Dreamer momentarily finds through the latest incarnation of his multivalent and triangulated desire. But even this moment of ravishment is insufficient to quell the Dreamer's polymorphous and bubbling desires: at the moment one earthly desire is quelled, another rises to take its place.

If earthly desires can never be quenched, if God has removed the very possibility of bliss from this world, humans must abandon the game of earthly desire. To teach this lesson, the Pearl Maiden apprises the Dreamer of the ubiquity of suffering and the necessity of abandoning the self in response to God's judgment:

> "The oghte better thyseluen blesse,
> And loue ay God, in wele and wo,
> For anger gaynez the not a cresse.
> Who nedez schal thole, be not so thro;
> For thogh thou daunce as any do,
> Braundysch and bray thy brathez breme,
> When thou no fyrre may, to ne fro,
> Thou moste abyde that He schal deme." (341–48)

("You ought to bless yourself better and always love God, both in times of prosperity and misfortune because anger gains you nothing at all. Whoever must suffer shall do so; be not so perverse. For though you may writhe as any deer—struggle and shout with wild ferocity—when you can go no further, neither to nor fro, you must endure what He shall decide.")

The focus of these lines on suffering ("Who nedez schal thole") and acceptance ("Thou moste abyde that He schal deme") call to mind the necessity of patience and humility during trials and tribulations. Resistance is futile, as humans must abide by and endure God's judgments, no matter how arbitrary or unkind they appear. The only proper response to this hierarchical relationship is willed sufferance leading to abject submission and a complete acceptance of God's will. Indeed, the Pearl Maiden reiterates this lesson when she reports, "'My Lorde ne louez not for to chyde'" ("'My Lord loves not to chide'"; 403); due to this divine propensity to forgo punishment of sinful humans, the proper response is meekness: "'Be dep deuote in hol mekenesse'" ("'Be deeply devout in complete meekness'"; 406). Although meekness as a heavenly virtue is not wholly congruent with the dynamics of abandon, they share a similar valence in their acceptance of a greater power. It is also somewhat ironic that, in this statement, the Pearl Maiden accords God the power to punish while simultaneously highlighting his mercy (in a dynamic congruent to Lacan's reading of Paul and the law). Thus, because one cannot trust that God will forever refrain from chiding, *Pearl* suggests that meekness and abandon are the appropriate responses. In this regard, the Pearl Maiden may be a queen in heaven, yet she nonetheless models Christian submission to Mary, the Heavenly Queen: "'Cortayse quen,' thenne sayde that gaye, / Knelande to grounde, folde vp hyr face" ("'Courteous queen,' then said that lovely one, / Kneeling to the ground and bowing her face"; 432–33). Submission eventually coexists with heavenly knowledge, yet it is never fully eclipsed in the creation of the normative Christian subject, as the Dreamer must learn.

At the moment when the Dreamer actively seeks to quench his desire by crossing the river and joining the Pearl Maiden, God intervenes and circumvents the fulfillment of that desire:

"Delyt me drof in yghe and ere,
My manez mynde to maddyng malte;
Quen I segh my frely, I wolde be there,
Byyonde the water thagh ho were walte.
I thoght that nothyng myght me dere
To fech me bur and take me halte,
And to start in the strem schulde non me stere,
To swymme the remnaunt, thagh I ther swalte.
Bot of that munt I watz bitalt;
When I schulde start in the strem astraye,
Out of that caste I watz bycalt:
Hit watz not at my Pryncez paye." (1153–64)

("Delight drove me in eye and ear; my mortal mind was reduced to madness. When I saw my maiden, I desired to be there—beyond the water—although she would be upset. I thought that nothing could thwart me, bring me grief and cause me to waver, and nothing should restrain me from leaping into the stream, to swim the remaining space,

even if I died there. But of that intention I was startled: when I was going
to jump impetuously into the stream, I was called back from that
opportunity. It was not my Prince's pleasure.")

The closing line of this stanza foreshadows the Dreamer's forthcoming
metamorphosis, when he will refashion himself as one of the "precious
perlez vnto His pay" (1212). Ann Chalmers Watts sees in this moment the
connection between the inexpressibility of the Dreamer's desires and the
shattering of the dream: "In *Pearl* too the dreamer uses inexpressibility as
a verbally doomed gesture toward the glory of heavenly things, but the
poet joins inexpressibility to failed vision, to experience so packed with
desire that desire breaks the vision."[49] But whose desires break the
vision—the Dreamer's or God's? This question is impossible to answer in
definite and mutually exclusive terms, as the *Pearl*-poet describes the
calamitous event as resulting both from the Dreamer following his own
desires ("Delyt me drof in yghe and er") and from Christ's decision ("Out
of that caste I watz bycalt / Hit watz not at my Pryncez paye"). These
desires appear antithetical, yet they immediately begin to dovetail as the
Dreamer abandons his own will to God's.

The conflict between internal desire and external force finally compels
the Dreamer to abandon his desires to God's pleasure. Rather than depicting the Dreamer's realization of the truth of the Pearl Maiden's lesson, the
Pearl-poet describes the Dreamer's reluctant privileging of divine desires
over his own:

> "I raxled, and fel in gret affray,
> And, sykyng, to myself I sayd:
> 'Now al be to that Pryncez paye.'" (1174–76)

> ("I stretched, and fell in great dismay, and sighing to myself, I said: 'Now
> all must be to the Prince's pleasure.'")

In this moment of (somewhat petulant) abandon, we sense no new knowledge of Christian revelation and its teleological purpose.[50] Rather, the
Dreamer simply gives up his pursuit of the Pearl Maiden and of answers
to his questions in favor of divine desires outside of himself:

> "Therfore my joye watz sone toriuen,
> And I kaste of kythez that lastez aye.
> Lorde, mad hit arn that agayn the stryuen,
> Other proferen the oght agayn thy paye." (1197–1200)

> ("Therefore, my joy was soon shattered and I was cast from lands that last
> forever. Lord, those who strive against you are foolish, as are those who
> propose anything against your pleasure.")

The "lesson," if one can call it that, is that human agency and human questions must be abandoned in deference to the Divine Will. Quite simply, one must be crazy to resist God's desires, and one must likewise suffer from madness to pursue earthly objectives.

If the moral lesson of *Pearl* is that God triumphs in all erotic triangles and that His desires always precede human ones, the Dreamer is nonetheless somewhat recalcitrant at the poem's conclusion. He declares forthrightly that he continues to suffer greatly in his expulsion from his dream:

> "Me payed ful ille to be outfleme
> So sodenly of that fayre regioun,
> Fro alle tho syghtez so quyke and queme.
> A longeyng heuy me strok in swone." (1177–80)

> ("It pleased me exceedingly poorly to be cast out so suddenly from that fair region, from all of those sights so vivid and pleasing. A heavy longing struck me into a swoon.")

Feeling the pangs of a "longeyng heuy," the Dreamer sees no immediate benefit to his marvelous experience. The dream vision mildly alleviates his suffering, but only that portion of his suffering predicated upon his concern for the Pearl Maiden:

> "If hit be ueray and soth sermoun
> That thou so strykez in garlande gay,
> So wel is me in thys doel-doungoun
> That thou art to that Prynsez paye." (1185–88)

> ("If it is a truthful and true speech that you are set so in beautiful garlands, then it is well for me in this doleful prison—because you are intended for the Prince's pleasure.")

The bleak depiction of life on earth as a "doel-doungoun" stresses the suffering of earthly life and reminds the reader that the dungeon is not to be escaped but embraced. The contrast between the Dreamer's and Christ's situations—the former grimly declaring that he endures a doleful prison on earth, the latter enjoying the pleasure of the Pearl Maiden's company in heaven—undermines the *Pearl*-poet's resolution, in which the moral lesson of the allegory cannot effectively undo the tremendous agony highlighted throughout the narrative.

The Dreamer then contemplates the paradox of this vision of Christian revelation in that one cannot seek knowledge. One must abandon oneself to God's will and never attempt to cross the boundaries—literal and metaphorical—between the human and the divine:

> "To that Pryncez paye hade I ay bente,
> And yerned no more then watz me geuen,
> And halden me ther in trwe entent,
> As the perle me prayed that watz so thryuen,
> As helde, drawen to Goddez present,
> To mo of His mysterys I hade ben dryuen." (1189–94)

> ("Had I always yielded to that Prince's pleasure, and yearned for no more than was given to me, and maintained myself there in true intent, as the Pearl that was so special prayed me to do, to more of his His mysteries I would have been driven.")

The Dreamer blames himself for his lack of obedience to God's will, but he also suggests that, had he been more patient, he might have been compelled to understand more of His mysteries. The use of passive voice ("To mo of His mysterys I hade ben dryuen") accentuates mortal power-lessness to direct spiritual quests. The Dreamer then again accepts culpability for his transgressions, but the small moment of possibility lingers: God could have shown him more, but He did not. The Dreamer reiterates his suffering, which ever more forcefully appears the result of divine privilege than of personal sin.

Suffering thus incarnates and re-eroticizes the Dreamer's desires for the Pearl Maiden because he believes pain increases heavenly rewards. The possibility of penance ironically promises pleasure:

> "What more honour moghte he acheue
> That hade endured in worlde stronge,
> And lyued in penaunce hys lyuez longe
> With bodyly bale hym blysse to byye?" (475–78)

> ("What more honor might a man achieve who has endured steadfastly in the world, and lived in penance the length of his life with bodily suffering buying him bliss?")

These lines transform bodily suffering into eternal bliss, calling to mind Christ's exemplary anguish and the salvation that He purchased for humanity. As the eroticized image of the Pearl Maiden fades from the text in the final stanzas, the Dreamer abandons desires and embraces suffering as a conduit to pleasure.

The poem concludes with a tableau inconceivable at its commence-ment: the Dreamer now finds delight and pleasure in the death of the

Pearl Maiden. The scene of her burial and his lamentations metamorphoses into the locus of a renewed commitment to his savior. Over the girl's
interred and corrupted body, the Dreamer finds Christ:

> "Ouer this hyul this lote I laghte,
> For pyty of my perle enclyin,
> And sythen to God I hit bytaghte,
> In Krystez dere blessyng and myn,
> That in the forme of bred and wyn
> The preste vus schewez vch a daye." (1205–10)

> ("On this mound I experienced this adventure for pity of my humble
> Pearl, and then I entrusted her to God--in Christ's dear blessing and
> mine that in the form of bread and wine the priest shows us everyday.")

The revelation, then, comes not from the lengthy sermon of the Pearl
Maiden but from a moment of will and desire met with the disciplining
hand of the divine. The focus on the Dreamer's individual suffering
metamorphoses into a vision of the Eucharist. David Aers analyzes the
mourning enacted in *Pearl* and concludes that "despite the closing reference to Eucharist, to priest, and to our potential participation in the com-
munion of saints, the poet's preoccupations have been thoroughly
individualistic, and his invocation of Corpus Christi extraneous to his
shaping concerns—psychological, spiritual, and theological."[51] Aers's
reading focuses on the ways in which mourning individuates the self; in
a complementary fashion, I explore the ways in which the Dreamer's
desires negate the self in favor of the divine. These divergent readings, I
believe, do not cancel each other out; rather, the ultimate convergence of
these interpretations enacts in narrative form the tension between self as
individual subject and as communal Christian in western medieval culture, in which one's personal desires do not always correlate uniformly
with Christian values. In contrast to the Pearl Maiden, who is now hidden from view, the Dreamer's desires focus on the priest sharing and
showing the Eucharist to the Christian community.

But what is left of the Dreamer after this vision in which all earthly
desires must be denied? He sees himself metamorphosing into a pearl at
an indeterminate time after the narrative history depicted in the poem:
"He gef vus to be His homly hyne / Ande precious perlez vnto His pay"
("He allows us to be His gracious servants and precious pearls unto His
pleasure"; 1211–12). The Dreamer shifts emphasis from his egocentric
focus on his individual pain to his perception of a wider Christian community of pearls that he joins in fellowship. Sacrificing himself as courtly
lover, the Dreamer is feminized into the position of a pearl, another Bride

of Christ in the Pearl of the New Jerusalem. Of course, gender matters little in this vision of the Kingdom of Heaven, in which female pearls are correspondingly described with terms gendered masculine: "Thise alder-men, quen He aproched, / Grouelyng to His fete thay felle" ("These elders, when He approached, fell to His feet groveling"; 1119–20). Likewise, the Pearl Maiden herself is queerly described in male terms— "Her semblaunt sade for doc other erle" ("Her appearance proclaimed her a duke or earl"; 211)—rendering her enigmatic form even less interpre-table. The Dreamer must correspondingly metamorphose into a Bride of Christ despite his male body. Earthly signifiers of gender and sexual roles are stripped away in the New Jerusalem, leaving abandoned and aban-doning selves freed of human appendages and their concomitant earthly desires. As the Dreamer's infant daughter is reconfigured and eroticized into a Bride of Christ, so too is the Dreamer himself bodily refashioned and eroticized into a new yet unimaginable corporeal form. As surprising as this glorious metamorphosis may be, in whatever form it will take, the anticipation of future glories seems to offer tepid comfort to the Dreamer, as his newfound relationship with Christ is voiced unconvinc-ingly. The passion that rang throughout his dialogues with the Pearl Maiden is lacking in his closing moralizations, which suggests that the queer process of becoming a normative Christian in eroticized submis-sion to Christ puts believers in the position of losing what they most desire in favor of desires forced upon them.

Readers, too, face both the cold comfort of a splash of water in our quest for the narrative's meaning and the eroticized transformation of our selves in the pearl's final transformation. As we assume the position of the Dreamer, his desires are our own, and we can no more understand his desires than we can understand our own narratival yearnings that have been repeatedly frustrated. The Dreamer's queerly triangulated desires for the Pearl Maiden are abandoned, as are the reader's desires for her to sig-nify, but as she is lost, the *Pearl*-poet allows readers to discover numinous desire. From a medieval Christian perspective, all desires not directed to God are false ones, but for the *Pearl*-poet, the false leads directly to the true, circuitously through the path of his protagonist's and the reader's own ultimately incomprehensible experiences of interpretive longing. Both the narratival and the metatextual erotic triangles fade from view, leaving only the divine to inspire abandon and devotion. The Dreamer and readers can achieve proper Christian subjectivity by reconfiguring sexual and textual desires in congruence with Christian spiritual norma-tivity, yet this process highlights the compulsory queerness of amorphous desires necessary to achieve an abandoned submission to divinity.

CHAPTER 3

QUEERING HARRY BAILLY: GENDERED CARNIVAL, SOCIAL IDEOLOGIES, AND MASCULINITY UNDER DURESS IN THE *CANTERBURY TALES*

Harry Bailly is a man's man. He serves as "governing figure, as ruler, as king" of the Canterbury pilgrimage,[1] and he also represents a "figure of bourgeois masculinity,"[2] as well as a "recognizable type of the proud man."[3] Walter Scheps asserts that "Harry is, even more than the monk, 'a manly man,' "[4] and William Keen sees in Harry a sufficiency of "heroic qualities... to recommend his services to pilgrims who must pass where perils may lie."[5] Indeed, Chaucer's first description of the Host underscores his vibrant masculinity:

> A semely man OURE HOOSTE was withalle
> For to been a marchal in an halle.
> A large man he was with eyen stepe—
> A fairer burgeys was ther noon in Chepe—
> Boold of his speche, and wys, and wel ytaught,
> And of manhod hym lakkede right naught. (1.751–56)[6]

Attractive, authoritative, large, forthright, wise, well educated—Harry Bailly appears to represent a strong and vibrant incarnation of masculinity. In Chaucer's statement "of manhod hym lakkede right naught," we appear to have conclusive evidence of Harry's masculinity and virility.[7]

But readers should be wary of trusting Chaucer—in his role either as narrator/pilgrim or as author—to speak directly and without irony in the *Canterbury Tales*. Given the way in which he praises outrightly malevolent characters (e.g., the Shipman-cum-Pirate is "certeinly... a good felawe"

[1.395]), Chaucer-the-narrator's statements about Harry's masculinity prove little about the validity of this masculinity or how it functions within the narrative arc of the *Canterbury Tales*. Rather than accepting Chaucer's appreciative assessment of Harry's manhood *ipso facto*, it behooves the reader to ponder whether his masculinity and sexual norma-tivity might be ironically imbued with the seeds of their own destruction.

In this chapter, I explore the ways in which Harry asserts his mascu-line and sexual identity by manipulating the gendered ideology of carni-val play. Although Harry attempts to control his tale-telling carnival, the carnivalesque is an ideological force fraught with queering potential that undermines his masculine bourgeois governance by troubling gender categories to the point of incomprehensibility. In outlining the queer potential of the carnivalesque, my aim is not to uncover a latent homo-sexuality in Harry or the pilgrims but to investigate the fault-lines between masculine sexual identity and social practice, a social chasm fraught with perils of insufficient manliness and threats of the queer.[8] As Lee Edelman declares, "The queer dispossesses the social order of the ground on which it rests. … [Q]ueerness exposes the obliquity of our relations to what we experience in and as social reality."[9] If the daily real-ity of the social order bubbles with queering potential, the carnival, a playful festival predicated upon ostensibly upending social reality, bears exponentially more queering possibilities in its exuberant social inver-sions. In a similar vein to Edelman's observations, Glenn Burger argues that the power of the queer lies in its ability to fracture categories of iden-tity, claiming that " 'gay' resists the oppressive power of dominant culture to 'other' dissident sexualities not by reproducing dominant culture's positivist historicism and stable identities, but by turning the categories of identity politics precisely against themselves."[10] Such inversions of cate-gorical identities, notably the deconstruction of masculinity and norma-tive sexuality through play and carnival, structure the ways in which Harry's identity is presented to the reader as insistently masculine yet ultimately queered from its heteronormative foundations. In regard to Harry's carnival and its accompanying subversion of his masculinity, the situation is all the more ironic in that Harry is queered into submissive Christian normativity by the carnival play he himself sets in motion. Through the carnival play of gender in the tale-telling game, Chaucer subverts Harry's masculinity through his (Harry's) confessional "readings" of the other pilgrims' tales.[11] Reading undermines Harry's masculinity, as the seductiveness of some tales forces him to confront the fictions of his own gender and sexual privilege.[12] At the end of the *Canterbury Tales,* Harry is not the gendered man he thought himself to be because queer-ness, as ensconced in carnival ideology, undermines the performance of

masculinity he puts forth, eliciting queer discontent in his position as the
failed alpha-male of the Canterbury pilgrimage.

The Host Queers: The Carnival Play
of Gender and the Pilgrims'
Masculinities under Duress

As John M. Ganim observes, the carnivalesque "seems an almost irresist-
ible metaphor for the *Canterbury Tales*. Bakhtin seems to uncover at a
stroke an entire social dynamic implicit in monastic satire, popular folk-
lore, and goliardic parody, all of which offer an 'unofficial' medieval
comic tradition for Chaucer's tales and frame."[13] Reading the *Canterbury
Tales* as a playful carnival bears much obvious merit, especially due to the
ways in which tensions between play and seriousness, game and earnest,
structure the narrative.[14] A sense of play coupled with freedom from the
standard social order should encourage the pilgrims to enjoy themselves
through the amusements of the tale-telling game, and Harry indeed presents his tale-telling game as a form of play. However, the inversions to the
social order endemic to carnival also camouflage his personal motiva-
tions of self-advancement in the game. In this way, play and carnival are
inextricably linked because Harry blurs the contours between the two.
At the same time, the sense of play inherent in carnivalesque inversions
frequently evaporates when Harry exploits carnival and play to pursue his
own serious objectives in retaining control of the pilgrimage.

The carnivalesque's utility as a playful metaphor for the *Canterbury
Tales* is simultaneously counterbalanced by its limitations. Although
carnival ostensibly represents the people's unlicensed play and popular
festival fun, Chaucer's tale-telling contest also parallels Umberto Eco's
critique of carnival, in that festival can simultaneously function as an
ideological mechanism of social restraint. By providing an authorized
framework for temporary rebellions against the quotidian power structure, carnival reifies prevailing ideological systems, at least in some
instances. Eco stresses this point, arguing that "comedy and carnival are
not instances of real transgressions: on the contrary, they represent para-
mount examples of law reinforcement."[15] Terry Eagleton likewise
observes that "carnival, after all, is a *licensed* affair in every sense, a per-
missible rupture of hegemony, a contained popular blow-off as disturbing
and relatively ineffectual as a revolutionary work of art. As Shakespeare's
Olivia remarks, there is no slander in an allowed fool."[16] Neither Bakhtin's
nor Eco's and Eagleton's views explain carnival in all of its complexity,
but if their approaches are united, they uncover in the carnivalesque a

heady nexus of competing social practices, in which popular play clashes with ideological regulation and control.[17]

In addition to the class issues inherent in carnival, the playful and contested communal space between lower and upper classes of society is gendered as well. Carnival's social class inversions are readily apparent, but carnival's gender play is somewhat occluded in that these inversions need not be between male and female gender roles but between different types of masculinities. Blatant inversions of male/female gender roles arise with relative frequency in medieval literature, such as when Aucassin and Nicolette visit an upside-down world where the queen fights in battle and the king lies pregnant in bed,[18] or when the eponymous heroine Silence gender-bends in assuming male roles, including jongleur and knight.[19] The greater visibility of these gendered inversions should not blind readers to similar inversions taking place among members of the same sex in other literary circumstances. For example, perhaps the most famous image of the carnival is that of the commoner assuming the role of king. But as social roles are changed in this instance, gender roles are altered as well, for the masculinity expected of and accorded to a commoner differs from the masculinity expected of and accorded to a king. As Ruth Mazo Karras explains in her study of medieval masculinities, "Concepts of what it meant to be a man not only changed over time, they also coexisted and competed within any given medieval culture or even subculture."[20] Chaucer's Monk embodies the ways in which social classes and genders clash, as this character's masculinity belongs more appropriately in the court than in the cloister (1.177–83); likewise, Chaucer's depictions of the Knight and the Miller in the *General Prologue* provide strikingly different models of masculinity. If the Miller, with his brutish version of masculinity, assumed the position of a knight or king, the gendered expectations of these positions would be subverted in a manner analogous to how class dynamics are subverted in carnival. As these examples demonstrate, gender circulates throughout carnival play with as much—or as little—potential for subversion as social class. Whether one agrees with Bakhtin or with Eco and Eagleton about the social ramifications of carnival, surely gender, sexuality, and social class are at stake and in flux during this social phenomenon, and it must be determined whether these inversions bear lasting ideological impact in each unique set of social circumstances. As carnival plays with genders, then, it also bears the likely potential for queering in that the slippage among gender roles invites manipulations and inversions of ostensibly stable categories of identity.

The carnivalesque's queering tensions between popular freedom and ideological control in relation to social class and gender drives the

Canterbury Tales in that Harry's motives for the tale-telling competition are mixed. First and foremost, he delights in play, as Chaucer reports: "Eek therto he was right a myrie man; / And after soper pleyen he bigan, / And spak of myrthe amonges othere thynges" (1.757–59).[21] Harry desires to bring festival fun to the pilgrims (along the lines of Bakhtin's carnival), but through this play, he also seeks to impose his own masculine governance on them (along the lines of Eco's and Eagleton's critique of carnival). For the Host, play and amusement are not merely innocent recreational pastimes designed for fun and frivolity; rather, they are inextricably linked to his desire to control the pilgrims, as evidenced by the agreement he offers them:

> "And therfore wol I maken yow disport,
> As I seyde erst, and doon yow som confort.
> And if yow liketh alle by oon assent
> For to stonden at my juggement,
> And for to werken as I shal yow seye,
> Tomorwe, whan ye riden by the weye,
> Now, by my fader soule that is deed,
> But ye be myrie, I wol yeve yow myn heed!
> Hoold up youre hondes, withouten moore speche." (1.775–83)

In this passage, the Host creates a powerful connection between the pilgrims' play and his authority. It is, in effect, a *quid pro quo,* in which Harry promises play in return for the players' sacrifice of self-governance, even to the extent that they may not discuss the offer among themselves ("withouten moore speche") before putting the motion to a vote. In his demand for unanimity ("oon assent"), Harry seeks to eradicate any dissenting voices that might subsequently threaten his rule. Play, in effect, camouflages the imposition of Harry's carnival authority over the other pilgrims in the tale-telling game. It also hides his attempts both to queer male identities so that they reflect his particular gendered and class desires and to protect his position as the alpha-male leader of the pilgrimage, which ultimately depends as much upon his ability to manipulate genders as upon his ability to encourage tales.

Harry's lexicon of rule and governance further demonstrates both how he establishes his authority through carnival play and how this "play" bears serious repercussions to the ideological underpinnings of the pilgrimage. Seeing immediate threats to his governance, despite that no pilgrims register discontent with his rule, Harry shores up his authority by outlining the penalties due to any pilgrim refusing to acquiesce to his decisions: " 'And whoso wole my juggement withseye / Shal paye al that we spenden by the weye' " (1.805–06). To cement this penalty in the minds of the pilgrims,

Harry quickly reiterates this condition in a nearly verbatim phrasing: "'Whoso be rebel to my juggement / Shal paye for al that by the wey is spent'" (1.833–34). With this repeated caveat, which is inserted only after the pilgrims accede to his authority, Harry establishes that his masculine governance is the primary rule of the tale-telling game, one that cannot be broken without incurring severe financial penalties. By seizing governance through the promise of play, Harry disguises the authoritarianism of his liminal ideology with a playful façade. It is somewhat of a tyrannical move, but perhaps not surprising for a man who soon adapts the demeanor of royalty in his interactions with his fellow pilgrims.

As the affirmed leader of the pilgrimage, Harry's opinions of his traveling companions and their tales influence their position within the pilgrimage. In this light, Carolyn Dinshaw sees in Harry the representative of ideology, in that "his function as master of ceremonies may well be to register unacknowledged ideology in the *Tales* as a whole."[22] By seizing the right of judging the competition he himself proposes, Harry positions himself as the ideological enforcer of the pilgrimage, and he subsequently directs the pilgrims' actions through the force of his masculine and authoritative presence. As a member of the rising bourgeoisie, however, Harry cannot effectively represent the dominant aristocratic and class-based ideology of medieval England. Within the traditional three estates model of English society of those who work, fight, and pray, Harry occupies a liminal position, perched on the borders between the peasant and aristocratic/clerical classes, and he accentuates this liminality by assuming the role of judge of the tale-telling contest.[23] In this role, Harry positions himself above his fellow bourgeois pilgrims (e.g., the Miller, the Cook, the Wife of Bath, and the Guildsmen), as he simultaneously positions himself above his social superiors, including the Knight, the Monk, and the Prioress. Harry's commands to the Man of Law, for example, stress the pilgrims' submission to his authority: "'Ye been submytted, thurgh youre free assent, / To stonden in this cas at my juggement'" (2.35–56). If Harry does indeed register ideology, as Dinshaw observes, one must ponder which ideology Harry represents—the nascent bourgeois ideology of the rising middle and merchant class or the aristocratic ideology of his social superiors? More interested in serving his personal desires than those of the aristocracy or the bourgeoisie, Harry speaks throughout the *Canterbury Tales* with a liminal voice that comprises both a bourgeois timbre disdainful of aristocratic manners and an aristocratic timbre mindful of such social privilege, depending upon his needs in a particular rhetorical situation.

By ruling his fellow pilgrims, Harry establishes the primacy of his masculinity, and here we see that gender and sexuality are implicated within the realm of the tale-telling carnival. As Chaucer first notes "of manhod hym lakkede right naught," the subsequent vision of Harry as the pilgrims' "aller cok" (1.823) who "gadrede us togidre alle in a flok" (1.824) further establishes Harry's phallic mastery. One need only think of the medieval lyric "I haue a gentil cok" to realize that the symbolic register of "cock" included penis in the Middle Ages.[24] As these lines magnify Harry's phallic manhood, they correspondingly queer the remaining pilgrims into apparent submission to his masculine rule. The vision of Harry as the "alpha" cock effectively emasculates his fellow pilgrims by accentuating the inability of their masculinities to match his. Aristocratic and clerical figures who now accept the authority of a bailiff are queered from the contours of both their social and their gender roles, and even Harry's fellow bourgeois pilgrims are emasculated as Harry demands their deference to him. (In referring to the pilgrims' collective masculinities, I am not forgetting the presence of the female pilgrims such as the Prioress and the Wife of Bath; rather, I am highlighting the performative valence of gender and identity, in that women may perform masculinity as effectively as men.)[25] At this early moment in the narrative, no one's masculinity yet seems sufficient to counteract the queering force of Harry's tale-telling carnival.

As Harry's ideology is liminal, so too is his occupational masculinity on the precarious borders between the aristocratic and the bourgeois. Chaucer highlights the liminal nature of Harry's social position by describing him as sufficiently "semely" to serve as a "marchal in an halle" (1.751–52, quoted previously). "Marchal" may simply denote that Harry is a master of ceremonies, and thus firmly ensconced in the world of the bourgeoisie as represented in the Tabard Inn; however, the word also refers to a more administrative and courtly position.[26] The accompanying phrase "in an halle" offers inconclusive contextual evidence to determine whether his hypothetically appropriate milieu is in the halls of courtiers or of commoners. Indeed, it is not clear that Harry *is* a marshal; Chaucer only indicates that he is attractive enough "for to been" one. This passage unclearly paints Harry either as a bourgeois master-of-ceremonies or as an aristocratic social climber with pretensions of employment in more courtly positions. In the ambiguous occupation of "marchal," masculinity and governance merge in Harry, but it is unclear how this occupation corresponds to his political sympathies and allegiances.

Harry's surname "Bailly" is likewise somewhat vague in its meaning, as the *Middle English Dictionary* indicates that the word refers to "an office held by delegation from a superior; delegated authority" and thus suggests a lower-level local administrative function. However, "bailly" also refers to "an official of the English crown with delegated administrative authority;

the king's officer in a county, hundred, or town." Chaucer observes of Harry that "a fairer burgeys was ther noon in Chepe," which again appears to be an ironic compliment. "Burgeys" dually associates men with merchants and trade guilds as well as with local governance.[27] Thus, with "marchal," "bailly," and "burgeys," Harry's social position appears decidedly liminal, and such liminality fits Harry well in his role as a social climber precisely because social climbers, by definition, occupy one social position but seek to move to a more prestigious one. Chaucer soon notes that Harry "gan to speke as lordly as a kyng" (1.3900) when he pressures the Reeve to tell his tale, which indicates that masculine and aristocratic self-aggrandizement is a primary goal of his carnival play. Usurping the ultimately regal role of masculine authority while in colloquy with a social peer who works in a similar low-level administrative position, Harry manipulates his carnival to alienate the social order from its foundational equations of particular social classes with corresponding masculinities; self-aggrandizement is achieved by queering his fellow pilgrims.

The multiple meanings of "marchal," "bailly," and "burgeys" in relation to Harry's social status capture semiotically the difficulty of assessing his masculinity in relation to economic class and ideology. If it is purposefully unclear where his loyalties lie, it is nonetheless apparent that Harry reifies his liminal ideology by providing a comic and carnival release that sutures over cultural and class tensions. As a member of the bourgeoisie, Harry Bailly may appear to represent Bakhtin's "language of the marketplace,"[28] but he also employs carnival play to establish his authority over the pilgrims. Harry's promise of play catalyzes the pilgrims' enthusiastic response to his governance, as his ploy is effective and they unanimously agree to his authority:

> Oure conseil was nat longe for to seche.
> Us thoughte it was noght worth to make it wys,
> And graunted hym withouten moore avys,
> And bad him seye his voirdit as hym leste. (1.784–87)

With the lure of play in front of them, the pilgrims cede their governance to Harry because "it was noght worth to make it wys." Although play appears to be an insufficiently weighty matter over which the pilgrims should worry, their decision, in fact, entails both play and governance. When governance is masked behind a façade of play, Eco's and Eagleton's critiques of carnival as a means of social control appear stunningly accurate. Furthermore, since this play is so strongly connected to the gendered identities of the pilgrims in that they are effectively queered by Harry's assertion of phallic mastery, readers might expect the subsequent narrative to address in some manner how various pilgrims reclaim their gendered identities.

The suspect nature of Harry Bailly's carnival is apparent in that it first reifies the dominant ideology of aristocratic class privilege before subsequently attacking aristocratic manners; that is, Harry deploys his carnival at times to heighten his own masculinity by ingratiating himself to an unquestionably masculine man of higher social class while nonetheless controlling his actions. In this move, Harry inverts typically carnivalesque inversions that offer freedom to the lower social classes, partially stripping festival form of its class inversions and retailoring it to an aristocratic taste. In inverting the inversions of carnival, it might appear that Harry thus reinstates the status quo of everyday society; however, since Harry himself retains control of the tale-telling game, the reader still sees the commoner in the role of the "king" of the contest. Carnivalesque inversions thus reinforce Harry's role as ruler of the pilgrimage, and the overarching structure of the carnival holds in effect even when he subsequently reifies or subverts other social hierarchies. Despite that all pilgrims will take turns in the tale-telling game, Harry manipulates his carnival more to reassert than to subvert social hierarchies when he calls for the Monk, who epitomizes masculinity as the "manly man" (1.167) of the pilgrimage, to follow the Knight in the tale-telling competition: "'Now telleth ye, sir Monk, if that ye konne, / Somwhat to quite with the Knyghtes tale'" (1.3118–19). By inviting the Monk to "quite" the Knight, Harry foments an intermasculine tension within the Canterbury pilgrimage that he then attempts to regulate throughout the game.[29] In so doing, he also reinforces the aristocratic bent of his liminal ideology by ingratiating himself to the aristocratic and priestly orders, as he simultaneously wields his as yet absolute control of masculinity. Harry shores up the aristocracy that he now controls, and in so doing, he reasserts his position as the "aller cok" of the pilgrimage.

Of course, with the Miller's drunken outburst (1.3125–27), a strident bourgeois voice denies Harry complete control of his game. Here conflicting notions of carnival converge, in that the Miller restructures the tale-telling game as a carnival for commoners rather than for aristocrats. This tension between the bourgeoisie and the aristocracy bubbles up frequently in the *Canterbury Tales,* and Harry is often caught in the middle. It must be noted, however, that Harry deliberately places himself between these two social classes to bolster his masculinity and his governance. In his dialogue with the Miller, Harry positions himself with the aristocratic orders, demanding that the Miller let a man of higher social class speak: "Oure Hooste saugh that [the Miller] was dronke of ale, / And seyde, 'Abyd, Robyn, my leeve brother; / Som bettre man shal telle us first another'" (1.3128–30). Here Harry sycophantically reinforces the social system that labels some men better than others, rejecting any social allegiance he might have with the Miller in order to cement aristocratic social privilege.

In contrast to his deference to the Monk, Harry's disdain for the priestly and aristocratic orders also appears in the *Canterbury Tales* when he upbraids the Friar and explains to him how he should behave: "Oure Hoost tho spak, 'A, sire, ye sholde be hende / And curteys, as a man of youre estaat'" (3.1286–87). As Harry chastises a representative of the religious orders for his inability to act with proper courtesy, so too does his bourgeois sensibility set him at odds with the aristocratic orders, as when he argues with the Franklin about the meaning of gentility. A member of the lower aristocracy and one himself dedicated to hosting and hospitality, the Franklin serves as Harry's aristocratic foil. But with his aristocratic status assured in his roles as "housholdere" (1.339), "lord and sire" (1.355), and "vavasour" (1.360), the Franklin highlights the limitations of Harry's aristocratic aspirations as an innkeeper. Contributing to the nascent tension between the two men, the Franklin indiscreetly attacks the rising bourgeois class while praising the virtues of gentility:

> "...Fy on possessioun,
> But if a man be vertuous withal!
> I have my sone snybbed, and yet shal,
> For he to vertu listeth nat entende;
> ....
> And he hath levere talken with a page
> Than to comune with any gentil wight
> Where he myghte lerne gentillesse aright." (5.686–89, 692–94)

The Franklin makes an opening gesture toward inclusiveness by stating that a man need not be wealthy to be genteel, but his overarching message is that lineage breeds honor, that blood matters. In this affirmation of the unbreakable connection between social class and character, the Franklin, in effect, denounces the pilgrims of lower social class as unworthy of aristocratic notice.

"'Straw for youre gentillesse!'" Harry shouts in response to the Franklin (5.695), thus deriding the Franklin's construction of aristocratic and masculine gentility.[30] If Harry previously inverted carnival, turning an upside-down social order right-side-up in his preferential treatment of the Knight and the Monk, here he returns to the tale-telling carnival the reversals of social strictures ostensibly endemic to festival form. Certainly, the Franklin's subsequent words indicate that he accepts his subordinated position to Harry within the tale-telling game:

> "Gladly, sire Hoost," quod he, "I wole obeye
> Unto your wyl; now herkneth what I seye.
> I wol yow nat contrarien in no wyse
> As fer as that my wittes wol suffyse.
> I prey to God that it may plesen yow;
> Thanne woot I wel that it is good ynow." (5.703–08)

The Franklin may somewhat exaggerate his deference to Harry in these lines, but this possibility of exaggeration does not therefore undo Harry's authority. The Host's play with carnival manipulates the social positions and masculine identities of others and estranges them from their gendered senses of self so that his authority is uncontested.

As Harry inverts the social class structure of carnival to shore up his desire for masculine authority, he also inverts the very meaning of play to support his rule. Harry frames his governance as play, but some of the pilgrims—notably the Clerk—do not want to play his game. I discuss the relationship between the Clerk and the Host in greater detail in the subsequent chapter, but at this point it is necessary to highlight that Harry scoffs at the Clerk's masculinity and sexuality as part of his carnival fun. He bullies the Clerk into an apparently powerless and thoroughly queered position by deriding his nonnormative gender: " 'Sire Clerk of Oxenford,' oure Hooste sayde, / 'Ye ryde as coy and stille as dooth a mayde / Were newe spoused, sittynge at the bord' " (4.1–3). As a "sire" who is also a "mayde," the Clerk's body is queerly reconstituted through Harry's playful rhetoric.[31] Queering the Clerk both through carnival play and through his gender-baiting lexicon, Harry's jibes at the Clerk underscore the ways in which conflicting masculinities resemble a zero-sum game: Harry aggrandizes his masculinity by queering the studious Clerk.

But as Harry will learn from the queering carnival he unleashes that tames his traveling companions, he who queers can be queered as well. A foreshadowing hint that carnival play can also be used to topple Harry's masculine governance appears in his dialogue with Roger the Cook, in which Harry reveals his belief that carnivalesque play allows serious matters to be considered under the guise of amusement. For Harry, the game is not mere play and festive fun; it is an avenue through which social truths may likewise be addressed: " 'Now telle on, gentil Roger by thy name. / But yet I pray thee, be nat wroth for game; / A man may seye ful sooth in game and pley' " (1.4353–55). Given the ways that Harry links his masculine identity as judge of the pilgrims to the tale-telling game, it is apparent that his masculinity and ideological control over the other pilgrims is at least one of the "truths" hidden behind the game. Roger's response, however, highlights that play—and the pilgrims—cannot be so easily tamed. The Cook agrees to play the tale-telling game but argues with the Host about the true nature of play: "'Thou seist ful sooth' quod Roger, 'by my fey! / But "sooth pley, quaad pley," as the Flemyng seith'" (1.4356–57). The Cook's rejoinder is a masterpiece of Chaucerian irony and double meaning. Roger first agrees wholeheartedly with Harry ("'Thou seist ful sooth'") and upholds the connection between truth and play. But in his subsequent citation of the Flemish proverb "sooth pley, quaad pley," Roger disagrees with Harry immediately subsequent to agreeing with him. In responding to Harry's playful governance, Roger points to the ways in which play simultaneously subverts that which it ostensibly supports.

Certainly, Roger plans a narratival revenge against Harry, perhaps in return for Harry's insults to him and his cooking (1.4344–52). He threatens Harry that he will tell a tale of a host similar to Harry, in a manner analogous to the hostile tale-telling exhibited in the narratival exchanges both between the Miller and the Reeve and between the Friar and the Summoner:

> "And therfore, Herry Bailly, by thy feith,
> Be thou nat wrooth, er we departen heer,
> Though that my tale be of an hostileer.
> But natheless I wol not telle it yit;
> But er we parte, ywis, thou shalt be quit." (1.4358–62)

In this threat to Harry, the promise of a true insult to Harry is concealed under the façade of a playful—and thus ostensibly unserious—tale. Since Harry has staked his masculine authority on a foundation of play, Roger highlights the evanescent and mercurial nature of carnival fun, and thus the ways in which Harry's authority and masculinity can be undermined through the very queering carnival forces that he himself has unleashed. Given the brevity and (likely) incompleteness of Roger's tale, it is difficult to draw any definitive conclusions, but it nonetheless appears probable that the tale would undermine the Host's narratival authority by casting him in a sexually laughable role. Despite Roger's statement that he will include an incarnation of Harry as a character in a later tale, the *Cook's Tale* is set "in Chepe" (1.4376), which recalls Harry's location in the same vicinity (1.754), and it contains at least the possibility of a queered innkeeper in its depiction of Perkyn Revelour's friend, his

> ...compeer of his owene sort,
> That lovede dys, and revel, and disport,

And hadde a wyf that heeld for contenance
A shoppe, and swyved for hir sustenance. (1.4419–22)

By constructing the "Harry" character as the husband of a prostitute,
Roger hints at a vision of the "compeer"-cum-Harry as undone by
uncontrolled female sexuality. As the *Canterbury Tales* continues and we
catch glimpses of Harry's home life with his overbearing wife, Roger's
evocative dig at Harry in this brief tale seems prescient in its queering
allegations.

Harry's carnival, as it exploits a sense of play and reflects the tensions
between the bourgeois and aristocratic orders of society, serves the needs
of one man: Harry Bailly. The gendered carnival that Harry unleashes
bears the potential to reconstitute the pilgrims' sense of their personal
identities, but such queerings do not only work in the direction of the
powerful to the less powerful. Rather, the force of queering lies in its
unpredictable and chaotic play, and Harry also learns that the carnival's
play, which he has used to emasculate and subjugate his fellow pilgrims
into discontented positions subservient to him, can be used as their tool
of liberation from his somewhat tyrannical authority.

The Host Queered: Narrative
Interpretation and Harry's
Masculinity under Duress

Carnival play is the means by which the Host attempts to control the
pilgrims through the imposition of his liminal ideology, but narrative
interpretation—a form of recreation and play—undoes his control and
reveals the fictions of his masculinity.[32] Reader-response theories examine the ways in which texts construct readers and compel them to reimagine themselves in light of the textual encounter. As Emma Wilson argues,
"The text may engage its reader in a process of fantasy construction and
voyeuristic participation as it literally arouses his/her imagination. The
text may thus offer the reader new images of him/herself as desiring subject with which to identify, and new scenarios for the performance of an
identity category."[33] Through the textual encounter, readers position
themselves vis-à-vis a text, but the text may, in effect, take control of this
encounter. In such a manner, Harry is forced to confront through his readings of his fellow pilgrims' tales the ways in which his carnival fails to
protect his masculine authoritarianism.

Harry's own masculinity is not his only concern, and he displays an
abundant interest in the masculinities and sexualities of his fellow
pilgrims by paying attention to the ways in which their tales bolster or

undermine their genders. John Plummer observes a desire on Harry's part to link textual fecundity with masculinity: "As master of ceremonies, Sir Mirthe seeks to engender in his fellow pilgrims both fruitful and mirthful texts, and he sees a perfectly natural connection between fruit and mirth ('sentence' and 'solas') in healthy masculinity."[34] Such a paradigm is readily observable in the gendered language with which Harry addresses his fellow pilgrims, as when Chaucer has Harry compliment the Knight for his tale: "Oure Hooste lough and swoor, 'So moot I gon, / This gooth aright; unbokeled is the male'" (1.3114–15). Harry defines the pilgrims' social and sexual normativity throughout the tale-telling competition, which is apparent in the phrase "unbokeled is the male" and its oblique reference to male genitalia and sexuality.[35] By so powerfully linking manhood to narrative, Harry, in effect, puts his own masculinity in jeopardy, since his "tale" in the Epilogue to the *Merchant's Tale* merely discloses his fear of his wife:

> "But wyte ye what? In conseil be it seyd,
> Me reweth soore I am unto hire teyd.
> For and I sholde rekenen every vice
> Which that she hath, ywis I were to nyce.
> And cause why? It sholde reported be
> And toold to hire of somme of this meynee." (4.2431–36)

More than describing his wife as a shrew, Harry hints that he fears her as well, or at the very least that he does not wish her to learn of his public denigrations of her lest he face her wrath. Harry then concludes: "'And eek my wit suffiseth nat therto / To tellen al; wherfore my tale is do'" (4.2439–40). This moment of confession, if Chaucer intended it to be considered a narrative on par with those of the other pilgrims, hardly meets the minimum expectations of a tale, such as a setting and a plot. In effect, Harry's narrative masculinity—as opposed to his authoritarian masculinity—is predicated upon absence, and it becomes increasingly linked to his failure to control his wife.

Harry's carnival is the means by which he asserts himself as arbiter of masculinity as well as of narrative. Again, I address the relationship between Harry and the Clerk in chapter 4, but it should be noted that the *Clerk's Tale* leads Harry to admit the limits of his domestic masculinity. As Harry constructs the Clerk as a "mayde" and impugns his masculinity, in response the Clerk leads the Host to reassess the meaning of his own maleness. The reader first learns of Harry's status as a henpecked husband through his response to the boundless marital suffering depicted in the *Clerk's Tale*: "Oure Hooste seyde, and swoor, 'By Goddes bones, / Me were levere than a barel ale / My wyf at hoom had herd this legende ones!'" (4.1212b–d). By describing his wife as a woman who needs to emulate Griselda, Harry admits that his wife dominates him, concomitantly hinting at his own lack of governance at home: "'This is a gentil tale for the nones, / As to my purpos, wiste ye my wille; / But thyng that wol nat be, lat it be stille'" (4.1212e–1212g). The Clerk's "gentil" tale is praised presumably for the ways in which it shores up masculine rule by constructing feminine suffering as a key domestic value, but Harry's final line registers the impossibility of his realizing this vision with his own wife. The seductive force of the Clerk's narrative, coupled with its apparent relevance to his own domestic experiences, leads Harry to confess a queer chink in his masculinity, and such chinks become increasingly apparent throughout the remainder of the *Canterbury Tales*.

With the males unbuckled in the tale-telling game, Harry's own troubled and queered masculinity appears plainly in view. In response to Chaucer's *Tale of Melibee*, Harry again wishes that his wife would learn a lesson in patience: "'I hadde levere than a barel ale / That Goodelief, my wyf, hadde herd this tale! / For she nys no thing of swich pacience'" (7.1893–95). He then reports that his wife queers him by reversing their traditional spheres:

"Whan she comth hoom she rampeth in my face,
And crieth, 'False coward, wrek thy wyf!
By corpus bones, I wol have thy knyf,
And thou shalt have my distaf and go spynne!'" (7.1904–07)

With his wife wielding his knife, Harry's subsequent claims of phallic mastery ("'For I am perilous with knyf in honde'" [7.1919]) serve only to undermine further his already beleaguered masculinity. Consigned to the feminine sphere of spinning with his wife's distaff, Harry's queered masculinity becomes a metaphor for his queering carnival: his wife inverts their gendered roles in the domestic space, and thus Harry attempts to invert his domestic effeminacy through his carnival manipulations of public masculinities.

Harry's response to the *Physician's Tale* offers another opportunity to witness his gendered readerly transformations. Chaucer reports that the Host's initial reaction to the tale suggests a loss of reason and excessive emotional investment ("Oure Hooste gan to swere as he were wood" [6.287]), which indicates that Harry responds emotionally and affectively to the Physician's mournful tale. To judge the tone of Harry's subsequent words is somewhat difficult, as his emotionally charged yet scholarly response could be read as heartfelt or ironic:

> "Algate this sely mayde is slayn, allas!
> Allas, to deere boughte she beautee!
> ....
> Hire beautee was hire deth, I dar wel sayn.
> Allas, so pitously as she was slayn!
> ....
> But trewely, myn owene maister deere,
> This is a pitous tale for to heere.
> But nathelees, passe over; is no fors.
> I pray to God so save thy gentil cors,
> And eek thyne urynals and thy jurdones,
> Thyn ypocras, and eek thy galiones,
> And every boyste ful of thy letuarie;
> God blesse hem, and oure lady Seinte Marie!
> So moot I theen, thou art a propre man,
> And lyk a prelat, by Seint Ronyan!
> Seyde I nat wel? I kan nat speke in terme." (6.292–93, 297–98, 301–11)

In this passage it is almost as if two Harrys are speaking, one with an affective discourse of heartfelt emotion and the other with a scientific discourse of medical terms. Of these two voices, however, the voice of science and reason falls short, as Harry confesses that he "kan nat speke in terme."[36] John David Burnley observes Harry's inability to express himself eloquently in this speech and argues that this failure in diction is tied to his social class: "It is to this implied challenge [of uniting eloquence and urbanity] that Harry is responding, and his failure to meet it...is part of the comedy of social status and aspiration which is adumbrated in the language of the Host."[37] Failing to speak correctly in the male discourse of rhetoric and science, Harry's affective words bear more real meaning in this speech, and thus they offer deeper insight into his character than his masculine discourse. In his faltering discourse of science, Harry's masculinity is again revealed to be a façade, and the force of his emotional response to the *Physician's Tale* thus reveals another queer chink in the alpha-male masculinity depicted in the *General Prologue*.

Regardless of Harry's tone and his sincerity in these lines, he attempts to regain control of himself and the tale-telling game by returning it to play and amusement. He denies the queering force of Virginia's story by asking the Pardoner to return the pilgrimage to the realm of carnival play and laughter, which ostensibly serves as his domain:

> "By corpus bones! but I have triacle,
> Or elles a draughte of moyste and corny ale,
> Or but I heere anon a myrie tale,

Myn herte is lost for pitee of this mayde.
Thou beel amy, thou Pardoner," [Harry] sayde,
"Telle us som myrthe or japes right anon." (6.314–19)

Requesting medicine, alcohol, or a merry tale, Harry redirects the tale-telling game to the realm of his masculine play. The Host, asserting the masculine authority that has been subverted by the queering force of affective and pathetic narrative, relies on carnival and the play of a merry tale to suture over his lapse into feminized discourse.

In his encounter with the Pardoner, Harry most clearly faces the limits of his masculine and bourgeois carnival due to the crippling blows that the Knight's aristocratic privilege directs against his masculinity.[38] After Harry threatens the Pardoner with castration ("'I wolde I hadde thy coillons in myn hond / In stide of relikes or of seintuarie'" [6.952–53]), the Pardoner is enraged ("This Pardoner answerde nat a word; / So wrooth he was, no word ne wolde he seye" [6.956–57]). The hilarious metaphorical exchange that Harry broaches—equating the Pardoner's blasphemous relics for his questionable testicles—points to Harry's deployment of fun and amusement for serious ends as he attempts to quiet the Pardoner into submission and thus to end his con game. Harry accentuates the seriousness of the situation by ending his carnival play: "'Now,' quod oure Hoost, 'I wol no lenger pleye / With thee, ne with noon oother angry man'" (6.958–59). Harry's attempt to end this play serves his desire to retain mastery over the pilgrimage, but it is certainly a moment of great hypocrisy as well. The reader might wonder why Harry refuses to play with an angry man, given his earlier statement to Roger the Cook that the arena of play can be used to address matters of truth and seriousness. Here it becomes apparent that Harry's insistence on play—and his willingness to end play that he cannot control—is merely an insistence on his particular form of self-servingly masculinist carnival. The Pardoner's play threatens Harry on many levels, but central to this threat is that Harry's masculinity is predicated on his authoritarian governance of the tale-telling game. Harry here calls for the play of carnival to end, but the game continues without pause.

With Harry's masculinity faltering and the breakdown of the tale-telling game impending, the Knight steps in to save the game by enforcing the rule of play. In much the same manner as Harry earlier compelled the Clerk to participate in the tale-telling game by effeminizing him, the Knight now queerly compels Harry to follow his (the Knight's) playful desires rather than his own:

But right anon the worthy Knyght bigan,
Whan that he saugh that al the peple lough,

"Namoore of this, for it is right ynough!
Sire Pardoner, be glad and myrie of cheere;
And ye, sire Hoost, that been to me so deere,
I prey yow that ye kisse the Pardoner.
And Pardoner, I prey thee, drawe thee neer,
And, as we diden, lat us laughe and pleye."
Anon they kiste, and ryden forth hir weye. (6.960–68)

This passage begins and ends with laughter, but it is the Knight's aristocratic power that directs the scene, not the humor itself. The Knight
first compels both Harry and the Pardoner to cease their bickering and
the pilgrims to cease their laughter (" 'Namoore of this' "), only to
subsequently allow the recommencement of the pilgrims' laughter (" 'lat
us laughe and pleye' "). The Knight's real accomplishment in this scene
is to establish the primacy of his authority over the Host's; that is to say,
the Knight reveals the limits of the Host's governance over play and
laughter by more effectively controlling the carnival that Harry himself
set in motion. Linking the pilgrims' laughter to the kiss between the
Pardoner and the Host, the Knight delineates the limits of bourgeois
carnival and queers its primary advocate, whose masculinity is undermined in this scene both in his failure to govern and in the enforced
male-male kiss with the Pardoner.[39] Carolyn Dinshaw reads this scene
and insightfully notes that the Pardoner's queerness "is silenced in a
reimposition of heterosexual order, [but] it is nonetheless still around
and, moreover, contagious. ...The Pardoner still walks by the side of
the other pilgrims, still goes where they go;...the Pardoner's very
person remains an unwelcome but insistent reminder of normative heterosexual unnaturalness."[40] Dinshaw's evocative interpretation of the
Pardoner's queer potential enlightens an understanding of how the
queer undermine normativity, and it is critical to add that such queerness now bleeds onto the reader's perception of Harry. As the pilgrims
must continually keep company with the Pardoner, so too must they
walk with Harry Bailly and the memory of the kiss that queered him.
Carnival, even as a staged and sanctioned social institution, creates a
lingering specter of disruption that can never be fully contained by the
resumption of the "proper" order, and in this instance, a carnival kiss
creates a compulsory queer out of the ostensibly normative and masculine
Harry Bailly.

   As Harry first directed the Knight's actions in the beginning of the
Canterbury Tales, he must now cede his alpha-male masculinity and accept
a queered position of secondary masculinity. The Knight asserts his masculine control as the head of the social order, and henceforth, Harry can

do little more than chirp up to reinforce his social superior's opinions. He has been, in effect, demoted to sidekick status, and thus his masculinity is systemically weakened because it serves to shore up the Knight's masculinity rather than to bolster his own. He is now Watson to the Knight's Sherlock Holmes, Robin to his Batman, Tonto to his Lone Ranger. For example, when the Knight calls for an end to the Monk's interminable tale ("'Hoo!...good sire, namoore of this! That ye han seyd is right ynough, ywis, / And muchel moore'" [7.2767–69]), Harry only pipes up in agreement after the Knight speaks. Sycophantically agreeing with the Knight, Harry's tenuous masculinity now relies on the Knight to bolster its flagging authority:

> "Ye," quod oure Hooste, "by Seint Poules belle!
> Ye seye right sooth; this Monk he clappeth lowde.
> ....
> Sire Monk, namoore of this, so God yow blesse!
> Youre tale anoyeth al this compaignye.
> Swich talkyng is nat worth a boterflye,
> For therinne is ther no desport ne game.
> ....
> I pray yow hertely telle us somwhat elles;
> ....
> Sir, sey somwhat of huntyng, I yow preye." (7.2780–81, 2788–91, 2793, 2805)

These lines document a bruised and queered masculinity, as the Host first reiterates the Knight's assessment of the Monk's endless tale and then derides the tale because it lacks "desport" and "game." The seriousness of the Monk's tragedies do little to reinforce the mirthful atmosphere necessary to maintain Harry's playfully carnivalesque masculine authority. In this episode, the final blow to Harry's authority lies in the Monk's refusal to obey Harry's request for a tale of hunting. Harry's masculinity is sufficient to force a tale out of the resistant yet somewhat effeminate Clerk, but it is insufficient to compel a suitable tale—or any tale—from the "manly man" Monk (1.167), whose gender and social standing ultimately remain unaffected by Harry's authoritarian efforts.

Due to the Knight's manipulation of Harry's manhood through the enforced kiss with the Pardoner and the Monk's refusal to acquiesce to his authority, Harry's masculinity is increasingly subverted. The Host has used his carnival to establish the primacy of his masculinity, but as it loses its phallic puissance, he increasingly praises the sexual prowess of other pilgrims, such as the Monk and the Nun's Priest. Harry describes these men as bounteously masculine, as when he extols the Monk as:

> "No povre cloysterer, ne no novys,
> But a governour, wily and wys,
> And therwithal of brawnes and of bones
> A wel farynge persone for the nones.
> I pray to God, yeve hym confusioun
> That first thee broghte unto religioun!
> Thou woldest han been a tredefowel aright.
> Haddestow as greet a leeve as thou hast myght
> To parfourne al thy lust in engendrure,
> Thou haddest bigeten ful many a creature." (7.1939–48)

In regard to the Nun's Priest, Harry more succinctly observes: "'See, whiche braunes hath this gentil preest, / So gret a nekke, and swich a large breest!'" (7.3455–56).[41] Praising the physical masculinity of these religious figures, who are depicted as potentially more sexually successful with women than the Host despite their vows of celibacy, Harry accentuates his beleaguered manhood. He calls both men a "'tredefowel'" (7.1944 and 3451), and by calling these men "chicken-fuckers," Harry again links masculinity and sexuality, coupling these identificatory markers with the narrative of Chauntecleer. In a joking manner, Harry compares the sexual prowess of the religious and lay orders: "'Religioun hath take up al the corn / Of tredyng, and we borel men been shyrmpes'" (7.1954–55). With this metaphor of "tredying corn" coming so soon after the image of the Monk as a "tredefowel," Harry obliquely but humorously laments the loss of sexual opportunity occasioned by the sexual appetites of the religious orders and the concomitant figuration of "shrimpy" bourgeois manhood. Constructing the bourgeois social order as sexually deprived by over-amorous religious men, Harry here queers himself. He then tells the Monk that he is merely joking ("'But be nat wrooth, my lord, though that I pleye'" [7.1963]), but in the very next line he also tells the Monk that his joke is serious ("'Ful ofte in game a sooth I have herd seye!'" [7.1964]). Is Harry joking or serious in these verbal games? Of course, he is joking (lest textual evidence arise that the Monk and the Nun's Priest do indeed copulate with chickens). But the serious aspect of Harry's joke emerges in his own sexual failures. Once the pilgrims' "aller cok" (1.823), Harry confesses his personal failings as a "tredefowel" soon after disclosing his emasculated, "knifeless" relationship with his wife (7.1904–07, quoted previously). No conclusive textual evidence corroborates that Harry is indeed cuckolded by a religious man, but his jokes with the Monk and the Nun's Priest nonetheless tell a deeper truth: whether his wife cuckolds him or not, she certainly does not obey him, and the greater virility embodied in the religious men bears the potential, even if unrealized, to queer bourgeois men.

As arbiter of masculinity, the Host determines the relative merits of the manliness of many pilgrims, which is evident in his encounters with the Monk and the Nun's Priest; in comparison to these macho men, Chaucer-the-pilgrim appears to offer little masculine competition for Harry. After abruptly confronting Chaucer with a derisive question that both asks his identity and interrogates his masculinity ("'What man artow?'" [7.695]), Harry jokes about Chaucer-the-pilgrim's attractiveness, masculinity, and sexual normativity:

> "Approche neer, and looke up murily.
> Now war yow, sires, and lat this man have place!
> He in the waast is shape as wel as I;
> This were a popet in an arm t'enbrace
> For any womman, smal and fair of face.
> He semeth elvyssh by his contenaunce,
> For unto no wight dooth he daliaunce." (7.698–704)

Again, Harry calls for play from the pilgrims, demanding that Chaucer "looke up murily," but this scene bears little real merriment for Chaucer, with the Host insulting him so blatantly. If the Host is large (1.753) and Chaucer-the-pilgrim is short (7.702), their shared waist size bespeaks Chaucer's immoderate girth. Beyond a mere fat joke, however, the Host also derides Chaucer's amatory affairs, noting that "unto no wight dooth he daliaunce."[42] By focusing on Chaucer's apparent celibacy, the Host buttresses his own queered masculinity, which has been undermined through his revelations of his status as a henpecked husband following the *Clerk's Tale* and the *Merchant's Tale*.

If Harry queers Chaucer from normative masculinity by casting him as a chubby celibate whom any woman could physically master, Chaucer resists the Host's play with his own queering sensibility. Certainly, Chaucer can play the same rhetorical games as Harry himself: as Harry queers Chaucer (as pilgrim) by denigrating his masculinity, so Chaucer (as narrator) likewise queers the Host by noting his feminine mannerisms when speaking to the Prioress: "and with that word [the Host] sayde, / As curteisly as it had been a mayde" (7.445–56). Furthermore, Chaucer's sense of play, as exemplified by both of his tales, is quite different than Harry's, with the "drasty speche" (7.923) of the *Tale of Sir Thopas* and the interminable moralizing of the *Tale of Melibee*. After Harry interrupts Chaucer's *Tale of Sir Thopas,* he demands a tale of mirth:

> "By God," quod he, "for pleynly, at a word,
> Thy drasty rymyng is nat worth a toord!

Thou doost noght elles but despendest tyme.
Sire, at o word, thou shalt no lenger ryme.
Lat se wher thou kanst tellen aught in geeste,
Or telle in prose somwhat, at the leeste,
In which ther be som murthe or som doctryne." (7.929–35)

In response, Chaucer lies, promising a "litel thyng in prose" (7.937) but delivering the very lengthy *Tale of Melibee.* As Harry's governance is predicated on play, his masculine control fails when pilgrims tell tales of moral seriousness in prose. For Chaucer, poetry is a more playful form than prose; with rhyme and meter, poetry incarnates a rule structure that paradoxically evokes the inherent play of language.[43] Certainly, prose may be playful as well, as Harry's own words indicate when he tells Chaucer to " 'telle in prose somwhat, at the leeste, / In which ther be som murthe or som doctryne' " (7.934–35). But within the *Canterbury Tales,* Chaucer's prose sections are almost unanimously agreed to be the least amusing of his tales. Indeed, Chaucer's use of prose in his Retraction at the end of the *Canterbury Tales* shuts down the primarily poetic play that has been unleashed throughout the preceding narrative.[44] Through prose, the fun of the tale-telling competition is subverted for Harry but not necessarily for Chaucer; as Harry's governance is predicated on play, prose serves as a narratival structure of resistance to his rule. Also, given the Host's near obsession with the passing of time, the very lengthy *Tale of Melibee* offers another opportunity for Chaucer to resist Harry's authority and thus to subvert his masculine control of the game.[45]

That the Parson tells his tale in prose provides further evidence that prose subverts the Host's masculine authority. When demanding that the Parson tell his tale, Harry insists that the tale be a playful one because play should bolster his (Harry's) masculine governance:

"Be what thou be, ne breke nat oure pley;
For every man, save thou, hath toold his tale.
Unbokele and shewe us what is in thy male;
For trewely, me thynketh by thy cheere
Thou sholdest knytte up wel a greet mateere.
Telle us a fable anon, for cokkes bones!" (10.24–29)

The Host again links narrative to masculinity, demanding that the Parson narratively expose his masculinity with the repeated pun on unbuckling his "male." Since Harry asserts his masculine and earthly governance through the repeated call to play and amusement, the Parson, as the earthly representative of spiritual and heavenly governance, emerges as the ultimate threat to his power. Earlier when the Parson upbraided Harry for his swearing ("The Parson him answerde, 'Benedicite! / What eyleth the man, so synfully to swere?'" [2.1170–71]), the Host quelled this rebellion against his masculine authority by assailing the Parson's religious normativity: "'I smelle a Lollere in the wynd / ... / This Lollere heer wil prechen us somwhat'" (2.1173–77). The exchange is dropped, as the Shipman interrupts and promises to tell his fabliau (2.1178–90). In this earlier scene, Harry's play triumphs, and his masculine control continues. The Parson's rebellion, however, is only delayed, not defeated, and his very lengthy, very serious prose sermon, which addresses several of Harry's own sins (such as cursing), effectively ends the tale-telling game in favor of spiritual sobriety and the cessation of carnival. The Parson also directly attacks the ethos of Harry's tale-telling game and its chaotic but purposeful conflation of seriousness and play when he discusses the sin of "double tonge," when people "maken semblant as though they speeke of good entencioun, or elles in game and pley, and yet they speke of wikked entente" (10.644). Throughout the Canterbury pilgrimage Harry has spoken with a double tongue, exploiting the liminal gap between seriousness and play to bolster his masculinity and to queer his fellow pilgrims. Although one may hesitate to construe Harry's motives as wicked, surely the Parson, whom Harry accuses of Lollard sympathies, would see his play as threatening.

Andrew Taylor argues that this moment "demands not just that the reader abandon early frivolity, but that the reader start using the book in a fundamentally different way."[46] As the "reader" most inscribed in the hermeneutic process of interpreting the tales, Harry thus textually models this readerly experience for the actual audience of the narrative, and Glenn Burger declares that "for the Host, the end to tale-telling is bound up not just with filling the stipulated terms of an idle game, but with manifesting the ordered web of social relations that such game playing represents."[47] Although Harry attempts to manipulate the masculinity and social authority of a range of men throughout the Canterbury Tales and concludes along these lines with his admonition to the Parson that he must "[b]eth fructuous, and that in litel space" (10.71), the Parson does not realign his spiritual goals in accordance with Harry's playful desires. The Parson's Tale may be fruitful in its spiritual message, but it is surely not delivered in "litel space," and its lack of play appears no accidental piece of narratival happenstance but a rhetorical ploy designed to offer the final word on the class and gendered tensions evident throughout the pilgrimage. The end of the Canterbury Tales depicts the end of Harry's play, and the Parson is the last man standing, with Harry disciplined through Christian instruction into a new position as a normative bourgeois male—that is, one who lacks any real power over his social superiors and cannot redirect their actions. Queerness offered a temporary respite from normativity when Harry ruled his fellow pilgrims' gendered and sexual identities, but now queerness tames Harry back into his pre-carnivalesque position as a bourgeois man.

Given the fragmented nature of the *Canterbury Tales,* we can never know whom Harry Bailly would have chosen as the winner of his tale-telling contest. The terms of the contest require that the winner "telleth... / Tales of best sentence and moost solaas" (1.797–98), which is generally understood to mean the most humorous tale with the best moral.[48] A strong argument can be made for the *Nun's Priest's Tale,* as Walter Scheps proposes,[49] but any such hypothesis must remain forever a hypothesis given the unfinished nature of the *Canterbury Tales.* Rather than depicting Harry Bailly choosing the winner and awarding the prize while speaking in verse, Chaucer declares his retraction in prose *in propria persona.* The absence of Harry's decision may indicate nothing more than that Chaucer did not manage to address this issue prior to his death, but it might also indicate that the final governance of the tales is beyond Harry's control. L. M. Leith observes that the resolution of the *Canterbury Tales,* fragmented as it is, presents a decrease of comedy and an increase of spiritual growth, with Harry losing governance of the game: "As Harry's power diminishes, as the concern for the company increases, the movement towards the affirmation of doctrine and spiritual edification emerges as the agent of resolution to the tensions developed throughout the *Canterbury Tales.*"[50] The transition from Harry's earthly guidance to the Parson's spiritual guidance creates a compelling end to the *Canterbury Tales,* but it ultimately neutralizes Harry's class struggles and masculine self-aggrandizement. All might ultimately be equal in the heavenly kingdom, but since the pilgrims remain on earth, the rejection of Harry's leadership ultimately benefits the aristocratic and religious orders, who gain the most from preserving the status quo. In a fashion somewhat similar to Milton's Satan in *Paradise Lost,* Harry appears a magnificently larger-than-life figure in the opening of the *Canterbury Tales*, only to appear less grand and more self-delusionally grandiose by the narrative's end.

In Harry Bailly's carnival, the reader sees that play offers a bourgeois man opportunities to refashion his masculinity in accordance with his perceptions of social advancement and governance. By demanding the tale-telling game, Harry simultaneously establishes his control over the pilgrims and unleashes a queering and ludic force beyond his control. With a masculinity that both guides and is subverted throughout the Canterbury pilgrimage, Harry's manhood serves as an ideological barometer of the limits of bourgeois power. Queering Harry Bailly: he is both active and passive in this formulation, both the provocative agent of sexual policing and the emasculated object of queering social praxis as enacted in carnival. As Harry himself would say, "[U]nbokeled is the male"; however, it is ultimately Chaucer, as narrator and as author, who unbuckles the male and queers his Host's bourgeois manhood.[51] With the pilgrimage's leading social climber tamed of his rebellious and gendered puissance, queerness reveals its ideological power to create masculine subjects appropriate to their social caste. Harry, then, is not only queered and queering; he is normatively masculine again, but this normativity hangs on the conjunction of a quelled social class rebellion through a queering sexual politics.

CHAPTER 4

"HE NEDES MOOT UNTO THE PLEY ASSENTE": QUEER FIDELITIES AND CONTRACTUAL HERMAPHRODITISM IN CHAUCER'S *CLERK'S TALE*

> *Faithful women are all alike, they think only of their fidelity, never of their husbands.*
>
> —Jean Giraudoux, *Amphitryon 38*

Readers of Chaucer's *Clerk's Tale* frequently ponder why Griselda so patiently acquiesces to Walter's outrageously cruel demands.[1] Her unqualified and unyielding assent to abject cruelty troubles today's sensibilities, and ample evidence suggests that this story proved likewise troubling to medieval readers. Mary Carruthers, for example, concludes that the story of Griselda "seems always to have left some of its readers in a state of puzzlement and with a feeling of distaste."[2] The same question, however, could also be directed to the Clerk himself: why does he consent to Harry Bailly's storytelling game? The Clerk appears initially resistant to playing the Canterbury tale-telling game, yet he nonetheless acquiesces to the Host's demands (4.21–25).[3] In many ways, the narrative force of the *Clerk's Tale* is predicated upon both the Clerk's and Griselda's stubborn refusal to refuse desires antithetical to their own. Although their respective acquiescences to external authority contrast sharply in degree—the Clerk succumbs to Harry Bailly's bullying for a story, whereas Griselda sacrifices her children in response to Walter's tyrannical cruelty—their shared disavowal of personal desires creates a troubling tension between submission and suffering that resonates throughout *Prologue* and *Tale*.

With Griselda acceding to wishes patently hostile to her personal desires, is there any pleasure in the *Clerk's Tale*? The bulk of the narrative focuses on the stoic acceptance of pain, but such adamantine self-denial as Griselda practices is not the traditional stuff of readerly pleasure. Griselda's unwavering commitment to Walter and to the suffering he inflicts upon her highlights the disparities between power and pleasure enacted in social contracts (such as marriage) that depend upon performing gender roles. Although one may question the likelihood of a person's fidelity to social contracts predicated upon his/her own disenfranchisement, one need only examine the contours and constructions of gender—within medieval or modern society—to see how social contracts and queer fidelities to them structure daily existence. Gender roles, especially in regard to their social context within heterosexual, homosexual, or even nonsexual relationships, bear queer potential, in that they demand individuals to subvert, exceed, or otherwise fracture the very binary of masculine/feminine upon which they are ostensibly predicated.[4] That is to say, maintaining gender as a heterosexual and heteronormative binary entails endless transgressions of the active/passive binary that serves as the bedrock of sexual difference. Thomas Laqueur argues that biological understandings of sex difference inevitably colored constructions of gender and other social relations in western culture:

> In a public world that was overwhelmingly male, the one-sex model displayed what was already massively evident in culture more generally: *man* is the measure of all things, and woman does not exist as an ontologically distinct category. Not all males are masculine, potent, honorable, or hold power, and some women exceed some men in each of these categories. But the standard of the human body and its representation is the male body.[5]

If we see gender as constructed upon fundamentally queer and queering foundations in its phantastic reliance upon a masculine standard for all people, regardless of their gender or sexuality, queer allegiances are necessary to maintain this social edifice that continually teeters under duress.

As Griselda's queer fidelity to her husband and her gender role paradoxically repositions her gender, pleasure finally appears at the moment she reaches the liminal threshold of hermaphroditism between genders. The social contract to which the Clerk remains queerly faithful—the tale-telling game—is both radically different from marriage yet fundamentally similar in that gender roles—Harry Bailly's overbearing masculinity, the Clerk's apparent acceptance of a feminized passivity—bear deep repercussions to their interactions. The Clerk, too, fractures gender through its enactment, remaining true to the feminized position accorded him by Harry Bailly while simultaneously undermining the constructions of gender throughout his tale. Reading Griselda and the Clerk hermaphroditically, we see that they are bound by gender roles yet paradoxically freed by them as well, as these characters ultimately deconstruct gender through its radical performance. Only by phantastically assuming the femininity accorded them by Walter and Harry can Griselda and the Clerk subvert gender's ostensible destruction of their agency.

Beyond the surface level of the *Clerk's Tale,* the audience of Canterbury pilgrims, engaged in the purportedly enjoyable act of sharing recreational tales, finds a narrative that denies its pleasure by intensely focusing on human suffering. Through the Clerk's queering play, the male pilgrims are coerced into a reenactment of the destruction of gender depicted in the tale. The gendered hostilities evident in the frame of the *Clerk's Tale* evince Chaucer's shrewd attention to the ways in which social contracts— from the play of the tale-telling contest to the underlying earnest of socially conditioned gender and sexual roles in marriage—call for individuals to subject themselves to external dominion within the gendered dynamics of personal interaction. Although Harry Bailly's aggressive rhetoric queers the Clerk, the Clerk's apparent submission to Harry's dominion then allows the Clerk to queer his masculine audience into a new awareness of the limitations of masculinity. The feminized Clerk thus repositions his primarily male audience into a feminized awareness by reconstructing their genders away from their ostensibly normative positions.

Along with these moments of coerced consent in the text and its frame, readers also acquiesce to the *Clerk's Tale* through the act of reading and rereading it, despite that the critical history of the *Clerk's Tale* demonstrates the ways in which it troubles readers, perhaps more than any other Canterbury narrative.[6] Readers are likewise queerly faithful to Chaucer's notoriously unlikable tale, as through the latent pleasures of hermaphroditic readings, character and readers alike are stripped of their genders.[7] After outlining a theoretical framework of queer fidelities and contractual hermaphroditism, along with their latent pleasures, I turn first to the *Clerk's Prologue* and then to his *Tale* to explore how queerings of desire enable its impossible fulfillments. The Clerk manipulates and exposes the ways in which gender is itself such a queer fidelity to an arbitrary social contract. By creating a hermaphroditic audience, the Clerk forecloses his tale's teleology to undermine the oppressive masculinity of his primarily male audience. The characters of the *Clerk's Tale* and both of its metatextual audiences—of Canterbury pilgrims and modern readers—all experience the compulsory queerness of desire as they progress to the story's

end, where a sense of normativity is attained only after a decidedly queering conclusion.

Engendering Queer Fidelities

The Clerk and Griselda deny their individual desires in service of larger
social obligations, sacrificing their personal wishes to ones exterior to their
selves. In these selfless acts, the characters display a latent awareness that
desire is doomed to failure.[8] In the teleological failure of desire, its multivalent force creates disharmonies between self and society. Queer fidelities
arise in the inevitable failure of desire, in that one is nonetheless faithful to
the power structure foreclosing the fulfillment of that desire. The utility
of queer theory for this investigation lies in its exploration of the nexus
between the unknowability of desire and the socially imposed limits of
gendered normativity. In his analysis of queer theory and desire, Lee
Edelman ponders, "Can desire survive its naming? Can it survive in the
place of its naming, in the state to which, and as which, by naming it, it is
named?"[9] From this perspective of the impossibility of ever naming desire,
queer desires must remain unknowable, and this unknowability of desire
highlights the ways in which it often queerly destabilizes norms of behavior, even "norms" of homosexuality. In applying a queer hermeneutic to
the Clerk's Tale, I am not attempting to locate submerged homosexual
desire in the tale but to uncover the ways in which gendered normativities
are revealed as chimerical fantasies dependent upon queerness. One might
expect Griselda to desire to save her children and the Clerk to desire not
to play the tale-telling game, but they both privilege the will of others in
their respective sacrificial decisions. Acting against their ostensible desires
queerly disrupts the contours of their characterological existence: how can
the reader comprehend Griselda, if she sates her desire by allowing her
children to be taken away and presumably executed? Why does the Clerk
succumb so readily to the Host's demands to sacrifice his personal desires
by joining the somewhat raucous tale-telling game?

If we see the Clerk's and Griselda's desires as a means for them to find
pleasure, such pleasure is frustrated because their pleasures conflict with
others' power. Pleasure and power are inextricably intertwined in the social
order: "Pleasure and power do not cancel or turn back against one another;
they seek out, overlap, and reinforce one another," as Michel Foucault
observes.[10] Given the intersection of pleasure and power, powerless people
have little ready access to pleasure because powerful people frequently control all access to pleasure. Within such a social network, how can desires
bring pleasure to the powerless? Articulated and enacted within its own
immediate cultural deconstruction, desires of the powerless shore up the

positions of the powerful. Furthermore, as both constitutive factor and escape route of all social structures, desire knows not what it desires, merely that it desires. If we see desire as such a destabilizing force, seeking its perpetuation rather than its satiation, it becomes increasingly apparent that desire leads the subject to unexpected avenues of "fulfillment," only then exposing the fraudulence of fulfillment as a real possibility. Given the polyvalent and conflicted structure of desire, endlessly circling yet never completing itself, it contains the potential to metamorphose into queerness when its false search for fulfillment directs the subject to ends antithetically structured to his/her own interests. If desires can never be quenched, if these desires are at times constructed by forces outside ourselves, fidelity to desire bears the likely burden of queerness, in that individuals will maintain allegiance to desires inscribed upon their selves yet adverse to their obvious needs.

Queer fidelities thus arise in one's participation in and maintenance of social systems and cultural arrangements directly antithetical to one's own interests. Such a dynamic is directly observable in modern life, in a variety of contradictory, if not self-negating, political, religious, and cultural affiliations (e.g., women in ultraconservative and patriarchal religions, Log Cabin Republicans).[11] As Molly Anne Rothenberg and Dennis Foster argue, "The category of the polymorphously perverse suggests that we are highly motivated to have varying forms of satisfaction and attachment to objects, including both human and nonhuman object relations. … We might even ask if the meaningful activities of social life would be possible without their perverse foundations."[12] Within the stunning multiplicity of object relations, desire wrenches the subject into perversion through personal alliances with antithetically constructed social networks. Also of critical interest in the construction of queer fidelities is the way in which the individual might realize the ever tentative collapse of identity as enacted in the queer fidelity, but other desires in play nevertheless structure a pleasure sufficient to overlook the queer construction of the self. As we will see, the moments when characters submit to domination can also be understood as moments when they convert submission to domination through a mastery of the masochistic dynamic at play in gender. The *Clerk's Tale* thus demonstrates that by playing out feminine passivity to such a radical degree, Griselda simultaneously demonstrates its impossibility and its undesirability for women—and for men as well. With queer fidelity, pleasure bubbles up in the act of self-sacrifice, whether that pleasure is confessed or not. This pleasure can be likened to a sadomasochistic contract in which a given individual plays both roles: Griselda is surely the masochistic victim of Walter's sadism, but the text's penchant for sadism extends to her in that she ultimately conquers Walter's tyranny. Readers might want her to rebel, to fight against Walter's tyranny, but the masochistic abjection she suffers cannot be entirely discounted as an unexpected conduit to authority and, eventually, to pleasure as well.

The Clerk's and Griselda's queer fidelities arise due to their virtual powerlessness. The Clerk, for all intents and purposes, does not appear to have sufficient power to decline Harry Bailly's storytelling game; likewise, despite that Walter requests Griselda's consent to their marriage ("'Wol ye assente, or elles yow avyse?'" [4.350]), she has little power due to the disparity in their social standings: a peasant cannot easily refuse the wishes of the nobility. In addition to the contractual levels in Harry's tale-telling game and Walter's marriage proposal, gender and sexual roles emerge as another ideological force to which these characters remain queerly faithful. Indeed, these queer constructions of identity arise due to the characters' parallel resistance to and embracing of gender roles inscribed by themselves and others. For in the *Clerk's Tale,* gender roles rigidly define the characters vis-à-vis one another. Although recent theoretical analyses of gender conceive it as a performative venue for self-construction and identity determination,[13] such a paradigm explains neither why Griselda adheres to her submissively feminized role nor why the Clerk inhabits the feminized position that Harry Bailly assigns him. By examining gender as a cultural contract to which these characters are queerly faithful, we see the ways in which the Clerk manipulates the exaggerated genders both of Griselda and of Walter to deflate the masculinity of his fellow pilgrims. That is to say, if characters are queerly faithful to gender within the Clerk's world, his pleasure surfaces in imbuing these individuals queerly faithful to gender with a new hermaphroditic sense of their selves. In her analysis of the Clerk, Carolyn Dinshaw hints at his hermaphroditism through his narratival translations: "The Clerk's identification of sympathy with the female—one who is fundamentally left out of patriarchal society—allows him to understand translation in this way, allows him to read with an eye to what is left out of the very reading he is performing—allows him to read, that is, like a woman."[14] As the Clerk represents a male capable of inhabiting a female reader's position, his complementary tale-telling goal is to teach other men to read hermaphroditically, to read as if they were women.

This hermaphroditism, however, does not refer to the heady gender play of alternating between cultural stereotypes of male and female as a sole result of the conscious decisions of the agent involved; rather, the hermaphroditism under discussion in this chapter teeters between cultural determinism and individual choice. Hermaphroditism can be envisioned in two complementary ways: either as the erasure of the dualistic construction of male/female through the embodiment of a merged, unified, and singular "gender" or as the oscillation between male and female gender roles. Both forms of hermaphroditism are at least somewhat culturally contingent, due to the ideological constructions of gender in effect in a given social contract. Such hermaphroditism is metaphoric, not biological, and so hermaphroditism bears a positive valence for agents desirous of gender play and subversion, but threatening to agents who benefit from maintaining traditional gender roles. Returning to marriage as an example, this social contract is certainly predicated upon gender and sexual roles, and traditionally gender roles have been rather bluntly demarcated in its enactment. But no social contract can take into account the countless permutations of identity necessary to face the day-to-day onslaught of ordinary and extraordinary circumstances, as no legal code can be constructed to take into account the multiplicity of permutations to which the law will be applied. Contractual hermaphroditism thus refers to the ambivalently gendered position that is accorded one by a social contract with the realization that this gender is both agreed to and forced upon one. Thus, depending upon the particular circumstances of the social contracts, the resulting hermaphroditism could be embodied through the erasure of gender or the oscillation between genders. Contractual hermaphroditism elicited by social contracts demands gendered adjustments and negotiations, as the Clerk and Griselda amply demonstrate.

Engendering Queer Fidelities
in the *Prologue*

Queer fidelities structure the *Prologue* of the *Clerk's Tale* both textually and metatextually, as the Canterbury game itself functions on both the surface level of game yet also allows its players a serious outlet for their aggressions.[15] Despite his cool response to the tale-telling game, the Clerk adheres to its rules, evincing his queer fidelity to the social contract in play. The description of him in the *General Prologue* hints strongly that he would find the storytelling game rather uninteresting:

> Of studie took he moost cure and moost heede.
> Noght o word spak he moore than was neede,
> And that was seyd in forme and reverence,
> And short and quyk and ful of hy sentence;
> Sownynge in moral vertu was his speche,
> And gladly wolde he lerne and gladly teche. (1.303–08)

Given the Clerk's tendency toward study, seriousness, and moral virtue, it is doubtful that he would appreciate the downward spiral of the

Canterbury Tales from the epic romance of the *Knight's Tale* to the fabliau licentiousness and ribaldry of the tales of the Miller, Reeve, Cook, and Summoner. Such a view is strengthened in light of his preference for serious study over the material gains or entertaining amusements represented by the "robes riche, or fithele, or gay sautrie" (1.296) that he rejects in favor of books and learning. From a preponderance of the evidence and in light of his preference for academic pursuits over frivolous amusements, it appears more likely that the Clerk would prefer to ignore the tale-telling contest altogether or to cede his turn to another pilgrim.

Certainly, Harry Bailly must go to greater lengths to convince the Clerk to play the tale-telling game than any other pilgrim. The *Prologue* of the *Clerk's Tale* commences with Harry twenty-line exhortation to the Clerk to begin his tale. This rhetorical scene is anomalous in the *Canterbury Tales,* as the other pilgrims willingly play the game and need little direct encouragement from the Host to begin their stories. In the *General Prologue,* Chaucer prepares the reader for the Clerk's resistance, as the Host's words to him ("'And ye, sire Clerk, lat be youre shamefastnesse, / Ne studieth noght'" [1.840–41]) establish the grounds of tension between the two characters early in the overarching narrative. The Clerk's studiousness riles Harry's sense of fun and play, and indeed, the Host sees in the Clerk a sullenness that must be corrected with his exasperated demand, "'For Goddes sake, as beth of bettre cheere! / It is no tyme for to studien heere'" (4.7–8). Emphasizing the Clerk's scholarly predilections, Chaucer depicts him as needing to be coerced into play by the Host, who then forces the tale-telling game upon him with a masterful elision of his own power: "'For what man that is entred in a pley, / He nedes moot unto the pley assente'" (4.10–11). These lines deprive the Clerk of the freedom to abstain from the game, as Harry Bailly turns the playful contest into a quasi-legal obligation.[16] Here emerges the frustrating tension of the *Clerk's Tale,* in that the characters are forced to participate in "pleasureful" social contracts—tale-telling in the frame and marriage in the tale— that they both do and do not want to play. The Clerk is subscribed into a relationship that refuses to address his desires, but his queer fidelity to the social contract entails that he must play according to the hypermasculine Host's demands. The Clerk could conceivably refuse to play the storytelling game, but such a response, although within the realm of the possible, shatters the realm of the likely, for he is involved in a pastime of ostensible play and pleasure. In this instance, what is presented as pleasureful is truly coercive: the Clerk expresses little individual agency in privileging exterior social desires over his own preferences.

If the Host's insistence to the Clerk that "'[h]e nedes moot unto the pley assente'" denies him his agency, the Clerk nonetheless undermines the social contract of gender by performing the very gender prescribed him by the Host. In addition to the tale-telling contest, gender is at stake throughout the *Canterbury Tales*.[17] The Host displays masculine aggression in his words as he feminizes the Clerk: "'Sire Clerk of Oxenford,' oure Hooste sayde, / 'Ye ryde as coy and stille as dooth a mayde / Were newe spoused, sittynge at the bord'" (4.1–3).[18] The hostility of these lines is perhaps not as rhetorically vicious as other moments during the Canterbury pilgrimage (such as when the Miller threatens, "'By armes, and by blood and bones, / I kan a noble tale for the nones, / With which I wol now quite the Knyghtes tale'" [1.3125–27]), but it nonetheless undermines the gendered normativity of the Clerk. By depicting him as a hermaphroditic figure, a "sire" who is also a "mayde," Harry subverts the Clerk's genital masculinity and feminizes him as a new bride, which ironically metamorphoses him into a foreshadowing of his protagonist Griselda. From the preceding tales of the Canterbury pilgrimage, clerks appear to be quite randy in their heterosexual pursuits, as evidenced by Nicholas in the *Miller's Tale* and Allen and John in the *Reeve's Tale*.[19] If we see gender as another social construction to which the Clerk queerly adheres, his sense of masculinity and sexuality is threatened by the Host's words that cast him as a bride apprehensively awaiting penetration. In the tale-telling that follows, the Clerk adheres to the precepts of the game, but he does so in a way that ultimately undermines the masculinity of his fellow male pilgrims and constructs them in the same hermaphroditic cast in which he finds himself.

In response to Harry Bailly's insult to the Clerk's masculinity, the Clerk leads the male pilgrims to reassess the meaning of their own maleness. The Clerk's reply to the Host stresses that he sees himself as coerced into the game, that he truly "nedes moot unto the pley assente." He is ruled by a man and a social structure beyond his individual control:

> "Hooste," quod he, "I am under youre yerde;
> Ye han of us as now the governance,
> And therfore wol I do yow obeisance,
> As fer as resoun axeth, hardily." (4.22–25)

As he submits to the Host's coercive play, the hermaphroditic Clerk's acceptance of the Host's orders prefigures Griselda's submission to Walter's cruel commands. Coercive play may appear oxymoronic,[20] but the Clerk's lexicon—"yerde," "governance," "obeisance"—stresses that he sees himself as contractually obligated to fulfill the parameters of the storytelling contest. At the same time the Clerk displays his queer fidelity to this antagonistic game that has so quickly been manipulated to rob him of his masculine and sexual normativity, he limits his participation with his caveat that he will play " 'as fer as resoun axeth.' " As Barrie Ruth Straus comments, "Adhering to a spirit of play different from what the Host might understand, the Clerk's caveat immediately undoes the obedience he has averred, by opening up a space for disobeying any demands that could be considered unreasonable."[21] If the Clerk accepts the feminine role that Harry Bailly accords him in his submission to the host's masculine authority, the Clerk nonetheless asserts a limitation to his new position. He will be feminized only as far as reason allows, which suggests that the Clerk performs his gender yet moves hermaphroditically between masculinity and femininity. As queer fidelity to a social system entails the possibility of maintaining allegiance to the system while simultaneously subverting its structure through this very allegiance, the Clerk's rhetoric straddles the border between acquiescence and rebellion.

Key to Harry Bailly's masculine command of the Canterbury pilgrimage and his manipulation of the pilgrims is his repeated insistence that the narratives must be amusing. In this way, patriarchal masculinity naturalizes its rule as enjoyable and beneficial to all, even though it is nonetheless structured without regard for egalitarianism. The Host, therefore, demands that the Clerk resist chiding the pilgrims for their sins: " 'But precheth nat, as freres doon in Lente, / To make us for oure olde synnes wepe, / Ne that thy tale make us nat to slepe' " (4.12–14). Of course, the pilgrims, through their participation in a religious tradition such as pilgrimage, should welcome opportunities to consider their sinfulness. Pleasure, not repentance, directs the Host's desires, and he then demands further that the Clerk " '[t]elle us som murie thyng of aventures' " (4.15) and that he " '[s]peketh so pleyn at this tyme, we yow preye, / That we may understonde what ye seye' " (4.19–20). In his request for plain speech, Harry explicitly rejects both sophisms (" 'I trowe ye studie aboute som sophyme' " [4.5]) and the deliberate study constitutive of clerkly life (" 'It is no tyme for to studien here' " [4.8]). In the *Prologue,* then, Harry's anti-intellectualism is conflated with his feminizing of the Clerk. As Harry bolsters his authoritarian masculinity by directing the Clerk's narrative actions, the Clerk's hermaphroditic liminality lies in the balance: conceptions of masculinity and femininity become increasingly blurred as he queerly adheres to the Host's orders.

If we see the Clerk's queer fidelity to the Canterbury game in his decision to play along, he also demonstrates the ways in which abundantly surpassing the rules of the game imbues him with subversive power in relation to the Host who demands the game. As the Clerk assumes control of the *Prologue,* we sense a sudden change in the gendered dynamics in effect, as the hermaphroditic Clerk then ignores Harry Bailly's orders. Before beginning his tale, the Clerk toys with the Host's request for a

simple and merry narrative by explicating his tale's origins, teaching his
fellow pilgrims a lesson about Petrarch and Giovanni da Lignano and
concluding it with a grim reminder of their deaths: " '[Death] Hem bothe
hath slayn, and alle shul we dye' " (4.38). He then devotes several lines to
detailing Petrarch's proem (4.39–54), but the Clerk himself cuts off this
introduction by declaring, " 'Me thynketh it a thyng impertinent' " (4.54).
If Petrarch's death and proem are irrelevant to his tale, what purpose do
they serve? Why does the Clerk employ this uninteresting, if not decidedly boring, material? Its very irrelevancy serves notice that the Clerk is
queerly faithful to the game but that his fidelity empowers rather than
enervates his rhetorical moves. Furthermore, by citing such a famous
textual authority, the Clerk frees himself from complete responsibility
for the tale's content. The masculine Host requests a "murie thyng of
aventure," but the hermaphroditic Clerk delivers a tale of his own choosing, thereby upsetting and subverting the meaning of gender that the
Host establishes. The game of the *Canterbury Tales* is predicated upon the
Host's primary embodiment of masculinity—he is, after all, the "aller
cok" of the pilgrimage (1.823)—but as within other social contracts, the
gendered borders of identity and behavior metamorphose in surprising
permutations. As we will see at the conclusion of the *Clerk's Tale,* the
"moral" so upsets the social contract of gender that no character can
maintain its normative demands without experiencing queerness.

Engendering Queer Fidelities in the *Tale*

Who is queerer, Griselda or Walter? Which one more flagrantly breeches
the codes of normativity—whether of marital or familial behavior—in
their relationship? Walter's inexplicable and abhorrent cruelty makes his
desires appear the less human of the two characters, but Griselda's inexplicable and aberrant constancy reveals tendencies as striking as her husband's cruelty. In her queer fidelity to their marriage, Griselda remains
true to her vows, despite the pain that it brings. In addition to the social
contract of marriage, she also adheres to gender constructions apparently
antithetical to her desires. Griselda is so passive in her actions, so acquiescent to Walter's every whim, that she appears to embody the worst cultural stereotypes regarding female submission. At the same time, however,
the contractual hermaphroditism evident in her queer fidelity to Walter
and her marriage arises in her deconstruction of gender as a hermeneutic
in the *Tale,* as the terms "male" and "female" mean very little by its
conclusion.

    In terms of Griselda's queer fidelity to Walter, it is crucial to realize
that she accepts his implacable wishes with neither hesitation nor resistance. Some scholars see traces of irony in Griselda's speeches, and these

moments of possible irony are used to argue for her resistance to Walter's cruelty. For example, Gail Ashton sees in Griselda's "perfect mimetic display" a strategy that "deceives the husband who represents patriarchy."[22] One such passage that can be read ironically involves Griselda's sacrifice of her son to Walter's pleasure:

> "Al youre plesance ferme and stable I holde;
> For wiste I that my deeth wolde do yow ese,
> Right gladly wolde I dyen, yow to plese.
> Deth may noght make no comparisoun
> Unto youre love." (4.663–67)

Griselda's somewhat bizarre statement that "'Deth may noght make no comparisoun / Unto youre love'" may be read ironically, as could her later declaration to Walter, "'How gentil and how kynde / Ye semed'" (4.852–53), but little in the text supports such readings through suggestions of intonation or phrasing. If any tinges of bitter irony bubble up to the surface in her words, they are insufficiently developed for Walter to catch, as he departs with his pleasure momentarily fulfilled:

> And whan this markys say
> The constance of his wyf, he caste adoun
> His eyen two, and wondreth that she may
> In pacience suffre al this array;
> And forth he goth with drery contenance,
> But to his herte it was ful greet plesance. (4.667–72)

That Walter misses Griselda's possible irony does not ensure its absence in her words, but readers are given insufficient textual clues to conclude definitively that she speaks with any ironic inflection. It is nonetheless evident that Walter is struck by the "constance of his wyf"; of course, he is somewhat bewildered ("wondreth") by her surprising constancy, and his wonder thus suggests that he finds her actions somewhat unnatural. Although he receives what he thinks he desires and momentarily finds "greet plesance," her fulfillment of this desire is somewhat unsettling to his perception of her, in that she allows the sacrifice to proceed without complaint. Both characters' desires obscure the contours of their identities: Griselda accedes to his brutal wishes, and thus her desires depend upon extreme self-abnegation, but Walter's desires appear unquenchable, in that their immediate fulfillment only stimulates a sense of bewildered wonder and momentary pleasure, but never satisfaction.

Reading against the grain of a story is often an essential part of the interpretive process, but in the instance of Griselda's "irony," very little in the narrative encourages us to concentrate on any potentially subversive qualities of Griselda's speech. Indeed, as the *Clerk's Tale* is problematically allegorized to the Book of Job, Griselda's "irony" would be theologically unsanctioned.[23] As Kathryn McKinley demonstrates, Griselda lacks the interiority necessary to construct her as a character capable of irony: "Griselda is something of a hagiographic 'Barbie'—idealized, perfect, virtuous, but incapable of manifesting subjectivity or agency through any type of authentic spiritual struggle."[24] As Jean Giraudoux's epigraph to this chapter indicates, however, Griselda's foremost goal is to maintain fidelity by shutting out any distraction to this fidelity, especially if her husband embodies the distraction: she thinks only of her fidelity, not of her husband. If there is no clear evidence of irony or subversion in Griselda's speeches, does she nonetheless offer any resistance to her fate? Her queer fidelity to her marriage, and her corresponding lack of fidelity to her children—implied in the act of birth but never formalized in a social contract—apparently trumps all other desires, leaving her wholly disconnected from her self yet wholly faithful to her persecutor. Certainly, she has evacuated herself of all personal desire:

> "Ne I desire no thyng for to have,
> Ne drede for to leese, save oonly yee.
> This wyl is in myn herte, and ay shal be;
> No lengthe of tyme or deeth may this deface,
> Ne chaunge my corage to another place." (4.507–11)

Realizing the dead end of desire, Griselda forsakes any wish that does not come from her husband. She evacuates her interiority in service of Walter, and Walter alone. In aligning Walter with her will and locating this desire in her heart, Griselda's vision of her fidelity and desire evacuates him as a human through his metaphoric encapsulation as an expression of her adamant will.

We appear to have in the *Clerk's Tale* a simple correspondence between male agency and female passivity, as well as between male cruelty and female submission. Such a pattern fails to hold throughout the narrative, and the fracturing of this gendered dynamic can be witnessed in the Clerk's manipulations of the figure of Job from an allegorical hermeneutic of Griselda's human suffering into a gendered interpretive decoy. The Clerk reminds his audience of Job's example to illuminate Griselda's torments:

> "Men speke of Job, and moost for his humblesse,
> As clerkes, whan hem list, konne wel endite,

Namely of men, but as in soothfastnesse,
Though clerkes preise wommen but a lite,
Ther kan no man in humblesse hym acquite
As womman kan, ne kan been half so trewe
As wommen been, but it be falle of newe." (4.932–38)

This passage offers several surprises, notably the Clerk's disparaging attitude toward his fellow clerks who praise women insufficiently. In the
highly gendered world of the *Canterbury Tales,* the Clerk here castigates
male patriarchal privilege as represented by his fellow clerks, echoing the
Wife of Bath's sentiment that "'it is an impossible / That any clerk wol
speke good of wyves, / But if it be of hooly seintes lyves'" (3.688–90).
The Clerk's words also suggest that he sees in Griselda a more successful
sufferer than Job: "'Ther kan no man in humblesse hym acquite / As
womman kan.'" Although men praise Job, he pales in comparison to
Griselda because she exemplifies suffering better than a male precisely
because she is a woman who should not be able to withstand such extreme
pain. Although suffering in itself need not be a gendered act, the Clerk's
rhetoric imbues pain with a gendered valence and concludes that women
more successfully embody the humility borne of suffering.

In this instance, the Clerk's message appears to be that a woman is
needed to do a man's work, if that work entails suffering. What, then, is
the gender of Job within the *Clerk's Tale?* He is a male who showcases the
vast potential for women to suffer, yet he is also a man insufficiently masculine to match Griselda's feminine suffering. Job then becomes not only
a model of male suffering but of a hermaphroditic allegorical figure highlighting the fragility of gender in relation to suffering. The Clerk's gendered observation that "'[m]en speke of Job'" suggests that men appreciate
masculine suffering, but men are insufficiently versed in suffering if Job—
not Griselda—serves as their role model because she should be deemed
the archetype of endurance. "Chaucer is exploring the antifeminist archetype to see whether some of its elements could be productively recuper-
ated," suggests Tara Williams.[25] Quite simply, Job symbolizes not the
superiority of masculine suffering but the failure of masculine suffering
to equal the queer potential of suffering as embodied in Griselda. As Ann
Astell demonstrates, such exegetes as Gregory the Great prefigured
Chaucer's depiction of a female Job: "Gregory's allegorical interpretation
of the Book of Job simultaneously genders and displaces its literal meaning as feminine in a way that admits and invites a Chaucerian reversal of
that reading and, thus, the return of a female Job in the form of Walter's
sorely tried wife."[26] Rather than trying to fix a certain gender to Job in
the *Clerk's Tale,* it is more important to realize that he and his gendered

suffering function as floating signifiers of hermaphroditic possibility. Since Job cannot teach a lesson about humility as well as Griselda can, he only serves as a negative example of male suffering and its insufficiency vis-à-vis female suffering. Job undermines gender in the Clerk's deployment of him, as he proves that the terms "male" and "female" collapse under the weight of human suffering and improperly aligned allegory. Furthermore, in terms of gendered allegory, Griselda can also be read as a Christ-figure based upon the narrator's assessment of how Walter's people perceive her:

> So wise and rype wordes hadde she,
> And juggementz of so greet equitee,
> That she from hevene sent was, as men wende,
> Peple to save and every wrong t'amende. (4.438–41)

Scholars such as Jill Mann see Griselda as a Christ figure, due to her exemplary suffering and salvific force;[27] however, given the ways in which gender fails to build meaning into this text, one may well wonder if even Christ's passion is insufficient to represent Griselda's feminine suffering.

In the collapse of gender, the hermaphroditism enacted in the tale focuses the reader's attention away from Griselda's feminine suffering to Walter's emasculated rebirth. His cruel actions foreclosing the reader's sympathy, Walter is often viewed in terms of his narrative function rather than in terms of his character development. Lynn Staley Johnson, for example, states that "we cannot relate personally to Walter; he embodies a function as an agent of test and as an image of authority."[28] Freudian and post-Freudian interpretations of the tale likewise construct Walter as an obstacle to be overcome rather than as a depiction of a human being.[29] Such readings illuminate the psychodynamics of the text, but they often do so at the expense of the characters. Allyson Newton observes that such an approach inevitably fails: "Attempts to explicate the seemingly incomprehensible Walter and Griselda in terms of individual psychologies are unsatisfactory because they divorce the characterological from the structural."[30] Yet it is critical to realize that Walter is a more fully realized character than Griselda. Her characterization is flat and undeveloped: as she acquiesces to paternal and phallic power at the beginning of the narrative, so she queerly continues to acquiesce throughout the narrative. As Kathryn Lynch points out, however, "On a closer look, balanced against the Clerk's self-conscious reference to Griselda's example at the tale's end...are numerous details, points of emphasis and structure, to indicate that Chaucer is interested in keeping Walter's experience before us more forcefully than Griselda's."[31] That is to say, the focus of the narrative lies more in Walter's decision to stop torturing Griselda than in Griselda's relief at its end. In a similar manner to which Job's masculine suffering cannot adequately compare to Griselda's feminine suffering, so too is Walter's masculine tyranny an insufficiently masculine force to crush her spirit. Of course, he could never do so because no one can act on or against Griselda. She is completely self-contained and impervious to outside forces. Her queer fidelity to Walter, in the end, is precisely the necessary protection to shield her from him. Griselda's agency—and this term is not used ironically or oxymoronically—arises in her sacrificial and queer fidelity, as it inexorably shields her from the passive femininity she ostensibly embodies. To put it bluntly, it takes balls—queer balls—to be such a faithful wife.

The degeneration and rebirth of Walter's sympathy and empathy from the beginning of the tale to its conclusion thus structures the narrative against a backdrop of Griselda's queer fidelity. When readers first meet Walter, he is a character capable of pity, as when his subjects ask him to marry: "Hir meeke preyere and hir pitous cheere / Made the markys herte han pitee" (4.141–42). In response, Walter sacrifices his personal desires for their benefit, despite his preference for a bachelor's life of freedom: " 'I me rejoysed of my liberte, / That seelde tyme is founde in mariage; / Ther I was free, I moot been in servage' " (4.145–47). Walter shows his obvious distaste for marriage, as the narrator reiterates that "he dide al this at hir requeste" (4.185); nevertheless, he sacrifices his pleasures to their demands.[32] Although Walter's demands on Griselda receive the lion's share of critical attention, these initial constraints placed upon Walter establish the ways in which, within this narrative world, virtually all of the characters' actions are conscripted to serve desires antithetical to their own. Thus, as Griselda's queer fidelity to Walter perplexes readers and denies them access to a coherently structured set of desires and concerns, so too does Walter's queer fidelity to his people's desires, which oppose his purported wishes, make his actions incomprehensible within any realm of rationality predicated upon one's attempt to pursue one's personal objectives. He is, after all, the ruler, and despite the historical relevance of the Peasants' Revolt of 1381 to Chaucer's view of governance, nothing in the poem suggests Walter's rule could be usurped by any fractious subjects.[33]

Griselda is more masculine in her suffering than Job, more capable of withstanding Walter's tyranny than he could have ever conceived, precisely because she is a woman. As Holly Crocker asserts, the performance of a credible female passivity often necessitates the dissemblance of masculine agency, as female passivity shatters the gendered paradigms of medieval thought.[34] Lynch also notes that "Griselda's constancy is itself chiefly a masculine virtue."[35] Walter exhibits the traits of a tyrant, yet his masculine tyranny eventually wavers in light of Griselda's endless capacity for suffering. Walter need do very little in the *Clerk's Tale* after marrying Griselda, as even his tormenting of her is carried out by proxy. In contrast to Griselda's determined passivity, Walter's apparently determined cruelty falters because he is incapable of *acting* upon her:

> And whan this Walter saugh hire pacience,
> Hir glade chiere, and no malice at al,
> And he so ofte had doon to hire offence,
> And she ay sad and constant as a wal,
> Continuynge evere hire innocence overal,
> This sturdy markys gan his herte dresse
> To rewen upon hire wyfly stedfastnesse. (4.1044–50)

In this moment, Walter feels pity and sympathy, and he is revealed to be capable of human growth and development. Incapable of defeating Griselda through his tyranny, Walter finally submits to her steadfastness. He maintains the power of patriarchy, yet simultaneously he is reconfigured into a feminized figure newly capable of feeling pity. Thomas Van suggests that Walter's "relentless testing of Griselda is an examination, by surrogate, of his own spiritual interior,"[36] and Elaine Tuttle Hansen similarly argues that Walter needs "to find the Other in Griselda, someone he can master in order to find himself."[37] If Walter's ultimate goal is self-knowledge, this revelation is predicated as much upon his own queer fidelity to marriage as Griselda's queer fidelity to him. Thus, the contractual hermaphroditism of their marriage circulates unevenly and awkwardly throughout the tale, as queer fidelities strip genders of their force through their aberrant and unconstrained yet always necessitated deployment.

In the end, gender is virtually meaningless within the *Clerk's Tale,* and contractual hermaphroditism reveals the ways in which social contracts enforce endless permutations of gender to the individuals so bound. As Gilbert D. Chaitin argues, "It is the impossibility of specifying sexual difference which, in the last analysis, makes it possible to subvert the totalitarian consequences of the logic of the signifier which otherwise rules the life of society."[38] Griselda suffers more capably than Job, simultaneously proving the superiority of her feminine masculinity and the limitations of male masculinity. Walter, on the other hand, cannot hold the position of masculine authority and eventually wavers in response to his wife's hypermasculine (and thus feminine) fidelity to suffering. Both Griselda and Walter must thus be seen as hermaphroditic figures, liminal characters who expose the fictionality of gender through the exaggerated enactments of feminine suffering and masculine tyranny as enacted in the social contract of marriage. They at last find normativity and happiness together when their domestic family unit joyfully reconciles and reunites, but the narrative journey to a joyful family life necessitated detours through ceaseless assaults to gender categories and the queer potential of fidelity. The Clerk's queering lesson about the impossibility of gender then bleeds beyond the borders of his narrative, causing the men of the Canterbury pilgrimage to reimagine their genders in light of Griselda's tale.

Engendering Hermaphroditic Audiences

As Walter and Griselda illustrate the Clerk's reconstruction of male and female identities into a genderless hermaphroditism that ultimately results in the normative bliss of a reunited family, so too does the Clerk deconstruct his audience's masculinity and compel them to reconsider the meaning of gender. Throughout his narrative, the Clerk addresses his audience with gendered terms to heighten its rhetorical effect. For example, after Griselda witnesses the sergeant taking her son to his "death," the Clerk appeals directly to the women in the audience:

> "But wel [Walter] knew that next hymself, certayn,
> She loved hir children best in every wyse.
> But now of wommen wolde I axen fayn
> If thise assayes myghte nat suffise?
> What koude a sturdy housbonde moore devyse
> To preeve hir wyfhod and hir stedefastnesse,
> And he continuynge evere in sturdinesse?" (4.694–700)

Although the Clerk categorically speaks to women with these words, it is critical to realize that only three women travel on the pilgrimage—the Wife of Bath, the Prioress, and the Prioress's nun. Thus, although the words are directed to women for increased rhetorical effect, the impact is nonetheless intended to be felt by the Clerk's audience in its entirety, which is comprised primarily of men, in a nine-to-one ratio. This direct address to women allows the Clerk to feminize his male auditors, as they must reposition their masculinity to ponder this question from a female perspective. Patrocinio Schweickart indicates that "feminist reading and writing alike are grounded in the interest of producing a community of feminist readers and writers,"[39] and such a goal appears reachable for the Canterbury pilgrims as a result of the Clerk's gendered play: would the answer to the Clerk's question be any different due to the gender of the auditor? How could the male pilgrims answer otherwise, since Job is insufficiently masculine to model male suffering? If the Clerk is simply asking a question here, its answer must be—can only be—a resounding *yes*: surely Griselda has suffered sufficiently, and all of her audience—both male and female—should concur with this point. By addressing his rhetorical question to women, the Clerk interpellates his male auditors into a female position and demands that they, like him, read like a woman with affective attention to female suffering, rather than assuming Walter's position in finding "greet plesance" in her pain.

Such a strategy is necessary because, from the Clerk's perspective, some men cannot understand a woman's capacity for suffering. As the Clerk criticizes Walter, he also criticizes the men who would praise the tyrant's actions:

> "He hadde assayed hire ynogh bifore,
> And foond hire evere good; what neded it
> Hire for to tempte, and alwey moore and moore,
> Though som men preise it for a subtil wit?
> But as for me, I seye that yvele it sit
> To assaye a wyf whan that it is no nede,
> And putten hire in angwyssh and in drede." (4.456–62)

The Clerk distinguishes between his interpretation of Walter's actions and other men's assessments, ultimately condemning these men for condoning evil. As Harry Bailly accentuated the Clerk's feminine characteristics in the *Prologue,* here the Clerk models for the rest of the Pilgrims the necessity of assuming a feminine position to interpret his story. Again, Dinshaw's point that the Clerk reads like a woman is certainly correct, but it is critical to add that his interpretive and rhetorical strategies reposition his audience away from their public masculinity into a new sense of hermaphroditism.

Exploiting further the gendered sensibilities of his auditors, the Clerk plays with the gender of his primarily male audience as he extracts the moral of his tale: "'For sith a womman was so pacient / Unto a mortal man, wel moore us oghte / Receyven al in gree that God us sent'" (4.1149–51). The gendered inflections of his words indicate that he establishes here a binary relationship between female accomplishment and masculine potentiality. Because women are already sufficiently masculine (as evidenced by Griselda), the men of the pilgrimage need to be like women. In this moment, we see that the Clerk demands the sacrifice of masculinity, its abandonment to a new construction of both genders. In this queering move to deny his male audience the privileges of masculinity, he demands that they reconstitute themselves along a different axis of maleness, one in which men may "ryde as coy and stille as dooth a mayde," yet still model a definitively Christian masculinity.

Such a hermaphroditic interpretation of *The Clerk's Tale* builds upon the ways in which the Clerk destroys gender in the explication of his tale, which is also set out in gendered terms:

> "This storie is seyd nat for that wyves sholde
> Folwen Grisilde as in humylitee,
> For it were inportable, though they wolde,
> But for that every wight, in his degree,
> Sholde be constant in adversitee
> As was Grisilde." (4.1142–47)

This paradoxical explication defies any sort of logic. The Clerk appears to say that women should not emulate Griselda's example as wives, but he then follows this statement with the claim that all human beings (presumably including wives) should indeed see her as an example. By denying that wives should imitate Griselda as a paragon of wifely suffering but then immediately employing her as an examplar of human constancy, the Clerk effectively effeminizes all humanity. But if humankind is effeminized in this rhetorical move, wives both are and are not excepted from this gendered construction because they always already inhabit the position of the hermaphrodite through their potential to incarnate masculine suffering better than Job. Wives, through Griselda and the failed allegory of Job, have already been proven capable of sufficient suffering. By first establishing the exception and then outlining the general precept, the Clerk prioritizes femininity to his masculine audience. If they are to understand his message, they must concede the greater power of female suffering.

At the close of the *Clerk's Tale,* the Clerk constructs his audience on the liminal threshold between genders, creating an audience of hermaphrodites through the collapsing of genders. The Clerk initially addresses his primarily male audience in a manner that assuages and comforts their masculinity:

> "But o word, lordynges, herkneth er I go:
> It were ful hard to fynde now-a-dayes
> In al a toun Grisildis thre or two;
> For if that they were put to swiche assayes,
> The gold of hem hath now so badde alayes
> With bras, that thogh the coyne be fair at ye,
> It wolde rather breste a-two than plye." (4.1163–69)

The Clerk urges patience and forbearance to men in their dealings with their wives, but it is crucial to note that his words coax his primarily male audience into an inflated conception of their own masculinities. Except for the aristocratic and religious pilgrims, primarily the Knight and the Monk, the Clerk need address very few of the men on the pilgrimage as if they were his "lordynges." Enhancing the masculinities of the men so addressed, the Clerk accords them a status greater than their actual place in the social order. His rhetoric makes lords out of commoners, as it also creates hermaphrodites out of men.

The closing section of the *Clerk's Tale,* marked textually as the "Lenvoy de Chaucer," establishes a determined shift in the Clerk's voice as he rhetorically positions his audience for their final re-gendering.[40] He prefaces his final remarks with a call for humor and play, declaring that it is time to " 'stynte of ernestful matere' " (4.1175). In this typically Chaucerian move from earnest to game, we nonetheless know to expect the game to contain latent seriousness. Having just placated his masculine audience with a bit of misogynistic contempt for women due to the scarcity of Griseldas within their ranks, the Clerk appears to continue in this mode with his call to wives to forebear emulating Griselda:

> "O noble wyves, ful of heigh prudence,
> Lat noon humylitee youre tonge naille,
> Ne lat no clerk have cause or diligence
> To write of yow a storie of swich mervaille
> As of Grisildis pacient and kynde,
> Lest Chichevache yow swelwe in hire entraille!" (4.1183–88)

But who are these "noble wyves" to whom the Clerk speaks? The most obvious answer is that the Clerk is apostrophizing to and creating a metatextual and idealized vision of a female audience who does not in fact exist, either in the tale itself or in the frame of the Canterbury narrative. Again, within the fictions of the *Canterbury Tales,* these wives are absent, as the Wife of Bath, the Prioress, and the Prioress's nun are the only females on the journey. It would be inappropriate to refer to the religious characters as wives, and the Wife of Bath, although certainly a larger–than–life figure, does not require the plural.[41] The Clerk later refers to "archewyves" (4.1195) and "sklendre wyves" (4.1198), who are also collectively missing from the pilgrimage. To whom is this repetitive direct address speaking, then, if not to the male pilgrims of the pilgrimage, now hermaphroditically created in the image of women they seek to control? Reading and responding to the *Clerk's Tale* entails reading like a woman, despite the biological sex of the auditor. As the Clerk previously indicted clerks for their disparaging attitude toward women, he now appears to warn men rhetorically constructed as female against providing material for tales such as his own. He also aligns his narratival authority with a call to the Wife of Bath (" 'For which heere, for the Wyves love of Bathe' " [4.1170]), which highlights the common ground between his fellow pilgrim and his suffering protagonist. Alison and Griselda could not appear more dissimilar at first glance, yet they ultimately share an ability to subvert masculine authority through the radical enactment of gender—Griselda through an impossibly incarnated passivity, and Alison through a comically insistent activity. They unquestionably represent opposite ends of a gendered spectrum, yet they share a similar ability to undermine masculinity through their determinedly gendered embodiments.

The success of the Clerk's hermaphroditic rhetoric is apparent in Harry Bailly's reaction to his words. The Host frequently serves as a touchstone to gauge the ways in which pilgrims and their tales affect one another, and his response to the *Clerk's Tale* likewise allows an opportunity to evaluate its rhetorical effect. Recalling Harry's masculine aggression in the *General Prologue* and *Prologue* of the *Clerk's Tale,* in which he attacked the Clerk's gender with imputations of femininity and dismissed his scholarly vocation, the reader now sees that the host himself suffers a similar gendered reconstruction. In his confession of his marital troubles, Harry reveals that he cannot control his wife:

> Oure Hooste seyde, and swoor, "By Goddes bones,
> Me were levere than a barel ale
> My wyf at hoom had herd this legende ones!
> This is a gentil tale for the nones,
> As to my purpose, wiste ye my wille;
> But thing that wol nat be, lat it be stille." (4.1212b–1212g)

This passage is frequently read as a standard misogynistic diatribe, but it also demonstrates that Harry himself represents a figure of Griselda who suffers in marriage. Since Harry's wife refuses the position of a suffering Griselda, and since Harry can, therefore, only wish that she would succumb to such a powerless position, it is apparent that she wields the power in their relationship and that the masculinity embodied and enacted by the Host is a façade, at least within the boundaries of the domestic sphere. The *Prologue* of the *Clerk's Tale* begins with a feminized Clerk and a hypermasculine Host, but in his narrative, the Clerk exposes the frailty of gender constructions through the hermaphroditism of Griselda and Walter. With the Host's confession, we see yet again the ways in which Chaucer's pilgrims' narratives bleed from tale to frame, from text to metatext. In the end, Harry serves as yet another example of a hermaphroditism catalyzed by queer fidelities. These lines hint that Harry is faithful to his marriage, not to his wife, but his queer fidelity to marriage keeps him bound to his domestic suffering.[42] Furthermore, the Clerk's role of telling a tale about a virtuous woman to a pilgrimage of mostly men is at least somewhat analogous to Chaucer's position as storyteller in the Ricardian court, which was likewise predominantly male.[43] In both instances, men are interpellated into a feminine position through the power of a narrative that asks them to think and interpret like a woman.

The themes of the *Clerk's Tale* resonate throughout the remainder of the *Canterbury Tales,* in that a clear dissolution of masculinity follows in the wake of the Clerk's narrative. If Fragment 1 focuses on masculine competition in amatory affairs, the tales of the so-called Marriage Group focus more on how feminine agency in marriage restructures masculinity than on masculine privilege within the domestic sphere.[44] Palamon and Arcite in the *Knight's Tale,* Nicholas, Absolon and John in the *Miller's Tale,* and John, Aleyn, and Symkyn in the *Reeve's Tale* all fight over women in their respective tales, and a "winner" typically emerges— Palamon wins Emily's hand in marriage, Nicholas sleeps with Alison, and John and Aleyn successfully "seduce" Symkyn's wife and daughter. But no men triumph in the marriage group in the same manner as these male victors of Fragment 1. Certainly, Walter does not "win" as a result of any of his actions; the dénouement depends upon Griselda's adamantine self-will more than upon Walter's embodiment of masculine control. January loses control of May's sexuality in the *Merchant's Tale,*[45] and neither Aurelius nor Arveragus "wins" in the *Franklin's Tale.* Indeed, in some ways the Merchant's disavowal of his suffering in marriage (" 'but of my owene soore, / For soory herte, I telle may namoore' " [4.1243–44]), which immediately follows the *Clerk's Tale,* may stand as a thematic touchstone for his tale. Simply put, the bravado of masculinity has been exposed as a lie through the Clerk's turn in the Canterbury game, and its tentative nature—its unfledged and faltering essence—is exposed for all to see in the remainder of the Marriage Group.

As the Clerk's audience is hermaphroditically reconfigured to understand the world of a feminized Clerk, a suffering woman, and an unsuccessfully masculine tyrant, readers must likewise face a text predicated upon the dissolution of gender through the depiction of wrenching agony and suffering. The difficulty of enjoying the *Clerk's Tale* arises in the difficulty of identifying with its characters: Griselda is too submissive, Walter is too cruel. Readers have no real entry point into the text's imaginative world, as it is simultaneously too fantastic in its depiction of suffering and tyranny and too real in the emotions it arouses. How then are audiences to react to the painful narrative of Griselda's suffering? Carolynn Van Dyke suggests that an appropriate response to the *Clerk's*

Tale is to reject it: "Conscious that Griselda's ordeal was unjustified but unpreventable, pressured by the narrative to regard her tormenter as also the agent of her reward, readers and witnesses can respond only by turning away."[46] Although this approach may also contain its pleasures, I would suggest that, at least among Chaucerians, the tale contains some kind of pleasure for the reader (lest the field of Chaucerians collectively confess ourselves subject to sadistic delight in repeatedly witnessing narrative cruelty). The *Clerk's Tale* appears to deny the possibility of narrative pleasure, yet readers continue to enjoy it nonetheless. Within the Canterbury pilgrimage, this tale is virtually unsurpassable in the way in which it aggressively denies readers any ready hope of narrative pleasure.[47] It establishes an impossible tension between the bulk of the narrative and its resolution, in which the end of the story refuses to signify as many readers wish it would.

As Linda Georgianna suggests in her groundbreaking study of the tale and its treatment of the "radical demands of Christian faith, [as] figured in Griselda's assent,"[48] the meaning of the text is ultimately found in our experience of it:

> It is not the tacked-on moral, nor Walter's cool account of his motives, but the experience of the narrative itself that bears the tale's meaning. Our experience of Griselda's mysterious assent, which will not yield to Walter's or to our critical *avysement,* forces us to confront the radical demands of faith, and our need, as fallen people to rationalize them.[49]

As readers witness the dissolution of gender in the *Clerk's Tale,* the only narrative pleasure the text offers is to maintain our queer fidelities to the text and to Chaucer and to join in the tale's hermaphroditic freedoms. We will never resolve the painful riddles of the *Clerk's Tale,* but our queer fidelity to it will keep us reading, even enjoying, this troubling text, with a newly conceived sense of our gendered selves. Readers "nedes moot unto the pley assente" as much as the Clerk and Griselda, with the hope that queer fidelity to the text's pains will likewise transform into hermaphroditic pleasures.

As the *Clerk's Tale* focuses so intensely on suffering, it is paradoxical yet fitting that it ends in pleasure. Griselda finds the bliss so long denied her, as her tribulations and ultimate triumph are celebrated by all: "Thus hath this pitous day a blisful ende, / For every man and womman dooth his myght / This day in murthe and revel to dispende" (4.1121–23). The Clerk, too, ends his tale with a note of uncircumscribed pleasure in his paean to personal happiness: "'Be ay of chiere as light as leef on lynde, / And lat hym care, and wepe, and wrynge, and waille!'" (4.1211–12).

Such pleasure was inconceivable at the beginning of the *Prologue* and *Tale,* but by outlining the ways in which queer fidelities simultaneously maintain and subvert sexual normativity and gender relations, the Clerk demonstrates that disavowals of gendered pleasure lead to reconceived hermaphroditic pleasures. In this tale normativity only becomes possible through the hermaphroditic figurings of the queer, as the queer bears the potential to reinforce social constructions of gendered and sexual normativity—whether or not pleasure can then be found within such normativity. The pleasure of a newly formulated normative marriage with Walter, one in which he no longer tests Griselda, is a queer pleasure indeed, as the spectral image of cruelty casts a long shadow over the happy ending.

CHAPTER 5

FROM BOYS TO MEN TO HERMAPHRODITES TO EUNUCHS: QUEER FORMATIONS OF ROMANCE MASCULINITY AND THE HAGIOGRAPHIC DEATH DRIVE IN *AMIS AND AMILOUN*

Medieval romances illustrate the ways in which culturally dominant paradigms of sexual identity structure and confine human relationships, thus exposing their audiences to sexuality's often coercive ideological force.[1] Anna Klosowska remarks that "romance is, to a good extent, a narrative that legitimates a symbolic order, a narrative that . . . legitimizes institutions,"[2] and sexuality serves as a primary measure of romance's ideological complicity with legitimating dominant modes of authority. The power of normative sexuality thus lies in its inextricable links to dominant modes of discourses, including those of politics, theology, and literature. An agonistic genre, romance narratives frequently depict knights fighting one another in battles and tournaments to prove their relative merits vis-à-vis one another and thus to win the praise of their female beloveds. Through the romance's combination of the amatory and the martial, readers readily discern the ideological function of romance sexuality in that these narratives teach men the necessary values of masculinist and heteronormative western culture, including bravery, strength, honor, and fidelity. A corresponding critical lesson in this regard is that knights need both enemies and women if they are to define themselves as sufficiently masculine. Ruth Mazo Karras affirms, "The successful man in the chivalric world was one who not only could fight but also knew how to behave appropriately at court, and this included behavior toward women."[3] A knight must both defeat his enemies as an invincible warrior and serve his lady as an aristocratic courtly lover, and the lady, therefore, provides tacit acknowledgment of the knight's heterosexuality, even when their love is chaste and not overtly sexualized.[4] Both his enemy and his lady thus construct in complementary fashion the knightly protagonist's masculinity; his identity needs public confirmation and reinforcement from those who hate him most viciously and love him most tenderly.

Sexual normativity circulates within the medieval romance tradition, but in no way does its ideological force operate uniformly in each text of this tradition. In the subset of medieval romances featuring homosocial brotherhoods in which two knights swear lifelong fidelity to each other and ostensibly serve as the dual protagonists of the tale, ideological sexuality circulates differently, though no less inexorably, throughout the narrative.[5] In this chapter, my goal is to examine the ways in which normative sexuality functions in *Amis and Amiloun*, a romance that foregrounds a different model of knightly protagonists in that the alpha-male model of masculinity so frequently depicted in the genre is replaced by two men who unite themselves under oaths of brotherhood and love. These pledges of brotherhood generate a cooperative model of heroic masculinity instead of the more typically agonistic vision of male-male relationships found in medieval romances, and the homosocial cast of such relationships alienates these protagonists from the ideologically normative structure of the romance genre.

In describing these brothers and their oaths as queer, I am not attempting to unmask the knights as homosexuals; on the contrary, *Amis and Amiloun* clearly depicts its protagonists' heterosexual marriages and amatory interests in members of the opposite sex along with their deep fraternal bonds. The issue of brotherhood oaths in the Middle Ages sparks a somewhat volatile scholarly debate, as John Boswell found with the publication of his *Same-Sex Unions in Premodern Europe*, in which he promulgates the view that "[m]any Christians may have understood such [same-sex] couplings as expressions of devoted friendship, while those whose own romantic interests were chiefly directed to their own gender doubtless understood them in a more personal way."[6] Critics have questioned Boswell's claims that same-sex unions were ritually performed in a manner somewhat analogous to heterosexual marriage throughout the Middle Ages. Camille Paglia accuses him, in virtually an *ad hominem* attack, of "slippery, self-interested scholarship, where propaganda and casuistry impede the objective search for truth,"[7] whereas Constance Woods refutes his translations with due equanimity to call into question his conclusions: "Boswell's readings of the rituals as homosexual marriages can hold up only if the plain sense of the words is ignored and 'brother' is consistently equated with 'lover.' "[8]

In *The Friend,* Alan Bray outlines a nuanced approach to such homo-social relationships by largely eschewing the question of homosexual identity in favor of analyzing such brotherhood oaths and friendships and teasing out the ways in which they must be accepted on their own historical terms, despite that those terms may remain obscure to today's viewers: "Viewed from outside, the strangeness to the modern eye in the [same-sex] friendship of traditional society lies in the formal and objective character that it evidently could possess."[9] These homosocial relationships of sworn brotherhood are indeed strange to the modern eye, and part of their fascination appears in the possibility that they could possibly include—yet simultaneously occlude—homosexual desires. In her critique of Boswell, Woods judiciously concedes that such deep ties between two people of the same sex might ignite the "suspicion that such exclusive friendships could lead to homosexual activity."[10] Thus, these sworn friendships straddle the border between the normative and the queer, as they reflect a culturally sanctioned social agreement between two men that nonetheless provides a possible cover for homoerotic desires to flourish.

The potential queerness in Amis and Amiloun's friendship—despite the characters' public performances of heterosexuality—causes tensions in the romance genre that must eventually be resolved. In this instance, romance sexuality ultimately negates the model of cooperative masculinity that might disrupt the ideological force of male competitiveness and violence. Queer brotherhood in *Amis and Amiloun* so troubles the narratival expectations of the romance genre and the ideological expectations of heterosexuality that the breach to the normative social order engendered by fraternal affection must be eradicated by revisioning the romance genre in line with hagiography. Although queer brotherhood at first undermines the alpha-male construction of male normativity by depicting the potential for masculinity to circulate in a less agonistic manner, the underlying narrative structure then quells these disruptions to the predominantly normative structure of medieval romance. In the end, it is virtually impossible both for this queer knightly friendship to remain a vibrant expression of male-male intimacy and for ideologically normative sexuality as embedded in the romance genre to remain in effect. Unsurprisingly, then, normative sexuality reemerges with a vengeance, ultimately reigning as the victor of this medieval romance of queer brotherhood. By reconfiguring the generic expectations of the narrative and queering the brothers first into hermaphroditic engenderings that effeminize them and then into a form of eunuchism that strips them of any lingering sexual desires for men or women, *Amis and Amiloun* showcases the ways in which compulsory queerness creates disruptions to normativity with the ultimate goal of reinforcing sexual complacency within prevailing ideological codes.

As it is a lesser studied romance, a brief plot review of *Amis and Amiloun* may be helpful to structure the ensuing analysis.[11] The narrative begins with the birth of its eponymous heroes, who resemble each other in many striking ways, especially in regard to their virtually identical physical appearance. As young men, they pledge oaths of brotherhood to each other, and these oaths are then tested throughout the narrative. Amis is coercively seduced by the duke's daughter Belisaunt, and when the duke's evil steward reveals their affair to her violent father and his court, Amis relies on Amiloun to save him by killing the steward. Amiloun is stricken with leprosy as divine retribution against his actions on Amis's behalf, and his wife cruelly evicts him from their territory. Suffering from his illness and ensuing impoverishment, Amiloun travels to Amis's lands under the care of his nephew Owaines, and there it is supernaturally revealed to Amis that he can save his friend from his leprous afflictions if he (Amis) sacrifices his two children. Amis concludes that his children must indeed be killed to alleviate Amiloun's suffering, but once Amiloun is restored to health, the children are miraculously restored to life. The romance ends with the death and burial of the two knights after they enjoy many years of chivalric brotherhood together.[12]

From Boys to Men

In the beginning of *Amis and Amiloun*, the narrator stresses the many similarities uniting the heroes, which ultimately helps the reader to appreciate their deep bond and subsequent oaths of queer brotherhood. As Edward Foster argues, Amis and Amiloun "are almost identical in their behavior as young 'flowers of chivalry.' It thus seems natural and proper that they should promise perpetual fidelity to each other."[13] As romances frequently feature the heroic accomplishments of a lone knight (such as the eponymous heroes of Chrétien de Troyes's *Lancelot, Cligès,* and *Yvain*), the focus of *Amis and Amiloun* on two apparently equal protagonists tweaks the reader's perceptions of the romance genre in favor of fraternal affection. The pair are both conceived and born on the same days ("Both they were getyn in oo nyght / And on oo day born aplyght" [40–41]),[14] and the narrator describes in detail additional similarities between the two, underscoring their almost identical appearance:

> In al the court was ther no wyght,
> Erl, baroun, squyer, ne knyght,
> Neither lef ne loothe,

So lyche they were both of syght
And of waxing, y yow plyght,
I tel yow for soothe,
In al thing they were so lyche
Ther was neither pore ne ryche,
Who so beheld hem both,
Fader ne moder that couth say
Ne knew the hend children tway
But by the coloure of her cloth. (85–96)

So similar that even their respective parents cannot distinguish them from each other, Amis and Amiloun are thus initially presented as equals. The twin-like appearance of the two knights reflects classical beliefs that male friendships should be predicated upon likeness; within this tradition, Cicero notes that physical similitude bolsters friendship: "When a man thinks of a true friend, he is looking at himself in the mirror."[15] Despite the agonistic pressures of many medieval romances, egalitarianism and brotherhood in *Amis and Amiloun* appear to undermine the genre's tendency to foment male competitiveness. Male–male violence will soon appear to generate the ensuing plot, but at this early point in the romance, the narrator underscores the ways in which the similarities between Amis and Amiloun define both their characters and the courtiers' reactions to them.

As romances frequently feature men in combat, they also depict men in homosocial and communal relationships with one another, and in *Amis and Amiloun*, this bond is predicated upon male beauty.[16] Here the homosocial foundation of the court reveals the queer possibilities of male eroticism, as physical attractiveness is the key feature of Amis and Amiloun's similarity. Their shared allure ignites the admiration of the men of the court:

Mony men gan hem byholde
Of lordynges that there were,
Of body how wel they were pyght
And how feire they were of syght,
Of hyde and hew and here. (77–81)

The men's unanimous reaction to Amis and Amiloun indicates that male beauty binds the court together in the creation of a unified homosocial milieu. The women of the court likewise admire beautiful men, and their appreciation of Amis's attractiveness subsequently plays a pivotal role in Belisaunt's decision to love him (457–80). At this early point of the narrative, the reader is encouraged to see the ways in which these two protagonists mirror each other, particularly in regard to their physical appearance; moreover, their similarities unite the court in a communal appreciation of the male form. Queer desires linger in the background of this scene, yet much like the desires for brotherhood between Amis and Amiloun, such affinities are cloaked under a veil of courtly normativity.

In light of such fraternal beauty, love blossoms between Amis and Amiloun. In describing their brotherhood, the narrator stresses their deep affection for each other: "Bituix hem tuai, of blod and bon, / Trewer love nas never non / In gest as so we rede" (142–44). With the narrator under-scoring that their queer brotherhood represents the epitome of true love beyond the bounds of consanguinity, this relationship is thus ostensibly unique within the generic field of medieval romance.[17] The two charac-ters soon undertake an oath of brotherhood to cement their love and fidelity to each other in an appropriate ritual of union:

> On a day the childer, war and wight,
> Trewethes togider thai gun plight,
> While thai might live and stond
> That bothe bi day and bi night,
> In wele and wo, in wrong and right,
> That thai schuld frely fond
> To hold togider at everi nede,
> In word, in werk, in wille, in dede,
> Where that thai were in lond,
> Fro that day forward never mo
> Failen other for wele no wo:
> Therto thai held up her hond. (145–56)

In its iteration of contrasting possibilities and conditions, the phrasing of this passage is reminiscent of Christian marriage rites. Amis and Amiloun's pledge to be true to each other "[i]n wele and wo" semantically captures the heterosexual marriage vow of "for bettere for wors."[18] Indeed, the oath bears such deep importance to the unfolding narrative that Amiloun soon restates its terms to Amis:

> "Brother, as we er trewthe plight
> Bothe with word and dede,
> Fro this day forward never mo
> To faile other for wele no wo,
> To help him at his nede,
> Brother, be now trewe to me,
> And y schal ben as trewe to the,
> Also God me spede!" (293–300)

In this scene Amiloun prepares to leave his beloved brother Amis so that he can return to his homeland. The repetition of the terms of their oath emphasizes that the queer bond between them should guide their every action, as it also guides the unfolding of the plot.

Through their vows, Amis and Amiloun pledge their primary allegiance to each other, although one may wonder why their primary allegiance does not belong to the duke they both serve. In privileging their status as brothers rather than as vassals, as Ojars Kratins notes, the text "exalts the virtue of friendship by debasing the virtue of feudal fidelity."[19] Concomitantly, when they both subsequently marry women, their primary bond remains to each other, and their respective wives never evolve beyond characters of secondary importance both for the titular heroes and for readers. Again, the queerness of Amis and Amiloun's oath does not arise in any latent adumbration of homosexuality but in the ways that their oath forever alters their childhood identities in a manner congruent to heterosexual marriage. As bachelors metamorphose into husbands through the rites of marriage, so too do Amis and Amiloun metamorphose into "brothers" through their oaths. This chaste oath thus subverts the narrative structure of romance, despite the absence of homosexuality between the two heroes, in that the privileged relationships both between knight and lord and between knight and lady are marginalized in light of Amis and Amiloun's overarching concern for each other as brothers. In the brief narratival space necessary to depict Amis and Amiloun's maturation from boys to men, readers see their deep similarities to and affection for each other, yet the primacy of this fraternal relationship queers their relationship with other men (such as the duke) and with women (such as their future wives) by marginalizing these relationships to secondary status, despite their critical role in defining knightly identity.

From Men to Hermaphrodites

As Amis and Amiloun's oath of queer fidelity marginalizes the traditional knightly concerns for lord and lady, it also immediately undermines the ostensible masculine equality shared between them. The reader might expect their pledge to fortify their similarities, and it is apparent that in their transition from boys to men, from children to knights, they are initially respected as equals: "For douhtiest in everi dede, / With scheld and spere to ride on stede, / Thai gat hem gret renoun" (178–80). Their childhood oath here helps them to transition successfully into men who are respected for their bravery and prowess in arms; however, soon after their pledge, the text differentiates between them in key ways and, in effect, queers the masculine normativity of knightly identity that has hitherto characterized their relationship by casting them into a more hermaphroditic model of gendered identity.[20] Their relationship has been predicated upon their great similarities, but these similarities now give way to differences as Amis loses his presumed status as Amiloun's partner in masculinity and combat. First, the duke gives them alternate duties in his household: Amis is "made his chef botelere" (188), whereas Amiloun serves as "chef steward in halle" (191).[21] These initial disparities appear slight, but as John C. Ford argues, Amis and Amiloun soon differ sharply from each other in terms of their genders despite the narrator's insistent presentation of the overarching similarities: "It is easy to recognise that the pair...fulfill separate gender roles: Amis the feminine counterpart to Amiloun's masculine one."[22] Within their relationship of queer brotherhood, Amis and Amiloun cannot serve simultaneously in the alpha-male position, and thus their oath of brotherhood not only queers the foundational relationships of knight to lord and lady, it now queers Amis's masculinity as well, as it will subsequently queer Amiloun's. Since both men cannot be fully masculine at the same time, they together inhabit a model of hermaphroditism in which male and female gender roles of knightly prowess and maidenly weakness oscillate between them.

On a number of occasions, the reader sees ready evidence that supports Ford's conclusions that Amis is feminized in relation to Amiloun's superior masculinity. When Belisaunt begins her determined courtship of Amis, he attempts to convince her that his loyalty to her father precludes him from pursuing an amatory relationship with her:

"And y dede mi lord this deshonour,
Than were ich an ivel traitour;
Ywis, it may nought be so.
Leve madame, do bi mi red
And thenk what wil com of this dede:
Certes, no thing bot wo." (607–12)

Amis's loyalty to Belisaunt's father guides his actions in this scene, and he attempts to bolster his masculinity predicated upon honorable behavior in deference to his lord rather than in submission to his courtly lady's demands. Choosing homosocial bonds over heterosexual ones, Amis demonstrates the primacy of male relationships in his personal construction of knightly honor and identity. The hierarchical construction of knightly masculinity is likewise tied to the peerage system, and Amis's lowly position in this field further establishes his feminized position in relation to other men, if not to Belisaunt as well. Certainly, Amis is of insufficient social status to woo Belisaunt, as he himself notes:

"Kinges sones and emperour
Nar non to gode to the;

Certes, than were it michel unright,
Thi love to lain opon a knight
That nath noither lond no fe." (596–600)

Belisaunt acknowledges the veracity of Amis's argument and assumes for herself the position of breadwinner: " 'No be thou never so pover of kinde, / Riches anough y may the finde' " (760–61). Promising to take care of Amis's future needs prior to consummating their relationship, Belisaunt further emasculates Amis's knightly identity. In relation both to Belisaunt's father and to the lady herself, Amis's social position limits the extent to which he can assert and attain his personal desires. Following his transformation from boy to man, Amis now queerly metamorphoses into a hermaphroditic figure who is male in body but female in narrative structure.

The tension between Amis's knightly identity as a loyal vassal and as a courtly lover eventually fractures his sexually normative sense of self. Since a knight must be perfectly faithful both to lord and to lady, Belisaunt puts Amis in an impossible bind when she demands that he forsake his loyalty to her father by loving her.[23] She rebukes Amis for his sexual cowardice and denigrates his knightly masculinity as more appropriate for a celibate member of the clergy than for an ostensibly heteronormative knight:

That mirie maiden of gret renoun
Answerd, "Sir knight, thou nast no croun;
For God that bought the dere,
Whether artow prest other persoun,
Other thou art monk other canoun,
That prechest me thus here?
Thou no schust have ben no knight,
To gon among maidens bright,
Thou schust have ben a frere!" (613–21)

Mocking Amis's apparent asexuality, which is predicated upon his homosocial loyalty to her father, Belisaunt taxonomizes a social and sexual caste system of lusty knights and celibate clerics.[24] Within her worldview of amatory pursuits, a man's social position reflects his sexual identity, and she attempts to cajole Amis into amatory action by pointing out the ways in which he fails to incarnate the knightly masculinity of courtly lover that she expects. Belisaunt's taunting of Amis is analogous to a similar scene in *Sir Gawain and the Green Knight,* when Bertilak's wife taunts Gawain, " 'Bot that ye be Gawan, hit gotz in mynde!' "[25] In both cases, it appears that a lady need only outline a knight's failures to act as a courtly lover ostensibly should to compel him to act in accordance with her sexual desires. In this manner, women mold men's masculinity and narrow the range of culturally viable actions available to them; in so doing, they hermaphroditically reposition men by highlighting the permeability of gender and then disciplining them into a masculinity amenable to female desires.

As Belisaunt coerces Amis into a sexual relationship with her, she also derides fraternal connections, noting that she would never listen to her brother if he advocated sexual abstinence. Continuing her tirade against male asexuality, she condemns brotherly ties in respect to male celibacy: "'He that lerd the thus to preche, / The devel of hell ichim biteche, / Mi brother thei he were!'" (622–24). Belisaunt disdains such familial restrictions on sexuality and romantic relationships, and this occluded reference to Amis's homosocial bond with Amiloun (in mentioning a hypothetical chastising brother) denigrates the primacy of the fraternal in Amis's construction of his knightly identity. Realizing that Amis will not succumb to her desires merely by insulting his masculinity, Belisaunt then threatens him with an accusation of rape, a crime for which he would be hanged (625–36). This crime also highlights a knight's failure to adhere to proper codes of sexually normative courtship in that the aggression that should be directed to the martial conquest of a man is wrongly redirected to the violent conquest of a woman.[26] Thus, by offering Amis contrasting models of masculinities incongruent with knightly chivalry—celibate cleric or rapist knight—Belisaunt restricts his options of personal identity to such an extent that he must acquiesce to her desires.

The end result of Belisaunt's coercive seduction of Amis is that she holds the power in their relationship at this point of the narrative, and she thus queers him from a position of masculine authority. Jacques Lacan argues that the courtly lady "is as arbitrary as possible in the tests she imposes on her servant" and that she thus represents a "terrifying, inhuman partner."[27] Belisaunt falls in line with such a pattern of terrifying courtly ladies, in that certain death will ensue if Amis does not accede to her desires. Amis merely operates as the object of her desires, and he appears incapable of acting with any real degree of agency. Even Belisaunt's hungry gaze feminizes Amis: "On Sir Amis, that gentil knight, / An hundred time sche cast hir sight, / For no thing wald sche lete" (694–96).[28] The feminized and ultimately powerless object of Belisaunt's gaze, Amis mounts little resistance to her ravenous seduction and is masculine only in corporeality, not in terms of the ideological privilege typically accorded to a powerful knight. Amis's masculine identity is now threatened, as his oath with Amiloun sets off numerous narratival circumstances underscoring his powerlessness, his failed masculinity, and his transformation into hermaphroditism.

As Amis's oath of brotherhood with Amiloun serves as a narrative catalyst for his effeminization, it also sparks a queer rival for his attentions that further attenuates his knightly masculinity. The evil steward, whom Amiloun will later be compelled to face in combat after he (the steward) reveals Amis's sexual relationship with Belisaunt, desires to engage in a queer relationship with Amis fundamentally similar to Amis's relationship with Amiloun. When we first meet this steward, he feels irrational jealousy toward Amis and Amiloun ("[h]e hadde therof gret envie" [213]) and thus determines to harm them ("[e]ver he proved to don hem schame / With wel gret felonie" [215–16]). After Amiloun's departure for his homeland, the evil steward's envy of the pair transforms into desire for Amis, and he proposes that Amis should join him in pledges of homosocial truth and fidelity:

> "Sir Amis," [the steward] seyd, "do bi mi red,
> And swere ous bothe brotherhed
> And plight we our trewthes to;
> Be trewe to me in word and dede,
> And y schal to the, so God me spede,
> Be trewe to the also." (361–66)

As with Amis and Amiloun's oaths of brotherhood, the queerness of the steward's proposal derives not from overt homosexual desire even though, as Sheila Delany observes, such desire is subtly hinted: "The emotional intensity suggests more at stake than a mere tactical alliance; the steward responds like the proverbial scorned woman." Delany also suggests that the steward's proposal brings the "emotional pitch" of the scene to such a degree that "eroticism seems to be at issue."[29] This oath appears queerer than the one between Amis and Amiloun in the hint of the steward's transgressive desires, but again, the more crucial point of queerness emerges in how this oath would further fracture Amis's masculine loyalties as a knight rather than in any latent hint of homosexuality. The text has already emphasized the difficulties of maintaining normative masculinity as predicated upon personal honor and loyalty enacted simultaneously to a sworn brother, a lord, and a lady; fecklessly multiplying one's social commitments, the text implies, prepares a knight for confusion and chaos that ultimately subverts his masculine identity.

In light of these multiplying commitments, as well as the fact that Amiloun warned him to avoid the steward (310–12), Amis quickly rejects the steward's proposal of pledged friendship:

> Sir Amis answered, "Mi treuthe y plight
> To Sir Amiloun, the gentil knight,

Thei he be went me fro.
Whiles that y may gon and speke,
Y no schal never mi treuthe breke,
Noither for wele no wo." (367–72)

Amis refrains from undertaking this suspiciously queer oath with the steward, and his allegiance to Amiloun thus constructs the deep singularity of their friendship and raises it tacitly to the equivalent of a monogamous marriage. Fraternal fidelity thus occludes hints of homosexuality in Amis and Amiloun's brotherhood while simultaneously adumbrating the queerness of the steward's desires. Amis is fully true to Amiloun, and thus his masculine honor remains intact; at the same time, the reader is becoming increasingly accustomed to viewing Amis as a sexualized and feminized object of both female and male desire.

A knight's masculinity finds reinforcement through the support of his fellow warriors, and this homosocial dynamic is initially depicted in the male members of the court and their appreciative assessment of Amis's and Amiloun's beauty. In this arena, too, Amis's masculinity is now subverted. No knights volunteer to serve as his seconds in the approaching battle with the evil steward, in contrast to the numerous men who stand by the steward: "Bot for the steward was so strong, / Borwes anowe he fond among, / Tuenti al bidene" (871–73). The only members of the court who support Amis are women—his lover Belisaunt and her mother—and these ladies face death if Amis fails to clear his name of the accusation of sexual misconduct with Belisaunt. A tournament between Amis and the evil steward is arranged to resolve their feud, and the description of this contest establishes the ways in which this ritualized performance of masculinity is arranged such "that mani man schuld it sen" (867). By judging one another in martial combat, men participate in a social system in which masculinity faces constant testing; it is always in flux and in need of reinforcement through the perpetual reenactment of knightly identity. But Amis is not merely insufficiently masculine to defeat his enemy, he is insufficiently honorable as well: the reader realizes that the evil steward's accusations, although grounded in a jealous desire for revenge, are nonetheless true. At this point of the narrative, the hermaphroditically effeminized Amis needs his sworn brother Amiloun to rescue him, and Amiloun, disguised as Amis, proves himself up to the task by quickly decapitating the steward.

As the preceding analysis demonstrates, *Amis and Amiloun* depicts Amis, following his metamorphosis from boy to man, assuming a feminized and hermaphroditic position in contrast to Amiloun's steadfast masculinity. In this part of the romance, Amis serves the narratival role of the maiden who must be rescued by a brave, daring, and masculine knight, and Amis's hermaphroditism is thus essential to the plot. If he were successfully masculine, he would not need his brother to rescue him; by inhabiting a femininely coded narrative position, Amis reveals the ways in which genders face duress in their daily performance. However, rather than seeing Amis as primarily feminine and Amiloun as primarily masculine throughout the romance, readers should perceive the two knights as oscillating in terms of their gendered identities and alternately—but rarely jointly—inhabiting the alpha-male position central to medieval romance. The dominant symbol of the narrative— the two golden cups that Amiloun buys, one of which he gives to Amis prior to his departure—iconically mark both men with feminine imagery, and the text stresses the joint similarity of the cups and the knights: "And bothe [the gold cups] weren as liche, ywis, / As was Sir Amiloun and Sir Amis" (250–51).[30] In much the same manner that Amis's divestment of his sword while sleeping with Amiloun's wife (1153–89)—a self-imposed metaphoric castration—signifies the fluidity of gendered identity, these two golden cups highlight the omnipresent possibility of hermaphroditic gender reassignments, whether this repositioning is self-chosen or outwardly imposed.

Similar to Amis's assumption of hermaphroditism after Amiloun's departure, Amiloun cannot maintain his position as the romance's alpha male when he is afflicted with leprosy as divine retaliation for defending Amis against the evil steward. Earlier in the narrative, a supernatural and divinely sanctioned voice warned Amiloun of a leprous punishment if he aided Amis in his combat with the steward (1251–60). Although Amis was formerly effeminized by his failure to control Belisaunt's seduction of him, by the evil steward's pursuit of his sworn friendship, and by his failure to find martial support within the homosocial network of knights, he immediately assumes the role of alpha male after marrying Belisaunt: "Over al that lond est and west / Than was Sir Amis helden the best / And chosen for priis in tour" (1522–24). Such a remarkable transformation into knight masculinity is especially surprising when one remembers scenes of Amis cowering and running away from Belisaunt's father (805–28). He rises in the peerage ("Ther Sir Amis, the bold baroun, / Was douke and lord in lond" [1865–66]),[31] and he is no longer depicted as feminized in his relationships with his wife or with his fellow knights. On the contrary, he is now a leader of men: "With knightes and with serjaunce fale / He went into that semly sale / With joie and blis to abide" (1894–96). Amis's dominant masculinity is now lauded throughout the land, but his elevation in masculinity is dependent upon, or at least in conjunction with, the quick devolution of Amiloun's physical manhood.

As Amis's humbled masculinity was signified by his courtship with Belisaunt, now Amiloun is likewise depicted as hermaphroditically effeminized through his relationship with his cruel wife. He is controlled by her, and she disparages him cruelly for his leprosy:

> "In this lond springeth this word,
> Y fede a mesel at mi bord,
> He is so foule a thing,
> It is gret spite to al mi kende,
> He schal no more sitt me so hende,
> Bi Jhesus, heven king!" (1591–96)

Additionally, Amiloun's wife supports the position of the now deceased evil steward, castigating Amiloun for killing him because she views him as an honorable and genteel man (1489–94, 1564–69). His wife's power is somewhat surprising in this scene, as she bears little claim to authority in their territory except through Amiloun, who inherited the land from his parents (216–28) and who brought her to live there (334–36). Nonetheless, Amiloun fails to assume a position of authority from which to reclaim his masculinity or to control her. As Amis was stripped of his masculinity earlier in the narrative, now Amiloun faces a similar construction as a hermaphrodite.

Leprosy infects Amiloun's body and concomitantly weakens his somatic masculinity, leaving him utterly incapable of defending himself. He weeps ineffectually against his wife's cruelty and begs for her charity (1603–08) because, as he admits, he cannot incarnate a masculinity capable of challenging her:

> "A, God help!" seyd that gentil knight,
> "Whilom y was man of might,
> To dele mete and cloth,
> And now icham so foule a wight
> That al that seth on me bi sight,
> Mi liif is hem ful loth." (1681–86)

Amiloun's definition of a "man of might" depends upon one's ability to fortify his social position through the distribution of such basic necessities as food and clothing to the men of his court. This paternalistic position as the provider for a male retinue should accord a man the privileges of masculinity, but Amiloun loses these privileges due to his leprosy, an illness that bears "the mark of moral corruption" in the Middle Ages.[32] Moreover, as Amis was feminized by Belisaunt and her mother acting as his seconds in combat with the evil steward, so too does Amiloun fail to find other knights who will now support him in his feminized state and help him to regain his masculine and patriarchal authority. Only his nephew, Child Owaines, stands by his side, and the appellation "Child" underscores this character's own inability to incarnate a fully functional vision of knightly masculinity.[33] According to the Middle English Dictionary, *child* may refer to "a youth of noble birth, esp[ecially] an aspirant to knighthood," and in this sense, the word can be used as a title rather than as a simple descriptor. Still, even with these aristocratic and courtly connotations, a child is not a man.

As Amiloun proved his masculinity by defeating Amis's enemy in combat, Amis must now prove his truth, honor, and masculinity in reference to his queer oath by successfully passing a test of masculine forbearance. An angel reveals to Amis that to save Amiloun from his leprous affliction, he (Amis) must kill his two children and anoint Amiloun with their blood.[34] For Amis, his roles as father to his children and as brother to Amiloun conflict: "Wel loth him was his childer to slo, / And wele lother his brother forgo, / That is so kinde ycorn" (2218–20). After deliberating his conflicting attachments to his children and Amiloun, Amis decides that he must kill his children to save his friend. The sacrifice of these children troubles many readers, especially given the romance's many references to Christian values, but the homosocial oath unites Amis and Amiloun to such an extent that the erasure of each other's hermaphroditic identities takes precedent over all other goals and relationships. As Kathryn Hume observes, "If we could agree that friendship should outweigh all other obligations, then *Amis and Amiloun* is fairly straightforward too: the number of victims is only an index of the strength of the tie."[35] But as Griselda's children are revealed to be alive at the end of the *Clerk's Tale,* so too are Amis's. The queer fidelity that structures Amis and Amiloun's brotherhood, as it earlier eclipsed the duties owed to lord and lady, here overshadows loyalty to religion—to Christ, the ultimate Lord of medieval Catholicism. Dale Kramer argues, "The testing of the friendship is amoral in that religion is not as influential as the troth in determining right behavior; but the implication of ignoring boundaries set by religion makes us more sensible of the meaningfulness of the survival of the troth."[36] All relationships must fall in deference to brotherhood, and the primacy of brotherhood, in this instance, is tied to the apotheosis of amorality.

From Hermaphrodites to Eunuchs

Hermaphroditism circulates between Amis and Amiloun after they pledge brotherhood to each other, but these two knights again appear to be true equals once Amiloun is cured of his leprosy. The text provides a battle in which they fight together, and this combat allows Amiloun to demonstrate publicly his renewed manhood and to divest himself of any lingering hermaphroditic traits. In his absence, Amiloun's wife became engaged to another man (2446–48), and Amis and Amiloun join together to defeat this usurper, demonstrating that their masculinities are jointly functional once more:

> Sir Amys and Sir Amylion
> And with hem mony a stout baron
> With knyghtes and squyers fale,
> With helmes and with haberyon,
> With swerd bryght and broun,
> They went in to the hale.
> Al that they there araught,
> Grete strokes there they caught,
> Both grete and smale.
> Glad and blyth were they that day,
> Who so myght skape away
> And fle fro that bredale. (2461–72)

Separately, Amis and Amiloun found great difficulties in enlisting men to support them, but they now find a host of knights and squires who join them in their cause. Then, in a fitting punishment reminiscent of her treatment of Amiloun, his wife is imprisoned until she dies (2476–83). Despite the vicissitudes they have faced in their fluctuating masculinities and hermaphroditic engenderings, both Amis and Amiloun once more embody knightly masculinity.

At this moment of triumph, when Amis and Amiloun are both fully healthy and fully masculine, as well as in control of their lands, the text then moves to circumscribe this vision of queer brotherhood by recasting them as saintly eunuchs. As with my discussion of hermaphroditism, I employ the figure of the eunuch as a metaphor to discuss the ways in which sexual identities fluctuate in a given narrative. Amis and Amiloun are not castrated physically, but they are indeed desexualized in the remainder of the narrative. Germaine Greer famously describes the cultural construction of the "female eunuch": "The castration of women has been carried out in terms of a masculine-feminine polarity, in which men have commandeered all the energy and streamlined it into an aggressive conquistatorial power, reducing all heterosexual contact to a sadomasochistic pattern."[37] So, too, can men be castrated by other men and by narrative genres through the male/female binarism of gender and sexual policing. Indeed, for Mathew Kuefler, the eunuch "reveal[s] the anxieties around sexual differentiation and at the same time question[s] its foundations, and bring[s] to the surface all of the uncertainties of masculine identity in public and private life."³⁸ Certainly, for Amis and Amiloun, it appears ideologically necessary to divest these knights of any hint of sexuality. As much as *Amis and Amiloun* celebrates homosocial brotherhood throughout the narrative, the text now circumscribes the elements of queerness that this powerful friendship unleashes by symbolically castrating its protagonists.

To quell the queer tensions seemingly intrinsic to such fraternal bonds, the final two stanzas of the romance depict the reinstitution of the alpha-male model of masculinity that the text simultaneously rejects in its celebration of brotherhood yet shores up through the hermaphroditic oscillations between the protagonists. First, Amiloun divests himself of his authority and gives his land to Owaines so that he (Amiloun) can live joyfully with Amis (with Belisaunt nowhere to be seen):

> Then Sir Amylion sent his sond
> To erles, barouns, fre and bond,
> Both feire and hende.
> When they com, he sesed in hond
> Child Oweys in al his lond,
> That was trew and kynde. (2485–90)

Here the text returns patriarchal control to a single male figure in Owaines. His connection to Amiloun seems at least partially negated, as he reverts to his earlier name of Owaines rather than "Amoraunt," the name he adopted when traveling with Amiloun that semantically linked him to his uncle. Judith Butler argues that "patronymic names...endure over time, as nominal zones of phallic control. Enduring and viable identity is thus purchased through subjection to and subjectivation by the patronym."³⁹ No longer a mere serving boy, Owaines symbolizes the reestablishment of the alpha-male model of masculinity that had apparently been transcended by Amis and Amiloun's queer brotherhood. Quite simply, the text cannot depict two "brothers" ruling together harmoniously, and so the final vision of governance within this romance returns to the ideologically normative structure of rulership in which one man—and one man alone—stands over and represents an entire territory.

With governance behind them, Amis and Amiloun finally enjoy a life of friendship and ease. This vision of fraternal mirth and joy is remarkably short-lived, lasting for only five lines of the narrative before the text reveals that God will call the men to receive their heavenly reward:

> And when [Amiloun] had do thus, ywys,
> With his brother, Sir Amys,
> Agen then gan he wende.
> In muche joy without stryf

Togeder ladde they her lyf,
Tel God after her dide send. (2491–96)

Indeed, God soon sends for Amis and Amiloun, and in so doing, divine intervention quells the queerness of their friendship. Before their mutual demise, however, the text's final stanza shows the two lords attending to matters of religious concern:

Anoon the hend barons tway,
They let reyse a faire abbay
And feffet it ryght wel thoo,
In Lumbardy, in that contray,
To senge for hem tyl Domesday
And for her eldres also.
Both on oo day were they dede
And in oo grave were they leide,
The knyghtes both twoo;
And for her trewth and her godhede
The blisse of hevyn they have to mede,
That lasteth ever moo. (2497–508)

This final image of Amis and Amiloun, buried and enjoying the blisses of heaven together, extols their queer brotherhood, and it is critical to realize that this vision of Amis and Amiloun celebrates them again as equals to each other. The hermaphroditism that denied them the possibility of coexisting as fully functional males disappears. But they cannot live as masculine and heteronormative equals; rather, they must die if they are to embody gendered equality simultaneously. Their knightly travails arose in large part because both men could not successfully incarnate knightly masculinity at the same time. To tame the vision of queer brotherhood unleashed in the text, the romance's concluding tableau relocates them from the masculinist court to the necessarily celibate environs of this abbey's grave. Dead, buried, and divested of governance, Amis and Amiloun may now lie together for all eternity, as they could never lie together in the body of the romance, but only when their status as rulers has been firmly displaced. Eunuchs typically guard one or more women who ostensibly "belong" to a man from other male suitors,[40] but in this instance, eunuchism protects Amis and Amiloun from themselves and the latent possibility of sexual desire between them.

In examining the functions of death in medieval romance, the reader realizes that death often serves as a narrative necessity: simply put, romances contain a narratival death drive, and normative sexuality kills in medieval romance. Of course, this pronouncement is not surprising on one level: readers—both medieval and modern—are accustomed to observing the ways in which knightly protagonists in traditional romances kill their enemies so that they can uphold the position of the text's alpha male and thus win female approbation. Such a scene occurs in Chrétien de Troyes' *Yvain* when Lunette admonishes Laudine to marry Yvain after he has defeated her husband in battle. By doing so, Yvain has proven himself the better warrior, as Lunette patiently explains:

"quant dui chevalier sont ansanble
venu a armes en bataille,
li quiex cuidiez vos qui mialz vaille,
quant li uns a l'autre conquis?
An droit de moi doing je ole pris
Au veinqueor. Et vos, que feites?"

("When two knights have come together in armed combat, which one do you think is more valiant, when one has conquered the other? As for me, I give the prize to the victor. And you? What do you do?")[41]

This trope of male/male competition resulting in death is resilient throughout western narrative, in other genres as diverse as epic and spy novel: as Lancelot must kill Meleagant in romance, so too must Beowulf kill Grendel in epic, as must James Bond kill Goldfinger in espionage fiction. But in medieval romances of queer brotherhood, the villains die (in accordance with the audience's expectations that they be punished for their transgressions), but romance sexuality here demands that the protagonists die as well.[42] Queer brotherhood so upsets the ideological force of heterosexuality that it must re-empower itself by destroying not only the text's villains, but its queer protagonists also. Amis and Amiloun achieve sexual normativity in death, but only when their queer hermaphroditism is stripped as they enter the grave.

Death, then, serves a regulatory function in narrative. It frequently codes characters as heroes and as villains, it provides a "natural" moment of climax and/or dénouement, and it sparks tensions that must be resolved before the text can end. As Herbert Marcuse argues, death bears deep cultural value and meaning:

Death is an institution and a value: the cohesion of the social order depends to a considerable extent on the effectiveness with which individuals comply with death as more than a natural necessity; on their willingness, even urge to die many deaths which are not natural; on their agreement to sacrifice themselves and not to fight death "too much. ... The established civilization does not function without a considerable degree of unfreedom; and death, the ultimate cause of all anxiety, sustains unfreedom.[43]

In this passage, Marcuse delineates death's cultural function, and death works in much the same way narratively. Certainly, the cohesion of a given narrative depends very much on the "willingness" of the proper characters to die—or to live—at the proper moment. Particular characters must respond appropriately to the death drive of the text, and thus the narratival structure of death sustains the author's unfreedom to tell a given story. In describing the author's unfreedom to create a text, I am not suggesting that authors cannot control their narratives. However, at the same time that authors are free to create, they must also respond to the pressures of narrative and narrative structure. For example, genres create and codify expectations for narratives to which authors must respond, whether by embracing or rejecting them. Anis Bawarshi claims that "we all function...within genre-constituted realities within which we assume genre-constituted identities," which captures the ways in which authors and their works both constitute and are constituted by genres.[44]

In *Amis and Amiloun*, death is the ultimate emasculator. It ends the evil steward's queer courtship of Amis, and it tames Amiloun's shrewish wife more effectively than her hermaphroditic husband ever managed. Most importantly, death castrates Amis and Amiloun such that their queer desire for brotherhood, which trumped all other courtly and sexual desires throughout the romance, is contained within the grave where it can retain its spiritual aspects yet be freed from any homoerotic or sexual aspersions. In the move to the grave, *Amis and Amiloun* fractures the generic expectation that the knightly protagonist will triumph—and remain alive—at the end of the romance. Here we see the ways in which this narrative merges romance with hagiography.[45] Ojars Kratins, for example, asks whether *Amis and Amiloun* generically represents a chivalric romance or a secular hagiography,[46] and it appears that the text occupies a liminal space between these two genres, both celebrating the chivalric world of knights and the heavenly afterlives of saints.[47]

In the end, however, the saintly chastity of hagiography trumps the romance's vision of homosocial brotherhood by recasting the protagonists as wholly asexual. Death represents the expected narrative end of saints' lives more than of romance, as the saint embraces a torturous death to win the glories of heaven, often proving his/her asexuality or chastity along the way.[48] As Simon Gaunt argues, "Sexuality—the configuration of discourses and drives that generate and regulate desire—is central to the construction of sanctity in the Middle Ages. Medieval saints' lives repeatedly celebrate virginity, celibacy, or repentance for past sexual activity."[49] By attaching a hagiographic conclusion to a secular romance, *Amis and Amiloun* recasts its eponymous heroes as sexless saints/eunuchs to disprove the queerness of their friendship. In the end, two knightly "brothers" who care so deeply for each other always carry the trace of the queer, and thus the conclusion of *Amis and Amiloun* seeks to put this queerness to rest, in quite a literal manner.

It is somewhat paradoxical to present eunuchism as a figure of sexual normativity, but here again we see the amorphousness of sexuality to signify clearly. Between the effeminization of hermaphroditism and the restored yet sexless masculinity of eunuchism, a greater ideological normativity is located in the latter, at least in this instance. Thus, in *Amis and Amiloun*, the compulsory queerness of a homosocial yet asexual fraternal oath engenders a romance quest for sexual normativity that can paradoxically only be located in the nonnormative figure of the eunuch. Queer tensions catalyze the hermaphroditic engenderings of Amis and Amiloun and spark every narrative development that eventually leads them to the safety and sanctity of sexlessness in hagiographic graves. For Amis and Amiloun to access the privileges of normativity as models of virtuous Christian knights, they must die as eunuchs, despite the fact that they were never really queer at all.

CHAPTER 6

QUEER CASTRATION, PATRIARCHAL
PRIVILEGE, AND THE COMIC PHALLUS
IN *EGER AND GRIME*

While the outlook of *Amis and Amiloun* is retrospective, probing the tale's roots in hagiography for the saintly chastity necessary to free its protagonists from the queer, *Eger and Grime* stresses the comic possibilities of the romance tradition.[1] This fifteenth-century Scottish romance similarly reveals narratival discomfort with its heroes' fraternal relationship, yet it seeks to rehabilitate them from the homoerotic undertones of their friendship through the regenerative force of heterosexual marriage. Illustrating a model of hermaphroditic knighthood similar to *Amis and Amiloun* in that the two brotherly protagonists cannot coexist as males fully invested with patriarchal authority, *Eger and Grime,* however, divests its eponymous protagonists from the aspersions of compulsory queerness through the generic prefiguring of romantic comedy rather than through the return to hagiography.[2]

The contours of queer brotherhood in *Eger and Grime* demonstrate how patriarchal politics limits the range of culturally viable identities for a range of characters. Within the patriarchal order, virtually all characters denied the power of primogeniture face queering exclusions from social privilege based upon their marginalized genders. In particular, Eger faces metaphoric castration when his little finger is hacked off as a souvenir of battle. By ridiculing the phallus's masculine aggressions and establishing it as a site for comic commentary, *Eger and Grime* disrupts the gendered construction of medieval romance as an agonistic genre and celebrates the regenerative and comic abilities of male generation and female fecundity. To offset patriarchy's deployment of compulsory queerness, the marginalized characters construct the phallus as a contested and comic site of public and performed masculinity. Certainly, *Eger and Grime* is quite a funny romance, yet its humor addresses serious matters within the courtly structures of the Middle Ages. Marcel Gutwirth argues for the interconnection of comedy with seriousness: "Inasmuch as laughter transmutes our frailty to euphoria, the comic 'take' on life bespeaks an undefeated awareness of even the worst that can befall us."[3] Such a perspective illustrates the mixture of comedy and seriousness in *Eger and Grime,* which humorously undermines values that it simultaneously upholds. In the end, *Eger and Grime* is a highly ambiguous text. At the same time that the romance so flagrantly celebrates homosocial masculine identity, it also undercuts the queer brotherhood of its protagonists, displaying unease with the fact that these two knights' primary relationship is with each other. It criticizes the political and ideological paradigms that necessitate agonistic constructions of phallic masculinity and subverts them by demonstrating their inherent comic potential, yet the conclusion of the romance fortifies and multiplies the problematic cultural mores that led to the marginalization of homosocial knights and unmarried maidens. Normativity triumphs at the end of this narrative, but only after it is revitalized by following a queerly circuitous route.

A brief plot summary will help to contextualize the ensuing argument. *Eger and Grime* begins as Eger returns home after suffering defeat at the hands of the villainous Grey Steele. His beloved Winglaine now scorns him for his humiliating loss in battle, which is marked on his body through the "castration" of his little finger; Grime, Eger's sworn brother, therefore, decides to fight Grey Steele to avenge his friend, and he disguises himself as Eger in an attempt to restore Eger to Winglaine's good graces. Following the martial advice of Loosepine, a widow whose husband and brother were both killed in battle with Grey Steele, Grime triumphs against his adversary and returns triumphantly home. After assuming their true identities, Eger and Grime respectively marry Winglaine and Loosepine, and Grime's "brother" Palyas likewise marries Grey Steele's daughter, thus uniting the lands torn asunder by war.[4] Homosocial brotherhood cedes to heterosexual marriage at the romance's close, with numerous children attesting to the fecundity of the women and the potency of the men.

Homosocial Brotherhood and
Queer Castration

As in *Amis and Amiloun, Eger and Grime* structures its depiction of knightly masculinities through a model of homosocial brotherhood. This focus on fraternal affection tweaks the typical parameters of romance, and David Faris notes that the author of *Eger and Grime*, "in emphasizing the theme

of sworn brotherhood, has focused on a story element that would inevitably conflict with the individualistic emphasis of more ordinary romance
adventure."[5] The perspective of *Eger and Grime* thus sacrifices a celebration of romance individualism to consider the benefits of communal
action. Upon meeting the romance's eponymous protagonists, the reader
learns that the two knights have sworn oaths of eternal brotherhood to
each other:

> they were nothing sib of blood,
> but they were sworne Bretheren good;
> they keeped a chamber together att home;
> better loue Loved there never none. (45–48)

Much like the friendship depicted in *Amis and Amiloun,* the homosocial
bond between Eger and Grime establishes their deep fraternal feelings for
each other, and their shared chamber paints a picture of the two men living together in domestic harmony.[6] The rhetorical deployment of exaggeration, in stressing the primacy of the knights' love for each other over
all other loves, highlights that their vow allows the two men to transcend
blood brotherhood.

A deeper bond between the two men appears inconceivable within the
romance's chivalric worldview, and the text also demonstrates that brotherhood in *Eger and Grime* promises both homosocial union and a defense
against external homosocial aggression. Grime describes their relationship
in terms of its shared intimacies for each other and its shared hostilities
against their enemies:

> "Egar," he said, "thou & I are brethren sworne,
> I loued neuer better brother borne;
> betwixt vs tow let vs make some cast,
> & find to make our formen fast,
> for of our enemies wee stand in dread,
> & wee Lye sleeping in our bedd." (489–94)

In their vow, Eger and Grime pledge to act in unison against their enemies, and through this fraternal intimacy, they create a masculine
authority that eventually succeeds in compensating for Grey Steele's
"castration" of Eger. The two knights appear to be two in body but one
in identity, as an attack against one is treated as an attack against both.
Indeed, the primacy of this relationship is such that the two men guard
each other's secrets from the outside world, as when they attempt to hide
the secret of Eger's defeat from Winglaine: "'from your loue & laydye

Lained this shalbee; / shee shall know nothing of our priuitye' " (361–62). Karma Lochrie trenchantly observes of medieval secrets between men that "[t]he value of masculine secrecy lies in the performance itself, with women as the pretext for the eroticization of knowledge."[7] Eger's defeat imbues their relationship with secrecy, and this secrecy defines and cements their mutual allegiance to each other. In this manner, homosocial privacy trumps heterosocial honesty.

The alliance between Eger and Grime is not solely directed to preserving their fraternal union before all other considerations; rather, they dismantle the primarily homosocial cast of their relationship by pursuing heterosexual amatory relationships. Such a move is crucial particularly for Eger, whose masculinity is under duress and faces compulsory queerness due to the patriarchal political structures in place. Because of primogeniture, Eger can ostensibly never attain the level of patriarchal privilege that his older brother enjoys:

> for [Eger] was but a poore bachlour,
> for his elder brother was liuande,
> & gouerned all his fathers Land.
> Egar was large of blood & bone,
> but broad Lands had hee none. (26–30)

The text does not provide many details about Eger's financial circumstances, and "poore" seems to reflect more his position vis-à-vis his brother than any suffering or poverty.[8] Still, his lack of broad lands to inhabit, despite his impressive physical form, bespeaks Eger's secondary status. Due to his elder brother's superior position in birth order, Eger must find a means to compensate for his relatively puny birthright, which is perpetually and incontrovertibly less than his brother's.[9] Given the emasculating structure of primogeniture, Eger's only chance to surpass his brother in patriarchal manhood is for this elder brother to die. Fratricide, however, does not appear to be a viable option within the text; indeed, Eger's brother barely registers in the narrative: he is briefly mentioned, but never introduced. The inclusion of this familial detail illustrates Eger's marginalized masculinity more than it delineates the character of the brother himself. The comparative focus of these lines— Eger's large body in contrast to his dearth of lands—stresses that primogeniture effectively emasculates younger brothers, whose bodies, therefore, carry little corresponding ideological power or privilege. Georges Duby outlines the situation of the *juvenes,* those "unmarried knights, turned out of the paternal home, gallivanting about, fantasizing about the various stages in their adventurous quest to find maidens who...would rouse them...but above all, anxiously and nearly always vainly, in search of a situation which would at last allow them to accede to the status of *senior*,"[10] and Eger faces similar challenges in his quest for manhood.

If Eger can never achieve full participation in patriarchal privilege as long as his brother lives, agonistic and knightly competition appears to offer him an avenue to success and privilege. A man cannot undo the queering force of primogeniture entirely, but he should nonetheless be able to buttress his masculinity through combat. The text explains that Eger's martial prowess, even if it cannot win him his brother's land, can nonetheless win him the love of a rich earl's daughter:

> but euermore he wan the honour
> through worshipp of his bright armour;
> & for loue that he was soe well taught,
> euer he Iusted & hee fought;
> & because he was soe well proued,
> the Erles daughter shee him Loued. (31–36)

By repeatedly proving his manhood in battle, Eger asserts his masculine position in the knightly and courtly arena. As primogeniture queers younger sons through its inexorable privileging of the eldest son over all his younger brothers, combat allows these disenfranchised sons the opportunity to fight back against the prevailing emasculating order.

Under cultural conditions in which manhood always needs to be proved, it faces the likelihood of eventually being disproved. Masculinity must be repeatedly performed, but the performance is so complex and demanding that even the most masculine of men will eventually trip up in its enactment. Such is the fate that Eger realizes after losing his battle with Grey Steele, as Grime observes ruefully:

> "for when wee parted att yonder yate
> thou was a mightye man, & milde of state;
> & well thou seemed, soe god me speede,
> to proue thy manhood on a steede." (65–68)

Unfortunately, Eger only *seemed* sufficiently worthy to assert his masculinity in battle; the defeat he suffers at Grey Steele's hands disproves the masculinity he sought to assert and proclaims his enemy's incontrovertible masculine superiority. Eger himself confesses that he has lost his manhood:

> "Now as it hath behappned mee,
> god let it neuer behappen thee
> Nor noe other curteous Knight
> That euer goeth to the feild to fight,

for to win worshipp as I haue done!
I haue bought it deare & lost it soone!
for other Lords haue biddn att home,
& saued their bodyes forth of shame,
& kepeed their manhood faire & cleane,
well broked my loue before mine eyen,
& I am hurt & wounded sore,
& manhood is lost for euermore." (73–84)

Eger's description of battle delineates the ways in which he believes that agonistic competition creates and discloses publicly masculine worth. He hoped to "win worship," but, in comparison to other men with "manhood[s] faire and cleane," his manhood now signifies only that these men do not suffer shame as he does. Other men have maintained their manhood in safety at home, but Eger has lost his, apparently forever. Defeated masculinity corresponds with a wounded male body that declares its failures through its publicly viewed corporeality, as Geraldine Heng asserts: "True horror, for men, arises from the diminution of status-power, a frightening loss of control that renders them vulnerable to abject humiliation—a loss signaled in narrative as symbolic abdication of male bodily integrity."[11] With his "manhood...lost for euermore," Eger now represents the queered shell of a formerly daunting knightly masculinity.

Eger's response to his defeated body highlights the ways in which *Eger and Grime* connects masculine power to the physical manifestation of a complete male body: masculine bodies distinguish varieties of manhood, and thus bodily markings and wounds reveal the vagaries that befall men who cannot adequately uphold the visible performance of masculinity. Homi Bhabha outlines the "prosthetic nature of masculinity," which entails "the 'taking up' of an enunciative position, the making up of a psychic complex, the assumption of a social gender, the supplementation of a historic sexuality, the apparatus of a cultural difference."[12] In regard to these masculinities that fail in their prosthetic performance, comic elements enter the text to invite the reader to laugh at the ways that masculinity is measured competitively. In Eger's battle with Grey Steele, we learn that size does indeed tell the reader who is the more phallic and masculine of the two combatants. Not only is Grey Steele's horse bigger than Eger's ("'my steed seemed to his but a fole'" [120]), but his phallic spear dwarfs Eger's: "'his speare that was both great & long, / faire in his brest he cold itt honge; / & I mine in my rest can folde'" (121–23). The reader can hear Eger's disappointment in his phallic spear's unmanly and comparatively puny size. As the battle continues, Eger's phallic weapons decrease in size ("'but with that stroke my sword was broken. / then

I drew a knife,—I had noe other'" [154–55]), yet Grey Steele's weapons
and phallic manhood endure throughout the combat:

> "for his sword was of Noble steele,
> he strake hard—& it lasted weele—
> through all my armour more & lesse,
> and neuer ceaced but in the fleshe." (175–78)

The long, hard strokes take on a sexual register (a metaphoric connection
that Loosepine soon makes explicit), suggesting that combat with phallic
weapons serves as a metaphor for a man's amatory prowess. When Eger
returns home to Grime after the battle, he is stripped of all his weapons
that might indicate phallic strength: "his knife was forth, his sheath was
gone, / his scaberd by his thigh was done, / a truncheon of a speare hee
bore" (55–57). Measuring a man's weapons certifies the condition of his
masculinity, with Grey Steele's phallic hardness commenting cruelly yet
humorously on Eger's increasingly queered manhood.

In this courtly romance in which prowess in battle is explicitly linked
to prowess in courtship, the sexualized depiction of combat accentuates
Grey Steele's superior manhood in knightly combat and hints at his
greater abilities in amatory acts. His hard strokes and noteworthy endurance at least tacitly register as metaphors of sexual prowess, and Loosepine
blatantly endorses this metaphoric parallelism between homosocial battle
and heterosocial sexuality when she describes the erotics of battle to
Grime prior to his battle with Grey Steele:

> "presse stiflye vpon him in that stoure
> as a Knight will thinke on his paramoure;
> but I will not bid you thinke on me,
> but thinke on your ladye whersoeuer shee bee;
> & let not that tyrant, if that he wold,
> lett you of that couenant that Ladye to holde." (901–06)

Loosepine directly equates knightly combat with courtly love: if a knight
is to be successful in battle, he must pursue combat as zealously as he
pursues his lover. With her admonishment to Grime that he must "presse
stiflye vpon him," male penetration merges as a descriptor both of
knightly combat and of sexual conquest. A knight's prowess in both martial and sexual affairs are thus constantly under duress because his com-
bats metaphorically adumbrate his abilities as a lover: if he fails in battle,
he correspondingly fails as a lover. Eger's defeat thus marks him as a
queered man, tainted by phallic weakness, in that Winglaine rejects him
as her lover after Grey Steele defeats him. Furthermore, the latent irony

in Loosepine's admonition for Grime to "thinke on your ladye" emerges in that Grime has no lady for whom to fight; he does not fight for a lady in a display of heterosexual courtship but for his brother in a display of homosocial affection.

To make the comic connection between Eger's phallus and his failure as a warrior explicit, the text symbolizes lost manhood in the castration that Eger suffers. When he regains consciousness after losing his battle with Grey Steele, he realizes his loss: "'then I looked on my right hand; / my litle fingar was lackand'" (191–92). The queer castration of his little finger, a crude representation of the penis, effectively marks Eger as less of a man than he was before.[13] Anna Klosowska states that "castration does play a crucial role in constituting the repressive, heteronormative order *specifically* with respect to same-sex desire,"[14] and thus it is important to realize that Eger's "castration" marks his body as an inappropriate object choice both for women and men. Lamenting the loss and mutilation of his formerly whole and wholly male body, Eger now realizes that his body only claimed manhood ("'I had a body that *seemed* well to doe'" [95, my italics]), but, in the end, he could not substantiate the claims that his body made. Now, his queered body humorously fails to denote full masculinity because it is measured against Grey Steele's and found wanting.

From a historically psychoanalytic perspective, the phallus is the chief signifier in discourse, and Eger's little finger continues the long metaphoric tradition of marking a man's phallic strength.[15] This ancient literary trope bears biblical precedent in the narratives of the Davidic kingships, when Rehoboam hears the advice of the young men who urge him to show no mercy to Jeroboam: "Thus you should say to this people who spoke to you, 'Your father made our yoke heavy, but you must lighten it for us'; thus you should say to them, 'My little finger is thicker than my father's loins. Now, whereas my father laid on you a heavy yoke, I will add to your yoke'" (I Kings 12: 10–11).[16] Although "phallus" should not be construed as a synonym for "penis," phallologocentrism conflates the ideological power of the phallus with the biological form of the penis. Thus, the phallus, as embodied in the penis, is the originary distinction, the *ur*-difference, from which all other culturally constructed distinctions arise. Of course, that these cultural distinctions are coincident with biological differences between the sexes "naturalizes" the workings of patriarchy. The penis is "there"; the vagina is "not." Through this distinction of whether a person is equipped with a pendulous flap of skin occasionally spurred to tumescence, access to patriarchal privilege is granted or denied. With Eger's metaphoric penis lost forever, so too do any hopes of compensating for his marginalization due to primogeniture disappear.

The phallus is such a powerful signifier in *Eger and Grime* that it appears impossible for a queered man to reassert his lost masculinity after a metaphoric castration. For example, Grime attempts to comfort Eger after his defeat, and in so doing, he suggests an alternative to the construction of agonistic manhood:

> "ye greeue you more then meete were;
> for that man was neuer soe well cladd,
> nor yett soe doughtye in armes dread,
> but in battell place he may be distayned.
> why shold his manhood be reproued,
> or his Ladye or his loue repine?" (86–91)

Grime's sensible response to martial defeat, in his realization that no man can win every battle every time, fails to disrupt the ideological construction of masculinity as registered through a man's phallic little finger. Grime poignantly reasserts this position later in the text:

> "that man was neuer so wise nor worthye
> nor yet soe cuning proued in clergye,
> nor soe doughtye of hart nor hand,
> nor yett soe bigg in stowre to stand,
> but in such companye he may put in
> but he is as like to loose as win." (349–54)

According to Grime, defeat in battle should not disenfranchise a man from his manhood and his lady, and, of course, his words make good sense: no man can maintain the position of alpha male forever. As reasonable a position as Grime posits, however, his words do not undermine the phallic system in play. Eger's manhood is lost through the queering force of metaphoric castration, and the only way it can be restored is through the reconstruction of his fractured masculinity. Eger himself, however, is too thoroughly queered to undertake this reconstruction himself, and he depends on Grime to avenge his queering.

Focusing so attentively on the male body and its phallic wholeness, *Eger and Grime* concomitantly dismisses constructions of phantastic masculinities to counteract the debilitating effects of phallic defeat. The equation of a little finger with the phallus is a phantastic social construction presented as an ideological truth: the phallus itself bears only the ideological weight that it is accorded in congruence with cultural constructions of masculinity and patriarchal privilege, and thus a pinky, serving as a symbol of the penis (which is itself a symbol of the phallus), depends upon people believing and responding to its ideological encoding. As much as this metaphor is based on social illusions about defining and performing masculinity, it nevertheless holds sway in this romance, and no contradictorily phantastic construction of manhood can quell the queering disturbance unleashed by Eger's metaphoric castration. Nevertheless, in an attempt to restore Eger's attenuated masculinity, Grime describes to the earl and his wife an imaginary scene in which Eger was honorably defeated in battle under circumstances in which no man could possibly triumph, rather than the actual events that transpired between his friend and Grey Steele:

> "then 15 theeves with Egar Mett;
> they thought Egar for to haue him sloe,
> his gold & his good to haue tooke him froe:
> thrise through them with a spere he ran,
> 7 he slew, & the master man.
> yett had hee scaped for all that dread;
> they shott att him & slew his steed;
> hee found a steed when they were gone,
> wheron Sir Egar is come home." (432–40)

The lie is a silly one, in which Grime casts Eger as an impossibly masculine figure capable of single-handedly defeating eight men in one battle. His goal here is to win back Winglaine's love for Eger by reconstituting his friend's queered masculinity, but he fails to accomplish this goal with his story, and its only effect is that Winglaine's father, the earl, seeks a doctor to tend to Eger's wounds. If Grime intended to impress Winglaine with her lover's fortitude in battle, she nonetheless dismisses her former lover and his queered manhood from her amatory attentions. Within this romance, the phallus is a phantastic ideological construction that nonetheless tells the truth about a man's social position; however, other lies about masculinity are immediately dismissed as the falsehoods that they are.

In another episode designed to restore Eger's flagging phallic manhood in the eyes of Winglaine, Palyas reminds her of Eger's triumphs over the sultan Gornordine:

> "Egar thought on you att home,
> & stale to that battell all alone;
> they fought together, as I heard tell,
> on a mountaine top till Gornordine fell." (697–700)

Here we see an instance of Eger's former successes in aggressive manhood, which is predicated upon the defeat and emasculation of a man coded racially and religiously as the Other. Regarding the roles of Saracen and eastern characters in medieval romance, Siobhain Bly Calkin suggests that "these [Saracen] characters provided their audience with the opportunity to examine purportedly exotic realism and people, but simultaneously ensured, through their inaccuracies and resemblances to Westerners, that such examination provided their audiences with ideas about, and clarifications of, the audiences' own concerns."[17] In such a manner, Eger's defeat of the sultan Gornordine testifies to constructions of both the Self and the Other. Again, however, past victories cannot reconstruct a masculinity later queered from patriarchal privilege. Gornordine's defeat, with its implied thematic message of Christian virtue triumphing over Saracen vice, no longer successfully communicates Eger's manliness.

Men's bodies are thus open texts, signifying to all the condition of their knightly prowess and disclosing their failures to the courtly community. When Loosepine nurses Eger back to health after his battle with Grey Steele, he realizes that she is aware that his manhood has been queered: "'& when shee saw my right hand bare, / alas! my shame is much the more!'" (253–54). Although shame, as a personal and private emotion, marks a character's internal response to a particular set of mortifying circumstances, shame bears the potential to bleed from the internal to the external when others perceive the internal emotion one feels. Derek Pearsall argues that the depiction of shame in *Sir Gawain and the Green Knight* is a relatively late development in medieval romance: "To show a fictional character capable of being embarrassed and humiliated...in the way that Gawain is embarrassed and humiliated is a new art of the interior self...that is being disentangled from the fictions of chivalry that had prevailed."[18] In both *Eger and Grime* and *Sir Gawain and the Green Knight,* shame is linked to the failure of masculinity to protect the heroic identity of the protagonist, although *Sir Gawain and the Green Knight* additionally links Gawain's failure of masculinity to his spiritual failure.

Eger realizes that, not only does Loosepine see that his finger is missing and perceive that this lacking digit detracts from his masculinity, but she senses his shame as well: "'the gloue was whole, the hand was nomen, / therby shee might well see I was ouercomen, / & shee perceiued that I thought shame'" (255–57). In response to this delicate situation in which an emasculated man must confront for the first time the social repercussions of his fallen masculinity, Loosepine pities him and allows him the sanctity of anonymity: "'therfore shee wold not aske me my name'" (258).[19] Michael Warner observes that shame typically demands some sort of retaliation: "What will we do with our shame?...the usual response is to pin it on someone else."[20] Compensating for Eger's shame thus guides the narrative, in that this shame must be removed from him and reassigned to Grey Steele, the man who caused it. Judith Halberstam also notes that "shame can be a powerful tactic in the struggle to make privileges (whiteness, masculinity, wealth) visible,"[21] and this dynamic of shame threatens to ostracize Eger from the patriarchal privileges due him (even if these privileges would remain incontrovertibly less than his brother's).

If a symbolic castration forever marking his emasculated body were insufficient to humiliate Eger, Loosepine's cure for his wounds additionally highlights the ways in which his defeat marks his body. Here his body is queered yet again, as it somatically registers his effeminizing conquest in battle through Loosepine's medicines:

> "the drinke shee gaue mee was grasse greene;
> soone in my wounds itt was seene;
> the blood was away, the drinke was there,
> & all was soft that erst was sore." (291–94)

Eger's wounds are bizarrely (if not grotesquely) accentuated, as the reader must imagine them shining grass–green all over his bruised and battered body. Loosepine's cure strips him of his hardened masculinity and replaces it with a feminized softness. As wounds are often metaphorically (and misogynistically) constructed as vaginas, Eger's body becomes a woman's, replete with an overabundance of vaginas that can never compensate for the loss of his castrated finger/penis. The queering wound of a missing finger, in effect, multiplies and metastasizes over his body. *Eger and Grime* thus focuses on a seemingly impossible quest: how can an emasculated, castrated, and queered man reclaim his lost manhood?

The Rise of the Comic Phallus

With the phallus serving as the defining symbol of *Eger and Grime*, a castrated man appears to have little hope of reclaiming either his lost member or his lost manhood.[22] Despite this bleak prognosis, *Eger and Grime* nonetheless creates the possibility of reclaimed masculinity through humor and the comic, first inviting readers to chuckle at Eger's lost member and then asking them to reimagine the meaning of the phallus through a comic vision of community and regeneration. A lost phallus may not appear to be a joking matter within a courtly community of aggressive knighthood, but by reconstructing its symbolic valence, Eger's tragedy of castration metamorphoses into a communal and comic celebration of procreation for both men and women.

Similar to Eger, the women of the narrative are likewise marginalized from full participation in the political structure, especially in terms of marriage, inheritance, and family dynasty.[23] When Winglaine and Loosepine are introduced, we learn that these female characters are seen as slightly better than nothing, with the corollary assumption, common to medieval culture and narratives, that sons are more highly prized than daughters.[24] The narrator introduces Winglaine with a cliché dismissal that undermines her very existence: "they had noe Child but a daughter younge" (7). The phrasing first erases female presence before, almost grudgingly, confessing this daughter's existence. Likewise, when Grime seeks information about the ruler of the land where he searches for Grey Steele, his interlocutor similarly dismisses Loosepine before admitting that she does, in fact, exist: "Grime sayd, 'how highteth that lords heyre?' / he sayd, 'he hath none but a daughter fayre'" (731–32). The repetition of this phrasing in reference to the text's two central female characters under-scores their cultural marginalization from patriarchal power. As the depiction of these female characters is founded on their refusal to be absent, we see a lingering hint of opposition to patriarchal politics. Constructed in absence (neither children nor heirs, yet nonetheless daughters), the women resist their erasure through their "real" presence in this fictional world; nevertheless, their female bodies create insurmountable obstacles against participation in the poem's masculine milieu. As their female bodies preclude them from the privileges of primogeniture, so too do their bodies preclude them from acting with full agency within the realm of masculine privilege.

Winglaine and Loosepine share a mutual construction as deficient in relation to patriarchal power, but these characters nonetheless assert agency through their ability to judge men and male bodies, and these scenes build sly humor into a narrative focused on male performances of knightly chivalry. Winglaine pays careful attention to a man's martial prowess in determining his suitability as her suitor:

They called that Ladye winglanye;
husband wold she neuer haue none,
Neither for gold nor yett for good,
nor for noe highnese of his blood,
without he would with swords dent
win euery battell where he went. (9–14)

The forbidding yet humorous feminine obstacle to Eger's full participa-tion in patrimony, Winglaine continually derides him for his defeat at the hands of Grey Steele and emasculates him beyond his initial male-induced humiliation. She represents the shrewish figure tamed in marriage at the romance's end, and her aggressive and harsh femininity sets her character at odds with the narrative's desire to restrain women to the domestic sphere.[25] Loosepine serves as Winglaine's foil, and she is depicted as a wise and capable woman, as well as an accomplished healer, but despite her ample and respected abilities, she is powerless to avenge Grey Steele's murder of her husband and brother. Medical knowledge may lie within a woman's purview in this romance, but acting to achieve her goals does not. Although Loosepine's words indicate that she might be capable of aggressively pursuing her objectives and of defending herself in an overwhelmingly masculine world (as when she fierily warns Grime, " 'If thou be comen to scorne mee, / ffull soone I can scorne thee' " [815–16]), the text fails to deliver on the promise of these words, and she never acts on her own behalf to conquer a male character.

The female body defines Winglaine's and Loosepine's limited agency in much the same manner that Eger's "castration" defines him, and thus the text pays close attention to female genitalia. Within the contours of medieval romance, a woman is accorded more ideological worth if she is a virgin. Although Loosepine is a widow, the texts assures the reader that she is nonetheless still fully virginal:

> the Knight sayd, "shee neuer came in mans bedd;
> but Sir Attelston, a hardye Knight,
> marryed that Lady fayre & bright;
> for he gaue battell, that wott I weele,
> vpon a day to Sir Gray Steele:
> a harder battell then there was done tho,
> was neuer betwixt Knights 2;
> but Gray steel killed Sir Attelstone." (734–41)

Loosepine's marriage should signify that she is no longer a virgin, but her body has nonetheless remained whole—with an intact hymen and her virginity unquestioned—because Sir Athelstone died before the consummation of their marriage. In a manner congruent yet inverse with Eger's social worth being measured by his phallic little finger, Loosepine is likewise measured by her intact hymen and given greater narratival respect for it.

In contrast to Loosepine's generosity to and nurturing of the castrated Eger, Winglaine's response to Eger—and to his body—underscores the importance of phallic representation on the male form and the ensuing comic possibilities when a man fails to embody knightly masculinity. Without his little finger, Eger is symbolically marked as effeminized and emasculated, and Winglaine, therefore, withdraws her amorous attentions immediately: "when shee heard that Egars bodye was in distresse, / shee loued his body mickle the worse" (373–74). In a real sense, Eger represents no more than a male body to Winglaine, and when his body suffers metaphoric castration, she drops all affection for the man who inhabits it. In a sarcastic rebuttal to Grime's defense of his defeated friend, she first brusquely queries about his condition ("shee saies, 'how doth that wounded Knight?'" [451]) and then snidely but humorously responds, "'he gaue a ffingar to lett him gange, / the next time he will offer vp the whole hand'" (457–58). When Eger pretends to depart for a new battle with Grey Steele, prior to Grime's assumption of his identity, Winglaine again comically humiliates Eger with her parting cry "'god keepe you better then he did ere!'" (638). It appears, indeed, that Winglaine sees no limit to the extent that Eger could further lose his masculine access to the phallus, and she repeatedly derides both him and his faltering manhood:

> "alas! hee may make great boast & shoure
> when there is noe man him before;
> but when there is man to man, & steed to steede,
> to proue his manhood, then were it neede!" (665–68)

As the comic shrew, Winglaine represents an obstacle for the male protagonists to overcome in their quest to attain proper masculine and knightly identities, but she also represents the brute force of comedy to puncture male posturings. Her satiric yet humorous barbs repeatedly rip through Eger's already tattered masculinity, exposing the ultimate failure of a man with an insufficient phallus.

Following her dismissal of Eger due to his battered manhood, Winglaine soon seeks a new and more masculine lover. Here the text appears to be developing an erotic triangle in which Winglaine's new suitor and Eger will compete in a tournament for her affections.[26] Grime tells Eger of this suitor, providing further evidence that his (Eger's) already weakened manhood faces new assaults:

> "I haue knowen priuie messengers come & gone
> betwixt your Ladye & Erle Olyes,
> a Noble Knight that doughtye is,
> of better blood borne then euer were wee,
> & halfe more liuings then such other 3." (504–08)

These lines focus on the ephemerality of Eger's manhood in comparison to men of better birth, in that masculinity necessitates that men constantly compare themselves to one another in terms of martial prowess, wealth, and other markers of social worth. Given Eger's faltering status as a man, he has little hope of achieving his goals of avenging himself on

Grey Steele, of marrying Winglaine, and now of defeating a rival suitor who descends from better blood. At this moment, his enemies are undefeatable, and his beloved is utterly disdainful of him. Without his own phallic power to support him, Eger's role in the romance withers as surely as his lost finger, and the narrative focuses almost exclusively on Grime.

Eger, Loosepine, and Winglaine are marginalized due to patriarchy and primogeniture, but Grime is wholly functional in the phallic world of medieval romance: whereas Eger's comically castrated finger denies him full patriarchal privilege, Grime's body accords him the benefits of proven manhood because his manhood is visually apparent to all onlookers. When Grime, disguised as Eger, travels to avenge Grey Steele's "castration" of his friend, Loosepine sees through his disguise because he bears the marker of his phallic masculinity in his little finger. Grime's assumption of Eger's identity appears remarkably clumsy, and in this humorous scene Loosepine refuses to recognize him as Eger, despite that he is disguised as his friend: "'Now, Sir,' sayd shee, 'soe haue I blisse: / how fareth the Knight that sent me this?'" (783–84). The humor here lies in Grime's willing assumption of a suspect and queered masculinity, as well as in Loosepine's perceptive puncturing of his ridiculous pretense. Once Grime removes his gloves, Loosepine realizes that the man before her could not possibly be Eger:

> "Sir," said shee, "it was noe marueill though you hidd you[r] hond!
> for such Leeches in this Land are none!
> there is noe Leeche in all this land
> can sett a fingar to a hand." (805–08)

It is physically impossible to reattach a severed finger, and thus it is metaphorically impossible to reconstruct a castrated manhood. Grime's masculinity is apparent through the semiotic wholeness of his body, and the narrative again focuses on the humor of a woman measuring a knight's masculinity by assessing his finger-*cum*-phallus.

Grime's little finger thus proves to Loosepine that he bears the bodily markings of knightly masculinity. He then quickly succeeds in defeating Grey Steele, thereby avenging Eger's "castration" and the deaths of Loosepine's husband and brother. However, as much as *Eger and Grime* focuses on the triumphs achieved by Grime's untainted masculinity in contrast to Eger's failure, it also underscores that Grime cannot defeat their mutual enemy alone. Eger and Loosepine rely on Grime to avenge their losses, but Grime likewise relies on women to kill Grey Steele. His phallus thus represents not merely the potent tool of a particular man but the intersected site of contributory desires, abilities, and agencies that are coordinated in and through his phallic authority. A phallus, as incarnated on a male body, is insufficient because it can be defeated: the threat of castration can never be fully eradicated, as each new combat potentially results in defeat. The embodied yet phantasmic construction of the comic phallus, which celebrates the female ability to deflate or to coordinate phallic manhood, explains the tensions and limitations enacted by Grime's manhood. In this light, the comic phallus serves as both a critique of patriarchal phallic authority and an alternative construction of ideological agency that is mediated through male and female desire.

In the humorous scenes in which characters appraise Eger's masculinity by observing his little finger as a phallus, *Eger and Grime* appears to uphold the ideologically phantastic construction between phallus and penis. This alleged corporeal connection between penis and phallus, however, does not obviate the need for women to participate in the cultural construction of the phallus. As Judith Butler observes: "Women are said to 'be' the Phallus in the sense that they maintain the power to reflect or represent the 'reality' of the self-grounding postures of the masculine subject, a power which, if withdrawn, would break up the foundational illusions of the masculine subject position."[27] That women are said to "be" the phallus, however, does not entail a corollary assumption of phallic power within phallologocentric constructions of ideological privilege. As Jacques Lacan points out,

> If the phallus is a signifier then it is in the place of the Other that the subject gains access to it. But in that the signifier is only there veiled and as the ratio of the Other's desire, so it is this desire of the Other as such which the subject has to recognize, meaning, the Other as itself a subject divided by the signifying *Spaltung*.[28]

But when women laugh at the phallus and when they cause readers to laugh at a lack of phallic puissance, they create alternative constructions of ideological power. Such a phantastic revisioning of the phallus renders it comic and affirmative rather than combative and destructive, and this comic phallus guides the remainder of *Eger and Grime*.

Within the masculine homosocial economy of *Eger and Grime,* in which the two male protagonists depend upon their mutual alliance and friendship to advance their cause, the narrator also demarcates male reliance on female capabilities. In the construction of a comic phallus capable of defeating Grey Steele, women play a pivotal role beyond their narrative function as commentators on phallic identity. Foremost, Loosepine's skills as a doctor allow her to nurse Eger back to health, and her medical abilities establish her in a position superior to male medical authorities, as when Eger praises her healing skills, "'a! deare good Madam, how may this be? / the conningest leeche in this land be yee'" (315–16).[29] In fact, Loosepine's healing talents are inscribed in her identity through her name: "why was she called Loospaine? / a better Leeche was none certaine" (1407–08). In a world with phalluses ostensibly attached to male bodies yet always liable to truncation, Loosepine's status as a healer marks her absolute necessity in shoring up faltering masculine authority. She may not be able to reattach a severed phallus, yet she can heal the wounds associated with such a loss. Loosepine saves the shreds of Eger's manhood from certain death, which sparks Grime's retributive quest, and his journey then becomes entangled with her own desires for revenge:

> "Sir" shee sayd, "I must neuer be weele
> till I be auenged on Sir Gray steele,
> for he slew my brother, my fathers heyre,
> & alsoe my owne Lord both fresh & fayre." (863–66)

Loosepine may not wield patriarchal authority herself, but her actions spur masculine power to act on her behalf. Through her intercessory powers, she creates new conduits of action hitherto unavailable to her, her family, and Eger.

Furthermore, if Grime were to fight Grey Steele without feminine assistance, he would likely suffer an ignominious defeat parallel to Eger's. Grime's victory depends on women symbolically shoring up his manhood, for he is insufficiently equipped to win the impending battle on his own. He borrows a sword from a woman prior to his combat with Grey Steele ("'I will goe thither to morrow at day / to borrow that sword if that I may'" [578–79]), which suggests that his own sword—and his own phallic manhood—are not yet ready for the fight. The woman grants him the use of her sword, but only on the condition that his masculinity is not tainted with cowardice: "'but I wold not for both your Lands / that Egeking came in a cowards hands'" (601–02). Here again a woman measures a man's masculinity and determines whether he sufficiently warrants her trust and allegiance. When Grime battles Grey Steele, the narrator emphasizes that his strength would be incomplete without this lady's lesson in wielding the phallic blade: "he thought on that Ladye yore, / how shee had taught him to doe before; / he shooke out his sword Egeking" (1003–05). The reader never sees the lady's martial lessons that teach Grime how to handle her weapon, but the line nonetheless intriguingly hints at feminine instruction in brandishing a phallic sword. Grime's manhood in itself was apparently deficient without such knowledge, but after the lady's pedagogy, he is ready to battle Grey Steele with a sword that has, in effect, been tempered with feminine aggression. His access to feminine weaponry through Edgeking contrasts directly with Eger's patrilineal weaponry (169–74), and in the ensuing comparison between Eger's masculine and Grime's feminized swords, Grime triumphs: he becomes a more capable warrior and, hence, a better man through the intercession of this female guardian of phallic power. The narrator then clearly demarcates that the sword's contribution to Grime's manhood plays a pivotal role in his subsequent victory over Grey Steele. Grey Steele himself admits that Eger would have won their earlier battle, if he (Eger) had been equipped with such a weapon as Grime now wields: "'& hee had beene weaponed as well as I, / he had beene worth both thee & mee'" (1039–40). Eger's defeat, then, is less a result of his own intrinsic worth as a man, but in his failure to supplement his masculinity with femininity. Had he taken the lady's sword into battle, the results of the combat would have proven quite different, and Grime now succeeds where Eger failed.

As the lady provides Grime with the symbolic and physical manifestation of the comic phallus with Edgeking, Loosepine correspondingly offers him the necessary knowledge to defeat their enemy, which once more highlights that Grime's manhood in itself is not powerful enough to triumph in the task at hand. Again, Grime's defeat of Grey Steele depends upon abilities beyond his own, for she knows the secret of Grey Steele's strength and reveals it to Grime:

> "there is noe woman aliue that knoweth so weele
> as I doe of the Condicions of Sir Gray Steele,
> for euerye houre from Midnight till noone,
> eche hower he increaseth the strenght of a man." (889–92)

Loosepine then reveals Grey Steele's weaknesses—that he weakens every hour after noon and that he is more easily defeated on foot than on horseback (893–904). These factors play a determinate role in Grey Steele's defeat, and they further accentuate the limitations of Grime's masculinity, which in itself could not have predicted such a handicap to his opponent's strength.

If the phallus is thus a floating signifier that circulates among the characters of the romance, castration, with its concomitant erasure of male privilege, similarly moves among the men of the text. When Grime defeats Grey Steele, he castrates him "more" than Grey Steele castrated Eger: "& smote of Sir Gray steeles hande: 'My brother left a fingar in this land with thee, / therfore thy whole hand shall he see'" (1107–08). Although castration may appear to be an "all or nothing" act—either a man is castrated or he is not—*Eger and Grime* highlights distinctions in degrees of castration, and Grey Steele is now "more" castrated than Eger in that he loses his entire hand—in effect, a fivefold castration. Comparatively, then, Eger's manhood begins to blossom again because he is physically more of a man than Grey Steele, even though Eger did not himself defeat his foe.

Grime triumphs in his battle against Grey Steele, yet surprisingly, the rewards of the combat go to his allies, not to himself. In terms of the material gains generated by Grime's labor, Loosepine and Eger reap more benefits from the battle than does the conqueror. Grime gives Eger the better prize for the defeat of Grey Steele: "[The robes] were all beaten gold begon;— / [Grime] gaue Egar the better when he came home" (1279–80). Indeed, this gift not only increases Eger's material assets but heightens his physical beauty as well: "[Grime] put the better [robe] Egar on; / then was Egar the seemlyest man / that was in all Christendonne" (1368–70). Here Grime revivifies Eger's faltering masculine attractiveness by reinvesting him with the physical allure that was lost in battle. In a similar vein, Loosepine wins more from Grey Steele's defeat than Grime, as Grime gives her the trophy of Grey Steele's hand: "he gaue her the hand & the gloue gay, / & sayd, 'lay vp this till itt be day' " (1171–72). Winglaine's earlier taunt that Eger would lose his entire hand in battle now underscores that his masculinity is on the mend in contrast to Grey Steele, who suffers the fivefold castration that she predicted for Eger. Grime marries Loosepine after defeating Grey Steele, but this action is more the consequence of her desires than his, for the text clearly records that she decides to marry him: "for euer thought that fayre Ladye / his wedded wife that shee shold bee" (1199–1200).[30] In terms of the physical and matrimonial rewards of Grey Steele's defeat, Eger and Loosepine, who were both unable to conquer their shared adversary through their own means, win more than the conqueror himself.

The narrator concludes that masculine accomplishment is impossible without feminine assistance: "that man was neuer borne of a woman / cold neuer kill Gray steele, one man to one" (1213–14). This line is foreshadowed by Grey Steele's own assessment that no man born of woman will ever defeat him: " 'that man shall I neuer see, / that man was neuer of woman borne / shall make me yeelde, one man to one' " (1064–66). Certainly, these words are true: no man could kill Grey Steele by himself. Only a man whose phallic puissance is buttressed by women and who thus gains access to the comic phallus can accomplish this task. As women face vast limitations in their access to ideological privilege and agency within the world of medieval romance and patriarchal politics, so too do queered men face barriers and obstructions in their efforts to assert masculine privilege. *Eger and Grime* thus outlines a complex view of medieval authority and masculine agency, in which misogynist and patriarchal structures deny women and marginalized men full privilege in the ideology of medieval romance; nonetheless, undercutting phallic pretense through comedy and community yields avenues to cultural privilege hitherto unexpected.

By outlining the comic potential of the phallus and modeling a vision of cooperative knighthood, *Eger and Grime* questions constructions of alpha-male masculinity, and it also removes any lingering queer aspersions against its protagonists by celebrating their marriages. Grime undertakes a new oath with Loosepine, as indicated in their handfasting ceremony (1274). The reader senses that this new oath transcends the brotherhood oaths between Eger and Grime, and the close of the narrative details the great fecundity of both men's wives:

> Winglaine bare to Sir Egar
> 15 Children that were fayre;
> 10 of them were sonnes wight,
> & 5, daughters fayre in sight.
> & Loosepine bare to Sir Grime
> 10 children in short time;
> 7 of them sonnes was,
> & 3 were daughters faire of face. (1453–60)

Eger and Grime thus ends with unity and fertility, erasing queer images of the two knights' homosocial domestic bliss and of Eger's battered and castrated masculinity. Indeed, since Eger produces more children—and, in particular, more sons—than Grime, any hint of his queered and castrated identity appears finally to be forgotten. The closing focus on marriage and fecundity foreshadows the rise of the romantic comedy tradition in the Renaissance, and this satirical and humorous romance presages comedies with heroines acting to advance their own amatory agendas. Further generic evolution of romance leads to new narrative forms, notably the novel,[31] and we can likewise see aspects of romantic comedy both in Winglaine's shrewishness and in Loosepine's agency.[32]

In this romance of homosocial brotherhood, compulsory queerness, as enacted through the dual signification of the phallus as castrated and comic, both disenfranchises men from normative privilege and goads them back on the path to such privilege. When two knights' primary relationship is with each other, the specter of queerness lurks in the background of their friendship, and this queerness must be exorcised by the narrative's end. Sexual normativity in marriage concludes the disruptions to the homosocial courtly community engendered by Eger and Grime's brotherhood, as brothers now metamorphose into husbands and fathers. Harriet Hudson declares that "the appeal of popular romance stems from its ability to create tension by questioning received values while offering reassurance by accepting them,"[33] and such a tension circulates throughout *Eger and Grime*: as much as the comic phallus disrupts constructions of agonistic masculinity, the patriarchal system of primogeniture remains fully functional at the close of *Eger and Grime*. We now see twenty-three out of twenty-five children who will face the uncomfortable force of compulsory queerness along their expected path to normativity.

As compulsory queerness thus guides protagonists and readers to a normative conclusion, a queer image of absence nonetheless haunts the narrative's close: Eger's missing pinky. As Loosepine observed earlier, no doctor can restore a castrated finger, and no number of children can ever attest to Eger's fully recovered phallic masculinity. Compulsory queerness leads Eger to normativity, but his missing finger provocatively hints at the potential of the queer to subvert even that which it has been conscripted to serve. The image of Eger's missing finger lingers for the reader, the spectral image of the impossibility of ever completely becoming a normal man.

CHAPTER 7

CONCLUSION: COMPULSORY
QUEERNESS AND THE PLEASURES
OF MEDIEVALISM

If one defines *queer* as that which is subversive of or otherwise resistant to normativity, medievalists are a decidedly queer bunch. In privileging intellectual passion over other vocational and avocational pursuits, we resist the tide of anti-intellectualism prevalent in today's culture and stake a claim for a decidedly atypical career.[1] Although I cannot make vast claims about the personal values of medievalists as a whole, our decisions to enter the ranks of academia for the life of research and teaching generally bespeak a willingness to forgo materialism for less tangible benefits. In the quest for the cerebral pleasures of solitary study in the library, medievalists model an appreciation for the historical humanities that locates pleasure in the past, with all of its scintillating mystery. In such a light, we must appear at least somewhat musty, if not altogether anachronistic, against the cyber backdrop of the brave, new era in which we now find ourselves.[2]

A retrospective outlook is necessary to medievalism, but such a vantage point should not entail the impossibility of merging the medievalist's passion for the past with a postmodern, if not futurist, perspective. Kathleen Biddick underscores the tension between the past and the future in medieval studies, in which "its melancholic fixation on an identity politics imagined as hard-edged alterity neither saves history (with the desire that it redeem us), nor ends it, but stifles it."[3] Medievalism coincident with postmodernism may sometimes appear to be phantastic,[4] and the difficulties inherent in bringing medievalism into postmodern scholarly focus appear at times well nigh impossible to resolve. Studying the Middle Ages elicits the inherent awkwardness of locating a position from which to advance such studies.[5] If we see the past as alien Other, we ignore congruencies between yesterday and today; however, if we embrace the similarities between the two vastly different historical periods, we risk solipsistically overlooking the chasm separating them. Medievalism is thus a queer profession counterpoised to and disruptive of the futurist bent of postmodernity, as it also resists prevalent ideological constructions of anti-intellectualism; it is a queering profession as well, in that it undermines the historical foundations necessary to construct oneself as an embedded agent in a given historical and cultural milieu. Such queerness is indeed compulsory, as we medievalists can in no measure define our profession exclusively for and by ourselves.

Medievalism need not—and cannot—be fully located either in the past or in the present. Medieval texts cannot be hermetically sealed in the archive, locked away from new interpretations and new readings that challenge their historical foundations. After all, as Alexandre Leupin observes, historical texts inexorably construct their modern readers, as they also formulated their medieval writers: "For the medieval writer and the modern critic are *equally* displaced in relation to the elusive Other whose trace and missing impression is the text; they each share the position of the subject of desire."[6] In the construction of writer and reader as desiring agents, texts bear the potential to queer their creator(s) and their consumer(s) from the formative fictions of identity. As a result of this dialectical historical bridge, the Middle Ages can never be fully illuminated by today's scholars, and, in fact, many scholars find a good deal of the allure of the past arises in its very inscrutability. Jeffrey Jerome Cohen outlines the difficulty in claiming a temporal perspective from which to analyze the past and suggests the middle as an appropriate solution: "Medieval studies as interminable, difficult middle must stress not difference (the past as past) or sameness (the past as present) but temporal interlacement, the impossibility of choosing alterity or continuity."[7] Cohen exposes the false dichotomy between past and present, and his vision of temporal interlacement opens the possibility for past and present to function together rather than to be cast in an antagonistic relationship of mutual alienation.

Following the reasoning of Leupin and Cohen, it becomes apparent that such temporal interlacements undermine easy constructions of medievalist as investigating subject and the Middle Ages as investigated object of critical inquiry; in this manner, as medievalists construct the past, so too does the past construct present identities. Such is the compulsory queerness of medievalism: to engage in academic study of the past is to become interpellated into a critical discipline that subverts the foundations of time itself. In constructing and reconstructing history, we are constructed and reconstructed as well. The binarism of subject and object merges into a duality, yet such ostensibly organic dualities are then subjected to incessant fracturings, in which academic identities are constantly reformulated in light of postmodern preconceptions of the medieval past. The compulsory queerness of medievalism elicits new conceptions of the self who undertakes the study of the past precisely because the connotative range of medievalism within society at large must include both our academic treatises on the past and pop-culture reconstitutions of history as well. Indeed, in the world beyond academia, a Hollywood flick affects, and effects, the meaning of the Middle Ages more than most scholarly exegesis. Regrettably, perhaps, *Braveheart* trumps Bynum in the popular imaginary.

On a personal level, I have repeatedly found that the simple statement "I am a medievalist" bears the potential to queer my identity, and one might as well deem such moments pleasurable rather than prickly. Both inside and outside the academy, medievalists are constructed as the Other, and such a candid declaration of vocational identity frequently leaves our interlocutors momentarily confused. Our friends both academic and lay seem to wonder at times, what *is* a medievalist? Although I have never been asked this particular question, the blank faces that confront me after confessing my vocational identity nonetheless seem to be pondering such a vacuous question. A question that I have indeed been asked repeatedly is, do medievalists attending the annual International Medieval Congress at Western Michigan University wear medieval garb? Obviously, my interlocutor is likely mistaking an academic conference for a medieval or Renaissance fair in this instance, but such moments nonetheless demonstrate how postmodern prejudices and pop-culture stereotypes of medievalism define us, whether we want them to or not. The pleasure of medievalism arises in our ability to queer time through the construction of its interlacements, as time also queers us.

If modern society often appears confused by medievalism as a scholarly profession, such confusion necessarily bleeds into perceptions of our genders. For as friends, colleagues, and new acquaintances are at times puzzled by meeting a medievalist, some of this confusion appears connected to latent questions about the genders and the gendered desires of medievalists. Pop-culture medievalisms, from Hollywood films to medieval fairs, provide a framework for nonspecialists to understand the Middle Ages in the broadest of strokes—brave knights defending maidens fair—and these conceptions inevitably color our interlocutors' perceptions of medievalists, too. In regard to the historicity of "medieval" films, Vivian Sobchack argues that "insistent dirt and squalor...comes to signify and fix the 'real' Middle Ages."[8] The mere presence of dirt in a "medieval" film serves as an iconic shorthand that creates, structures, and fulfills viewerly expectations and responses to the Middle Ages. Dirt cosmetically attached to an actor playing a medieval character in a film sufficiently constructs the appropriate historicity of the "Dark Ages" for its audience, and so too do such conceptions bleed onto perceptions of medieval scholars. Sobchack's argument focuses on the iconic construction of sufficient verisimilitude for a film audience to identify a specific mise-en-scène as appropriately medieval, but we medievalists are fooling ourselves if we think that we, as a profession, are not constructed through a similar process of pop-culture interpellation. Thankfully, I have not found that many of my interlocutors expect me to be dirty, but they do nonetheless make certain assumptions about my identity based upon my interest in the Middle Ages. The dominant characters of brave knights and virtuous damsels are at times projected on to us, as people assume our present-day gendered desires are reflected through their preconceptions of the medieval past rather than through our own understandings of the historical conditions of the era.

Taking pop-culture assumptions about medievalism seriously may seem to be making scholarly mountains out of mole hills, but the questions that emerge from pop-culture bear deep repercussions to the place of the academy in today's society. And so, we might ask ourselves: what *is* the gender of a medievalist? Are we twenty-first century scholars or fourteenth-century knights and damsels? Most medievalists would presumably claim the former identity over the latter, but we are not free to define ourselves. We can strive for the status of a "normative" academic identity (although many of us would willingly concede the oxymoronic flavor of that coinage), but in the heady play between self and society, queering perceptions strip us of the full autonomy of self-definition.

We are the products both of the modern twenty-first-century world that incarnates us and of the medieval world that enlivens us: twenty-first-century selves queered by the medieval past and medieval souls queered by the twenty-first century. Such transhistoricity defies the boundaries of linear time and fractures identity as a result, and such transhistorical literary experiences necessitate mutual construction and reconstruction of the self and the past, as Paul Zumthor hypothesizes about reading:

> Thus, reading is, at least potentially a dialogue; but in it two agents confront one another: I am in some way produced by this text, and in the same moment, as a reader, I construct it. A relationship of active solidarity rather than a mirror-effect; a solidarity promised rather than given, pleasurably

felt at the end of the long preparatory work required by the traversing of
two historical distances, going and coming back.[9]

This vision of union, of "active solidarity" between reader and text, but
also between reader and the occluded historical agent who wrote and/or
transcribed the text, creates a new reader. External and compulsory forces
construct a reader in line with the text's desires, and these newly formed
readers—whether resistant or acquiescent to this new identity—are
queered from their previous senses of self.

For if writing does not bear as its objective the metamorphosis of the
reader in line with the writer's agenda—whether that agenda be pleasureful or political, enlightening or indoctrinating—what is the purpose of
the text? Roland Barthes rightly reminds us of the pleasures of the texts,
but texts bear purposes as well.[10] As Clifton Fadiman famously observes
of literature, "When you reread a classic you do not see more in the book
than you did before; you see more in *you* than there was before."[11] Such
is the pleasure of literature, in the constant renewal of the self through the
textual encounter, but the literary encounter, ostensibly one engaged in
mutual comfort and familiarity, bears the real potential for unexpected
results. Literary texts bear pleasureful purposes, and purposeful pleasures,
and both pleasures and purposes are constructed with the potential for
queerness. By disrupting the gendered construction of self through the
study of gendered enactments and embodiments within given historical
and cultural conditions, new paradigms of identity are effected by
embodying this temporal interlacement. No text can strip itself of gender, including the genders of its characters and of its readers, and thus all
texts are implicated by the mechanisms and ideologies of gender circulat-
ing within their culture and zeitgeist.

Zumthor's model of reading establishes the potential for pleasure in
the head-to-head encounter between medieval text and modern reader,
and this pleasure is everywhere apparent in popular culture today. The
tension between academic and popular medievalisms, a frequently unnec-
essary intervention into the pleasure of both fields, establishes a binary
relationship between scholarship and popular culture. Scholars produce
the learned exegeses on the medieval world, advancing through discussion, disputation, and peer review a rational understanding of the past,
albeit one perpetually through a glass darkly. But popular culture creates
a medievalism of sheer pleasure, and this pleasure should serve as the
nexus between the two worlds. "What would it feel like to be colonized
by the Middle Ages?" asks Catherine Brown in her provocative meditation on the meaning of studying the Middle Ages and the ways in which

the past reaches out to touch the present.[12] Following Brown's lead, we might also wonder what it would feel like to be queered by the Middle Ages. Are not our genders touched by the act of reading and interpreting literature? For reading, when done well, frequently demands hermaphroditism. It requires the ability to switch subject positions and inhabit alien worlds. One must feel the Dreamer's loss in *Pearl,* Harry Bailly's tenuous masculinity in the *Canterbury Tales,* Griselda's suffering and Walter's metamorphosis in the *Clerk's Tale,* Amis's sacrifice of his children and Amiloun's leprous affliction in *Amis and Amiloun,* and Eger's humiliating castration in *Eger and Grime,* if one is to experience the queering potential of these narratives. Texts seduce and tease, remain recalcitrant and then turn playful, as all the while they inexorably act upon their readers' senses of self. For all of us who cannot put down a book once opened, it is impossible to deny literature's compulsory force. Couple the compulsory nature of reading with its almost inherent gender play, and the compulsory queerness of medieval literature emerges as one of the chief pleasures of our discipline.

For certainly, discipline defines our profession both in terms of its structure and its practice. We discipline students into our discipline, as we were disciplined into it as well. Foucault observes the disciplinary confluence of teaching and surveillance: "A relation of surveillance, defined and regulated, is inscribed at the heart of the practice of teaching, not as an additional or adjacent part, but as a mechanism that is inherent to it and which increases its efficiency."[13] In Foucault's playful elision of the differences between students and prisoners in the disciplinary construction of ideologically pliant subjects, a truth nonetheless emerges in that discipline structures both fields of knowledge and of social practice, as well as the subjects participating in and building these fields. "We enjoy the rigor of discipline, but for some of us this enjoyment would be spoiled if we acknowledged it," trenchantly observes Aranye Fradenburg.[14]

Queer pleasure belongs in the academy, even though the rigors of the disciplines demand that such pleasures at times be denied. Of course, pleasures—including literary pleasures, a sense of wonder, intellectual curiosity, pedagogical excitement, and communal discovery—continually draw scholars into the academy in the first place. Maintaining (or in some instances, returning) pleasure to the academy need not entail a slackening of scholarly rigor in deference to pop-culture play; it should merely serve to stimulate more passion for our fields. Through the compulsory queerness of the Middle Ages, our genders bear the potential to be reformulated and reconstructed through phantastic engagement with texts. If queer pleasure is there, why would we forgo it?

NOTES

Chapter 1 Introduction: Sexuality and Its Queer Discontents in Middle English Literature

1. William Shakespeare, *Twelfth Night, The Norton Shakespeare: Comedies*, ed. Stephen Greenblatt et al. (New York: Norton, 1997), 653–713, at 2.5.126.

2. Men and women have historically faced different forms of social construction in relation to ideological normativity, and this study focuses on men to uncover the ways in which social privilege is granted and taken away from the privileged sex of patriarchal society. Queerness presents unique barriers to social privilege depending upon a wide array of social and cultural factors, and these conditions shift based upon the biological sex and its concomitant engendering of the agent in question. By addressing the ways in which men metamorphose through queerness into normativity, I hope to expose how ideologically sanctioned masculinity, in some instances, depends upon the enactment of queerness.

3. For a theoretical conception of discipline, see Michel Foucault, *Discipline and Punish: The Birth of the Prison*, trans. Richard Sheridan, 2nd edn. (New York: Vintage, 1995), in which he observes, "Discipline 'makes' individuals; it is the specific technique of a power that regards individuals both as objects and as instruments of its exercise. It is not a triumphant power, which because of its own excess can pride itself on its omnipotence; it is a modest, suspicious power, which functions as a calculated, but permanent economy" (p. 170).

4. Describing medieval masculine normativity in regard to gender and (hetero)sexuality presupposes its existence, and such a phantastic construction of masculine identity calls forth deep debates about the nature of sexual identities in the medieval past. Studies of medieval sexuality, homosexuality, and queerness include Christopher A. Jones, "Monastic Identity and Sodomotic Danger in the *Occupatio* by Odo of Cluny," *Speculum* 92 (2007): 1–53; James A. Schultz, *Courtly Love, the Love of Courtliness, and the History of Sexuality* (Chicago, IL: University of Chicago Press, 2006); Susan Schibanoff, *Chaucer's Queer Poetics: Rereading the Dream Trio* (Toronto: University of Toronto Press, 2006); Ruth Mazo Karras, *Sexuality in Medieval Europe: Doing unto Others* (New York: Routledge, 2005); Karma

Lochrie, *Heterosyncrasies: Female Sexuality When Normal Wasn't* (Minneapolis: University of Minnesota Press, 2005); Anna Klosowska, *Queer Love in the Middle Ages* (New York: Palgrave Macmillan, 2005); William E. Burgwinkle, *Sodomy, Masculinity, and Law in Medieval Literature: France and England, 1050–1230* (Cambridge: Cambridge University Press, 2004); Glenn Burger, *Chaucer's Queer Nation* (Minneapolis: University of Minnesota Press, 2003); Richard E. Zeikowitz, *Homoeroticism and Chivalry: Discourses of Male Same-Sex Desire in the Fourteenth Century* (New York: Palgrave Macmillan, 2003); Glenn Burger and Steven F. Kruger, eds., *Queering the Middle Ages* (Minneapolis: University of Minnesota Press, 2001); Francesca Canadé Sautman and Pamela Sheingorn, eds., *Same-Sex Love among Women in the Middle Ages* (New York: Palgrave Macmillan, 2001); Carolyn Dinshaw, *Getting Medieval: Sexualities and Communities, Pre- and Postmodern* (Durham, NC: Duke University Press, 1999); Allen J. Frantzen, *Before the Closet: Same-Sex Love from* Beowulf *to* Angels in America (Chicago, IL: University of Chicago Press, 1998); Mark Jordan, *The Invention of Sodomy in Christian Theology* (Chicago, IL: University of Chicago Press, 1997); Karma Lochrie, Peggy McCracken, and James A. Schultz, eds., *Constructing Medieval Sexuality* (Minneapolis: University of Minnesota Press, 1997); Theresa Tinkle, *Medieval Venuses and Cupids: Sexuality, Hermeneutics, and English Poetry* (Stanford, CA: Stanford University Press, 1996); Louise Fradenburg and Carla Freccero, eds., *Premodern Sexualities* (New York: Routledge, 1996); and my *Queering Medieval Genres* (New York: Palgrave Macmillan, 2004). This list is by no means exhaustive, but it points to the variety of discourses addressing intersections of sexuality and the medieval past. For a casebook of primary sources on medieval gender and sexuality, see Martha A. Brozyna, ed., *Gender and Sexuality in the Middle Ages: A Medieval Source Documents Reader* (Jefferson, NC: McFarland, 2005).

5. Sigmund Freud, *Civilization and Its Discontents: The Standard Edition,* trans. and ed. James Strachey (New York: Norton, 1961), p. 106.

6. Secular and religious authorities have historically enacted penalties for sexual transgressions, but such rules highlight the arbitrariness of the connection between transgression and punishment. For example, see Allen J. Frantzen's illuminating study of the ways in which sexual acts were penalized differently depending upon the perceived identity of the sexual agent in his "Between the Lines: Queer Theory, the History of Homosexuality, and Anglo-Saxon Penitentials," *Journal of Medieval and Renaissance Studies* 26.2 (1996): 255–96. See also the U.S. Supreme Court decision, *Lawrence v. Texas,* for the ways in which the various justices respond to historical constructions of sex and sexuality (539 U.S. 558 [2003]. *Lawrence v. Texas,* 123 S. Ct. 2472; 156 L. Ed. 2d 508).

7. Leo Bersani, *Homos* (Cambridge, MA: Harvard University Press, 1995), p. 113. Bersani posits the antisocial potential of queerness in this book, a theoretical position in contrast with queer utopianists. For an example of this debate, see Robert Caserio, Tim Dean, Lee Edelman, Judith

Halberstam, and José Estaban Munoz, "The Antisocial Thesis in Queer Theory," *PMLA* 121.3 (2006): 819–28.

8. Bersani's stances on homosexuality, queerness, and culture opened up new frontiers in queer criticism. For example, Robert Caserio credits Bersani with "formulat[ing] what might be called 'the antisocial thesis' in contemporary queer theory" ("The Antisocial Thesis in Queer Theory," p. 819).

9. Paul Smith defines the *subject* as "the term inaccurately used to describe what is actually the series or the conglomeration of positions, subject-positions, provisional and not necessarily indefeasible, into which a person is called momentarily by the discourses and the world that he/she inhabits." Smith also distinguishes the subject from the agent: "The term 'agent,' by contrast...mark[s] the idea of a form of subjectivity where, by virtue of the contradictions and disturbances in and among subject-positions, the possibility (indeed, the actuality) of resistance to ideological pressure is allowed for" (*Discerning the Subject* [Minneapolis: University of Minnesota Press, 1988], pp. xxvii and xxxv). Within this framework, the subject is subjected by and into ideology, whereas the agent finds the potential to resist ideological inculcation.

10. Exodus International is the leading "reformation" ministry attempting to convince homosexuals of the sinful nature of their behavior. Such publications as Bob Davies and Lori Rentzel's *Coming Out of Homosexuality: New Freedom for Men and Women* (Downers Grove, IL: Intervarsity, 1993) and Jeff Konrad's *You Don't Have to Be Gay: Hope and Freedom for Males Struggling with Homosexuality or for Those Who Know of Someone Who Is* (Hilo, HI: Pacific, 1992) lionize heterosexuality as a cure for homosexual desires.

11. David M. Halperin, *Saint Foucault: Towards a Gay Hagiography* (Oxford: Oxford University Press, 1995), p. 47; his italics.

12. Scientific studies of homosexuality and its ubiquity throughout nature include Joan Roughgarden, *Evolution's Rainbow: Diversity, Gender, and Sexuality in Nature and People* (Berkeley: University of California Press, 2004); J. Michael Baily, *The Man Who Would Be Queen: The Science of Gender-Bending and Transsexualism* (Washington, DC: Joseph Henry, 2003); Edward Stein, *The Mismeasure of Desire: The Science, Theory, and Ethics of Sexual Orientation* (Oxford: Oxford University Press, 1999); Bruce Bagemihl, *Biological Exuberance: Animal Homosexuality and Natural Diversity* (New York: St. Martin's, 1999); Timothy F. Murphy, *Gay Science: The Ethics of Sexual Orientation Research* (New York: Columbia University Press, 1997); and Dean Hamer and Peter Copeland, *The Science of Desire: The Search for the Gay Gene and the Biology of Behavior* (New York: Simon & Schuster, 1994).

13. Biblical quotations are taken from *The Holy Bible: Douay Rheims* (Fitzwilliam, NH: Loreto, 2004). Other passages of biblical homophobia include Leviticus 20:13, 3 Kings 14:24, Romans 1:26–27, I Corinthians 6:9–10, and I Timothy 1:9–10. Studies of biblical depictions of sexuality

include David M. Carr, *The Erotic Word: Sexuality, Spirituality, and the Bible* (Oxford: Oxford University Press, 2003); Martti Nissinen, *Homoeroticism in the Biblical World: A Historical Perspective* (Minneapolis, MN: Fortress, 1998), pp. 37–56; and Steven Greenberg, *Wrestling with God and Men: Homosexuality in the Jewish Tradition* (Madison: University of Wisconsin Press, 2004), esp. pp. 41–112.

14. Ovid, *The Erotic Poems,* trans. Peter Green (London: Penguin, 1982), p. 182, ll. 523–24. The Latin reads "cetera lasciuae faciant concede puellae / et si quis male uir quaerit habere uirum" (*Ars Amatoria,* ed. A. S. Hollis [Oxford: Clarendon, 1977], p. 20, ll. 523–24). For a discussion of this passage and other Roman writers' depictions of male effeminacy and sexuality, see Craig A. Williams, *Roman Homosexuality: Ideologies of Masculinity in Classical Antiquity* (Oxford: Oxford University Press, 1999), pp. 125–59.

15. Peter Damian, *Book of Gomorrah: An Eleventh-Century Treatise against Clerical Homosexual Practices,* trans. Pierre J. Payer (Waterloo, Ont.: Wilfrid Laurier University Press, 1982). See also Jordan, *The Invention of Sodomy,* pp. 29–66.

16. Distinguishing between homophobia and heterosexism enlightens the different ways in which ideological regimes enforce sexual discipline in a "carrot and stick" manner. Homophobia encompasses acts directed against queers and homosexuals, ranging from social ostracism to imprisonment and execution, whereas heterosexism entails the rewards and preferential treatment granted to heterosexuals, including social approbation enacted through ritual and law.

17. Biblical passages describing David and Jonathan's love include I Kings 18:1–3, 20:12–17, and 23:18, and 2 Kings 1:23, 26. (In a modern Bible, I and II Kings are referred to as I and II Samuel.) For a recent study of David and Jonathan's relationship, see Susan Ackerman, *When Heroes Love: The Ambiguity of Eros in the Stories of Gilgamesh and David* (New York: Columbia University Press, 2005).

18. Martial, *Epigrams: Volume III,* ed. and trans. D. R. Shackleton Bailey (Cambridge, MA: Harvard University Press, 1993), p. 53. For analysis of Martial's homosexual desires, see Williams, *Roman Homosexuality*, esp. pp. 32–33.

19. Marbod's lyrics are included in *Patrologia Latina*, ed. J.-P. Migne (Paris, 1844–1904), vol. 171, cols. 1458–1782; Baudri's lyrics are found in *Les Oeuvres poétiques de Baudri de Bourgueil*, ed. Phyllis Abrahams (Paris: Champion, 1926). Thomas Stehling translates many of their poems in his *Medieval Poems of Male Love and Friendship* (New York: Garland, 1984). For studies of homoeroticism in Marbod's and Baudri's poetry, see my *Queering Medieval Genres,* pp. 21–43; M. J. Ailes, "The Medieval Male Couple and the Language of Homosociality," *Masculinity in Medieval Europe,* ed. D. M. Hadley (London: Longman, 1999), pp. 214–37; C. Stephen Jaeger, *Ennobling Love: In Search of a Lost Sensibility* (Philadelphia: University of Pennsylvania Press, 1999), pp. 71–73; Gerald Bond, *The*

Loving Subject: Desire, Power, and Eloquence in Romanesque France
(Philadelphia: University of Pennsylvania Press, 1995), pp. 42–98; and
Thomas Stehling, *Medieval Poems of Male Love and Friendship*, pp. xvii–xxx
and his "To Love a Medieval Boy," *Journal of Homosexuality* 8 (1983):
151–70.

20. In the Middle Ages, David and Jonathan's friendship was frequently used
as a model of proper homosocial affection and reciprocal duty, as in the
writings of Dhuoda, *Manuel pour mon fils: introduction, texts, critique, notes,*
ed. Pierre Riché, trans. Bernard de Vregille and Claude Mondésert, 2nd
edn. (Paris: Cerf, 1991), pp. 166–68; Abelard, *Medieval Latin Lyrics,*
ed. and trans. Helen Waddell (New York: Norton, 1948), 162–69, at
p. 169; and *The Cambridge Songs: Carmina Cantabrigiensia,* ed. and trans.
Jan Ziolkowski (New York: Garland, 1994).

21. Laurie Shannon, *Sovereign Amity: Figures of Friendship in Shakespearian
Contexts* (Chicago, IL: University of Chicago Press, 2002), p. 19.

22. Mathew S. Kuefler, "Male Friendship and the Suspicion of Sodomy in
Twelfth-Century France," *Gender and Difference in the Middle Ages,* ed.
Sharon Farmer and Carol Braun Pasternack (Minneapolis: University of
Minnesota Press, 2003), 145–81, at p. 145. Kuefler illustrates the tensions
between homosociality and queerness in that the former frequently gives
rise to suspicions of the latter. I aim to demonstrate how this tension
enables queerness to function in the construction of heterosexuality.

23. Studies of male friendship and homosexuality in the classical, medieval,
and early modern periods include John Boswell, *Christianity, Social
Tolerance, and Homosexuality: Gay People in Western Europe from the Beginning
of the Christian Era to the Fourteenth Century* (Chicago, IL: University of
Chicago Press, 1980) and his *Same-Sex Unions in Premodern Europe* (New
York: Villard, 1994); Alan Bray, *The Friend* (Chicago, IL: University of
Chicago Press, 2003), esp. "Wedded Brother," pp. 13–41; Michael Rocke,
Forbidden Friendships: Homosexuality and Male Culture in Renaissance Florence
(New York: Oxford University Press, 1996); Reginald Hyatte, *The Arts
of Friendship: The Idealization of Friendship in Medieval and Early Renaissance
Literature* (Leiden: Brill, 1994); and Laurens J. Mills, *One Soul in Bodies
Twain: Friendship in Tudor and Stuart Drama* (Bloomington, IN: Principia,
1937). See also Jaeger, *Ennobling Love,* in which he proposes that such
homosocial relationships are normative expressions of respect, honor, and
affection (pp. 11–26); nonetheless, in the gap between homonormativity
and desire, queer potential occasionally appears.

24. Lee Edelman, *Homographesis: Essays in Gay Literary and Cultural Theory*
(New York: Routledge, 1994), p. 10; his italics.

25. Numerous scientific studies indicate that biology plays a role in the construction of gender differences. For an illuminating perspective, see Anne
Campbell, *A Mind of Her Own: The Evolutionary Psychology of Women*
(Oxford: Oxford University Press, 2002), esp. pp. 1–33, in which she
discusses how "biophobia" inhibits analysis of the role of biology in sexual difference. Given the interplay of biology, bodies, culture, ideology,

and individuals, it would be simplistic to assume that any one of these factors could necessarily trump the others. For the purposes of this study, however, it is prudent to note that the ensuing analysis proceeds primarily from a social constructionist perspective.

26. David L. Eng, Judith Halberstam, and José Esteban Munoz, "What's Queer about Queer Studies Now?" *Social Text* 23.3–4 (2005): 1–17, at p. 1.

27. Michael Warner, "Introduction," *Fear of a Queer Planet: Queer Politics and Social Theory,* ed. Michael Warner (Minneapolis: University of Minnesota Press, 1993), vii–xxxi, at p. xxvi. See also Warner's *The Trouble with Normal: Sex, Politics, and the Ethics of Gay Life* (New York: Free Press, 1999).

28. See Michel Foucault, *The History of Sexuality: Volume I: An Introduction,* trans. Robert Hurley (New York: Vintage, 1990), pp. 53–73, as well as David Halperin, *One Hundred Years of Homosexuality and Other Essays on Greek Love* (New York: Routledge, 1990); Eve Kosofsky Sedgwick, *Epistemology of the Closet* (Berkeley: University of California Press, 1990), esp. pp. 157–67; and Jonathan Ned Katz, *The Invention of Heterosexuality* (New York: Penguin, 1995) and *Love Stories: Sex between Men before Homosexuality* (Chicago, IL: University of Chicago Press, 2001). Karma Lochrie's "Have We Ever Been Normal" is particularly enlightening on this topic (*Heterosyncrasies,* pp. 1–25.).

29. Lochrie, *Heterosyncrasies,* p. xxiii.

30. Schultz, *Courtly Love, the Love of Courtliness,* p. 56.

31. Michel Foucault, *The Use of Pleasure: Volume 2 of The History of Sexuality,* trans. Robert Hurley (New York: Vintage, 1990), p. 3.

32. Jonathan Goldberg and Madhavi Menon, "Queering History," *PMLA* 120.5 (2005): 1608–17, at p. 1608.

33. The premier study of chaste marriages in the Middle Ages remains Dyan Elliott, *Spiritual Marriage: Sexual Abstinence in Medieval Wedlock* (Princeton, NJ: Princeton University Press, 1993). Additional studies of medieval marriage include D. L. D'Avray, *Medieval Marriage: Symbolism and Society* (Oxford: Oxford University Press, 2005); Conor McCarthy, *Marriage in Medieval England: Law, Literature, and Practice* (Woodbridge, England: Boydell, 2004); and Christopher N. L. Brooke, *The Medieval Idea of Marriage* (Oxford: Oxford University Press, 1989). At the same time that chaste marriages model an ideal Christian relationship, they also conflict with the concept of the marital debt. In this example, we see that when normativities collide, queering potential emerges.

34. Geoffrey Chaucer, "The Second Nun's Tale," *The Riverside Chaucer,* ed. Larry D. Benson, 3rd edn. (Boston, MA: Houghton Mifflin, 1987), pp. 262–29, esp. lines 134–231.

35. Sanford Brown Meech, ed., *The Book of Margery Kempe* (London: Early English Text Society, 1997), p. 23. I have modernized thorn and yogh.

36. Along the lines of this analysis of spiritual marriage, Robert Sturges's reading of Gottfried von Strassburg's *Tristan* exposes the ways in which

queerness is at times eclipsed in the production of normative heterosexuality, in that "The love triangle composed of Tristan, Isolde, and King
Mark is the means by which Gottfried introduces heterosexual desire into
a fictional social world from which it is at first notably absent. He does so,
in a complex series of rhetorical and narrative moves, primarily, though
not exclusively, through the displacement of a same-sex desire imagined
as the enabling (and preexisting) condition of male-female love—a condition that the text must forget once it has performed its function in the
construction of other-sex desire" ("The Construction of Heterosexual
Desire in Gottfried von Strassburg's *Tristan*," *Exemplaria* 10.2 [1998]:
243–69, at p. 244).

37. Judith Bennett, " 'Lesbian-Like' and the Social History of Lesbianisms,"
Journal of the History of Sexuality 9.1–2 (2000): 1–24.

38. Studies of gender in the Middle Ages are numerous, and recent texts in
the field include Lisa Perfetti, ed., *The Representation of Women's Emotions
in Medieval and Early Modern Culture* (Gainesville: University Press of
Florida, 2005); Virginia Chieffo Raguin and Sarah Stanbury, eds.,
Women's Space: Patronage, Place, and Gender in the Medieval Church (Albany:
State University of New York Press, 2005); Leslie Brubaker and Julia M.
H. Smith, eds., *Gender in the Early Medieval World: East and West, 300–900*
(Cambridge: Cambridge University Press, 2004); Peggy McCracken, *The
Curse of Eve, the Wound of the Hero: Blood, Gender, and Medieval Literature*
(Philadelphia: University of Pennsylvania Press, 2003); Rebecca L. R.
Garber, *Feminine Figurae: Representations of Gender in Religious Texts by
Medieval German Women Writers, 1100–1375* (New York: Routledge,
2003); and Sharon Farmer and Carol Braun Pasternack, eds., *Gender and
Difference in the Middle Ages*.

39. The passages in Genesis relevant to McNamara's argument are as follows:
"And God created man to his own image; to the image of God he created
him. Male and female he created them" (1:27) and "And the Lord God
built the rib which he took from Adam into a woman: and brought her to
Adam" (2:22).

40. Jo Ann McNamara, "An Unresolved Syllogism: The Search for a Christian
Gender System," *Conflicted Identities and Multiple Masculinities: Men in the
Medieval West,* ed. Jacqueline Murray (New York: Garland, 1999), 1–24,
at p. 1.

41. Studies of gender and masculinity in the Middle Ages include Ruth Mazo
Karras, *From Boys to Men: Formations of Masculinity in Late Medieval Europe*
(Philadelphia: University of Pennsylvania Press, 2003); Jacqueline
Murray, ed., *Conflicted Identities and Multiple Masculinities: Men in the
Medieval West* (New York: Garland, 1999); D. M. Hadley, ed., *Masculinity
in Medieval Europe* (London: Longman, 1999); Peter G. Beidler, ed.,
Masculinities in Chaucer: Approaches to Maleness in the Canterbury Tales *and*
Troilus and Criseyde (Cambridge: D. S. Brewer, 1998); Jeffrey Jerome
Cohen and Bonnie Wheeler, eds., *Becoming Male in the Middle Ages* (New
York: Garland, 1997); and Clare Lees, ed., *Medieval Masculinities: Regarding*

Men in the Middle Ages (Minneapolis: University of Minnesota Press, 1994).

42. Ruth Mazo Karras, "Separating the Men from the Goats: Masculinity, Civilization, and Identity Formation in the Medieval University," *The Animal/Human Boundary: Historical Perspectives,* ed. Angela N. H. Creager and William Chester Jordan (Rochester, NY: University of Rochester Press, 2002), 50–73, at p. 50.

43. Studies of the ways in which medieval chivalry and conduct books construct identities include Richard E. Zeikowitz, *Homoeroticism and Chivalry;* Kathleen Ashley and Robert L. A. Clark, eds., *Medieval Conduct* (Minneapolis: University of Minneapolis Press, 2001); and Margaret Hallissy, *Clean Maids, True Wives, Steadfast Widows: Chaucer's Women and Medieval Codes of Conduct* (Westport, CT: Greenwood, 1993).

44. For example, see Jeffrey Jerome Cohen's insightful analysis of Lancelot's masochistic pleasure in "Masoch/Lancelotism," *Medieval Identity Machines* (Minneapolis: University of Minnesota Press, 2003), pp. 78–115. Another example can be found in Marie de France's *Lanval,* in which the eponymous knightly hero finds alienation in the world of homosocial chivalry yet is queerly rescued and effeminized by the Fairy Queen, despite that heterosexual desire sparks their relationship (*The Lais of Marie de France,* trans. Robert Hanning and Joan Ferrante [Durham, NC: Labyrinth, 1978], pp. 105–25).

45. Adrienne Rich, "Compulsory Heterosexuality and Lesbian Existence," *Journal of Women's History* 15.3 (2003): 11–48. Rich also admonishes that "to equate lesbian existence with male homosexuality because each is stigmatized is to erase female sexuality once again" (p. 38). I hope that Rich would not accuse this study of a similar erasure of women and lesbianism, in that it uses some of her ideas as a starting point to consider the ways in which queerness constructs normative men; by focusing on men, however, such a criticism of this analysis is indeed warranted. Explicating the deleterious effects of normativity in the construction of men and masculinity seems to me a laudable goal, and I hope that the benefits of this study outweigh its masculinist bent.

46. Louis Althusser, "Ideology and Ideological State Apparatuses," *Lenin and Philosophy and Other Essays,* trans. Ben Brewster (London: NLB, 1971), p. 157; his italics.

47. Althusser, "Ideology and Ideological State Apparatuses," p. 165.

48. Judith Butler, *Bodies That Matter* (New York: Routledge, 1993), p. 122; her italics.

49. Warren Montag, "'The Soul Is the Prison of the Body': Althusser and Foucault, 1970–1975," *Yale French Studies* 88 (1995): 53–77, at p. 60.

50. Additional critiques of Althusser include Slavoj Žižek, *The Sublime Object of Ideology* (London: Verso, 1989); Michel Pêcheux, *Language, Semantics and Ideology* (New York: St. Martin's, 1982); Goran Therborn, *The Ideology of Power and the Power of Ideology* (London: Verso, 1980); and Paul Hirst, *On Law and Ideology* (New Jersey: Humanities, 1979).

51. Of these films, *Some Like It Hot* offers perhaps the queerest ending. Sugar
Kane (Marilyn Monroe) and Joe (Tony Curtis) end the narrative in heterosexual bliss, but Jerry (Jack Lemmon) must still fend off the advances
of Osgood (Joe E. Brown). Jerry gives a litany of reasons why he cannot
marry Osgood, declaring finally, "Well, you don't understand, Osgood.
I'm a man," as he takes off his wig. Osgood cheerily responds, "Well,
nobody's perfect." The queerness of this moment dilutes the otherwise
heteronormative ending expected when a man returns from drag to
"straight" attire, as depicted in the storyline of Sugar Kane and Joe.

52. Richard O'Brien, *The Rocky Horror Picture Show: Music from the Original
Soundtrack of the Twentieth Century Fox Presentation of the Lou Adler/Michael
White Production* (Santa Monica, CA: Ode Records, 1975).

53. Peter Haidu, "Althusser Anonymous in the Middle Ages," *Exemplaria* 7.1
(1995): 55–74, at p. 74.

54. Carla Freccero, *Queer/Early/Modern* (Durham, NC: Duke University
Press, 2006), p. 5.

Chapter 2   Abandoning Desires, Desiring
Readers, and the Divinely Queer Triangle of *Pearl*

1. In analyzing readerly desires, I am not arguing that *Pearl*'s readers are
uniform in their responses to the text. Various readers interpret texts in a
multitude of exciting, harmonious, and disparate manners. The goal of
this chapter is certainly not to establish a sole, exclusive, and definitive
account of this masterpiece, but rather to point out similarities between
the Dreamer's and the reader's desires arising from the ways that the *Pearl*-
poet manipulates them simultaneously.

2. Psychoanalytical studies of *Pearl* include George Edmondson, "*Pearl*: The
Shadow of the Object, the Shape of the Law," *Studies in the Age of Chaucer*
26 (2004): 29–63; Sarah Stanbury, "The Body and the City in *Pearl*,"
Representations 48 (1994): 30–47; and David Aers, "The Self Mourning:
Reflections on *Pearl*," *Speculum* 68 (1993): 54–73. I am indebted to the
insights of these scholars, and my goal is to build upon their observations
in order to explore the queer workings of desire in the text. Queerness
provides a basis for investigating the narratological and metatextual structures of the poem in their compulsory construction of Dreamer and
reader.

3. Slavoj Žižek, *The Puppet and the Dwarf: The Perverse Core of Christianity*
(Cambridge, MA: MIT Press, 2003), p. 43.

4. L. O. Aranye Fradenburg, *Sacrifice Your Love: Psychoanalysis, Historicism,
Chaucer* (Minneapolis: University of Minnesota Press, 2002), pp. 4–5.

5. Phyllis Hodgson, ed., *The Cloud of Unknowing and The Book of Privy
Counselling* (London: Early English Text Society, 1944), pp. 132–33.
I have modernized thorn and yogh in all quotations of Middle English,
including subsequent quotations of *Pearl*.

6. Translations of Middle English are my own, including those of *Pearl*. In all translations I aim for clarity of expression rather than for retaining poetic qualities of the texts.

7. Studies addressing the collisions of religion, gender, and sexuality in medieval mysticism include Amy Hollywood, *Sensible Ecstasy: Mysticism, Sexual Difference, and the Demands of History* (Chicago, IL: University of Chicago Press, 2002); Karma Lochrie, "Mystical Acts/Queer Tendencies," *Constructing Medieval Sexuality*, ed. Karma Lochrie, Peggy McCracken, and James A. Schultz (Minneapolis: University of Minnesota Press, 1997), pp. 180–200; and Grace M. Jantzen, *Power, Gender and Christian Mysticism* (Cambridge: Cambridge University Press, 1995).

8. Quotations of *Pearl* are taken from *The Poems of the* Pearl *Manuscript*, ed. Malcolm Andrew and Ronald Waldron (Berkeley: University of California Press, 1978).

9. Philological interpretations, translations, and contextualizations are based on the definitions in the *Middle English Dictionary*.

10. Queer theory assists this study in examining the ways in which the text plays with normative and nonnormative desires; I am not employing it to uncover a latent homosexuality to the Dreamer's and/or the reader's desires. As Richard Zeikowitz argues, "'Queer' can thus…describe an alternative form of desire that threatens the stability of the dominant norm" ("Befriending the Medieval Queer," *College English* 65.1 [2002]: 67–80, at p. 67). The Dreamer's desires for the dead Pearl Maiden undoubtedly subvert medieval Christian normativity in that he questions God's divine plan in his insistent and latently incestuous desire for his daughter.

11. Eve Sedgwick, *Between Men: English Literature and Male Homosocial Desire* (New York: Columbia University Press, 1985), p. 21.

12. Sedgwick, *Between Men*, p. 22.

13. As Michel Foucault succinctly observes, "Where there is desire, the power relation is already present" (*The History of Sexuality, Vol I: An Introduction*, trans. Robert Hurley [New York: Vintage, 1990], p. 81).

14. Such an eroticized conception of an individual's relationship with Christ is apparent in much medieval thought. See such studies as Lara Farina, *Erotic Discourse and Early English Religious Writing* (New York: Palgrave Macmillan, 2006); Miri Rubin, *Corpus Christi: The Eucharist in Late Medieval Culture* (Cambridge: Cambridge University Press, 1991); Caroline Walker Bynum, *Jesus as Mother: Studies in the Spirituality of the High Middle Ages* (Berkeley: University of California Press, 1982); Bernard McGinn, "The Language of Love in Christian and Jewish Mysticism," *Mysticism and Language*, ed. Steven Katz (New York: Oxford University Press, 1992), pp. 202–35; and Rosemary Woolf, "The Theme of Christ the Lover-Knight in Medieval English Literature," *Review of English Studies* 13 (1962): 1–16.

15. Edmondson, "*Pearl*: The Shadow of the Object," p. 42.

16. Of course, the Pearl Maiden quickly upbraids the Dreamer for his mistake, asserting that she is in no way superior to the other heavenly

maidens: "Vnblemyst I am, wythouten blot, / And that may I with mensk
menteene, / Bot 'makelez quene' thenne sade I not" ("Unblemished I am,
without stain, and that I may with honor maintain. But 'matchless queen'
then said I not"; 782–84).

17. Madhavi Menon, *Wanton Words: Rhetoric and Sexuality in English Renaissance
Drama* (Toronto: University of Toronto Press, 2004), pp. 129–30.

18. Stanley Fish, *Surprised by Sin: The Reader in* Paradise Lost, 2nd edn.
(Cambridge, MA: Harvard University Press, 1997), p. 21. Fish's ideas
about how readers are constructed through textual encounters are
especially relevant to medieval allegories and their construction of ideal
readers. The quotation of Milton is taken from *Tetrachordon, Complete
Prose Works of John Milton, Vol. II: 1643–1648,* ed. Ernest Sirluck (New
Haven, CT: Yale University Press, 1959), 571–718, at p. 642.

19. J. Hillis Miller, *The Ethics of Reading: Kant, de Man, Eliot, Trollope, James,
and Benjamin* (New York: Columbia University Press, 1987), p. 43; his
italics.

20. Helen Phillips and Nick Havely, eds., *Chaucer's Dream Poetry* (Essex,
England: Longman, 1997), p. 13.

21. For an analysis of the ways in which medieval generic forms can be used
to queer texts and audiences, see my *Queering Medieval Genres* (New York:
Palgrave Macmillan, 2004), esp. pp. 1–20.

22. Biblical quotations are taken from *The Holy Bible: Douay Rheims*
(Fitzwilliam, NH: Loreto, 2004).

23. The *Pearl*-poet consistently plays with semantic and semiotic sense by
packing multiple meanings into one word, and the primary significations
of "perle" include gem, Pearl Maiden, New Jerusalem, and the Dreamer
himself. Edward Condren observes that the mathematical architecture of
the poem constructs it as a pearl itself: "The obvious circularity of
Pearl...creates an overwhelming sense of something round with a seam-
less surface, like its main subject the pearl" (*The Numerical Universe of the
Gawain-Pearl Poet* [Gainesville: University Press of Florida, 2002], p. 63).
See also Laurence J. Krieg, "Levels of Symbolic Meaning in *Pearl*,"
Mythlore 5 (1978): 21–23; Cary Nelson, *The Incarnate Word: Literature as
Verbal Space* (Urbana: University of Illinois Press, 1973), pp. 25–49; and
Maud Burnett McInerney, "Opening the Oyster: Pearls in *Pearl*," *Aestel* 1
(1993): 19–54.

24. Lawrence Clopper, "*Pearl* and the Consolation of Scripture," *Viator* 23
(1991): 231–45, at p. 245.

25. Do readers desire meaning? We probe texts in endless quests to comprehend them more fully, but like the Dreamer's desire for the Pearl Maiden,
what would we do if we established a definitive and monological end to
this desire? As with other desires, readerly desires establish an eternal
circuit that often staves off closure. Certainly, the opacity of *Pearl* is one
of its most alluring features.

26. Sarah Stanbury, ed., *Pearl* (Kalamazoo, MI: Medieval Institute Publications,
2001), p. 4.

27. Hugh White offers a striking counterargument to claims of the Pearl's perfection in both poetic form and symbolic meaning, arguing that

> Pearl, then, seems to set out to be a pearl and thus to represent formally its content, but that representation actually involves a different form and a different content. Formal perfection seems to me to be purposefully breached so that the form can insist on a qualification of the claims of simple monistic perfection to be at the centre of an explanation of the world. ("Blood in Pearl," Review of English Studies 38 [1987]: 1–13, at p. 8)

As with so many interpretive cruxes within the Pearl-poet's corpus, we are compelled to look for complementary both/and rather than binary either/or readings, which ultimately underscores the paradox of truly understanding heavenly Christian revelation from an earthly perspective.

28. Genre studies of Pearl include Ian Bishop, Pearl in Its Setting (Oxford: Blackwell, 1968), pp. 16–26; Laurance Eldridge, "The State of Pearl Studies since 1933," Viator 6 (1975): 171–94, at pp. 172–78; Constance Hieatt, "Pearl and the Dream-Vision Tradition," Studia Neophilologica 37 (1965): 139–45; Sandra Pierson Prior, The Pearl-Poet Revisited (New York: Twayne, 1994), pp. 21–26; and Michael Means, The Consolatio Genre in Medieval English Literature (Gainesville: University Press of Florida, 1972), pp. 49–59. Lawrence Clopper sees in Pearl a hybrid form, "an epistemological poem which incorporates consolatio into a meditative scheme" ("Pearl and the Consolation of Scripture," p. 232).

29. Studies of medieval allegory include Suzanne Conklin Akbari, Seeing through the Veil: Optical Theory and Medieval Allegory (Toronto: University of Toronto Press, 2004); Ann W. Astell, Political Allegory in Late Medieval England (Ithaca, NY: Cornell University Press, 1999); and Jon Whitman, Allegory: The Dynamics of an Ancient and Medieval Technique (Cambridge, MA: Harvard University Press, 1987).

30. Studies of medieval dreams and dream visions include Phillips and Havely, eds., Chaucer's Dream Poetry; Peter Brown, ed., Reading Dreams: The Interpretation of Dreams from Chaucer to Shakespeare (New York: Oxford University Press, 1999); Kathryn L. Lynch, The High Medieval Dream Vision: Poetry, Philosophy, and Literary Form (Stanford, CA: Stanford University Press, 1988); and Steven F. Kruger, Dreaming in the Middle Ages (Cambridge: Cambridge University Press, 1992).

31. Studies of medieval elegies contemporary to Pearl include Ardis Butterfield, "Lyric and Elegy in the Book of the Duchess," Medium Aevum 60 (1991): 33–60 and Ellen E. Martin, "Spenser, Chaucer, and the Rhetoric of Elegy," Journal of Medieval and Renaissance Studies 17.1 (1987): 83–109. Martin notes that the critical tradition mistakenly attempts to divorce elegy from dream vision: "Both [Chaucer's Book of the] Duchess and Pearl, where elegy effects vision without departing from the sense of loss, have inspired long debates on whether their genre is dream-vision or elegy, the critical assumption being that grief and inspired knowledge are mutually exclusive" (p. 108, n. 33).

32. Does the fact that allegories and dream visions often depict the fulfillment of desire disprove the theoretical basis of this chapter—that desires do not seek their satiation but rather their perpetuation and that they wantonly pursue arbitrary objectives? It is not possible to answer this question definitively, but I would suggest that frequently within these genres, the protagonists' desires reflect mirrored and exterior desires rather than interior ones arising from a coherently structured subjectivity.

33. Seminal studies of genre and its functions include Tzvetan Todorov, *Genres in Discourse,* trans. Catherine Porter (Cambridge: Cambridge University Press, 1990); Thomas Beebee, *The Ideology of Genre: A Comparative Study of Generic Instability* (University Park: Pennsylvania State University Press, 1994); Alastair Fowler, *Kinds of Literature: An Introduction to the Theory of Genres and Modes* (Oxford: Oxford University Press, 1982); and Heather Dubrow, *Genre* (London: Methuen, 1982).

34. Jim Rhodes, "The Dreamer Redeemed: Exile and the Kingdom in the Middle English *Pearl,*" *Studies in the Age of Chaucer* 16 (1994): 119–42, at p. 128.

35. Jane Beal, "The Pearl Maiden's Two Lovers," *Studies in Philology* 100.1 (2003): 1–21, at p. 2.

36. The *Middle English Dictionary* defines *debonair* as "kindly, mercifully; courteously, graciously; humbly, modestly." One need not assume the word carries modern connotations of urbanity for it nonetheless to characterize the Pearl Maiden inappropriately, if she is indeed an infant. Infants express a rather limited range of attitudes and emotions and cannot properly embody any of the range of characteristics contained within the semantic field of *debonair.*

37. María Bullón-Fernández, "'Byyonde the Water': Courtly and Religious Desire in *Pearl,*" *Studies in Philology* 91 (1994): 35–49, at p. 39.

38. Jacques Lacan, *The Seminar of Jacques Lacan: Book VII: The Ethics of Psychoanalysis, 1959–1960,* ed. Jacques-Alain Miller, trans. Dennis Porter (New York: Norton, 1986), p. 76.

39. Lacan, *The Seminar of Jacques Lacan,* p. 84.

40. Žižek, *The Puppet and the Dwarf,* p. 53.

41. Hodgson, ed., The Cloud of Unknowing *and* The Book of Privy Counselling, pp. 154–55.

42. The biblical quotation in this passage is taken from Luke 9:23. The translation of the Middle English is my own, but the translation of the Vulgate is taken from the Douay Rheims Bible.

43. In this masochistic self-degradation, does the Christian subject act through individual agency? Many scholars believe that masochists express agency in their sacrifice of will to another. Linda Williams, for one, declares that "what is tricky about masochism, however, is that this search for recognition through apparent passivity is a ruse intended to disavow what the masochist actually knows to exist but plays the game of denying: his (or her) very real sexual agency and pleasure" (*Hard Core: Power, Pleasure, and the "Frenzy of the Visible"* [Berkeley: University of California

Press, 1989], p. 212). However, when human subjects masochistically sacrifice their earthly desires at the insistence of the divine, we see a very different construction of masochism, one that does indeed deprive the human subject of meaningful agency.

44. Phillips and Havely, eds., *Chaucer's Dream Poetry*, pp. 13–14.

45. J. Stephen Russell, "*Pearl's* 'Courtesy': A Critique of Eschatology," *Renascence* 35 (1983): 183–95, at p. 186.

46. Anne Howland Schotter addresses the paradoxical meaning of equal rewards yet unequal ranking in *Pearl* and argues that a solution can be found in the medieval feast, which "embodies the paradox by providing the missing term of hierarchy. It thus serves as a metaphor for a heaven which is simultaneously equal in its reward and unequal in its rank" ("The Paradox of Equality and Hierarchy of Reward in *Pearl*," *Renascence* 33 [1981]: 172–79, at p. 172). This ingenious solution to the Pearl Maiden's spiritual puzzle resolves the interpretive difficulty of this passage for the reader, but the Dreamer nonetheless continues to face the paradox of Christianity. If the reader identifies with the protagonist (and the dream vision explicitly sets this readerly dynamic in motion), we must feel his confusion at the mystery of Christianity rather than resolve it. Schotter is smarter than the Dreamer, but the *Pearl*-poet relies on our enforced bewilderment in light of divine mysteries.

47. Glending Olson, "'Nawther reste ne trauayle': The Psychology of *Pearl* 1087," *Neuphilologische Mitteilungen* 83.4 (1982): 422–25, at p. 425.

48. Kathryn Gravdal, *Ravishing Maidens: Writing Rape in Medieval French Literature and Law* (Philadelphia: University of Pennsylvania Press, 1991), p. 14.

49. Ann Chalmers Watts, "*Pearl*, Inexpressibility, and Poems of Human Loss," *PMLA* 99 (1984): 26–40, at p. 32.

50. If we presume common authorship to the works of MS Cotton Nero A.x, we find a shared thematic interest in the Dreamer's and Gawain's need for abandon. A similar moment occurs in *Sir Gawain and the Green Knight,* when Gawain determines to accept his fate at the Green Knight's hands, despite his real fear of his impending death: "'Bi Goddez self,' quoth Gawayn, / 'I wyl nauther grete ne grone; / To Goddez wylle I am ful bayn, / And to hym I haf me tone'" ("'By God Himself,' says Gawain, 'I will neither weep nor groan. I am fully obedient to God's will, and to him I have given myself'"; *Sir Gawain and the Green Knight,* ed. J. R. R. Tolkien and E. V. Gordon, 2nd edn., ed. Norman Davis [Oxford: Clarendon, 1967], lines 2156–59). Subsequently Gawain exclaims, "Let God worche!" ("Let God work!"; 2208). These moments indicate that Gawain no longer looks inwardly to his own desires—for courtly play with the lady, for homosocial play with the host, for the preservation of his life—but places primacy on God's desires, unknown though they may be. Of course, he still wears the green girdle for additional protection, but he now appears ready to accept God's will.

51. Aers, "The Self Mourning," p. 73.

Chapter 3   Queering Harry Bailly: Gendered Carnival, Social Ideologies, and Masculinity under Duress in the *Canterbury Tales*

1. David R. Pichaske and Laura Sweetland, "Chaucer on the Medieval Monarchy: Harry Bailly in the *Canterbury Tales*," *Chaucer Review* 11 (1976–77): 179–200, at p. 198.

2. Mark Allen, "Mirth and Bourgeois Masculinity in Chaucer's Host," *Masculinities in Chaucer: Approaches to Maleness in the* Canterbury Tales *and* Troilus and Criseyde, ed. Peter G. Beidler (Cambridge: D. S. Brewer, 1998), 9–21, at p. 9.

3. Barbara Page, "Concerning the Host," *Chaucer Review* 4 (1970): 1–13, at p. 5.

4. Walter Scheps, "'Up roos oure Hoost, and was oure aller cok': Harry Bailly's Tale-Telling Competition," *Chaucer Review* 10 (1975–76): 113–28, at p. 114.

5. William Keen, "'To doon yow ese': A Study of the Host in the *General Prologue* of the *Canterbury Tales*," *Topic* 17 (1969): 5–18, at p. 10.

6. All references to and citations of Chaucer are taken from *The Riverside Chaucer,* ed. Larry D. Benson, 3rd edn. (Boston: Houghton Mifflin, 1987) and are noted parenthetically.

7. According to the *Middle English Dictionary,* "manhed" and "manhod(e)" are used as abstract nouns referring to "manly virtue, character, or dignity; manliness" and "the character befitting a knight or monarch; chivalric nature or dignity; courageous behavior, bravery, valor." Chaucer's reference to Harry Bailly's manhood thus likely carries connotations of courage and bravery to accompany his attractive physical appearance, as well as possible allusions to his assumption of aristocratic manners.

8. Recent studies of homosexuality and queerness in Chaucer's oeuvre include Susan Schibanoff, *Chaucer's Queer Poetics: Rereading the Dream Trio* (Toronto: University of Toronto Press, 2006); Glenn Burger, *Chaucer's Queer Nation* (Minneapolis: University of Minnesota Press, 2003); Richard E. Zeikowitz, *Homoeroticism and Chivalry: Discourses of Male Same-Sex Desire in the Fourteenth Century* (New York: Palgrave, 2003); John Bowers, "Queering the Summoner: Same-Sex Union in Chaucer's *Canterbury Tales*," *Speaking Images: Essays in Honor of V. A. Kolve,* ed. Robert F. Yeager and Charlotte C. Morse (Asheville, NC: Pegasus, 2001), pp. 301–24; Carolyn Dinshaw, "Chaucer's Queer Touches / A Queer Touches Chaucer," *Exemplaria* 7 (1995): 75–92; and my *Queering Medieval Genres* (New York: Palgrave, 2004), pp. 45–106.

9. Lee Edelman, *No Future: Queer Theory and the Death Drive* (Durham, NC: Duke University Press, 2004), pp. 6–7.

10. Burger, *Chaucer's Queer Nation,* p. xvi. Burger here uses the term *gay* where I would employ *queer,* but we agree on the disruptive potential of renegade sexualities.

11. With full awareness of its limitations to describe medieval auditory hermeneutics, I use the term "reading" as an appropriate lexical shorthand to discuss Harry's adventures in literary interpretation. Obviously, Harry is an auditor, not a reader; however, my interest lies more in his confessional responses than in the particular interpretive process—ocular or auditory—involved. Scholarship on medieval textual and auditory communities includes Brian Stock, "Textual Communities" in his *The Implications of Literacy: Written Language and Models of Interpretation in the Eleventh and Twelfth Centuries* (Princeton, NJ: Princeton University Press, 1983), pp. 88–240; M. T. Clanchy, "Hearing and Seeing," *From Memory to Written Record: England, 1066–1307* (Cambridge, MA: Harvard University Press, 1979), pp. 253–93; and Janet Coleman, "Vernacular Literacy and Lay Education," *Medieval Readers and Writers* (New York: Columbia University Press, 1981), pp. 18–57.

12. Judith Ferster sees Harry's failures as host arising from his difficulties in interpretation in her *Chaucer on Interpretation* (Cambridge: Cambridge University Press, 1985), pp. 139–49. See also Robert Sturges, *Medieval Interpretation: Models of Reading in Literary Narrative, 1100–1500* (Carbondale, IL: Southern Illinois University Press, 1991).

13. John M. Ganim, "Bakhtin, Chaucer, Carnival, Lent," *Studies in the Age of Chaucer Proceedings* 2 (1986): 59–71, at p. 61. Ganim's article also addresses Chaucer's literature in relation to other Bakhtinian theories, notably the dialogic. See also Jon Cook, "Carnival and the *Canterbury Tales:* 'Only Equals May Laugh,'" *Medieval Literature: Criticism, Ideology, and History,* ed. David Aers (New York: St. Martin's, 1986), pp. 169–91 and the essays on Chaucer in *Bahktin and Medieval Voices,* ed. Thomas J. Farrell (Gainesville: University Press of Florida, 1995), including Robert M. Jordan, "Heteroglossia and Chaucer's *Man of Law's Tale,*" pp. 81–93; Steve Guthrie, "Dialogics and Prosody in Chaucer," pp. 94–108, and Thomas J. Farrell, "The Chronotypes of Monology in Chaucer's *Clerk's Tale,*" pp. 141–57.

14. For the theoretical underpinnings of play and carnival, see Johan Huizinga, *Homo Ludens: A Study of the Play Element in Culture* (Boston, MA: Beacon, 1950) and Mikhail Bakhtin, *Rabelais and His World,* trans. Hélène Iswolsky (Bloomington: Indiana University Press, 1984). Huizinga establishes the ways in which play is a civilizing force (pp. 46–75); Bakhtin explores the ways in which social class is a determinate feature of humor and carnival (pp. 145–95). Although play and carnival can be employed as separate hermeneutics, their intersection allows a clearer view of Harry Bailly's exploitation of play, carnival, and the comic to serve his own ends.

15. Umberto Eco, "The Frames of Comic Freedom," *Carnival!* ed. Thomas A. Sebeok (Berlin: Mouton, 1984), 1–9, at p. 6.

16. Terry Eagleton, *Walter Benjamin, or, Towards a Revolutionary Criticism* (London: Verso, 1981), pp. 145–46; his italics.

17. For additional studies of carnival, see Chris Humphrey, "Social Protest or Safety Valve? Critical Approaches to Festive Misrule," *The Politics of*

Carnival: Festival Misrule in Medieval England (Manchester: Manchester University Press, 2001), pp. 11–37 and Aron Gurevich, "'High' and 'Low': The Medieval Grotesque," *Medieval Popular Culture: Problems of Belief and Perception,* trans. János M. Bak and Paul A. Hollingsworth (Cambridge: Cambridge University Press, 1988), pp. 176–210.

18. Jean Dufournet, ed., *Aucassin and Nicollette* (Paris: Flammarion, 1984), pp. 132–35.

19. Sarah Roche-Mahdi, ed. and trans., *Silence: A Thirteenth-Century French Romance* (East Lansing, MI: Colleagues, 1992); see lines 2823–30.

20. Ruth Mazo Karras, *From Boys to Men: Formations of Masculinity in Late Medieval Europe* (Philadelphia: University of Pennsylvania Press, 2003), p. 3. For additional studies of medieval masculinities, see Peter G. Beidler, ed., *Masculinities in Chaucer: Approaches to Maleness in the* Canterbury Tales *and* Troilus and Criseyde (Cambridge: D. S. Brewer, 1998); Jacqueline Murray, ed., *Conflicted Identities and Multiple Masculinities: Men in the Medieval West* (New York: Garland, 1999); D. M. Hadley, ed., *Masculinity in Medieval Europe* (London: Longman, 1999); Jeffrey Jerome Cohen and Bonnie Wheeler, eds., *Becoming Male in the Middle Ages* (New York: Garland, 1997); and Clare Lees, ed., *Medieval Masculinities: Regarding Men in the Middle Ages* (Minneapolis: University of Minnesota Press, 1994).

21. As is well documented, Harry's pleasure in play and mirth is one of his most salient characteristics. For example, Thomas C. Richardson observes that "the narrator uses 'myrie' or 'myrthe' seven times in his twenty-six-line introduction to the Host in the 'General Prologue'" ("Harry Bailly: Chaucer's Innkeeper," *Chaucer's Pilgrims: An Historical Guide to the Pilgrims in the* Canterbury Tales, ed. Laura C. Lambdin and Robert T. Lambdin [Westport, CT: Greenwood, 1996], 324–39, at p. 330). S. S. Hussey also documents Harry's penchant for mirth ("Chaucer's Host," *Medieval English Studies Presented to George Kane,* ed. Edward Donald Kennedy, Ronald Waldron, and Joseph S. Wittig [Cambridge: D. S. Brewer, 1988], 153–61, at pp. 157–60). Studies of Chaucerian play and game include Laura Kendrick, *Chaucerian Play* (Berkeley: University of California Press, 1988); Malcolm Andrew, "Games," *A Companion to Chaucer,* ed. Peter Brown (Oxford: Blackwell, 2000), pp. 167–79; Richard F. Green, "Troilus and the Game of Love," *Chaucer Review* 13 (1979): 201–20; Gerhard Joseph, "Chaucerian 'Game'—'Earnest' and the 'Argument of Herbergage' in the *Canterbury Tales,*" *Chaucer Review* 5 (1970): 83–96; G. D. Josipovici, "Fiction and Game in the *Canterbury Tales,*" *Critical Quarterly* 7 (1965): 185–97; Richard Lanham, "Game, Play, and High Seriousness in Chaucer's Poetry," *English Studies* 48 (1967): 1–24; Carl Lindahl, *Earnest Games: Folkloric Patterns in the* Canterbury Tales (Bloomington: Indiana University Press, 1987); Stephen Manning, "Rhetoric, Game, Morality, and Geoffrey Chaucer," *Studies in the Age of Chaucer* 1 (1979): 105–18; Glending Olson, "Chaucer's Idea of a Canterbury Game," *The Idea of Medieval Literature,* ed. James M. Dean and Christian Zacher (Newark: University of Delaware Press, 1992), pp. 72–90; and my

"Christian Revelation and the Cruel Game of Courtly Love in *Troilus and Criseyde*," *Chaucer Review* 39 (2005): 379–401.

22. Carolyn Dinshaw, *Chaucer's Sexual Poetics* (Madison: University of Wisconsin Press, 1989), p. 94.

23. The three estates model both describes the structure of medieval English society and points to how social structures were fundamentally shifting. Jill Mann argues in relation to the intersection of social estates and Chaucer's literature that "estates stereotypes also afford an explanation for Chaucer's ability to conceive of his estates representatives in topical situations; they are not fixed types whose features are determined *solely* by their existence in a literary tradition, and must be consciously brought up to date" (*Chaucer and Medieval Estates Satire: The Literature of Social Classes and the* General Prologue *to the* Canterbury Tales [Cambridge: Cambridge University Press, 1973], p. 9). Chaucer's literature thus reflects both his knowledge of estates tradition and his awareness of its transformations within his social world. See also David Wallace, *Chaucerian Polity: Absolutist Lineages and Associational Forms in England and Italy* (Stanford, CA: Stanford University Press, 1997) and Paul Olson, *The* Canterbury Tales *and the Good Society* (Princeton, NJ: Princeton University Press, 1986).

24. John C. Hirsh, ed., "I haue a gentil cok," *Medieval Lyric: Middle English Lyrics, Ballads, and Carols* (Oxford: Blackwell, 2005), p. 118. For a study of the phallic imagery in this lyric, see Lorrayne Y. Baird-Lange, "Symbolic Ambivalence in 'I haue a gentil cok,'" *Fifteenth-Century Studies* 11 (1985): 1–5, in which she concludes that "the barnyard cock in all his gorgeousness" symbolizes "the Christ-cock who awakens the priest, the priest-cock who performs his matins, and the phallic cock who stirs the priest and puts to flight all other cocks" (p. 5). For Chaucer's use of cock imagery, see André Crépin, "The Cock, the Priest, and the Poet," *Drama, Narrative, and Poetry in the* Canterbury Tales, ed. Wendy Harding (Toulouse: Presses Universitaires du Mirail, 2003), pp. 227–36. The *Medieval English Dictionary* attests an idiomatic usage of "ben aller cok" as "to wake everybody," and the phallic connotations of "cock" in the Middle Ages are amply demonstrated by Louise O. Vasvari, "Fowl Play in My Lady's Chamber: Textual Harassment of a Middle English Pornithological Riddle and Visual Pun," *Obscenity: Social Control and Artistic Creation in the European Middle Ages,* ed. Jan M. Ziolkowski (Leiden: Brill, 1998), pp. 108–35. See also the entries on the symbolic valences of cocks in Jack Tresidder, *Dictionary of Symbols: An Illustrated Guide to Traditional Images, Icons, and Emblems* (San Francisco, CA: Chronicle, 1998) and Jean Chevalier and Alain Gheerbrant, eds., *A Dictionary of Symbols,* trans. John Buchanan-Brown (Oxford: Blackwell, 1994).

25. Judith Butler succinctly characterizes gender as "a practice of improvisation within a scene of constraint," which nicely captures the tension between gender play and social expectation (*Undoing Gender* [New York: Routledge, 2004], at p. 1). See also Butler's *Bodies That Matter: On the*

Discursive Limits of "Sex" (New York: Routledge, 1993) and *Gender Trouble: Feminism and the Subversion of Identity* (New York: Routledge, 1990). For analysis of gender performance in Chaucer's literature, see Holly Crocker, *Chaucer's Visions of Manhood* (New York: Palgrave Macmillan, 2007); Elaine Tuttle Hansen, *Chaucer and the Fictions of Gender* (Berkeley: University of California Press, 1992) and Dinshaw, *Chaucer's Sexual Poetics.*

26. "Marshal" is defined simply as a "master of ceremonies" by both *The Riverside Chaucer,* p. 35 and Norman Davis et al., *A Chaucer Glossary* (Oxford: Clarendon, 1979), p. 93. The *Middle English Dictionary,* however, offers a more expansive definition that focuses primarily on the upper levels of society: "The chief officer of a kingdom, steward;...one of the high officers of the royal court," with a secondary definition as "An official in a royal or noble household in charge of ceremonies, protocol, seating, service, etc." The brief definitions of *The Riverside Chaucer* and *A Chaucer Glossary* foreclose analysis of Harry's position, which Chaucer seems, in characteristic fashion, to have constructed with deep ambiguity.

27. Again deferring to the authority of the *Middle English Dictionary,* we see that "burgeis" is dually defined as "a freeman of a town, a citizen with full rights and privileges; also, an inhabitant of a town;—usually used of city merchants and master craftsmen in the guilds," as well as "a magistrate or other official of a town; a member of the council or assembly governing a town...the representative of a town in the House of Commons."

28. Bakhtin, *Rabelais and His World,* pp. 145–95.

29. This aggression in the tale-telling competition is one of the more notable characteristics of the *Canterbury Tales.* Scholarship on this narratival aggression includes Anne Laskaya, "Men in Love and Competition: The *Miller's Tale* and the *Merchant's Tale,*" *Chaucer's Approach to Gender in the Canterbury Tales* (Cambridge: D. S. Brewer, 1995), pp. 78–98; Emily Jensen, "Male Competition as a Unifying Motif in Fragment A of the *Canterbury Tales,*" *Chaucer Review* 24 (1990): 320–28; and Lindahl, "Conventions of a Narrative War," *Earnest Games,* pp. 73–155.

30. Stephen Partridge intriguingly suggested to me that, in the phrase " 'Straw for youre gentillesse,' " the emphasis in Harry's words should be placed on "youre," which would suggest that Harry is not attacking gentility as a social value in itself as much as he is attacking the Franklin's particular construction of aristocratic gentility. Such an observation is consistent with the ways in which Harry's liminal ideology reflects his attempts to turn rhetorical situations to his advantage.

31. According to the *Middle English Dictionary,* "mayde" denotes a male virgin as well as a young woman, and so it is possible that Harry is commenting more on the Clerk's virginity than on his apparent femininity. The corresponding depiction of this maid apprehensively awaiting the impending loss of virginity after the marriage feast nonetheless suggests stereotypical depictions of femininity rather than of masculinity.

32. For scholarship on the medieval connections among reading, literature, and play, see Glending Olson, *Literature as Recreation in the Later Middle Ages* (Ithaca, NY: Cornell University Press, 1982), esp. pp. 90–127.

33. Emma Wilson, *Sexuality and the Reading Encounter* (Oxford: Clarendon, 1996), p. 5.

34. John Plummer, "'Beth fructuous and that in litel space': The Engendering of Harry Bailly," *New Readings of Chaucer's Poetry,* ed. Robert G. Benson and Susan J. Ridyard (Cambridge: D. S. Brewer, 2003), 107–18, at p. 117.

35. Although "male" means "bag" or "pouch" in a medieval lexicon, the *Oxford English Dictionary* attests that its meaning as "masculine" was developing in the 1380s, which makes likely a bawdy yet typically Chaucerian pun. The *Middle English Dictionary* likewise documents that the word can mean either a "male human being" or a "bag, pouch." Such a sexual interpretation of the phrase "unbokeled is the male" gains further credence when compared with the Pardoner's more openly suggestive pun in his request to Harry Bailly: "'Com forth, sire Hoost, and offre first anon, / And thou shalt kisse the relikes everychon, / Ye, for a grote! Unbokele anon thy purs'" (6.943–45). For further discussion of this passage, see Robert Sturges, *Chaucer's Pardoner and Gender Theory: Bodies of Discourse* (New York: St. Martin's, 2000), pp. 74–76.

36. Edwin Stieve argues that the phrase "in terme" indicates Harry's failure to use rhetorical and medical terminology correctly ("A New Reading of the Host's 'In terme' [*Canterbury Tales* VI, line 311]," *Notes and Queries* 34.1 [1987]: 7–10).

37. John David Burnley, "Chaucer's Host and Harry Bailly," *Chaucer and the Craft of Fiction,* ed. Leigh A. Arrathoon (Rochester, MI: Solaris, 1986), 195–218, at p. 210. For additional studies of the gap between expectations of social conduct and behavior, see the essays in *Medieval Conduct,* ed. Kathleen Ashley and Robert L. A. Clark (Minneapolis: University of Minnesota Press, 2001).

38. This scene receives a great deal of critical scrutiny. Studies that most inform my analysis include Sturges, *Chaucer's Pardoner and Gender Theory;* Alastair Minnis, "Chaucer and the Queering Eunuch," *New Medieval Literatures* 6 (2003): 107–29; Richard E. Zeikowitz, "Silenced but Not Stifled: The Disruptive Queer Power of Chaucer's Pardoner," *Dalhousie Review* 82.1 (2002): 55–73; Lee Patterson, "Chaucer's Pardoner on the Couch: Psyche and Clio in Medieval Literary Studies," *Speculum* 76.3 (2001): 638–80; Steven F. Kruger, "Claiming the Pardoner: Toward a Gay Reading of Chaucer's *Pardoner's Tale*," *Exemplaria* 6.1 (1994): 115–39; Glenn Burger, "Kissing the Pardoner," *PMLA* 107.4 (1992): 1143–56; Monica McAlpine, "The Pardoner's Homosexuality and How It Matters," *PMLA* 95.1 (1980): 8–22; and Richard Firth Green, "Further Evidence for Chaucer's Representation of the Pardoner as a Womanizer," *Medium Ævum* 71.2 (2002): 307–09, as well as his "The Pardoner's Pants (and Why They Matter)," *Studies in the Age of Chaucer* 15 (1993): 131–45.

39. Studies of homosocial relationships in the Middle Ages readily demon-
    strate that the simple act of two men kissing need not disclose any homo-
    erotic valence. For example, see C. Stephen Jaeger, *Ennobling Love: In
    Search of a Lost Sensibility* (Philadelphia: University of Pennsylvania Press,
    1999), esp. pp. 128–33. For a study of kissing and its cultural meanings in
    the Middle Ages, see Yannick Carré, *Le Baiser sur la bouche au moyen age:
    rites, symboles, mentalités, à travers les texts et les images, XIe-XVe siècles* (Paris:
    Léopard d'Or, 1992), as well as Michael Philip Penn, *Kissing Christians:
    Ritual and Community in the Late Ancient Church* (Philadelphia: University
    of Pennsylvania Press, 2005). The queerness of the kiss between Harry
    and the Pardoner lies not in the physical act itself as much as in the fact
    that they are compelled to act against their will in an act with sexual
    implications.
40. Carolyn Dinshaw, *Getting Medieval: Sexualities and Communities, Pre- and
    Postmodern* (Durham, NC: Duke University Press, 1999), p. 136.
41. For a reading of Harry's relationship to the Nun's Priest in terms of
    authorial and sexual positioning, see Peter W. Travis, "The Body of the
    Nun's Priest, or, Chaucer's Disseminal Genius," *Reading Medieval Culture:
    Essays in Honor of Robert W. Hanning,* ed. Robert Stein and Sandra Pierson
    Prior (Notre Dame, IN: University of Notre Dame Press, 2005),
    pp. 231–47.
42. In Chaucer's lexicon, "daliaunce" often connotes sexual flirtations, as in
    the short poem "To Rosemounde," in which Chaucer complains to his
    eponymous beloved that "ye to me ne do no daliaunce" (8, 16, 24). The
    Middle English Dictionary defines "daliaunce" as "polite, leisurely, inti-
    mate conversation or entertainment"; "serious, edifying, or spiritual
    conversation"; and "amorous talk or to-do; flirting, coquetry; sexual
    union." For a discussion of the sexual overtones of "daliaunce," see my
    Queering Medieval Genres, pp. 57–58. "Daliaunce" appears eleven times
    in Chaucer's canon, according to Larry D. Benson, ed., *A Glossarial
    Concordance to the* Riverside Chaucer (New York: Garland, 1993); it car-
    ries the distinct connotation of sexual courtship and flirtation in eight of
    these instances.
43. Bernard Suits observes that the rules of a game make its objectives diffi-
    cult to achieve for the sheer fun of this added difficulty: "To play a game
    is to attempt to achieve a specific state of affairs (prelusory goal), using
    only means permitted by rules (lusory means), where the rules prohibit
    use of more efficient in favour of less efficient means (constitutive rules),
    and where the rules are accepted just because they make possible such
    activity (lusory attitude)" (*The Grasshopper: Games, Life, and Utopia*
    [Toronto: University of Toronto Press, 1978], p. 41). Poetry shares a sim-
    ilar gamelike structure, as rhythm, meter, and rhyme add a rule structure
    to a communicative mode for playful and aesthetic rather than utilitarian
    purposes.
44. Of course, the Retraction itself could be viewed as ironic. Donald Howard
    observes that "at the end of his life [Chaucer] revokes in the Retraction

such of the Canterbury tales as 'sownen into sin.' There is that much evidence that he was hesitant about the ironic stance" (*The Idea of the Canterbury Tales* [Berkeley: University of California Press, 1975], p. 55). Whether ironic or not in regard to Chaucer's poetic play, however, the Retraction certainly ends Harry Bailly's governance.

45. In Harry's tale-telling carnival, the passing of time promises the end of his masculine authority; in order to assert his rule over as many pilgrims as possible, he carefully monitors the "schedule" of the tale-telling competition. For example, in response to time's inexorable passing, Harry pressures the tale-tellers to hurry, as in his admonition to the Reeve:

> "Sey forth thy tale, and tarie nat the tyme.
> Lo Depeford, and it is half-wey pryme!
> Lo Grenewych, ther many a shrewe is inne!
> It were al tyme thy tale to bigynne." (1.3905–08)

Likewise, Harry's words in the Introduction to the *Man of Law's Tale* convey his urgent desire to maintain the game's quick tempo (2.28–32). The pilgrims may well wonder why they may not "mowlen thus in ydelnesse" (2.32), especially as play is more aligned with idleness and recreation than seriousness and earnest. As Cynthia Richardson notes, "[Harry] chides others for wasting time, but wastes it himself giving speeches on various topics, including one on wasting time" ("The Function of the Host in the *Canterbury Tales*," *Texas Studies in Literature and Language* 12 [1970]: 325–44, at p. 333). The reader thus perceives again that the tale-telling competition serves Harry more in his desire to govern with his newly seized masculine authority than in his desire to play.

46. Andrew Taylor, "The Curious Eye and the Alternative Endings of the *Canterbury Tales*," *Part Two: Reflections on the Sequel*, ed. Paul Budra and Betty A. Schellenberg (Toronto: University of Toronto Press, 1998), 34–52, at p. 38.

47. Burger, *Chaucer's Queer Nation*, p. 188.

48. For considerations of the meaning of "sentence" and "solaas," see Alan Gaylord, "*Sentence* and *Solaas* in Fragment VII of the *Canterbury Tales*: Harry Bailly as Horseback Editor," *PMLA* 82 (1967): 226–35 and L. M. Leith, "Sentence and Solaas: The Function of the Hosts in the *Canterbury Tales*," *Chaucer Review* 17 (1982): 5–20.

49. Scheps, "'Up roos oure Hoost,'" pp. 123–26.

50. Leith, "Sentence and Solaas," p. 10.

51. For studies of the interplay between Harry and Chaucer as narrative voices, see Leo Carruthers, "Narrative Voice, Narrative Framework: The Host as 'Author' of the *Canterbury Tales*," *Drama, Narrative and Poetry in the Canterbury Tales*, ed. Wendy Harding (Toulouse: Presses Universitaires du Mirail, 2003), pp. 51–67 and Barbara Nolan, "'A Poet Ther Was': Chaucer's Voices in the *General Prologue* to *The Canterbury Tales*," *PMLA* 101 (1986): 154–69.

Chapter 4   "He nedes moot unto the pley assente": Queer Fidelities and Contractual Hermaphroditism in Chaucer's *Clerk's Tale*

1. Recent critical discussions of the *Clerk's Tale* addressing the question of Griselda's will and her submission to Walter's demands include J. Allan Mitchell, "Chaucer's *Clerk's Tale* and the Question of Ethical Monstrosity," *Studies in Philology* 102.1 (2005): 1–26; William McClellan, "'Ful pale face': Agamben's Biopolitical Theory and the Sovereign Subject in Chaucer's *Clerk's Tale*," *Exemplaria* 17.1 (2005): 103–34; Mark Miller, "Love's Promise: The *Clerk's Tale* and the Scandal of the Unconditional," *Philosophical Chaucer: Love, Sex, and Agency in the* Canterbury Tales (Cambridge: Cambridge University Press, 2004), pp. 216–48; Rodney Delasanta, "Nominalism and the *Clerk's Tale* Revisited," *Chaucer Review* 31 (1997): 209–31, at pp. 214–18; Linda Georgianna, "The *Clerk's Tale* and the Grammar of Assent," *Speculum* 70.4 (1995): 793–821; Carolynn Van Dyke, "The Clerk's and Franklin's Subjected Subjects," *Studies in the Age of Chaucer* 17 (1995): 45–68; Andrew Sprung, "'If it youre wille be': Coercion and Compliance in Chaucer's *Clerk's Tale*," *Exemplaria* 7.2 (1995): 345–69; and Robert Emmett Finnegan, "'She Should Have Said No to Walter': Griselda's Promise in the *Clerk's Tale*," *English Studies* 75.4 (1994): 303–21.

2. Mary Carruthers, "The Lady, the Swineherd, and Chaucer's Clerk," *Chaucer Review* 17.3 (1983): 221–34, at p. 222. For medieval constructions of Griselda's story, see Amy W. Goodwin, "The Griselda Game," *Chaucer Review* 39 (2004): 41–69; Charlotte C. Morse, "The Exemplary Griselda," *Studies in the Age of Chaucer* 7 (1985): 51–86; and Anne Middleton, "The Clerk and His Tale: Some Literary Contexts," *Studies in the Age of Chaucer* 2 (1980): 121–50.

3. All references to and citations of Chaucer are taken from *The Riverside Chaucer,* ed. Larry D. Benson, 3rd edn. (Boston: Houghton Mifflin, 1987) and are noted parenthetically.

4. I use the terms "heterosexual" and "homosexual" as appropriate lexical shorthands for describing sexual relationships in the Middle Ages, with full awareness of their limitations in regard to pre-Foucauldian sexualities. For a discussion of the issues inherent in discussing medieval sexualities, see the Introduction, pp. 7–11.

5. Thomas Laqueur, *Making Sex: Body and Gender from the Greeks to Freud* (Cambridge, MA: Harvard University Press, 1990), p. 62.

6. Charlotte Morse reviews the critical history of the tale in "Critical Approaches to *The Clerk's Tale*," *Chaucer's Religious Tales*, ed. C. David Benson and Elizabeth Robertson (Cambridge: D. S. Brewer, 1990), pp. 71–83.

7. The notorious limitation of reader-response hermeneutics arises in that they can in no measure account for the virtually infinite number of interpretive possibilities of a given text. In outlining a theoretical reader's

response parallel to the dynamics of the characters in the frame and in the tale itself, I hope to enlighten the textual and metatextual structure of the *Clerk's Tale* in its demand for queer fidelity. By offering such a reading, however, I make no claims about the universality of the ways in which the text works on every unique and individual reader. For recent studies of reader-response criticism, see Patrocinio P. Schweickart and Elizabeth A. Flynn, eds., *Reading Sites: Social Difference and Reader Response* (New York: MLA, 2004); Gerry Brenner, *Performative Criticism: Experiments in Reader Response* (Albany: State University of New York Press, 2004); and Todd F. Davis and Kenneth Womack, *Formalist Criticism and Reader-Response Theory* (Basingstoke, Hampshire: Palgrave Macmillan, 2002).

8. In terms of medieval literature, Aranye Fradenburg explores the sacrificial nature of desire in *Sacrifice Your Love: Psychoanalysis, Historicism, Chaucer* (Minneapolis: University of Minnesota Press, 2002). Cultural and psychoanalytic theorists who investigate desire through a similar lens include Slavoj Žižek, *The Sublime Object of Ideology* (New York: Verso, 1989) and *Metastases of Enjoyment: Six Essays on Women and Causality* (London: Verso, 1994); Jacques Lacan, *The Seminar of Jacques Lacan: Book VII: The Ethics of Psychoanalysis, 1959–1960,* ed. Jacques-Alain Miller, trans. Dennis Porter (New York: Norton, 1992); and Gilles Deleuze and Félix Guattari, *A Thousand Plateaus: Capitalism and Schizophrenia,* trans. Brian Massumi (Minneapolis: University of Minnesota Press, 1987). The insights of these scholars and theorists provide a psychoanalytical structure for illustrating how queer fidelities structure characterological and metatextual hermaphroditism.

9. Lee Edelman, "Queer Theory: Unstating Desire," *GLQ: A Journal of Lesbian and Gay Studies* 2.4 (1995): 343–46, at p. 345.

10. Michel Foucault, *The History of Sexuality: An Introduction,* trans. Robert Hurley (New York: Vintage, 1990), p. 48.

11. Octave Mannoni addresses this tension between conflicting layers of knowledge and desire in the essay "I Know Well, But All the Same" (*Perversion and the Social Relation*, ed. Molly Anne Rothenberg, Dennis Foster, and Slavoj Žižek [Durham, NC: Duke University Press, 2003], pp. 68–92). The very title of this essay captures the stunning disjointure between oppositional senses of knowledge and desire.

12. Molly Anne Rothenberg and Dennis Foster, "Introduction: Beneath the Skin: Perversion and Social Analysis," *Perversion and the Social Relation*, p. 3.

13. See Judith Butler, *Undoing Gender* (New York: Routledge, 2004), *Bodies That Matter: On the Discursive Limits of "Sex"* (New York: Routledge, 1993), and *Gender Trouble: Feminism and the Subversion of Identity* (New York: Routledge, 1990). Primary texts of Chaucerian gender criticism include Elaine Tuttle Hansen, *Chaucer and the Fictions of Gender* (Berkeley: University of California Press, 1992); Carolyn Dinshaw, *Chaucer's Sexual Poetics* (Madison: University of Wisconsin Press, 1989); and Holly Crocker, *Chaucer's Visions of Manhood* (New York: Palgrave Macmillan, 2007).

14. Dinshaw, *Chaucer's Sexual Poetics,* p. 154.

15. Scholarship on aggression in the *Canterbury Tales* includes Anne Laskaya, "Men in Love and Competition: The *Miller's Tale* and the *Merchant's Tale*," *Chaucer's Approach to Gender in the* Canterbury Tales (Cambridge: D. S. Brewer, 1995), pp. 78–98; Emily Jensen, "Male Competition as a Unifying Motif in Fragment A of the *Canterbury Tales*," *Chaucer Review* 24 (1990): 320–28; and Carl Lindahl, "Conventions of a Narrative War," *Earnest Games: Folkloric Patterns in the* Canterbury Tales (Bloomington: Indiana University Press, 1987), pp. 73–155.

16. Of course, Harry Bailly established the contractual nature of the game much earlier, when he declared in the *General Prologue*, " 'And therfore wol I maken yow disport, / As I seyde erst, and doon yow som confort. / And if yow liketh alle by oon assent / For to stonden at my juggement, / And for to werken as I shal yow seye' " (1.775–79). For a discussion of this passage, see chapter 3, pp. 52–54.

17. For scholarship on the ways in which gender and sexuality structure the *Canterbury Tales,* see my "Chaucer's Queering Fabliaux," *Queering Medieval Genres,* pp. 45–79; Susan Schibanoff, *Chaucer's Queer Poetics: Rereading the Dream Trio* (Toronto: University of Toronto Press, 2006); Glenn Burger, *Chaucer's Queer Nation* (Minneapolis: University of Minnesota Press, 2003); Richard E. Zeikowitz, *Homoeroticism and Chivalry: Discourses of Male Same-Sex Desire in the Fourteenth Century* (New York: Palgrave, 2003); Angela Jane Weisl, *Conquering the Reign of Femeny: Gender and Genre in Chaucer's Romance* (Cambridge: D. S. Brewer, 1995); and Susan Crane, *Gender and Romance in Chaucer's* Canterbury Tales (Princeton, NJ: Princeton University Press, 1994).

18. According to the *Middle English Dictionary,* "mayde" may refer to a female or a male virgin: "1(a) An unmarried woman, usually young;... 2(a) A Virgin; (b) a virgin by religious vocation; (c) the Virgin Mary...; (d) a man who abstains from sexual experience for religious reasons; also a man lacking sexual experience." Despite the possible ambiguity of "mayde" in relation to gender, the Host's words contextually paint the Clerk as a newly wed bride in this brief tableau of marital jitters at the reception table, a typical scene that Chaucer parodies in the *Merchant's Tale* (4.1750–82).

19. These clerks appear in fabliaux, and the generic expectations of such tales in some manner necessitate such lusty clerics. Still, the Clerk of the pilgrimage stands in direct contrast to the sexually frisky clerks depicted elsewhere in the *Canterbury Tales.*

20. Johan Huizinga argues that play is a "free activity standing quite consciously outside 'ordinary' life." He proceeds to describe play "as being 'not serious,' but at the same time absorbing the player intensely and utterly" (*Homo Ludens: A Study of the Play-Element in Culture* [Boston, MA: Beacon, 1950], p. 13). This conception of play's voluntary and free qualities does not mesh well with the Host's coercive sense of fun and amusement.

21. Barrie Ruth Straus, "Reframing the Violence of the Father: Reverse Oedipal Fantasies in Chaucer's *Clerk's, Man of Law's,* and *Prioress's Tales,*" *Domestic Violence in Medieval Texts,* ed. Eve Salisbury, Georgiana Donavin, and Merrall Llewelyn Price (Gainesville: University Press of Florida, 2002), 122–38, at p. 124.

22. Gail Ashton, "Patient Mimesis: Griselda and the *Clerk's Tale,*" *Chaucer Review* 32 (1998): 232–38, at p. 236.

23. Kathy Lavezzo notes how the allegorization of Griselda disguises the historical conditions of the peasantry by constructing her as a female incarnation of Job: "Chaucer situates Griselda within an oppressive Christian discourse that hides the anguished historical reality of medieval peasant everyday life through the transcendental logic of typology, whereby Griselda's mangerlike home renders a type of Mary, and her nakedness throughout the tale makes her a figure of Job" ("Chaucer and Everyday Death: The *Clerk's Tale,* Burial, and the Subject of Poverty," *Studies in the Age of Chaucer* 23 [2001]: 255–87, at p. 271).

24. Kathryn L. McKinley, "The *Clerk's Tale:* Hagiography and the Problematics of Lay Sanctity," *Chaucer Review* 33 (1998): 90–111, at p. 96.

25. Tara Williams, " 'T'assaye in thee thy wommanheede': Griselda Chosen, Translated, and Tried," *Studies in the Age of Chaucer* 27 (2005): 93–127, at p. 103.

26. Ann W. Astell, "Translating Job as Female," *Translation Theory and Practice in the Middle Ages,* ed. Jeanette Beer (Kalamazoo, MI: Medieval Institute, 1997), 59–69, at p. 60.

27. Jill Mann, "Satisfaction and Payment in Middle English Literature," *Studies in the Age of Chaucer* 5 (1983): 17–48, at pp. 43–45.

28. Lynn Staley Johnson, "The Prince and His People: A Study of the Two Covenants in the *Clerk's Tale,*" *Chaucer Review* 10 (1975): 17–29, at p. 27.

29. Psychoanalytical readings of the *Clerk's Tale* are common. Patricia Cramer, e.g., interprets "Walter and Griselda as an 'ideal' Oedipal couple whose sadomasochistic rituals of dominance and submission enact gender roles prescribed by patriarchal social structures which Freud recognized and propagated through his Oedipal models of mental health" ("Lordship, Bondage, and the Erotic: The Psychological Bases of Chaucer's *Clerk's Tale,*" *Journal of English and Germanic Philology* 89 [1990]: 491–511, at p. 491). In a similar vein, Andrew Sprung sees in the tale "a pre-Oedipal search for recognition from the mother" (" 'If it youre will be,' " p. 348). Norman Lavers views Walter as the "analyst" who treats the "old neurotic Griselda" by encouraging her "to step aside for the new, healthy Griselda" ("Freud, the Clerkes Tale, and Literary Criticism," *College English* 26 [1964]: 180–87, at pp. 186–87), while Carol Heffernan reverses these roles in her declaration that "like many a psychiatric relationship between doctor and patient, Griselda's conversion of Walter takes time" ("Tyranny and Commune Profit in the *Clerk's Tale,*" *Chaucer Review* 17.4 [1983]: 332–40, at p. 336). See also Barrie Ruth Straus, "Reframing the

Violence of the Father: Reverse Oedipal Fantasies in Chaucer's *Clerk's, Man of Law's,* and *Prioress's Tales.*"

30. Allyson Newton, "The Occlusion of Maternity in Chaucer's *Clerk's Tale,*" *Medieval Mothering,* ed. John Carmi Parsons and Bonnie Wheeler (New York: Garland, 1996), 63–75, at p. 69.

31. Kathryn L. Lynch, "Despoiling Griselda: Chaucer's Walter and the Problem of Knowledge in the *Clerk's Tale,*" *Studies in the Age of Chaucer* 10 (1988): 41–70, at p. 44.

32. The crowd, however, displays little consistency in their desires, first asking Walter to marry and approving of Griselda, then disapproving of Walter, and finally approving of him again. The crowd can thus be seen to embody the fickleness and unknowability of desire, as well as the need for governance, as Michaela Paasche Grudin observes: "Contrasted with both Walter and Griselda, the diversity and changeability of the crowd becomes a powerful argument for the need for authority" ("Chaucer's *Clerk's Tale* as Political Paradox," *Studies in the Age of Chaucer* 11 [1989]: 63–92, at p. 81).

33. Studies of the Peasants' Revolt of 1381 in relation to Chaucer and fourteenth-century literature include Marion Turner, "*Troilus and Criseyde* and the 'Treasonous Aldermen' of 1382: Tales of the City in Late Fourteenth-Century London," *Studies in the Age of Chaucer* 25 (2003): 225–57; J. Stephen Russell, "Is London Burning?: A Chaucerian Allusion to the Rising of 1381," *Chaucer Review* 30.1 (1995): 107–09; Susan Crane, "The Writing Lesson of 1381," *Chaucer's England: Literature in Historical Context,* ed. Barbara Hanawalt (Minneapolis: University of Minnesota Press, 1992), pp. 201–21; and Steven Justice, *Writing and Rebellion: England in 1381* (Berkeley: University of California Press, 1996).

34. Crocker's argument focuses on the *Merchant's Tale* as she considers the ways in which

> the tale sets up a series of contrasts designed to distinguish between men in terms of their control of (ideas about) women. This project perpetually fails...because May's femininity exposes the fictionality of gender distinctions based on displays of agency or passivity. May's conduct does not shift from passive to active; instead, her behavior demonstrates that feminine passivity always requires agency. ("Performative Passivity and Fantasies of Masculinity in the *Merchant's Tale,*" *Chaucer Review* 38 [2003]: 178–98, at p. 179)

Despite the differences in genre between the *Clerk's Tale* and the *Merchant's Tale,* Crocker's findings in regard to female agency apply well to the *Clerk's Tale.* Crocker addresses the tensions between the *Clerk's Tale* and the *Merchant's Tale* on pp. 180–82; Carol Heffernan similarly notes the demands for agency in passivity, observing that, in the *Clerk's Tale,* "what is seemingly passive in actuality contains potent, even catalytic, force" ("Tyranny and Commune Profit in the *Clerk's Tale,*" pp. 335–36). In "The Pornographic Imagination," Susan Sontag suggests that the *Story of O* depicts its eponymous protagonist as "profoundly active in her own passivity," which suggests both the power inherent in passivity and its link to pornographic pleasures (*Styles of Radical Will* [New York: Farrar, Straus & Giroux, 1969], p. 53). To describe the *Clerk's Tale* as pornographic would stretch the boundaries of the text, but it is nonetheless critical to see the ways in which Griselda is eroticized through her passivity, as measured by Walter's inability to free himself of her.

35. Lynch, "Despoiling Griselda," p. 46.

36. Thomas A. Van, "Walter at the Stake: A Reading of Chaucer's *Clerk's Tale*," *Chaucer Review* 22.3 (1988): 214–24, at p. 215.

37. Hansen, *Chaucer and the Fictions of Gender*, p. 192.

38. Gilbert D. Chaitin, *Rhetoric and Culture in Lacan* (Cambridge: Cambridge University Press, 1996), p. 253.

39. Patrocinio Schweickart, "Reading Ourselves: Toward a Feminist Theory of Reading," *Contemporary Literary Criticism*, ed. Robert Con Davis and Ronald Schliefer, 2nd edn. (New York: Longman, 1989), 118–41, at p. 137.

40. Although noted textually as the "Lenvoy de Chaucer" by a scribal heading, the passage nonetheless "belongs dramatically to the Clerk" (*Riverside Chaucer*, p. 883, n. 1177). John Ganim suggests that the "Envoy represents a strikingly different voice than the one we expect from the Clerk, but that taken as a type, the Clerk could be expected to speak in that latter voice" ("Carnival Voices and the Envoy to the *Clerk's Tale*," *Chaucer Review* 22.2 [1987]: 111–27, at p. 113); Dinshaw sees this scribal heading as "articulat[ing] a double reading, a double perspective associated with the feminine, that describes larger Chaucerian poetic concerns as well" (*Chaucer's Sexual Poetics*, p. 154).

41. According to the *Middle English Dictionary*, "wif" refers generally to a "human biological female, a woman" with the more contextual sense of a "female partner in procreation," "mother," and "mistress of a household." It is, therefore, possible that the Clerk's use of "wyves" refers to all women and not specifically to married women. The context of his tale, however, indicates that he uses the word in its matrimonial and familial denotation.

42. That Harry refers to the Clerk's tale as "gentil" also highlights the social class issues inherent in the tale-telling competition, as the ostensibly aristocratic trait of gentility that Harry praises is one which he is culturally denied as a bourgeois man. For a discussion of gentility in regard to Harry, see chapter 3, esp. pp. 57–59.

43. See Richard Firth Green, "Women in Chaucer's Audience," *Chaucer Review* 18 (1983): 146–60.

44. The foundational study of the Marriage Group remains G. L. Kittredge, "Chaucer's Discussion of Marriage," *Modern Philology* 9 (1912): 435–67. Scholarly consensus sees this group of tales—from the Wife of Bath's to the Franklin's—as participating in a debate about marriage.

45. One could label Damian the masculine winner of the *Merchant's Tale* in that he sates his lascivious desires with May at January's expense. However,

Damian's hasty retreat from the scene of his sexual liaison and January's ignorance regarding the exact nature of the events that transpired focus the narrative's attention more on May's defeat of January's sexual authoritarianism than on male-male rivalries.

46. Van Dyke, "The Clerk's and Franklin's Subjected Subjects," p. 58.

47. Other *Canterbury Tales* also deny narrative pleasure, such as the *Squire's Tale,* the *Tale of Sir Thopas,* and the *Tale of Melibee,* but the ways in which the *Clerk's Tale* refuses readerly pleasures appears to be a unique instance of an aggression bleeding into the tale and foreclosing easy enjoyment of the text. Enjoyment of the *Clerk's Tale* can nonetheless be found queerly, freed from the bounds of normative readings.

48. Georgianna, "The *Clerk's Tale* and the Grammar of Assent," p. 794.

49. Georgianna, "The *Clerk's Tale* and the Grammar of Assent," p. 818.

Chapter 5   From Boys to Men to Hermaphrodites to Eunuchs: Queer Formations of Romance Masculinity and the Hagiographic Death Drive in *Amis and Amiloun*

1. As Tony Davenport trenchantly observes of the genre of romance, "Romance is notoriously difficult to define, largely because there is so much of it that it spills over and needs subcategories and overflow tanks. The central medieval sense is of narratives of chivalry, in which knights fight for honour and love" (*Medieval Narrative* [Oxford: Oxford University Press, 2004], p. 130). Given the vast field of medieval romance as outlined by Davenport, the goal of this chapter is to contextualize the ways in which *Amis and Amiloun,* a romance of male brotherhood, differs narratively from more typical romantic plots. I return to the question of genre and the ways in which it functions with romance sexuality throughout this chapter. Additional studies of romance include Helen Cooper, *The English Romance in Time: Transforming Motifs from Geoffrey of Monmouth to the Death of Shakespeare* (Oxford: Oxford University Press, 2004); Derek Pearsall, *Arthurian Romance: A Short Introduction* (Oxford: Blackwell, 2003); D. H. Green, *The Beginnings of Medieval Romance: Fact and Fiction, 1150–1220* (Cambridge: Cambridge University Press, 2002); Ad Putter and Jane Gilbert, eds., *The Spirit of Medieval English Popular Romance* (Harlow, England: Longman, 2000); Roberta Krueger, ed., *The Cambridge Companion to Medieval Romance* (Cambridge: Cambridge University Press, 2000); Douglas Kelly, *Medieval French Romance* (New York: Twayne, 1993); and Eugene Vinaver, *The Rise of Romance* (Oxford: Clarendon, 1971).

2. Anna Klosowska, *Queer Love in the Middle Ages* (New York: Palgrave Macmillan, 2005), p. 40.

3. Ruth Mazo Karras, *From Boys to Men: Formations of Masculinity in Late Medieval Europe* (Philadelphia: University of Pennsylvania Press, 2003),

p. 25. See esp. "Mail Bonding: Knights, Ladies, and the Proving of Manhood," pp. 20–66.

4. In terms of a lexicon describing sexuality in the Middle Ages, I use the terms *heterosexual* and *homosexual* to refer respectively to those acts and actors featuring members of the opposite sex and to those featuring members of the same sex. (See the discussion of queer critical lexicons in the Introduction, pp. 7–10.) I do not use these terms to indicate any sense of modern identity politics or subject formation. Despite the vast differences in views of sexuality between the medieval and the postmodern eras, sexuality nevertheless serves as a tool of ideological indoctrination and regulation in both time periods, and romances provide an appropriate venue for analyzing the ways in which medieval sexualities regulate narratival identities.

5. Beyond *Amis and Amiloun,* additional examples of medieval romances featuring two knights who have sworn brotherhood to each other include *Eger and Grime* and Chaucer's *Knight's Tale.* Romances such as *Guy of Warwick, Athelston,* and *King Horn* also depict a homosocial world of deep male friendships, yet these eponymous protagonists do not share the stage equally with their various male friends. Another subset of homosocial romances include narratives such as "The Tale of Balyn and Balan" in Malory's *Morte D'Arthur,* in which the brothers are united through consanguinity. For a discussion of the brotherhood oaths depicted in such texts, see Alan Bray, *The Friend* (Chicago, IL: University of Chicago Press, 2003), esp. "Wedded Brother," pp. 13–41.

6. John Boswell, *Same-Sex Unions in Premodern Europe* (New York: Villard, 1994), pp. 218–19.

7. Camille Paglia, "Plighting Their Troth," Review of John Boswell, *Same Sex Unions in Pre-Modern Europe* (*The Washington Post,* July 17 1994, p. wkb1).

8. Constance Woods, "Same-Sex Unions or Semantic Illusions?" *Communio* 22 (1995): 316–42, at p. 321.

9. Bray, *The Friend,* p. 40. Additional studies of homosocial brotherhood include Michael Rocke, *Forbidden Friendships: Homosexuality and Male Culture in Renaissance Florence* (New York: Oxford University Press, 1996); Reginald Hyatte, *The Arts of Friendship: The Idealization of Friendship in Medieval and Early Renaissance Literature* (Leiden: Brill, 1994); and Laurens J. Mills, *One Soul in Bodies Twain: Friendship in Tudor and Stuart Drama* (Bloomington, IN: Principia, 1937). See also C. Stephen Jaeger, *Ennobling Love: In Search of a Lost Sensibility* (Philadelphia: University of Pennsylvania Press, 1999), for his study of the ways in which homosocial love could tame culturally nonnormative sexualities in the Middle Ages: "Ennobling love had to manage sexuality, hold it in its place by severe discipline" (p. 7).

10. Woods, "Same-Sex Unions or Semantic Illusions," p. 320.

11. *Amis and Amiloun* survives in four manuscripts, Auchinleck (Advocates Library, Edinburgh), BM Egerton 2862 (British Library), Bodleian 21900

(Bodleian Library), and BM Harley 2386 (British Library). Auchinleck is
the basis for the editions both of MacEdward Leach (*Amis and Amiloun*
[London: Early English Text Society, 1937; reprint, 2001]) and of
Edward E. Foster (Amis and Amiloun, Robert of Cisyle, *and* Sir Amadace
[Kalamazoo, MI: Medieval Institute, 1997]). Studies of the Auchinleck
manuscript include Laura Hibbard Loomis, "The Auchinleck Manuscript
and a Possible London Bookshop of 1330–1340," *PMLA* 57.3 (1942):
595–627; Timothy A. Shonk, "A Study of the Auchinleck Manuscript:
Bookmen and Bookmaking in the Early Fourteenth Century," *Speculum*
60 (1985): 71–91; and Ralph Hanna, "Reconsidering the Auchinleck
Manuscript," *New Directions in Later Medieval Manuscript Studies: Essays
from the 1998 Harvard Conference*, ed. Derek Pearsall (York: York Medieval
Press, 2000), pp. 91–102 and his "Reading Romance in London: The
Auchinleck Manuscript and Laud misc. 622," *London Literature, 1300–
1380* (Cambridge: Cambridge University Press, 2005), pp. 104–47.

12. The basic plot of *Amis and Amioun* is cognate with the French romance
Ami et Amile. For a plot summary of the French version of the narrative,
see William Calin, "Women and Their Sexuality in *Ami et Amile:* An
Occasion to Deconstruct?" *Olifant* 16.1–2 (1991): 77–89, at p. 77. For
comparative studies of the French and English versions of the tale, see
Susan Dannenbaum, "Insular Tradition in the Story of *Amis and Amiloun*,"
Neophilologus 67 (1983): 611–22 and Susan Crane, *Insular Romance: Politics,
Faith, and Culture in Anglo-Norman and Middle English Literature* (Berkeley:
University of California Press, 1986), pp. 117–28.

13. Edward Foster, "Simplicity, Complexity, and Morality in Four Medieval
Romances," *Chaucer Review* 31.4 (1997): 401–19, at p. 411. Despite the
apparent propriety of Amis and Amiloun's pledge, the tale must eventually dismantle the queer potential in such brotherhoods.

14. Quotations of *Amis and Amiloun* are cited parenthetically and are taken
from Edward E. Foster, ed., Amis and Amiloun, Robert of Cisyle, *and* Sir
Amadace.

15. Cicero, *On the Good Life,* ed. Michael Grant (London: Penguin, 1971),
p. 189; qtd. in Robert Sturges, *Dialogue and Deviance: Male-Male Desire in
the Dialogue Genre* (New York: Palgrave Macmillan, 2005), p. 45.

16. For studies of chivalric communities, see Kenneth Hodges, *Forging
Chivalric Communities in Malory's* Le Morte D'Arthur (New York: Palgrave
Macmillan, 2005); Dorsey Armstrong, *Gender and the Chivalric Community
of Malory's* Morte d'Arthur (Gainesville: University Press of Florida,
2003); and Richard Zeikowitz, *Homoeroticism and Chivalry: Discourses of
Male Same-Sex Desire in the Fourteenth Century* (New York: Palgrave
Macmillan, 2003).

17. As a genre, romance is given to hyperbole and exaggeration, as the protagonist of each tale typically assumes the role of the bravest knight in the
land fighting for his lady, who is the most beautiful. It is nevertheless instructive to observe which narratival moments in a given romance rely on
exaggeration to make a critical point to its audience; in this instance, the

audience is intended to respond appropriately to the uniqueness and deep affection embodied in Amis and Amiloun's love for each other. Douglas Kelly notes that "romance descriptions are *merveilles,* extraordinary persons and things," and traces the trope of exaggeration through rhetoricians including Priscian, Isidore of Seville, and Matthew of Vendôme ("Exaggeration, Abrupt Conversion, and the Uses of Description in *Jaufre* and *Flamenca," Studia Occitanica in Memoriam Paul Remy,* ed. Hans-Erich Keller [Kalamazoo, MI: Medieval Institute, 1986], pp. 107–19, at p. 107).

18. For medieval marriage vows, see Barbara A. Hanawalt, *The Ties That Bound: Peasant Families in Medieval England* (New York: Oxford University Press, 1986), p. 203. Recent studies of medieval marriage include D. L. D'Avray, *Medieval Marriage: Symbolism and Society* (Oxford: Oxford University Press, 2005); Conor McCarthy, *Marriage in Medieval England: Law, Literature, and Practice* (Woodbridge: Boydell, 2004); and Christopher N. L. Brooke, *The Medieval Idea of Marriage* (Oxford: Oxford University Press, 1989).

19. Ojars Kratins, "The Middle English *Amis and Amiloun:* Chivalric Romance or Secular Hagiography?" *PMLA* 81.5 (1966): 347–54, at p. 348.

20. In analyzing hermaphroditism and intersexuality, Cheryl Chase states,

> Many people familiar with the ideas that gender is a phenomenon not adequately described by male/female dimorphism and that the interpretation of physical sex differences is culturally constructed remain surprised to learn just how variable sexual anatomy is. Though the male/female binary is constructed as natural and presumed to be immutable, the phenomenon of intersexuality offers clear evidence to the contrary and furnishes an opportunity to deploy "nature" strategically to disrupt heteronormative systems of sex, gender, and sexuality. ("Hermaphrodites with Attitude," *Queer Studies: An Interdisciplinary Reader,* ed. Robert J. Corber and Stephen Valocchi [Oxford: Blackwell, 2003], pp. 31–45, at p. 31)

Within the arena of compulsory queerness, however, the resistant force of hermaphroditism is shackled in service of normativity, and Amis and Amiloun's hermaphroditic figurings, in the end, shore up more than subvert ideological normativity. See also the discussion of contractual hermaphroditism in chapter 4, "'He nedes moot unto the pley assente': Queer Fidelities and Contractual Hermaphroditism in Chaucer's *Clerk's Tale,*" pp. 78–81.

21. Amiloun serves as the Duke's "chef steward in halle," in contrast to Amis's enemy, the "chef steward of alle [the Duke's] lond" (206). It is potentially confusing for the reader to disentangle these two chief stewards, but it appears that the author distinguishes between them in their respective domains of interior household and exterior lands.

22. John C. Ford, "Contrasting the Identical: Differentiation of the 'Indistinguishable' Characters of *Amis and Amiloun," Neophilologus* 86 (2002): 311–23, at pp. 320–21.

23. For a study of the women of *Amis and Amiloun,* see Jean Jost, "Hearing the Female Voice: Transgression in *Amis and Amiloun,*" *Medieval Perspectives* 10 (1995): 116–32. Jost argues that "these disarmingly strong wives...high-light...the indecisive or ineffective behavior of their weak but sensitive husbands" (p. 130). In a complementary manner, my goal is to outline the ways in which Amis's and Amiloun's enervated masculinities reflect their hermaphroditic relationship with each other. For studies of the women in the French tale *Ami et Amile,* see William Calin, "Woman and Their Sexuality in *Ami et Amile*"; Sarah Kay, "Seduction and Suppression in *Ami et Amile,*" *French Studies* 44 (1990): 129–42; and Michel Zink, "Lubias et Belissant dans la chanson d'*Ami et Amile,*" *Littératures* 17 (1987): 11–24.

24. Comic tensions between knights and clerics appear frequently in medieval debate literature. Critical studies of this tradition include Oleg V. Bychkov, "The Debate between the Knight and the Cleric: Emendation and Translation," *Cithara* 40.1 (2000): 3–36; Charles Oulmont, *Les débats du clerc et du chevalier dans la littérature poétique du Moyen-Age* (Paris: Honore Champion, 1911); and H. Walther, *Das Streitgedicht in der lateinischen Literatur des Mittelalters* (München: Beck, 1920).

25. J. R. R. Tolkien and E. V. Gordon, eds., *Sir Gawain and the Green Knight,* 2nd edn., ed. Norman Davis (Oxford: Clarendon, 1967), line 1293. I have modernized thorn and yogh.

26. In his treatise on courtly love, Andreas Capellanus rejects rape as inappropriate behavior for a knight: "That which a lover takes against the will of his beloved has no relish" (*The Art of Courtly Love,* trans. John Jay Parry [New York: Columbia University Press, 1960], p. 184). Of course, Andreas's highly ironic tone often makes deciphering his meaning difficult, but one need only remember Chaucer's *Wife of Bath's Tale* to see the ways in which rape fractures a courtly construction of appropriate knightly masculinity. See also Kathryn Gravdal, *Ravishing Maidens: Writing Rape in Medieval French Literature and Law* (Philadelphia: University of Pennsylvania Press, 1991), esp. pp. 104–21, for her discussion of rape as a "game." For visual depictions of rape in the Middle Ages, see Diane Wolfthal, *Images of Rape: The "Heroic" Tradition and Its Alternatives* (Cambridge: Cambridge University Press, 1999), esp. pp. 60–98.

27. Jacques Lacan, *The Seminar of Jacques Lacan, Book VII: The Ethics of Psychoanalysis 1959–1960,* ed. Jacques-Alain Miller, trans. Dennis Potter (New York: Norton, 1992), p. 150.

28. For medieval studies of the gaze and the ways in which gender roles are enacted through it, see Sarah Stanbury, *Seeing the* Gawain-*Poet* (Philadelphia: University of Pennsylvania Press, 1991) and her "Regimes of the Visual in Premodern England: Gaze, Body, and Chaucer's *Clerk's Tale,*" *New Literary History* 28.2 (1997): 261–89; David C. Lindberg, *Theories of Vision from Al-Kindi to Kepler* (Chicago, IL: University of Chicago Press, 1981); and Dallas G. Denery, *Seeing and Being Seen in the Later Medieval World: Optics, Theology, and Religious Life* (Cambridge: Cambridge University Press, 2005). Many current theoretical approaches

to the gaze are based on the ideas of Laura Mulvey, *Visual and Other Pleasures* (Bloomington: Indiana University Press, 1989), esp. "Visual Pleasure and Narrative Cinema," pp. 14–26. Mulvey argues that a masculinist gaze typically takes pleasure in constructing a vision of a feminized object. Such a paradigm of vision, though pervasive, is neither historically nor culturally universal, and critics must also take into account when such dynamics are subverted.

29. Sheila Delany, "A, A, and B: Coding Same-Sex Union in *Amis and Amiloun*," *Pulp Fictions of Medieval England: Essays in Popular Romance,* ed. Nicola McDonald (Manchester: Manchester University Press, 2004), 63–81, at p. 68.

30. For the feminine symbolism of cups, see Robert E. Bell, *Dictionary of Classical Mythology: Symbols, Attributes, and Associations* (Santa Barbara, CA: ABC Clio, 1982), pp. 59–60. Additionally, these golden cups also link Amis and Amiloun to queerness, as cupbearers (such as Ganymede) were frequently viewed as homosexual.

31. Both Amis and Amiloun are descended from barons ("Her faders were barons hende" [7]), and thus it is apparent that Amis successfully climbs the peerage through his advantageous marriage to Belisaunt. In contrast, Amiloun is never described as a duke.

32. Saul Nathaniel Brody, *The Disease of the Soul: Leprosy in Medieval Literature* (Ithaca, NY: Cornell University Press, 1974), p. 147. See also pp. 159–73 for a discussion of leprosy in *Amis and Amiloun*. Other studies of medieval leprosy include Carole Rawcliffe, *Leprosy in Medieval England* (Suffolk, Woodbridge: Boydell, 2006); Paul Remy, "La Lèpre, thème littéraire au moyen age," *Le Moyen Age* 52 (1946): 195–242; and Peter Richards, *The Medieval Leper and His Northern Heirs* (Cambridge: D. S. Brewer, 1977).

33. Although Child Owaines may not yet be a man within courtly circles, his beauty elicits great praise from other men (1909–20, 1969–80). As with Amis and Amiloun earlier in the text, the reader again sees the ways in which male beauty, as appreciated by other men, establishes a man's worth, honor, and masculinity.

34. For a study of child sacrifice in medieval literature, see Peggy McCracken, "Engendering Sacrifice: Blood, Lineage, and Infanticide in Old French Literature," *Speculum* 77 (2002): 55–75. McCracken analyzes the French forebears of the *Amis and Amiloun* legend and concludes, "Medieval narratives about sacrifice suggest that the blood of sacrifice is gendered symbolically, not according to the identity of the sacrifice—in both *Ami et Amile* and *Philomena* the murdered children are sons—but by the identity of the sacrificer" (p. 74).

35. Kathryn Hume, "*Amis and Amiloun* and the Aesthetics of Middle English Romance," *Studies in Philology* 70 (1973): 19–41, at p. 28.

36. Dale Kramer, "Structural Artistry in *Amis and Amiloun*," *Annuale Mediaevale* 9 (1968): 103–22, at p. 118.

37. Germaine Greer, *The Female Eunuch* (London: MacGibbon & Kee, 1970), p. 16.

38. Mathew Kuefler, *The Manly Eunuch: Masculinity, Gender Ambiguity, and Christian Ideology in Late Antiquity* (Chicago, IL: University of Chicago Press, 2001), p. 14.

39. Judith Butler, *Bodies That Matter: On the Discursive Limits of "Sex"* (New York: Routledge, 1993), p. 153.

40. Gary Taylor sardonically observes that "the eunuch was a prosthesis, a weapon used by one man in his sexual rivalry with other males: more eyes, more minds and hands, guardians of all those precious uteruses" (*Castration: An Abbreviated History of Western Manhood* [New York: Routledge, 2000], p. 35).

41. Mario Roques, ed., *Les romans de Chrétien de Troyes, édités d'après la copie de Guiot (Bibl. Nat. fr 794), 4: Le Chevalier au lion (Yvain)* (Paris: Champion, 1965), lines 1698–1703. Camilla Rachal assisted with this translation.

42. Many romances follow this pattern, with the heteronormative hero living "happily ever after" with his beloved. Within the vast field of romance, however, exceptions also appear. Heteronormative hero King Horn and his queen, e.g., are dispatched to heaven as well: "Nu ben hi bothe dede— / Crist to hevene hem lede!" (*Four Romances of England: King Horn, Havelock the Dane, Bevis of Hampton, Athelston,* ed. Ronald B. Herzman, Graham Drake, and Eve Salisbury [Kalamazoo, MI: Medieval Institute, 1999], lines 1537–38). The difference between the deaths of Horn and Rymenhild and of Amis and Amiloun is quite simply the difference between the heteronormative and the queer. Horn and Rymenhild can be focused on as an exemplary couple obtaining the graces of heaven, but Amis's and Amiloun's deaths include a disciplinary element that precludes their relationship from displaying any hint of sexuality.

43. Herbert Marcuse, "The Ideology of Death," *The Meaning of Death,* ed. Herman Feifel (New York: McGraw-Hill, 1959), p. 74.

44. Anis Bawarshi, "The Genre Function," *College English* 62 (2000): 335–60, at p. 354.

45. Recent studies of hagiography include Sarah Salih, ed., *A Companion to Middle English Hagiography* (Cambridge: D. S. Brewer, 2006); Gail Ashton, *The Generation of Identity in Late Medieval Hagiography: Speaking the Saint* (London: Routledge, 2000); Paul Szarmach, ed., *Holy Men and Holy Women: Old English Prose Saints' Lives and Their Contexts* (Albany: State University of New York Press, 1996); Renate Blumenfeld-Kosinski and Timea Szell, eds., *Images of Sainthood in Medieval Europe* (Ithaca, NY: Cornell University Press, 1991); Sandro Sticca, ed., *Saints: Studies in Hagiography* (Binghamton, NY: Medieval and Renaissance Texts and Studies, 1996); and Thomas J. Heffernan, *Sacred Biography: Saints and Their Biographers in the Middle Ages* (New York: Oxford University Press, 1988).

46. Kratins, "The Middle English *Amis and Amiloun*," esp. pp. 353–54. See also Delany, "A, A, and B: Coding Same-Sex Union in *Amis and Amiloun*," in which she declares that the narrative "is loosely framed as hagiography" (p. 165); and Dieter Mehl, *The Middle English Romances of the*

Thirteenth and Fourteenth Centuries (London: Routledge & Kegan Paul, 1968), pp. 110–11.

47. *Amis and Amiloun* bears hagiographic roots, as early avatars of the story include a Latin verse epistle by the French monk Radulfus Tortarius (before 1114) and the *Vita sanctorum Amici et Amelii* (ca. 1150). These texts can be found in Francis Bar, ed., *Les epîtres latines de Raoul le Tourntier: etude de sources; la légende d'Ami et d'Amile* (Paris: Droz, 1937) and Eugen Kölbing, ed., *Amis and Amiloun, zugleich mit der altfranzösischen Queele* (Heilbronn: Henninger, 1884). For a study of hagiographic romance, see Alison Goddard Elliott, *Roads to Paradise: Reading the Lives of Early Saints* (Hanover, NH: University Press of New England, 1987), esp. pp. 42–76.

48. For recent studies of gender and sexuality in saints' lives, see Samantha J. E. Riches and Sarah Salih, eds., *Gender and Holiness: Men, Women, and Saints in Late Medieval Europe* (London: Routledge, 2002); Julie E. Fromer, "Spectators of Martyrdom: Corporeality and Sexuality in the *Liflade ant te Passiun of Seinte Margarete*," *Intersections of Sexuality and the Divine in Medieval Culture: The Word Made Flesh,* ed. Susannah Mary Chewning (Aldershot, UK: Ashgate, 2005), pp. 89–106; Theresa Coletti, "Genealogy, Sexuality, and Sacred Power: The Saint Anne Dedication of the Digby *Candlemas Day and the Killing of the Children of Israel*," *Journal of Medieval and Early Modern Studies* 29.1 (1999): 25–59; and Ruth Mazo Karras, "Holy Harlots: Prostitute Saints in Medieval Legend," *Journal of the History of Sexuality* 1.1 (1990): 3–22.

49. Simon Gaunt, "Straight Minds/Queer Wishes in Old French Hagiography: *La vie de Sainte Euphrosine*," *Premodern Sexualities,* ed. Louise Fradenburg and Carla Freccero (New York: Routledge, 1996), 155–73, at p. 155.

Chapter 6   Queer Castration, Patriarchal Privilege, and the Comic Phallus in *Eger and Grime*

1. *Eger and Grime* survives in two manuscripts, the Percy and the Huntington-Laing editions. For comparisons of the two editions, see James Ralston Caldwell, ed., *Eger and Grime: A Parallel-Text Edition of the Percy and the Huntington-Laing Versions of the Romance* (Cambridge, MA: Harvard University Press, 1933), pp. 20–51; Antony J. Hasler, "Romance and Its Discontents in *Eger and Grime,*" *The Spirit of Medieval English Popular Romance,* ed. Ad Putter and Jane Gilbert (Harlow, England: Longman, 2000), 200–18, at p. 202; and Matthew McDiarmid, "The Metrical Chronicles and Non-Alliterative Romances," *The History of Scottish Literature: Origins to 1660, Vol. 1,* ed. R. D. S. Jack (Aberdeen: Aberdeen University Press, 1988), p. 34. The Huntington-Laing manuscript, with 2860 lines, is almost twice as long as the 1474 lines of Percy. Antony Hasler summarizes that "[Huntington-Laing] presents a fuller and more—though by no means wholly—coherent narrative. Some of

[Percy's] readers have nevertheless found it tersely suggestive rather than messily over-packed" (p. 202). In this study, I focus on the Percy version of the narrative, primarily because its terse style complements its sardonic perspective on male patriarchal privilege. Documentary evidence details that *Eger and Grime* was performed for King James IV in April 1497. This date does not tell us the time of the poem's composition, but it nonetheless provides a useful point for contextualizing its historical circumstances (Caldwell, *Eger and Grime,* pp. 6–12).

2. Mabel Van Duzee outlines points of congruency between *Eger and Grime* and such other medieval narratives as *Amis and Amiloun, Saduis and Galo,* and *Pwyll* (*A Medieval Romance of Friendship*: Eger and Grime [New York: Burt Franklin, 1963], pp. 18–40).

3. Marcel Gutwirth, *Laughing Matter: An Essay on the Comic* (Ithaca, NY: Cornell University Press, 1993), p. 164.

4. Grime describes Palyas as his brother ("'I haue a brother that men call Palyas, / a noble squire & worthye is'" [523–24]), but it is never explicitly revealed whether Palyas is a brother by blood (like Eger's older brother) or by oaths (like Eger and Grime's relationship). Brotherhood is the central model of homosocial fidelity in this romance, but its parameters and permutations are at times surprisingly nebulous. Certainly, though, Grime's relationship with Palyas in no way undermines the primacy of his fraternal relationship with Eger. (Quotations of *Eger and Grime* are cited parenthetically and are taken from Caldwell, ed., *Eger and Grime,* which transcribes both the Percy and the Huntington-Laing editions. Unless otherwise noted, all citations refer to the Percy manuscript.)

5. David E. Faris, "The Art of Adventure in the Middle English Romance: *Ywain and Gawain, Eger and Grime,*" *Studia Neophilologica* 53.1 (1981): 91–100, at p. 100.

6. For analysis of knightly brotherhood oaths, see chapter 5, pp. 102–3. Richard Zeikowitz examines chivalric treatises and the cultural conditions that necessitate their endorsement of homosocial intimacy and friendship (*Homoeroticism and Chivalry: Discourses of Male Same-Sex Desire in the Fourteenth Century* [New York: Palgrave Macmillan, 2003], esp. pp. 18–43). Caldwell addresses the topic of "Artificial Brotherhood" in his introduction to the poem (64–79). See also C. Stephen Jaeger, *Ennobling Love: In Search of a Lost Sensibility* (Philadelphia: University of Pennsylvania Press, 1999), esp. pp. 54–58.

7. Karma Lochrie, *Covert Operations: The Medieval Uses of Secrecy* (Philadelphia: University of Pennsylvania Press, 1999), p. 123. Lochrie refers here to medieval medical texts, but her observation captures well the ways that male secrets also eroticize the generic structures of romance.

8. For a brief review of medieval primogeniture and its disenfranchising impact on younger sons, see Frances and Joseph Gies, "The Aristocratic Lineage: Perils of Primogeniture," *Marriage and the Family in the Middle Ages* (New York: Harper and Row, 1987), pp. 186–95.

9. Tension between blood brothers appears frequently in romances. For example, see Susan Crane's analysis of *Gamelyn* in *Insular Romance: Politics, Faith, and Culture in Anglo-Norman and Middle English Literature* (Berkeley: University of California Press, 1986), pp. 73–74.

10. Georges Duby, *Love and Marriage in the Middle Ages,* trans. Jane Dunnett (Chicago, IL: University of Chicago Press, 1994), p. 14. It should be noted that this quotation refers specifically to the cultural milieu of twelfth-century northern France, but these social practices continued to influence romances throughout the Middle Ages. See also Noël James Menuge, *Medieval English Wardship in Romance and Law* (Cambridge: D. S. Brewer, 2001).

11. Geraldine Heng, *Empire of Magic: Medieval Romance and the Politics of Cultural Fantasy* (New York: Columbia University Press, 2003), p. 121.

12. Homi K. Bhabha, "Are You a Man or a Mouse?" *Constructing Masculinity,* ed. Maurice Berger, Brian Wallis, and Simon Watson (New York: Routledge, 1995), 57–65, at p. 58.

13. For scholarship on castration in the Middle Ages, see Mathew Kuefler, "Castration and Eunuchism in the Middle Ages," *Handbook of Medieval Sexuality,* ed. Vern Bullough and James Brundage (New York: Garland, 1996), pp. 279–306; Gary Taylor, *Castration: An Abbreviated History of Western Manhood* (New York: Routledge, 2000); David DeVries, "Fathers and Sons: Patristic Exegesis and the Castration Complex," *Gender Rhetorics: Postures of Dominance and Submission in History,* ed. Richard Trexler (Binghamton, NY: Center for Medieval and Renaissance Texts and Studies, 1994), pp. 33–45; Jacqueline Murray, "Mystical Castration: Some Reflections on Peter Abelard, Hugh of Lincoln and Sexual Control," *Conflicted Identities and Multiple Masculinities: Men in the Medieval West,* ed. Jacqueline Murray (New York: Garland, 1999), pp. 73–91; and Anna Klosowska, "Grail Narratives: Castration as a Thematic Site," *Queer Love in the Middle Ages* (New York: Palgrave Macmillan, 2005), pp. 21–67.

14. Klosowska, *Queer Love in the Middle Ages,* p. 55.

15. Much psychoanalytic and postmodern theory is predicated upon the phallus, as constructed by Sigmund Freud in *The Interpretation of Dreams* (New York: Gramercy, 1996). The topic of psychoanalytic theory and its application to literature is vast, but representative critical works include Jacques Lacan, *Feminine Sexuality: Jacques Lacan and the école freudienne,* ed. Juliet Mitchell and Jacqueline Rose (New York: Norton, 1982); Julia Kristeva, *Desire in Language: A Semiotic Approach to Literature and Art,* ed. Leon S. Roudiez, trans. Thomas Gora, Alice Jardine, and Leon S. Roudiez (New York: Columbia University Press, 1980); Judith Butler, *Gender Trouble: Feminism and the Subversion of Identity* (New York: Routledge, 1990) and *Bodies That Matter: On the Discursive Limits of "Sex"* (New York: Routledge, 1993). In considering the phallus as a signifier in *Eger and Grime,* my goal is to explore the connections between queered men and sneering women, as mediated through the comedy of the phallus

and its metaphors. For a psychoanalytic reading of *Eger and Grime,* see Antony J. Hasler, "Romance and Its Discontents in *Eger and Grime,*" who argues "that loss and fantasy structure the narrative of *Eger,* and...that *Eger* strives to accommodate loss through reliance on a common romance pattern of *compagnonnage* or male companionship" (pp. 202–03). This study complements Hasler's by focusing on the comic potential in castration and the phallus.

16. This biblical quotation is taken from Michael Coogan, ed., *The New Oxford Annotated Bible,* 3rd edn. (Oxford: Oxford University Press, 2001). For a study of the early phallus, see Daniel Boyarin, "On the History of the Early Phallus," *Gender and Difference in the Middle Ages,* ed. Sharon Farmer and Carol Braun Pasternack (Minneapolis: University of Minnesota Press, 2003), pp. 3–44, in which he states, "The first Adam is not a male body but rather the male androgyne represented as pure Mind and as an Idea of the male, so also, the Phallus is not the penis, but it is a disembodied idealization of the penis, a Platonic Idea of the penis" (p. 9). See also his "What Does a Jew Want? or, The Political Meaning of the Phallus," *The Psychoanalysis of Race,* ed. Christopher Lane (New York: Columbia University Press, 1998), pp. 211–40.

17. Siobhain Bly Calkin, *Saracens and the Making of English Identity: The Auchinleck Manuscript* (New York: Routledge, 2005), p. 211. Additional postcolonial studies of medievalism include Patricia Clare Ingham and Michelle R. Warren, eds., *Postcolonial Moves: Medieval through Modern* (New York: Palgrave Macmillan, 2003); Ananya Jahanara Kabir and Deanne Williams, eds., *Postcolonial Approaches to the European Middle Ages: Translating Cultures* (Cambridge: Cambridge University Press, 2005); and Jeffrey Jerome Cohen, ed., *The Postcolonial Middle Ages* (New York: St. Martin's, 2000).

18. Derek Pearsall, "Courtesy and Chivalry in *Sir Gawain and the Green Knight:* The Order of Shame and the Invention of Embarrassment," *A Companion to the* Gawain-*Poet,* ed. Derek Brewer and Jonathan Gibson (Cambridge: D. S. Brewer, 1997), 351–62, at p. 361.

19. The author of *Eger and Grime* repeatedly delays identifying characters by name, a fairly common trope of medieval romance (as in Chrétien de Troyes's *Lancelot*). Grey Steele is not named until line 345, after he has defeated Eger. Loosepine is not named until line 1406, when she marries Grime. In *Eger and Grime,* the narratival reticence to name characters builds suspense, but it also underscores the ways in which characters are constructed through their relationships—whether combative or nurturing—to Eger's and Grime's masculinities.

20. Michael Warner, *The Trouble with Normal: Sex, Politics, and the Ethics of Queer Life* (New York: Free Press, 1999), p. 3.

21. Judith Halberstam, "Shame and White Gay Masculinity," *Social Text* 23.3–4 (2005): 219–33, at p. 220.

22. In an analysis of film and phallic comedy, Peter Lehman suggests the possibility of masochistic pleasure for men through phallic jokes: "When

beautiful, desirable women erotically look at and make evaluative judgments about the penis, the structure may be masochistically pleasurable
for men" ("Penis Jokes and Hollywood's Unconscious," *Comedy/Cinema/
Theory,* ed. Andrew Horton [Berkeley: University of California Press,
1991], 43–59, at p. 57). Such a viewpoint is intriguing, and one might
indeed locate latent pleasure in Eger's queered identity; nonetheless, the
narrative trajectory of *Eger and Grime* focuses on removing the shame
kindled by his metaphoric castration rather than finding latent pleasure in
his humiliation.

23. Women's position in medieval society and marriage is a vast topic.
Representative works that inform my analysis include Helen Jewell,
Women in Dark Age and Early Medieval Europe, c. 500–1200 (Basingstoke,
Hampshire: Palgrave Macmillan, 2007); Kim M. Phillips, *Medieval
Maidens: Young Women and Gender in England, 1270–1540* (Manchester:
Manchester University Press, 2003); Mavis Mate, *Women in Medieval
English Society* (Cambridge: Cambridge University Press, 1999); Robert
Edwards and Vickie Ziegler, eds., *Matrons and Marginal Women in Medieval
Society* (Suffolk, UK: Boydell, 1995); Emilie Amt, ed., *Women's Lives in
Medieval Europe: A Sourcebook* (New York: Routledge, 1993); Constance
Rousseau and Joel Rosenthal, eds., *Women, Marriage, and Family in
Medieval Christendom* (Kalamazoo, MI: Medieval Institute, 1998);
Christopher N. L. Brooke, *The Medieval Idea of Marriage* (Oxford: Oxford
University Press, 1989); Georges Duby, *Love and Marriage in the Middle
Ages,* trans. Jane Dunnett (Chicago, IL: University of Chicago Press,
1988); and Shulamith Shahar, *The Fourth Estate: A History of Women in the
Middle Ages,* trans. Chaya Galai (London: Methuen, 1983).

24. In medieval romance, the need for a son to inherit his family's estate and
to continue the family dynasty often casts daughters in the position of
unwanted or problematic heirs. For example, this cultural preference for
sons catalyzes Silence's transvestism in *Roman de Silence.* Studies of the
connection between *Roman de Silence* and patriarchal inheritance customs
include Christopher Callahan, "Canon Law, Primogeniture, and the
Marriage of Ebain and Silence," *Romance Quarterly* 49.1 (2002): 12–20;
and Sharon Kinoshita, "Male-Order Brides: Marriage, Patriarchy, and
Monarchy in the *Roman de Silence*," *Arthuriana* 12.1 (2002): 64–75 and her
"Heldris de Cornuâlle's *Roman de Silence* and the Feudal Politics of
Lineage," *PMLA* 110.3 (1995): 397–409.

25. As noted in chapter 5 regarding the construction of the courtly lady,
Jacques Lacan argues that she "is as arbitrary as possible in the tests she
imposes on her servant" and that she thus represents a "terrifying, in-
human partner" (*The Seminar of Jacques Lacan, Book VII: The Ethics of
Psychoanalysis 1959–1960,* ed. Jacques-Alain Miller, trans. Dennis Potter
[New York: Norton, 1992], p. 150). Like Belisaunt in *Amis and Amiloun,*
Winglaine similarly serves as an arbitrary obstacle to Eger's attainment of
masculine privilege.

26. For a discussion of the erotic triangle, see chapter 2, pp. 22–26.

27. Butler, *Gender Trouble,* p. 45.
28. Lacan, *Feminine Sexuality,* p. 83.
29. Additional passages addressing Loosepine's status as a healer include 385–88 and 395–96.
30. Although Loosepine determines to marry Grime, her father then "awards" her to Grime:
    > "for I haue a daughter that is my heyre
    > of all my Lands, that is soe faire;
    > & if thou wilt wed that Ladye free,
    > with all my hart I will giue her thee." (1267–70)

    Here again we see the limitations of female agency within the world of romance.
31. Studies of the connection between romance and the novel include Caroline A. Jewers, *Chivalric Fiction and the History of the Novel* (Gainesville: University Press of Florida, 2000) and David H. Richter, *The Progress of Romance: Literary Historiography and the Gothic Novel* (Columbus: Ohio State University Press, 1996). Primary sources can be found in Ioan Williams, ed., *Novel and Romance, 1700–1800: A Documentary Record* (New York: Barnes & Noble, 1970).
32. The influence of medieval romance on later dramatic traditions is well documented. For bibliographic sources, see J. Paul McRoberts, *Shakespeare and the Medieval Tradition: An Annotated Bibliography* (New York: Garland, 1985), esp. pp. 87–94. The connection between medieval romance and comedy has been widely studied, as in E. Talbot Donaldson, *The Swan at the Well: Shakespeare Reading Chaucer* (New Haven, CT: Yale University Press, 1985), esp. pp. 30–49, and Michael Hays has recently linked chivalric romances to tragedy as well, in his *Shakespearian Tragedy as Chivalric Romance: Rethinking* Macbeth, Hamlet, Othello, *and* King Lear (Cambridge: D. S. Brewer, 2003).
33. Harriet Hudson, ed., *Four Middle English Romances:* Sir Isumbras, Octavian, Sir Eglamour of Artois, Sir Tryamour (Kalamazoo, MI: Medieval Institute, 1996), p. 118.

Chapter 7   Conclusion: Compulsory Queerness and the Pleasures of Medievalism

1. The definitive study of American anti-intellectualism remains Richard Hofstadter's *Anti-Intellectualism in American Life* (New York: Knopf, 1963). Sadly, many of the trends that he documents remain readily apparent in today's society.
2. In delineating the potential dichotomy between medievalism and the cyber-present, I do not wish to occlude the fascinating work on cyber-constructions of the Middle Ages nor the scholars who are undertaking such groundbreaking work. Numerous studies illustrate the ways in which the past is increasingly illuminated by modern technologies, such as Martin Foys, ed., *The Bayeux Tapestry on CD-Rom* (Cambridge: Boydell & Brewer,

2002); Daniel Paul O'Donnell, *Cædmon's Hymn: A Multimedia Study, Archive and Edition* (Cambridge: D. S. Brewer, 2005); *The Piers Plowman Electronic Archive: Huntington Library Ms Hm 128 (Hm)*, ed. Michael Calabrese, Hoyt N. Duggan, and Thorlac Turville-Petre, SEENET Series A.9 (Boston, MA: Medieval Academy of America and Boydell & Brewer, 2006). Also, medieval websites abound.

3. Kathleen Biddick, *The Shock of Medievalism* (Durham, NC: Duke University Press, 1998), p. 12.

4. In contrast, Bruce Holsinger demonstrates that much postmodern thought depends upon a dialectic yet somewhat sentimentalized engagement with medievalism; see his *The Premodern Condition: Medievalism and the Making of Theory* (Chicago, IL: University of Chicago Press, 2005).

5. This dynamic is compellingly explored in such studies as Allen J. Frantzen, *Desire for Origins: New Language, Old English, and Teaching the Tradition* (New Brunswick, NJ: Rutgers University Press, 1990).

6. Alexandre Leupin, "The Middle Ages, the Other," *Diacritics* 13.3 (1983): 21–31, at p. 30.

7. Jeffrey Jerome Cohen, "Introduction: Midcolonial," *The Postcolonial Middle Ages*, ed. Jeffrey Jerome Cohen (New York: Palgrave, 2000), pp. 1–17, at p. 5.

8. Vivian Sobchack, "The Insistent Fringe: Moving Images and Historical Consciousness," *History and Theory* 36.4 (1997): 4–20, at p. 9.

9. Paul Zumthor, *Speaking of the Middle Ages* (Lincoln: University of Nebraska Press, 1986), p. 66.

10. As Barthes writes, "What pleasure wants is the site of a loss, the seam, the cut, the deflation, the *dissolve* which seizes the subject in the midst of bliss" (*The Pleasure of the Text,* trans. Richard Miller [New York: Hill & Wang, 1975], p. 7).

11. Clifton Fadiman, *Any Number Can Play* (Cleveland, OH: World Publishing, 1957), p. 367.

12. Catherine Brown, "In the Middle," *Journal of Medieval and Early Modern Studies* 30.3 (2000): 547–74, at p. 551.

13. Michel Foucault, *Discipline and Punish: The Birth of the Prison*, trans. Alan Sheridan, 2nd edn. (New York: Vintage, 1995), p. 176.

14. L. O. Aranye Fradenburg, *Sacrifice Your Love: Psychoanalysis, Historicism, Chaucer* (Minneapolis: University of Minnesota Press, 2002), p. 45.

BIBLIOGRAPHY

Abelard. *Medieval Latin Lyrics*. Ed. and trans. Helen Waddell. New York: Norton, 1948. 162–69.

Ackerman, Susan. *When Heroes Love: The Ambiguity of Eros in the Stories of Gilgamesh and David*. New York: Columbia University Press, 2005.

Aers, David. "The Self Mourning: Reflections on *Pearl*." *Speculum* 68 (1993): 54–73.

Ailes, M. J. "The Medieval Male Couple and the Language of Homosociality." Hadley, *Masculinity* 214–37.

Akbari, Suzanne Conklin. *Seeing through the Veil: Optical Theory and Medieval Allegory*. Toronto: University of Toronto Press, 2004.

Allen, Mark. "Mirth and Bourgeois Masculinity in Chaucer's Host." Beidler, *Masculinities in Chaucer* 9–21.

Althusser, Louis. *Lenin and Philosophy and Other Essays*. Trans. Ben Brewster. London: NLB, 1971.

Amt, Emilie, ed. *Women's Lives in Medieval Europe: A Sourcebook*. New York: Routledge, 1993.

Andreas Capellanus. *The Art of Courtly Love*. Trans. John Jay Parry. New York: Columbia University Press, 1960.

Andrew, Malcolm. "Games." *A Companion to Chaucer*. Ed. Peter Brown. Oxford: Blackwell, 2000. 167–79.

Andrew, Malcolm and Ronald Waldron, eds. *The Poems of the* Pearl *Manuscript*. Berkeley: University of California Press, 1978.

Armstrong, Dorsey. *Gender and the Chivalric Community of Malory's* Morte d'Arthur. Gainesville: University Press of Florida, 2003.

Ashley, Kathleen and Robert L. A. Clark, eds. *Medieval Conduct*. Minneapolis: University of Minneapolis Press, 2001.

Ashton, Gail. *The Generation of Identity in Late Medieval Hagiography: Speaking the Saint*. London: Routledge, 2000.

———. "Patient Mimesis: Griselda and the *Clerk's Tale*." *Chaucer Review* 32 (1998): 232–38.

Astell, Ann W. *Political Allegory in Late Medieval England*. Ithaca, NY: Cornell University Press, 1999.

———. "Translating Job as Female." *Translation Theory and Practice in the Middle Ages*. Ed. Jeanette Beer. Kalamazoo, MI: Medieval Institute, 1997. 59–69.

Bagemihl, Bruce. *Biological Exuberance: Animal Homosexuality and Natural Diversity.* New York: St. Martin's, 1999.

Baily, J. Michael. *The Man Who Would Be Queen: The Science of Gender-Bending and Transsexualism.* Washington, DC: Joseph Henry, 2003.

Baird-Lange, Lorrayne Y. "Symbolic Ambivalence in 'I haue a gentil cok.'" *Fifteenth-Century Studies* 11 (1985): 1–5.

Bakhtin, Mikhail. *Rabelais and His World.* Trans. Hélène Iswolsky. Bloomington: Indiana University Press, 1984.

Baldwin, Dean R. *"Amis and Amiloun:* The Testing of Treuthe." *Papers on Language and Literature* 16 (1980): 353–65.

Bar, Francis, ed. *Les epîtres latines de Raoul le Tourntier: etude de sources; la légende d'Ami et d'Amile.* Paris: Droz, 1937.

Barthes, Roland. *The Pleasure of the Text.* Trans. Richard Miller. New York: Hill & Wang, 1975.

Bawarshi, Anis. "The Genre Function." *College English* 62 (2000): 335–60.

Baudri of Bourgueil. *Les Oeuvres poétiques de Baudri de Bourgueil.* Ed. Phyllis Abrahams. Paris: Champion, 1926.

Beal, Jane. "The Pearl Maiden's Two Lovers." *Studies in Philology* 100.1 (2003): 1–21.

Beebee, Thomas. *The Ideology of Genre: A Comparative Study of Generic Instability.* University Park: Pennsylvania State University Press, 1994.

Beidler, Peter G., ed. *Masculinities in Chaucer: Approaches to Maleness in the* Canterbury Tales *and* Troilus and Criseyde. Cambridge: D. S. Brewer, 1998.

Bell, Robert E. *Dictionary of Classical Mythology: Symbols, Attributes, and Associations.* Santa Barbara, CA: ABC Clio, 1982.

Bennett, Judith. "'Lesbian-Like' and the Social History of Lesbianisms." *Journal of the History of Sexuality* 9.1–2 (2000): 1–24.

Benson, Larry D., ed. *A Glossarial Concordance to the* Riverside Chaucer. New York: Garland, 1993.

Bersani, Leo. *Homos.* Cambridge, MA: Harvard University Press, 1995.

Bhabha, Homi K. "Are You a Man or a Mouse?" *Constructing Masculinity.* Ed. Maurice Berger, Brian Wallis, and Simon Watson. New York: Routledge, 1995. 57–65.

Biddick, Kathleen. *The Shock of Medievalism.* Durham, NC: Duke University Press, 1998.

Bishop, Ian. Pearl *in Its Setting.* Oxford: Blackwell, 1968.

Blumenfeld-Kosinski, Renate and Timea Szell, eds. *Images of Sainthood in Medieval Europe.* Ithaca, NY: Cornell University Press, 1991.

Bond, Gerald. *The Loving Subject: Desire, Power, and Eloquence in Romanesque France.* Philadelphia: University of Pennsylvania Press, 1995.

Boswell, John. *Christianity, Social Tolerance, and Homosexuality: Gay People in Western Europe from the Beginning of the Christian Era to the Fourteenth Century.* Chicago, IL: University of Chicago Press, 1980.

———. *Same-Sex Unions in Premodern Europe.* New York: Villard, 1994.

Bowers, John. "Queering the Summoner: Same-Sex Union in Chaucer's *Canterbury Tales.*" *Speaking Images: Essays in Honor of V. A. Kolve.* Ed. Robert F. Yeager and Charlotte C. Morse. Asheville, NC: Pegasus, 2001. 301–24.

Boyarin, Daniel. "On the History of the Early Phallus." Farmer and Pasternack, eds., *Gender* 3–44.

———. "What Does a Jew Want? or, The Political Meaning of the Phallus." *The Psychoanalysis of Race.* Ed. Christopher Lane. New York: Columbia University Press, 1998. 211–40.

Bray, Alan. *The Friend.* Chicago, IL: University of Chicago Press, 2003.

Brenner, Gerry. *Performative Criticism: Experiments in Reader Response.* Albany: State University of New York Press, 2004.

Brody, Saul Nathaniel. *The Disease of the Soul: Leprosy in Medieval Literature.* Ithaca, NY: Cornell University Press, 1974.

Brooke, Christopher N. L. *The Medieval Idea of Marriage.* Oxford: Oxford University Press, 1989.

Brown, Catherine. "In the Middle." *Journal of Medieval and Early Modern Studies* 30.3 (2000): 547–74.

Brown, Peter, ed. *Reading Dreams: The Interpretation of Dreams from Chaucer to Shakespeare.* New York: Oxford University Press, 1999.

Brozyna, Martha A. *Gender and Sexuality in the Middle Ages: A Medieval Source Documents Reader.* Jefferson, NC: McFarland, 2005.

Brubaker, Leslie and Julia M. H. Smith, eds. *Gender in the Early Medieval World: East and West, 300–900.* Cambridge: Cambridge University Press, 2004.

Bullón-Fernández, María. "'Byyonde the Water': Courtly and Religious Desire in *Pearl.*" *Studies in Philology* 91 (1994): 35–49.

Burger, Glenn. *Chaucer's Queer Nation.* Minneapolis: University of Minnesota Press, 2003.

———. "Kissing the Pardoner." *PMLA* 107.4 (1992): 1143–56.

Burger, Glenn and Steven F. Kruger, eds. *Queering the Middle Ages.* Minneapolis: University of Minnesota Press, 2001.

Burgwinkle, William E. *Sodomy, Masculinity, and Law in Medieval Literature: France and England, 1050–1230.* Cambridge: Cambridge University Press, 2004.

Burnley, John David. "Chaucer's Host and Harry Bailly." *Chaucer and the Craft of Fiction.* Ed. Leigh A. Arrathoon. Rochester, MI: Solaris, 1986. 195–218.

Butler, Judith. *Bodies That Matter: On the Discursive Limits of "Sex."* New York: Routledge, 1993.

———. *Gender Trouble: Feminism and the Subversion of Identity.* New York: Routledge, 1990.

———. *Undoing Gender.* New York: Routledge, 2004.

Butterfield, Ardis. "Lyric and Elegy in the *Book of the Duchess.*" *Medium Aevum* 60 (1991): 33–60.

Bychkov, Oleg V. "The Debate between the Knight and the Cleric: Emendation and Translation." *Cithara* 40.1 (2000): 3–36.

Bynum, Caroline Walker. *Jesus as Mother: Studies in the Spirituality of the High Middle Ages.* Berkeley: University of California Press, 1982.

Caldwell, James Ralston, ed. Eger and Grime: *A Parallel-Text Edition of the Percy and the Huntington-Laing Versions of the Romance*. Cambridge, MA: Harvard University Press, 1933.

Calin, William. "Women and Their Sexuality in *Ami et Amile:* An Occasion to Deconstruct?" *Olifant* 16.1–2 (1991): 77–89.

Calkin, Siobhain Bly. *Saracens and the Making of English Identity: The Auchinleck Manuscript*. New York: Routledge, 2005.

Callahan, Christopher. "Canon Law, Primogeniture, and the Marriage of Ebain and Silence." *Romance Quarterly* 49.1 (2002): 12–20.

Campbell, Anne. *A Mind of Her Own: The Evolutionary Psychology of Women*. Oxford: Oxford University Press, 2002.

Carr, David M. *The Erotic Word: Sexuality, Spirituality, and the Bible*. Oxford: Oxford University Press, 2003.

Carré, Yannick. *Le Baiser sur la bouche au moyen age: rites, symboles, mentalités, à travers les texts et les images, XIe-XVe siècles*. Paris: Léopard d'Or, 1992.

Carruthers, Leo. "Narrative Voice, Narrative Framework: The Host as 'Author' of the *Canterbury Tales*." Harding, *Drama, Narrative and Poetry* 51–67.

Carruthers, Mary. "The Lady, the Swineherd, and Chaucer's Clerk." *Chaucer Review* 17.3 (1983): 221–34.

Caserio, Robert, Tim Dean, Lee Edelman, Judith Halberstam, and José Estaban Munoz. "The Antisocial Thesis in Queer Theory." *PMLA* 121.3 (2006): 819–28.

Chaitin, Gilbert D. *Rhetoric and Culture in Lacan*. Cambridge: Cambridge University Press, 1996.

Chase, Cheryl. "Hermaphrodites with Attitude." *Queer Studies: An Interdisciplinary Reader*. Ed. Robert J. Corber and Stephen Valocchi. Oxford: Blackwell, 2003. 31–45.

Chaucer, Geoffrey. *The Riverside Chaucer*. Ed. Larry Benson. 3rd edn. Boston, MA: Houghton Mifflin, 1987.

Chevalier, Jean and Alain Gheerbrant, eds. *A Dictionary of Symbols*. Trans. John Buchanan-Brown. Oxford: Blackwell, 1994.

Chrétien de Troyes. *Les romans de Chrétien de Troyes, édités d'après la copie de Guiot (Bibl. Nat. fr 794), 4: Le Chevalier au lion (Yvain)*. Ed. Mario Roques. Paris: Champion, 1965.

Cicero. *On the Good Life*. Ed. Michael Grant. London: Penguin, 1971.

Clanchy, M. T. *From Memory to Written Record: England, 1066–1307*. Cambridge, MA: Harvard University Press, 1979.

Clopper, Lawrence. "*Pearl* and the Consolation of Scripture." *Viator* 23 (1991): 231–45.

Cohen, Jeffrey Jerome. *Medieval Identity Machines*. Minneapolis: University of Minnesota Press, 2003.

———, ed. *The Postcolonial Middle Ages*. New York: St. Martin's, 2000.

Cohen, Jeffrey Jerome and Bonnie Wheeler, eds. *Becoming Male in the Middle Ages*. New York: Garland, 1997.

Coleman, Janet. *Medieval Readers and Writers*. New York: Columbia University Press, 1981.

Coletti, Theresa. "Genealogy, Sexuality, and Sacred Power: The Saint Anne Dedication of the Digby *Candlemas Day and the Killing of the Children of Israel.*" *Journal of Medieval and Early Modern Studies* 29.1 (1999): 25–59.

Condren, Edward. *The Numerical Universe of the* Gawain-Pearl *Poet.* Gainesville: University Press of Florida, 2002.

Coogan, Michael, ed. *The New Oxford Annotated Bible.* 3rd edn. Oxford: Oxford University Press, 2001.

Cook, Jon. "Carnival and the *Canterbury Tales*: 'Only Equals May Laugh.'" *Medieval Literature: Criticism, Ideology, and History.* Ed. David Aers. New York: St. Martin's, 1986. 169–91.

Cooper, Helen. *The English Romance in Time: Transforming Motifs from Geoffrey of Monmouth to the Death of Shakespeare.* Oxford: Oxford University Press, 2004.

Cramer, Patricia. "Lordship, Bondage, and the Erotic: The Psychological Bases of Chaucer's *Clerk's Tale.*" *Journal of English and Germanic Philology* 89 (1990): 491–511.

Crane, Susan. *Gender and Romance in Chaucer's* Canterbury Tales. Princeton, NJ: Princeton University Press, 1994.

———. *Insular Romance: Politics, Faith, and Culture in Anglo-Norman and Middle English Literature.* Berkeley: University of California Press, 1986.

———. "The Writing Lesson of 1381." *Chaucer's England: Literature in Historical Context.* Ed. Barbara Hanawalt. Minneapolis: University of Minnesota Press, 1992. 201–21.

Crépin, André. "The Cock, the Priest, and the Poet." Harding, *Drama, Narrative and Poetry* 227–36.

Crocker, Holly. *Chaucer's Visions of Manhood.* New York: Palgrave Macmillan, 2007.

———. "Performative Passivity and Fantasies of Masculinity in the *Merchant's Tale.*" *Chaucer Review* 38 (2003): 178–98.

Dannenbaum, Susan. "Insular Tradition in the Story of *Amis and Amiloun.*" *Neophilologus* 67 (1983): 611–22.

Davenport, Tony. *Medieval Narrative.* Oxford: Oxford University Press, 2004.

Davies, Bob and Lori Rentzel. *Coming Out of Homosexuality: New Freedom for Men and Women.* Downers Grove, IL: Intervarsity, 1993.

Davis, Norman, ed. *Sir Gawain and the Green Knight.* 2nd edn. Ed. J. R. R. Tolkien and E. V. Gordon. Oxford: Clarendon, 1967.

Davis, Norman, Douglas Gray, Patricia Ingham, and Anne Wallace-Hadrill. *A Chaucer Glossary.* Oxford: Clarendon, 1979.

Davis, Todd F. and Kenneth Womack. *Formalist Criticism and Reader-Response Theory.* Basingstoke, Hampshire: Palgrave Macmillan, 2002.

D'Avray, D. L. *Medieval Marriage: Symbolism and Society.* Oxford: Oxford University Press, 2005.

Delany, Sheila. "A, A, and B: Coding Same-Sex Union in *Amis and Amiloun.*" *Pulp Fictions of Medieval England: Essays in Popular Romance.* Ed. Nicola McDonald. Manchester: Manchester University Press, 2004. 63–81.

Delasanta, Rodney. "Nominalism and the *Clerk's Tale* Revisited." *Chaucer Review* 31 (1997): 209–31.

Deleuze, Gilles and Félix Guattari. *A Thousand Plateaus: Capitalism and Schizophrenia.* Trans. Brian Massumi. Minneapolis: University of Minnesota Press, 1987.

Denery, Dallas G. *Seeing and Being Seen in the Later Medieval World: Optics, Theology, and Religious Life.* Cambridge: Cambridge University Press, 2005.

DeVries, David. "Fathers and Sons: Patristic Exegesis and the Castration Complex." *Gender Rhetorics: Postures of Dominance and Submission in History.* Ed. Richard Trexler. Binghamton, NY: Center for Medieval and Renaissance Texts and Studies, 1994. 33–45.

Dhuoda. *Manuel pour mon fils: introduction, texts, critique, notes.* Ed. Pierre Riché. Trans. Bernard de Vregille and Claude Mondésert. 2nd edn. Paris: Cerf, 1991.

Dinshaw, Carolyn. "Chaucer's Queer Touches / A Queer Touches Chaucer." *Exemplaria* 7 (1995): 75–92.

———. *Chaucer's Sexual Poetics.* Madison: University of Wisconsin Press, 1989.

———. *Getting Medieval: Sexualities and Communities, Pre- and Postmodern.* Durham, NC: Duke University Press, 1999.

Donaldson, E. Talbot. *The Swan at the Well: Shakespeare Reading Chaucer.* New Haven, CT: Yale University Press, 1985.

Dubrow, Heather. *Genre.* London: Methuen, 1982.

Duby, Georges. *Love and Marriage in the Middle Ages.* Trans. Jane Dunnett. Chicago, IL: University of Chicago Press, 1994.

Dufournet, Jean, ed. *Aucassin and Nicollette.* Paris: Flammarion, 1984.

Eagleton, Terry. *Walter Benjamin, or, Towards a Revolutionary Criticism.* London: Verso, 1981.

Eco, Umberto. "The Frames of Comic Freedom." *Carnival!* Ed. Thomas A. Sebeok. Berlin: Mouton, 1984. 1–9.

Edelman, Lee. *Homographesis: Essays in Gay Literary and Cultural Theory.* New York: Routledge, 1994.

———. *No Future: Queer Theory and the Death Drive.* Durham, NC: Duke University Press, 2004.

———. "Queer Theory: Unstating Desire." *GLQ: A Journal of Lesbian and Gay Studies* 2.4 (1995): 343–46.

Edmondson, George. "*Pearl:* The Shadow of the Object, the Shape of the Law." *Studies in the Age of Chaucer* 26 (2004): 29–63.

Edwards, Robert and Vickie Ziegler, eds. *Matrons and Marginal Women in Medieval Society.* Suffolk, UK: Boydell, 1995.

Eldridge, Laurance. "The State of *Pearl* Studies since 1933." *Viator* 6 (1975): 171–94.

Elliott, Alison Goddard. *Roads to Paradise: Reading the Lives of Early Saints.* Hanover, NH: University Press of New England, 1987.

Elliott, Dyan. *Spiritual Marriage: Sexual Abstinence in Medieval Wedlock.* Princeton, NJ: Princeton University Press, 1993.

Eng, David L., Judith Halberstam, and José Esteban Munoz. "What's Queer about Queer Studies Now?" *Social Text* 23.3–4 (2005): 1–17.

Fadiman, Clifton. *Any Number Can Play.* Cleveland, OH: World Publishing, 1957.

Farina, Lara. *Erotic Discourse and Early English Religious Writing*. New York: Palgrave Macmillan, 2006.

Faris, David E. "The Art of Adventure in the Middle English Romance: *Ywain and Gawain, Eger and Grime*." *Studia Neophilologica* 53.1 (1981): 91–100.

Farmer, Sharon and Carol Braun Pasternack, eds. *Gender and Difference in the Middle Ages*. Minneapolis: University of Minnesota Press, 2003.

Farrell, Thomas J., ed. *Bahktin and Medieval Voices*. Gainesville: University Press of Florida, 1995.

———. "The Chronotypes of Monology in Chaucer's *Clerk's Tale*." Farrell, *Bakhtin* 141–57.

Ferster, Judith. *Chaucer on Interpretation*. Cambridge: Cambridge University Press, 1985.

Finnegan, Robert Emmett. "'She Should Have Said No to Walter': Griselda's Promise in the *Clerk's Tale*." *English Studies* 75.4 (1994): 303–21.

Fish, Stanley. *Surprised by Sin: The Reader in* Paradise Lost. 2nd edn. Cambridge, MA: Harvard University Press, 1997.

Ford, John C. "Contrasting the Identical: Differentiation of the 'Indistinguishable' Characters of *Amis and Amiloun*." *Neophilologus* 86 (2002): 311–23.

Foster, Edward E. Amis and Amiloun, Robert of Cisyle, *and* Sir Amadace. Kalamazoo, MI: Medieval Institute, 1997.

———. "Simplicity, Complexity, and Morality in Four Medieval Romances." *Chaucer Review* 31.4 (1997): 401–19.

Foucault, Michel. *Discipline and Punish: The Birth of the Prison*. Trans. Alan Sheridan. 2nd edn. New York: Vintage, 1995.

———. *The History of Sexuality, Volume I: An Introduction*. Trans. Robert Hurley. New York: Vintage, 1990.

———. *The Use of Pleasure: Volume 2 of The History of Sexuality*. Trans. Robert Hurley. New York: Vintage, 1990.

Fowler, Alastair. *Kinds of Literature: An Introduction to the Theory of Genres and Modes*. Oxford: Oxford University Press, 1982.

Foys, Martin, ed. *The Bayeux Tapestry on CD-Rom*. Cambridge: Boydell and Brewer, 2002.

Fradenburg, L. O. Aranye. *Sacrifice Your Love: Psychoanalysis, Historicism, Chaucer*. Minneapolis: University of Minnesota Press, 2002.

Fradenburg, Louise and Carla Freccero, eds. *Premodern Sexualities*. New York: Routledge, 1996.

Frantzen, Allen J. *Before the Closet: Same-Sex Love from* Beowulf *to* Angels in America. Chicago, IL: University of Chicago Press, 1998.

———. "Between the Lines: Queer Theory, the History of Homosexuality, and Anglo-Saxon Penitentials." *Journal of Medieval and Renaissance Studies* 26.2 (1996): 255–96.

———. *Desire for Origins: New Language, Old English, and Teaching the Tradition*. New Brunswick, NJ: Rutgers University Press, 1990.

Freccero, Carla. *Queer/Early/Modern*. Durham, NC: Duke University Press, 2006.

Freud, Sigmund. *Civilization and Its Discontents: The Standard Edition*. Trans. and ed. James Strachey. New York: Norton, 1961.

Freud, Sigmund. *The Interpretation of Dreams.* New York: Gramercy, 1996.

Fromer, Julie E. "Spectators of Martyrdom: Corporeality and Sexuality in the *Liflade ant te Passiun of Seinte Margarete.*" *Intersections of Sexuality and the Divine in Medieval Culture: The Word Made Flesh.* Ed. Susannah Mary Chewning. Aldershot, UK: Ashgate, 2005. 89–106.

Ganim, John M. "Bakhtin, Chaucer, Carnival, Lent." *Studies in the Age of Chaucer Proceedings* 2 (1986): 59–71.

———. "Carnival Voices and the Envoy to the *Clerk's Tale.*" *Chaucer Review* 22.2 (1987): 111–27.

Garber, Rebecca L. R. *Feminine Figurae: Representations of Gender in Religious Texts by Medieval German Women Writers, 1100–1375.* New York: Routledge, 2003.

Gaunt, Simon. "Straight Minds/Queer Wishes in Old French Hagiography: *La vie de Sainte Euphrosine.*" Fradenburg and Freccero, eds., *Premodern Sexualities* 155–73.

Gaylord, Alan. "Sentence and Solaas in Fragment VII of the *Canterbury Tales*: Harry Bailly as Horseback Editor." *PMLA* 82.2 (1967): 226–35.

Georgianna, Linda. "The *Clerk's Tale* and the Grammar of Assent." *Speculum* 70.4 (1995): 793–821.

Gies, Frances and Joseph Gies. *Marriage and the Family in the Middle Ages.* New York: Harper and Row, 1987.

Giraudoux, Jean. *Amphitryon 38: comédie en trois actes.* Paris: Bélier, 1931.

Goldberg, Jonathan and Madhavi Menon. "Queering History." *PMLA* 120.5 (2005): 1608–17.

Goodwin, Amy W. "The Griselda Game." *Chaucer Review* 39 (2004): 41–69.

Gravdal, Kathryn. *Ravishing Maidens: Writing Rape in Medieval French Literature and Law.* Philadelphia: University of Pennsylvania Press, 1991.

Green, D. H. *The Beginnings of Medieval Romance: Fact and Fiction, 1150–1220.* Cambridge: Cambridge University Press, 2002.

Green, Richard Firth. "Further Evidence for Chaucer's Representation of the Pardoner as a Womanizer." *Medium Ævum* 71.2 (2002): 307–09.

———. "The Pardoner's Pants (and Why They Matter)." *Studies in the Age of Chaucer* 15 (1993): 131–45.

———. "Troilus and the Game of Love." *Chaucer Review* 13 (1979): 201–20.

———. "Women in Chaucer's Audience." *Chaucer Review* 18 (1983): 146–60.

Greenberg, Steven. *Wrestling with God and Men: Homosexuality in the Jewish Tradition.* Madison: University of Wisconsin Press, 2004.

Greer, Germaine. *The Female Eunuch.* London: MacGibbon & Kee, 1970.

Grudin, Michaela Paasche. "Chaucer's *Clerk's Tale* as Political Paradox." *Studies in the Age of Chaucer* 11 (1989): 63–92.

Gurevich, Aron. *Medieval Popular Culture: Problems of Belief and Perception.* Trans. János M. Bak and Paul A. Hollingsworth. Cambridge: Cambridge University Press, 1988.

Guthrie, Steve. "Dialogics and Prosody in Chaucer." Farrell, *Bakhtin* 94–108.

Gutwirth, Marcel. *Laughing Matter: An Essay on the Comic.* Ithaca, NY: Cornell University Press, 1993.

Hadley, D. M., ed. *Masculinity in Medieval Europe*. London: Longman, 1999.

Haidu, Peter. "Althusser Anonymous in the Middle Ages." *Exemplaria* 7.1 (1995): 55–74.

Halberstam, Judith. "Shame and White Gay Masculinity." *Social Text* 23.3–4 (2005): 219–33.

Hallissy, Margaret. *Clean Maids, True Wives, Steadfast Widows: Chaucer's Women and Medieval Codes of Conduct*. Westport, CT: Greenwood, 1993.

Halperin, David M. *One Hundred Years of Homosexuality and Other Essays on Greek Love*. New York: Routledge, 1990.

———. *Saint Foucault: Towards a Gay Hagiography*. Oxford: Oxford University Press, 1995.

Hamer, Dean and Peter Copeland. *The Science of Desire: The Search for the Gay Gene and the Biology of Behavior*. New York: Simon & Schuster, 1994.

Hanawalt, Barbara A. *The Ties That Bound: Peasant Families in Medieval England*. New York: Oxford University Press, 1986.

Hanna, Ralph. *London Literature, 1300–1380*. Cambridge: Cambridge University Press, 2005.

———. "Reconsidering the Auchinleck Manuscript." *New Directions in Later Medieval Manuscript Studies: Essays from the 1998 Harvard Conference*. Ed. Derek Pearsall. York: York Medieval Press, 2000. 91–102.

Hansen, Elaine Tuttle. *Chaucer and the Fictions of Gender*. Berkeley: University of California Press, 1992.

Harding, Wendy, ed. *Drama, Narrative, and Poetry in the* Canterbury Tales. Toulouse: Presses Universitaires du Mirail, 2003.

Hasler, Antony J. "Romance and Its Discontents in *Eger and Grime*." Putter and Gilbert, eds., *Spirit* 200–18.

Hays, Michael. *Shakespearian Tragedy as Chivalric Romance: Rethinking* Macbeth, Hamlet, Othello*, and* King Lear. Cambridge: D. S. Brewer, 2003.

Heffernan, Carol. "Tyranny and Commune Profit in the *Clerk's Tale*." *Chaucer Review* 17.4 (1983): 332–40.

Heffernan, Thomas J. *Sacred Biography: Saints and Their Biographers in the Middle Ages*. New York: Oxford University Press, 1988.

Heng, Geraldine. *Empire of Magic: Medieval Romance and the Politics of Cultural Fantasy*. New York: Columbia University Press, 2003.

Herzman, Ronald B., Graham Drake, and Eve Salisbury, eds. *Four Romances of England:* King Horn, Havelok the Dane, Bevis of Hampton, Athelston. Kalamazoo, MI: Medieval Institute, 1999.

Hieatt, Constance. "*Pearl* and the Dream-Vision Tradition." *Studia Neophilologica* 37 (1965): 139–45.

Hirsh, John C., ed. *Medieval Lyric: Middle English Lyrics, Ballads, and Carols*. Oxford: Blackwell, 2005.

Hirst, Paul. *On Law and Ideology*. New Jersey: Humanities, 1979.

Hodges, Kenneth. *Forging Chivalric Communities in Malory's* Le Morte D'Arthur. New York: Palgrave Macmillan, 2005.

Hodgson, Phyllis, ed. The Cloud of Unknowing *and* The Book of Privy Counselling. London: Early English Text Society, 1944.

202   BIBLIOGRAPHY

Hofstadter, Richard. *Anti-Intellectualism in American Life.* New York: Knopf, 1963.

Hollywood, Amy. *Sensible Ecstasy: Mysticism, Sexual Difference, and the Demands of History.* Chicago, IL: University of Chicago Press, 2002.

Holsinger, Bruce. *The Premodern Condition: Medievalism and the Making of Theory.* Chicago, IL: University of Chicago Press, 2005.

The Holy Bible: Douay Rheims. Fitzwilliam, NH: Loreto, 2004.

Howard, Donald. *The Idea of the* Canterbury Tales. Berkeley: University of California Press, 1975.

Hudson, Harriet, ed. *Four Middle English Romances:* Sir Isumbras, Octavian, Sir Eglamour of Artois, Sir Tryamour. Kalamazoo, MI: Medieval Institute, 1996.

Huizinga, Johan. *Homo Ludens: A Study of the Play-Element in Culture.* Boston, MA: Beacon, 1950.

Hume, Kathryn, "*Amis and Amiloun* and the Aesthetics of Middle English Romance." *Studies in Philology* 70 (1973): 19–41.

Humphrey, Chris. *The Politics of Carnival: Festival Misrule in Medieval England.* Manchester: Manchester University Press, 2001.

Hussey, S. S. "Chaucer's Host." *Medieval English Studies Presented to George Kane.* Ed. Edward Donald Kennedy, Ronald Waldron, and Joseph S. Wittig. Cambridge: D. S. Brewer, 1988. 153–61.

Hyatte, Reginald. *The Arts of Friendship: The Idealization of Friendship in Medieval and Early Renaissance Literature.* Leiden: Brill, 1994.

Ingham, Patricia Clare and Michelle R. Warren, eds. *Postcolonial Moves: Medieval through Modern.* New York: Palgrave Macmillan, 2003.

Jaeger, C. Stephen. *Ennobling Love: In Search of a Lost Sensibility.* Philadelphia: University of Pennsylvania Press, 1999.

Jantzen, Grace M. *Power, Gender and Christian Mysticism.* Cambridge: Cambridge University Press, 1995.

Jensen, Emily. "Male Competition as a Unifying Motif in Fragment A of the *Canterbury Tales.*" *Chaucer Review* 24 (1990): 320–28.

Jewell, Helen. *Women in Dark Age and Early Medieval Europe, c. 500–1200.* Basingstoke, Hampshire: Palgrave Macmillan, 2007.

Jewers, Caroline A. *Chivalric Fiction and the History of the Novel.* Gainesville: University Press of Florida, 2000.

Johnson, Lynn Staley. "The Prince and His People: A Study of the Two Covenants in the *Clerk's Tale.*" *Chaucer Review* 10 (1975): 17–29.

Jones, Christopher A. "Monastic Identity and Sodomitic Danger in the *Occupatio* by Odo of Cluny." *Speculum* 92 (2007): 1–53.

Jordan, Mark. *The Invention of Sodomy in Christian Theology.* Chicago, IL: University of Chicago Press, 1997.

Jordan, Robert M. "Heteroglossia and Chaucer's *Man of Law's Tale.*" Farrell, *Bakhtin* 81–93.

Joseph, Gerhard. "Chaucerian 'Game'—'Earnest' and the 'Argument of Herbergage' in the *Canterbury Tales.*" *Chaucer Review* 5 (1970): 83–96.

Josipovici, G. D. "Fiction and Game in the *Canterbury Tales.*" *Critical Quarterly* 7 (1965): 185–97.

Jost, Jean. "Hearing the Female Voice: Transgression in *Amis and Amiloun*." *Medieval Perspectives* 10 (1995): 116–32.

Justice, Steven. *Writing and Rebellion: England in 1381*. Berkeley: University of California Press, 1996.

Kabir, Ananya Jahanara and Deanne Williams, eds. *Postcolonial Approaches to the European Middle Ages: Translating Cultures*. Cambridge: Cambridge University Press, 2005.

Karras, Ruth Mazo. *From Boys to Men: Formations of Masculinity in Late Medieval Europe*. Philadelphia: University of Pennsylvania Press, 2003.

———. "Holy Harlots: Prostitute Saints in Medieval Legend." *Journal of the History of Sexuality* 1.1 (1990): 3–22.

———. "Separating the Men from the Goats: Masculinity, Civilization, and Identity Formation in the Medieval University." *The Animal/Human Boundary: Historical Perspectives*. Ed. Angela N. H. Creager and William Chester Jordan. Rochester, NY: University of Rochester Press, 2002. 50–73.

———. *Sexuality in Medieval Europe: Doing unto Others*. New York: Routledge, 2005.

Katz, Jonathan Ned. *The Invention of Heterosexuality*. New York: Penguin, 1995.

———. *Love Stories: Sex between Men before Homosexuality*. Chicago, IL: University of Chicago Press, 2001.

Kay, Sarah. "Seduction and Suppression in *Ami et Amile*." *French Studies* 44 (1990): 129–42.

Keen, William. "'To doon yow ese': A Study of the Host in the *General Prologue* of the *Canterbury Tales*." *Topic* 17 (1969): 5–18.

Kelly, Douglas. "Exaggeration, Abrupt Conversion, and the Uses of Description in *Jaufre* and *Flamenca*." *Studia Occitanica in Memoriam Paul Remy*. Ed. Hans-Erich Keller. Kalamazoo, MI: Medieval Institute, 1986. 107–19.

———. *Medieval French Romance*. New York: Twayne, 1993.

Kendrick, Laura. *Chaucerian Play*. Berkeley: University of California Press, 1988.

Kinoshita, Sharon. "Heldris de Cornuâlle's *Roman de Silence* and the Feudal Politics of Lineage." *PMLA* 110.3 (1995): 397–409.

———. "Male-Order Brides: Marriage, Patriarchy, and Monarchy in the *Roman de Silence*." *Arthuriana* 12.1 (2002): 64–75.

Kittredge, G. L. "Chaucer's Discussion of Marriage." *Modern Philology* 9 (1912): 435–67.

Klosowska, Anna. *Queer Love in the Middle Ages*. New York: Palgrave Macmillan, 2005.

Kölbing, Eugen, ed. Amis and Amiloun, *zugleich mit der altfranzösischen Quelle*. Heilbronn: Henninger, 1884.

Konrad, Jeff. *You Don't Have to Be Gay: Hope and Freedom for Males Struggling with Homosexuality or for Those Who Know of Someone Who Is*. Hilo, HI: Pacific, 1992.

Kramer, Dale. "Structural Artistry in *Amis and Amiloun*." *Annuale Mediaevale* 9 (1968): 103–22.

Kratins, Ojars. "The Middle English *Amis and Amiloun*: Chivalric Romance or Secular Hagiography?" *PMLA* 81.5 (1966): 347–54.

Krieg, Laurence J. "Levels of Symbolic Meaning in *Pearl*." *Mythlore* 5 (1978): 21–23.

Kristeva, Julia. *Desire in Language: A Semiotic Approach to Literature and Art*. Ed. Leon S. Roudiez. Trans. Thomas Gora, Alice Jardine, and Leon S. Roudiez. New York: Columbia University Press, 1980.

Krueger, Roberta, ed. *The Cambridge Companion to Medieval Romance*. Cambridge: Cambridge University Press, 2000.

Kruger, Steven F. "Claiming the Pardoner: Toward a Gay Reading of Chaucer's *Pardoner's Tale*." *Exemplaria* 6.1 (1994): 115–39.

———. *Dreaming in the Middle Ages*. Cambridge: Cambridge University Press, 1992.

Kuefler, Mathew. "Castration and Eunuchism in the Middle Ages." *Handbook of Medieval Sexuality*. Ed. Vern Bullough and James Brundage. New York: Garland, 1996. 279–306.

———. "Male Friendship and the Suspicion of Sodomy in Twelfth-Century France." Farmer and Pasternack, ed., *Gender* 145–81.

———. *The Manly Eunuch: Masculinity, Gender Ambiguity, and Christian Ideology in Late Antiquity*. Chicago, IL: University of Chicago Press, 2001.

Lacan, Jacques. *Feminine Sexuality: Jacques Lacan and the école freudienne*. Ed. Juliet Mitchell and Jacqueline Rose. New York: Norton, 1982.

———. *The Seminar of Jacques Lacan: Book VII: The Ethics of Psychoanalysis, 1959–196*. Ed. Jacques-Alain Miller. Trans. Dennis Porter. New York: Norton, 1992.

Lanham, Richard. "Game, Play, and High Seriousness in Chaucer's Poetry." *English Studies* 48 (1967): 1–24.

Laqueur, Thomas. *Making Sex: Body and Gender from the Greeks to Freud*. Cambridge, MA: Harvard University Press, 1990.

Laskaya, Anne. *Chaucer's Approach to Gender in the* Canterbury Tales. Cambridge: D. S. Brewer, 1995.

Lavers, Norman. "Freud, the Clerkes Tale, and Literary Criticism." *College English* 26 (1964): 180–87.

Lavezzo, Kathy. "Chaucer and Everyday Death: The *Clerk's Tale,* Burial, and the Subject of Poverty." *Studies in the Age of Chaucer* 23 (2001): 255–87.

Leach, MacEdward, ed. *Amis and Amiloun*. 1937. London: Early English Text Society, 2001.

Lees, Clare, ed. *Medieval Masculinities: Regarding Men in the Middle Ages*. Minneapolis: University of Minnesota Press, 1994.

Lehman, Peter. "Penis Jokes and Hollywood's Unconscious." *Comedy/Cinema/Theory*. Ed. Andrew Horton. Berkeley: University of California Press, 1991. 43–59.

Leith, L. M. "Sentence and Solaas: The Function of the Hosts in the *Canterbury Tales*." *Chaucer Review* 17.1 (1982): 5–20.

Leupin, Alexandre. "The Middle Ages, the Other." *Diacritics* 13.3 (1983): 21–31.

Lindahl, Carl. *Earnest Games: Folkloric Patterns in the* Canterbury Tales. Bloomington: Indiana University Press, 1987.

Lindberg, David C. *Theories of Vision from Al-Kindi to Kepler.* Chicago, IL: University of Chicago Press, 1981.

Lochrie, Karma. *Covert Operations: The Medieval Uses of Secrecy.* Philadelphia: University of Pennsylvania Press, 1999.

———. *Heterosyncrasies: Female Sexuality When Normal Wasn't.* Minneapolis: University of Minnesota Press, 2005.

———. "Mystical Acts/Queer Tendencies." Lochrie, McCracken, and Schultz, eds., *Constructing Medieval Sexuality* 180–200.

Lochrie, Karma, Peggy McCracken, and James A. Schultz, eds. *Constructing Medieval Sexuality.* Minneapolis: University of Minnesota Press, 1997.

Loomis, Laura Hibbard. "The Auchinleck Manuscript and a Possible London Bookshop of 1330–1340." *PMLA* 57.3 (1942): 595–627.

Lynch, Kathryn L. "Despoiling Griselda: Chaucer's Walter and the Problem of Knowledge in the *Clerk's Tale.*" *Studies in the Age of Chaucer* 10 (1988): 41–70.

———. *The High Medieval Dream Vision: Poetry, Philosophy, and Literary Form.* Stanford, CA: Stanford University Press, 1988.

Malory, Thomas. *Works.* Ed. Eugène Vinaver. 2nd edn. London: Oxford University Press, 1971.

Mann, Jill. *Chaucer and Medieval Estates Satire: The Literature of Social Classes and the* General Prologue *to the* Canterbury Tales. Cambridge: Cambridge University Press, 1973.

———. "Satisfaction and Payment in Middle English Literature." *Studies in the Age of Chaucer* 5 (1983): 17–48.

Manning, Stephen. "Rhetoric, Game, Morality, and Geoffrey Chaucer." *Studies in the Age of Chaucer* 1 (1979): 105–18.

Mannoni, Octave. "I Know Well, But All the Same." Rothenberg, Foster, and Žižek, eds., *Perversion* 68–92.

Marbod of Rennes. In *Patrologia Latina.* Ed. J.-P Migne. Paris, 1844–1904. Vol. 171, cols. 1458–1782.

Marcuse, Herbert. "The Ideology of Death." *The Meaning of Death.* Ed. Herman Feifel. New York: McGraw-Hill, 1959. 64–76.

Marie de France. *The Lais of Marie de France.* Trans. Robert Hanning and Joan Ferrante. Durham, NC: Labyrinth, 1978.

Martial. *Epigrams: Volume III.* Ed. and trans. D. R. Shackleton Bailey. Cambridge, MA: Harvard University Press, 1993.

Martin, Ellen E. "Spenser, Chaucer, and the Rhetoric of Elegy." *Journal of Medieval and Renaissance Studies* 17.1 (1987): 83–109.

Mate, Mavis. *Women in Medieval English Society.* Cambridge: Cambridge University Press, 1999.

McAlpine, Monica. "The Pardoner's Homosexuality and How It Matters." *PMLA* 95.1 (1980): 8–22.

McCarthy, Conor. *Marriage in Medieval England: Law, Literature, and Practice.* Woodbridge, England: Boydell, 2004.

McClellan, William. "'Ful pale face': Agamben's Biopolitical Theory and the Sovereign Subject in Chaucer's *Clerk's Tale.*" *Exemplaria* 17.1 (2005): 103–34.

McCracken, Peggy. *The Curse of Eve, the Wound of the Hero: Blood, Gender, and Medieval Literature*. Philadelphia: University of Pennsylvania Press, 2003.

———. "Engendering Sacrifice: Blood, Lineage, and Infanticide in Old French Literature." *Speculum* 77 (2002): 55–75.

McDiarmid, Matthew. "The Metrical Chronicles and Non-Alliterative Romances." *The History of Scottish Literature: Origins to 1660, Volume 1.* Ed. R. D. S. Jack. Aberdeen: Aberdeen University Press, 1988.

McGinn, Bernard. "The Language of Love in Christian and Jewish Mysticism." *Mysticism and Language*. Ed. Steven Katz. New York: Oxford University Press, 1992. 202–35.

McInerney, Maud Burnett. "Opening the Oyster: Pearls in *Pearl*." *Aestel* 1 (1993): 19–54.

McKinley, Kathryn L. "The *Clerk's Tale*: Hagiography and the Problematics of Lay Sanctity." *Chaucer Review* 33 (1998): 90–111.

McNamara, Jo Ann. "An Unresolved Syllogism: The Search for a Christian Gender System." Murray, *Conflicted Identities* 1–24.

McRoberts, J. Paul. *Shakespeare and the Medieval Tradition: An Annotated Bibliography*. New York: Garland, 1985.

Means, Michael. *The Consolatio Genre in Medieval English Literature*. Gainesville: University Press of Florida, 1972.

Meech, Sanford Brown, ed. *The Book of Margery Kempe*. London: Early English Text Society, 1997.

Mehl, Dieter. *The Middle English Romances of the Thirteenth and Fourteenth Centuries*. London: Routledge & Kegan Paul, 1968.

Menon, Madhavi. *Wanton Words: Rhetoric and Sexuality in English Renaissance Drama*. Toronto: University of Toronto Press, 2004.

Menuge, Noël James. *Medieval English Wardship in Romance and Law*. Cambridge: D. S. Brewer, 2001.

Middleton, Anne. "The Clerk and His Tale: Some Literary Contexts." *Studies in the Age of Chaucer* 2 (1980): 121–50.

Miller, J. Hillis. *The Ethics of Reading: Kant, de Man, Eliot, Trollope, James, and Benjamin*. New York: Columbia University Press, 1987.

Miller, Mark. *Philosophical Chaucer: Love, Sex, and Agency in the* Canterbury Tales. Cambridge: Cambridge University Press, 2004.

Mills, Laurens J. *One Soul in Bodies Twain: Friendship in Tudor and Stuart Drama*. Bloomington, IN: Principia, 1937.

Milton, John. *Tetrachordon*. *Complete Prose Works of John Milton, Vol. II: 1643–1648*. Ed. Ernest Sirluck. New Haven, CT: Yale University Press, 1959. 571–718.

Minnis, Alastair. "Chaucer and the Queering Eunuch." *New Medieval Literatures* 6 (2003): 107–29.

Mitchell, J. Allan. "Chaucer's *Clerk's Tale* and the Question of Ethical Monstrosity." *Studies in Philology* 102.1 (2005): 1–26.

Montag, Warren. "'The Soul Is the Prison of the Body': Althusser and Foucault, 1970–1975." *Yale French Studies* 88 (1995): 53–77.

Morse, Charlotte C. "Critical Approaches to the *Clerk's Tale*." *Chaucer's Religious Tales*. Ed. C. David Benson and Elizabeth Robertson. Cambridge: D. S. Brewer, 1990. 71–83.

———. "The Exemplary Griselda." *Studies in the Age of Chaucer* 7 (1985): 51–86.

Mrs. Doubtfire. Dir. Chris Columbus. Perf. Robin Williams and Sally Field. 1993. Videocassette. Beverly Hills, CA: Fox, 1994.

Mulvey, Laura. *Visual and Other Pleasures*. Bloomington: Indiana University Press, 1989.

Murphy, Timothy F. *Gay Science: The Ethics of Sexual Orientation Research*. New York: Columbia University Press, 1997.

Murray, Jacqueline, ed. *Conflicted Identities and Multiple Masculinities: Men in the Medieval West*. New York: Garland, 1999.

———. "Mystical Castration: Some Reflections on Peter Abelard, Hugh of Lincoln and Sexual Control." Murray, *Conflicted Identities* 73–91.

Nelson, Cary. *The Incarnate Word: Literature as Verbal Space*. Urbana: University of Illinois Press, 1973.

Newton, Allyson. "The Occlusion of Maternity in Chaucer's *Clerk's Tale*." *Medieval Mothering*. Ed. John Carmi Parsons and Bonnie Wheeler. New York: Garland, 1996. 63–75.

Nissinen, Martti. *Homoeroticism in the Biblical World: A Historical Perspective*. Minneapolis, MN: Fortress, 1998.

Nolan, Barbara. "'A Poet Ther Was': Chaucer's Voices in the *General Prologue* to the *Canterbury Tales*." *PMLA* 101.2 (1986): 154–69.

O'Brien, Richard. *The Rocky Horror Picture Show: Music from the Original Soundtrack of the Twentieth Century Fox Presentation of the Lou Adler/Michael White Production*. Santa Monica: Ode Records, 1975.

O'Donnell, Daniel Paul. *Cædmon's Hymn: A Multimedia Study, Archive and Edition*. Cambridge: D. S. Brewer, 2005.

Olson, Glending. "Chaucer's Idea of a Canterbury Game." *The Idea of Medieval Literature*. Ed. James M. Dean and Christian Zacher. Newark: University of Delaware Press, 1992. 72–90.

———. *Literature as Recreation in the Later Middle Ages*. Ithaca, NY: Cornell University Press, 1982.

———. "'Nawther reste ne trauayle': The Psychology of *Pearl* 1087." *Neuphilologische Mitteilungen* 83.4 (1982): 422–25.

Olson, Paul. *The* Canterbury Tales *and the Good Society*. Princeton, NJ: Princeton University Press, 1986.

Oulmont, Charles. *Les débats du clerc et du chevalier dans la littérature poétique du Moyen-Age*. Paris: Honore Champion, 1911. Geneva: Slatkine Reprints, 1974.

Ovid. *Ars Amatoria*. Ed. A. S. Hollis. Oxford: Clarendon, 1977.

———. *The Erotic Poems*. Trans. Peter Green. London: Penguin, 1982.

Page, Barbara. "Concerning the Host." *Chaucer Review* 4 (1970): 1–13.

Paglia, Camille. "Plighting Their Troth." Review of John Boswell, *Same Sex Unions in Premodern Europe*. *Washington Post* July 17, 1994: wkb1.

Patterson, Lee. "Chaucer's Pardoner on the Couch: Psyche and Clio in Medieval Literary Studies." *Speculum* 76.3 (2001): 638–80.

Pearsall, Derek. *Arthurian Romance: A Short Introduction*. Oxford: Blackwell, 2003.

———. "Courtesy and Chivalry in *Sir Gawain and the Green Knight*: The Order of Shame and the Invention of Embarrassment." *A Companion to the* Gawain-*Poet*. Ed. Derek Brewer and Jonathan Gibson. Cambridge: D. S. Brewer, 1997. 351–62.

Pêcheux, Michel. *Language, Semantics and Ideology*. New York: St. Martin's, 1982.

Penn, Michael Philip. *Kissing Christians: Ritual and Community in the Late Ancient Church*. Philadelphia: University of Pennsylvania Press, 2005.

Perfetti, Lisa, ed. *The Representation of Women's Emotions in Medieval and Early Modern Culture*. Gainesville: University Press of Florida, 2005.

Peter Damian. *Book of Gomorrah: An Eleventh-Century Treatise against Clerical Homosexual Practices*. Trans. Pierre J. Payer. Waterloo, Ontario: Wilfrid Laurier University Press, 1982.

Phillips, Helen, and Nick Havely, eds. *Chaucer's Dream Poetry*. Essex, England: Longman, 1997.

Phillips, Kim M. *Medieval Maidens: Young Women and Gender in England, 1270–1540*. Manchester: Manchester University Press, 2003.

Pichaske, David R. and Laura Sweetland. "Chaucer on the Medieval Monarchy: Harry Bailly in the *Canterbury Tales*." *Chaucer Review* 11.3 (1976–77): 179–200.

Plummer, John. "'Beth fructuous and that in litel space': The Engendering of Harry Bailly." *New Readings of Chaucer's Poetry*. Ed. Robert G. Benson and Susan J. Ridyard. Cambridge: D. S. Brewer, 2003. 107–18.

Prior, Sandra Pierson. *The* Pearl-*Poet Revisited*. New York: Twayne, 1994.

Pugh, Tison. "Christian Revelation and the Cruel Game of Courtly Love in *Troilus and Criseyde*." *Chaucer Review* 39 (2005): 379–401.

———. *Queering Medieval Genres*. New York: Palgrave Macmillan, 2004.

Putter, Ad. "Transvestite Knights in Medieval Life and Literature." Cohen and Wheeler, eds. *Becoming Male* 279–302.

Putter, Ad and Jane Gilbert, eds. *The Spirit of Medieval English Popular Romance*. Harlow, England: Longman, 2000.

Raguin, Virginia Chieffo and Sarah Stanbury, eds. *Women's Space: Patronage, Place, and Gender in the Medieval Church*. Albany: State University of New York Press, 2005.

Rawcliffe, Carole. *Leprosy in Medieval England*. Suffolk, Woodbridge: Boydell, 2006.

Remy, Paul. "La Lèpre, thème littéraire au moyen age." *Le Moyen Age* 52 (1946): 195–242.

Rhodes, Jim. "The Dreamer Redeemed: Exile and the Kingdom in the Middle English *Pearl*." *Studies in the Age of Chaucer* 16 (1994): 119–42.

Rich, Adrienne. "Compulsory Heterosexuality and Lesbian Existence." *Journal of Women's History* 15.3 (2003): 11–48.

Richards, Peter. *The Medieval Leper and His Northern Heirs*. Cambridge: D. S. Brewer, 1977.

Richardson, Cynthia. "The Function of the Host in the *Canterbury Tales*." *Texas Studies in Literature and Language* 12 (1970): 325–44.

Richardson, Thomas C. "Harry Bailly: Chaucer's Innkeeper." *Chaucer's Pilgrims: An Historical Guide to the Pilgrims in the* Canterbury Tales. Ed. Laura C. Lambdin and Robert T. Lambdin. Westport, CT: Greenwood, 1996. 324–39.

Riches, Samantha J. E. and Sarah Salih, eds. *Gender and Holiness: Men, Women, and Saints in Late Medieval Europe*. London: Routledge, 2002.

Richter, David H. *The Progress of Romance: Literary Historiography and the Gothic Novel*. Columbus: Ohio State University Press, 1996.

Roche-Mahdi, Sarah, ed. and trans. *Silence: A Thirteenth-Century French Romance*. East Lansing, MI: Colleagues, 1992.

Rocke, Michael. *Forbidden Friendships: Homosexuality and Male Culture in Renaissance Florence*. New York: Oxford University Press, 1996.

Rothenberg, Molly Anne and Dennis Foster. "Introduction: Beneath the Skin: Perversion and Social Analysis." Rothenberg, Foster, and Žižek, eds., *Perversion* 1–14.

Rothenberg, Molly Anne, Dennis Foster, and Slavoj Žižek, eds. *Perversion and the Social Relation*. Durham, NC: Duke University Press, 2003.

Roughgarden, Joan. *Evolution's Rainbow: Diversity, Gender, and Sexuality in Nature and People*. Berkeley: University of California Press, 2004.

Rousseau, Constance and Joel Rosenthal, eds. *Women, Marriage, and Family in Medieval Christendom*. Kalamazoo, MI: Medieval Institute, 1998.

Rubin, Miri. *Corpus Christi: The Eucharist in Late Medieval Culture*. Cambridge: Cambridge University Press, 1991.

Russell, J. Stephen. "Is London Burning?: A Chaucerian Allusion to the Rising of 1381." *Chaucer Review* 30.1 (1995): 107–09.

———. "*Pearl*'s 'Courtesy': A Critique of Eschatology." *Renascence* 35 (1983): 183–95.

Salih, Sarah, ed. *A Companion to Middle English Hagiography*. Cambridge: D. S. Brewer, 2006.

Sautman, Francesca Canadé and Pamela Sheingorn, eds. *Same-Sex Love among Women in the Middle Ages*. New York: Palgrave Macmillan, 2001.

Scheps, Walter. "'Up roos oure Hoost, and was oure aller cok': Harry Bailly's Tale-Telling Competition." *Chaucer Review* 10.2 (1975–76): 113–28.

Schibanoff, Susan. *Chaucer's Queer Poetics: Rereading the Dream Trio*. Toronto: University of Toronto Press, 2006.

Schotter, Anne Howland. "The Paradox of Equality and Hierarchy of Reward in *Pearl*." *Renascence* 33 (1981): 172–79.

Schultz, James A. *Courtly Love, the Love of Courtliness, and the History of Sexuality*. Chicago, IL: University of Chicago Press, 2006.

Schweickart, Patrocinio. "Reading Ourselves: Toward a Feminist Theory of Reading." *Contemporary Literary Criticism*. Eds. Robert Con Davis and Ronald Schliefer. 2nd edn. New York: Longman, 1989. 118–41.

Schweickart, Patrocinio P. and Elizabeth A. Flynn, eds. *Reading Sites: Social Difference and Reader Response*. New York: MLA, 2004.

Sedgwick, Eve Kosofsky. *Between Men: English Literature and Male Homosocial Desire*. New York: Columbia University Press, 1985.

———. *Epistemology of the Closet*. Berkeley: University of California Press, 1990.

Shahar, Shulamith. *The Fourth Estate: A History of Women in the Middle Ages*. Trans. Chaya Galai. London: Methuen, 1983.

Shakespeare, William. *Twelfth Night. The Norton Shakespeare: Comedies*. Ed. Stephen Greenblatt, et al. New York: Norton, 1997. 653–713.

Shannon, Laurie. *Sovereign Amity: Figures of Friendship in Shakespearian Contexts*. Chicago, IL: University of Chicago Press, 2002.

Shonk, Timothy A. "A Study of the Auchinleck Manuscript: Bookmen and Bookmaking in the Early Fourteenth Century." *Speculum* 60 (1985): 71–91.

Smith, Paul. *Discerning the Subject*. Minneapolis: University of Minnesota Press, 1988.

Sobchack, Vivian. "The Insistent Fringe: Moving Images and Historical Consciousness." *History and Theory* 36.4 (1997): 4–20.

Some Like It Hot. Dir. Billy Wilder. Perf. Jack Lemmon, Tony Curtis, and Marilyn Monroe. 1959. DVD. Culver City, CA: MGM, 2001.

Sontag, Susan. *Styles of Radical Will*. New York: Farrar, Straus & Giroux, 1969.

Sprung, Andrew. "'If it youre wille be': Coercion and Compliance in Chaucer's *Clerk's Tale*." *Exemplaria* 7.2 (1995): 345–69.

Stanbury, Sarah. "The Body and the City in *Pearl*." *Representations* 48 (1994): 30–47.

———, ed. *Pearl*. Kalamazoo, MI: Medieval Institute, 2001.

———. "Regimes of the Visual in Premodern England: Gaze, Body, and Chaucer's *Clerk's Tale*." *New Literary History* 28.2 (1997): 261–89.

———. *Seeing the* Gawain-*Poet*. Philadelphia: University of Pennsylvania Press, 1991.

Stehling, Thomas, trans. *Medieval Poems of Male Love and Friendship*. New York: Garland, 1984.

———. "To Love a Medieval Boy." *Journal of Homosexuality* 8 (1983): 151–70.

Stein, Edward. *The Mismeasure of Desire: The Science, Theory, and Ethics of Sexual Orientation*. Oxford: Oxford University Press, 1999.

Sticca, Sandro, ed. *Saints: Studies in Hagiography*. Binghamton, NY: Medieval and Renaissance Texts and Studies, 1996.

Stieve, Edwin. "A New Reading of the Host's 'In terme' (*Canterbury Tales* VI, line 311)." *Notes and Queries* 34.1 (1987): 7–10.

Stock, Brian. *The Implications of Literacy: Written Language and Models of Interpretation in the Eleventh and Twelfth Centuries*. Princeton, NJ: Princeton University Press, 1983.

Straus, Barrie Ruth. "Reframing the Violence of the Father: Reverse Oedipal Fantasies in Chaucer's *Clerk's, Man of Law's,* and *Prioress's Tales*." *Domestic Violence in Medieval Texts*. Ed. Eve Salisbury, Georgiana Donavin, and

Merrall Llewelyn Price. Gainesville: University Press of Florida, 2002. 122–38.

Sturges, Robert. *Chaucer's Pardoner and Gender Theory: Bodies of Discourse.* New York: St. Martin's, 2000.

———. "The Construction of Heterosexual Desire in Gottfried von Strassburg's *Tristan.*" *Exemplaria* 10.2 (1998): 243–69.

———. *Dialogue and Deviance: Male-Male Desire in the Dialogue Genre.* New York: Palgrave Macmillan, 2005.

———. *Medieval Interpretation: Models of Reading in Literary Narrative, 1100–1500.* Carbondale, IL: Southern Illinois University Press, 1991.

Suits, Bernard. *The Grasshopper: Games, Life, and Utopia.* Toronto: University of Toronto Press, 1978.

Szarmach, Paul, ed. *Holy Men and Holy Women: Old English Prose Saints' Lives and Their Contexts.* Albany: State University of New York Press, 1996.

Taylor, Andrew. "The Curious Eye and the Alternative Endings of the *Canterbury Tales.*" *Part Two: Reflections on the Sequel.* Ed. Paul Budra and Betty A. Schellenberg. Toronto: University of Toronto Press, 1998. 34–52.

Taylor, Gary. *Castration: An Abbreviated History of Western Manhood.* New York: Routledge, 2000.

Therborn, Goran. *The Ideology of Power and the Power of Ideology.* London: Verso, 1980.

Tinkle, Theresa. *Medieval Venuses and Cupids: Sexuality, Hermeneutics, and English Poetry.* Stanford, CA: Stanford University Press, 1996.

Todorov, Tzvetan. *Genres in Discourse.* Trans. Catherine Porter. Cambridge: Cambridge University Press, 1990.

Tootsie. Dir. Sydney Pollack. Perf. Dustin Hoffman, Jessica Lange, and Teri Garr. 1982. Videocassette. Burbank, CA: Columbia Tristar, 1993.

Travis, Peter W. "The Body of the Nun's Priest, or, Chaucer's Disseminal Genius." *Reading Medieval Culture.* Ed. Robert Stein and Sandra Pierson Prior. Notre Dame, IN: University of Notre Dame Press, 2005. 231–47.

Tresidder, Jack. *Dictionary of Symbols: An Illustrated Guide to Traditional Images, Icons, and Emblems.* San Francisco, CA: Chronicle, 1998.

Turner, Marion. "*Troilus and Criseyde* and the 'Treasonous Aldermen' of 1382: Tales of the City in Late Fourteenth-Century London." *Studies in the Age of Chaucer* 25 (2003): 225–57.

Van, Thomas A. "Walter at the Stake: A Reading of Chaucer's *Clerk's Tale.*" *Chaucer Review* 22.3 (1988): 214–24.

Vance, Eugene. *Mervelous Signals: Poetics and Sign Theory in the Middle Ages.* Lincoln: University of Nebraska Press, 1986.

Van Duzee, Mabel. *A Medieval Romance of Friendship: Eger and Grime.* New York: Burt Franklin, 1963.

Van Dyke, Carolynn. "The Clerk's and Franklin's Subjected Subjects." *Studies in the Age of Chaucer* 17 (1995): 45–68.

Vasvari, Louise O. "Fowl Play in My Lady's Chamber: Textual Harassment of a Middle English Pornithological Riddle and Visual Pun." *Obscenity: Social*

Control and Artistic Creation in the European Middle Ages. Ed. Jan M. Ziolkowski. Leiden: Brill, 1998. 108–35.

Vinaver, Eugene. *The Rise of Romance.* Oxford: Clarendon, 1971.

Wallace, David. *Chaucerian Polity: Absolutist Lineages and Associational Forms in England and Italy.* Stanford, CA: Stanford University Press, 1997.

Walther, H. *Das Streitgedicht in der lateinischen Literatur des Mittelalters.* München: Beck, 1920.

Warner, Michael, ed. *Fear of a Queer Planet: Queer Politics and Social Theory.* Minneapolis: University of Minnesota Press, 1993.

———. *The Trouble with Normal: Sex, Politics, and the Ethics of Queer Life.* New York: Free Press, 1999.

Watts, Ann Chalmers. "*Pearl,* Inexpressibility, and Poems of Human Loss." *PMLA* 99 (1984): 26–40.

Weisl, Angela Jane. *Conquering the Reign of Femeny: Gender and Genre in Chaucer's Romance.* Cambridge: D. S. Brewer, 1995.

White, Hugh. "Blood in *Pearl.*" *Review of English Studies* 38 (1987): 1–13.

Whitman, Jon. *Allegory: The Dynamics of an Ancient and Medieval Technique.* Cambridge, MA: Harvard University Press, 1987.

Williams, Craig A. *Roman Homosexuality: Ideologies of Masculinity in Classical Antiquity.* Oxford: Oxford University Press, 1999.

Williams, Ioan, ed. *Novel and Romance, 1700–1800: A Documentary Record.* New York: Barnes & Noble, 1970.

Williams, Linda. *Hard Core: Power, Pleasure, and the "Frenzy of the Visible."* Berkeley: University of California Press, 1989.

Williams, Tara. "'T'assaye in thee thy wommanheede': Griselda Chosen, Translated, and Tried." *Studies in the Age of Chaucer* 27 (2005): 93–127.

Wilson, Emma. *Sexuality and the Reading Encounter.* Oxford: Clarendon, 1996.

Wolfthal, Diane. *Images of Rape: The "Heroic" Tradition and Its Alternatives.* Cambridge: Cambridge University Press, 1999.

Woods, Constance. "Same-Sex Unions or Semantic Illusions?" *Communio* 22 (1995): 316–42.

Woolf, Rosemary. "The Theme of Christ the Lover-Knight in Medieval English Literature." *Review of English Studies* 13 (1962): 1–16.

Zeikowitz, Richard E. "Befriending the Medieval Queer." *College English* 65.1 (2002): 67–80.

———. *Homoeroticism and Chivalry: Discourses of Male Same-Sex Desire in the Fourteenth Century.* New York: Palgrave Macmillan, 2003.

———. "Silenced but Not Stifled: The Disruptive Queer Power of Chaucer's Pardoner." *Dalhousie Review* 82.1 (2002): 55–73.

Zink, Michel. "Lubias et Belissant dans la chanson d'*Ami et Amile.*" *Littératures* 17 (1987): 11–24.

Ziolkowski, Jan, ed. and trans. *The Cambridge Songs: Carmina Cantabrigiensia.* New York: Garland, 1994.

Žižek, Slavoj. *Metastases of Enjoyment: Six Essays on Women and Causality.* London: Verso, 1994.

————. *The Puppet and the Dwarf: The Perverse Core of Christianity.* Cambridge, MA: MIT Press, 2003.

————. *The Sublime Object of Ideology.* New York: Verso, 1989.

Zumthor, Paul. *Speaking of the Middle Ages.* Lincoln: University of Nebraska Press, 1986.

INDEX